Karen Ross is .... ter and advertising copywriter. Her first book, a comedy memoir of her career as a professional spread better and written under a pseudonym, was a surprise bestseller.

Mother of the Year

KAREN ROSS

EBURY
PRESS

1 3 5 7 9 10 8 6 4 2

First published in the UK in 2014 by Ebury Press,
an imprint of Ebury Publishing
A Random House Group Company

Copyright © 2014, Karen Ross

The Random House Group Limited Reg. No. 954009

Addresses for companies within the Random House Group can be found at:
www.randomhouse.co.uk

A CIP catalogue record for this book is
available from the British Library

The Random House Group Limited supports The Forest Stewardship
Council® (FSC®), the leading international forest-certification organisation.
Our books carrying the FSC label are printed on FSC® -certified paper.
FSC is the only forest-certification scheme supported by the leading
environmental organisations, including Greenpeace. Our paper procurement
policy can be found at: www.randomhouse.co.uk/environment

Printed and bound by CPI Group (UK) Ltd, Croydon, CR0 4YY

ISBN   9780091956400

To buy books by your favourite authors and register for offers visit:
www.randomhouse.co.uk

For Beverly.
And for my own mother – Rita Bauchwitz Croucher –
who would have been so proud.

Book One
That that is...

Chapter One

I often think my mother would prefer colonic irrigation to hanging out with me.

Ever since I was knee high to a handbag, she's squeezed me in around her clockwork schedule, leaving me to cool my heels while she enjoys more exciting obligations: garden parties at Buckingham Palace, Fashion Weeks in New York, Paris and Rome, and – on three ironic occasions – collecting her Mother of the Year award.

I'm definitely no match for the Beautiful People who populate Mum's universe, so I don't really blame her for wanting to spend time with them rather than me. Even so, when I showed up unexpectedly last weekend, all I got was, 'Darling, you really ought to know by now that you need to phone first. Dad and I are on our way to the Dorchester. Business meeting to discuss the launch of my charitable foundation. Mustn't keep the President of the International Red Cross from his cucumber sandwiches.'

Mum and I both know charity is *not* supposed to begin in Geneva (or the Dorchester) but still, it is what it is.

Despite Mum's latest brush-off, I've spent the whole week hoping today would be different. That at the eleventh hour she might turn round and announce, 'Sorry chaps, you'll have to find someone else. I'd rather be with JJ.'

In my dreams…

Which is how I come to be pretending it's an ordinary Sunday.

Any old Sunday.

In fact, a typical Sunday in March, when the rain beats down and paints everything it touches a deeper shade of grey, and all you really want to do is snuggle up to your other half and sleep off Saturday night's hangover. Except Rob left hours ago to spend the day with his folks in Sussex, so it's just Theodora and me.

Theodora is in the kitchen putting together some sort of brunch, while I add another item to the Everest of ironing in front of me. Unlike Mum's glad rags, the random assortment of clothes I wore to work last week will never feature in *Vogue* or *Vanity Fair* (in truth, they'd be hard pressed to make it onto Topshop's last-chance sale rail), but at least they smell delicious.

Theodora waltzes in balancing a tray piled high with mystery meat – possibly the kebabs we couldn't finish on Friday – surrounded by crisps, olives, dippy things and chocolate mini-rolls. The bottle of iced vodka that usually lives in the freezer is tucked under one arm, and a four-pack of Red Bull dangles precariously from a spare finger.

'I love the way you do the ironing when you're stressed,' she laughs. 'Makes you the perfect flatmate!'

'I'm not stressed.' The vapour trail of steam hovering above the ironing board tells a different story. 'Working up an appetite,' I insist. 'Let's eat.'

'On or off?' My best friend gestures towards the giant slab of plasma that holds court in the corner of our living room. She hits the remote without waiting for an answer and some bloke who used to be Dr Who appears on our giant screen. Before I can protest she tells me, 'You know you want to watch it, JJ.'

Theodora's right. I want to watch it in the same way that after coughing up my intestines for three days, I'm almost ready to concede defeat, and register with a GP; it's the least worst option.

We don't have long to wait. Before either of us can say, 'Pass the Pringles,' a Liverpool accent announces, 'And now, on this very special Sunday, we join Beth Jackson for an extra-special edition of *At Home.*'

The familiar music plays.

I reach for the vodka.

And Beth Jackson joins us in the living room.

I fidget with the rip in my jeans, listening to her opening gambit. 'Hello and welcome.' She shoots me a perfect smile. 'Mothering Sunday is one of my favourite days of the year. A tradition that has lasted through the centuries. A time for family. A time to show how much we all care.'

I feel the heat flash through my body. Not the alcohol. Just a red-hot haze of disappointment. You'd think that by the age of twenty-four, and after so much practice, I'd be used to it but—

Theodora keeps glancing between the television and me like she's watching the tennis at Wimbledon. 'Is that a spot on the side of her nose? To the right?' She points. I know she's trying to help, but my mother's complexion is – as always – flawless. I get up and remove a few specks of dust from the screen, rubbing them away with a freshly ironed tea towel.

Yep.

Beth Jackson's my mum.

She's hardly ever out of the headlines, so you're as familiar with her face as you are with your own mother's. And since Mum has been sharing the story of *my* life with the public since the day I was born, you probably think you know me too.

The camera cuts to a Mother's Day card.

Home-made.

Shaky pink writing that declares: '*You are the prettyest mother in the world.*'

Along with a particularly inept crayoned scribble that looks like a cat.

Just as I am preparing to sneer, my mum tells the

world, 'That's the card Juliet sent me when she was eight.'

'Oh my God. She's done it again, Theodora. That's fifty pence you owe me! I've never seen that card in my life. I bet the props department made it ten minutes ago. Now everyone will think I can't even spell. I mean, I wouldn't mind if Mum teased me about my ability to cook. But spelling's one of the few things I *can* do.'

I bite my bottom lip to shut myself up (a technique I use in the office, whenever I know I'm talking myself into trouble) and brace myself for whatever's coming next.

'...And even though Juliet burned the toast, forgot I'm allergic to peanuts and was too young to know instant coffee tastes better when the water hasn't come straight from the hot tap—'

With a flick of the remote control, I banish my mother from the room.

If only it were that easy to get her out of my head.

I picture Rob, sitting down for a home-made roast beef Sunday lunch with all the trimmings, his mother appreciatively eyeing the forest of white roses he bought yesterday in Borough Market. Whereas when I offered to visit my mum any time today, the best she could manage was 'Darling, I'm afraid I'm busy for the whole weekend. Working both days, then straight off to Egypt. Maybe we could squeeze in Mother's Day some time the week after next. How are you fixed on the Friday?'

My answer was deliberately vague, because that's the best way to avoid the disappointment of being blown out nearer the time.

It's mean even to think it, but I sometimes feel that in our family there's an unwritten rule that *every* day is Mother's Day.

At least Theodora's mum is consistent in her neglect. She lives in Honolulu with her fourth husband, barely sees her daughter from one year to the next, and sends irregular but large sums of money by way of compensation.

'Shall we watch *America's Got Talent* instead, babes?' Theodora knows I am mysteriously fascinated by Piers Morgan. I don't even understand the attraction myself. I mean, he's seriously middle-aged. Looks like he eats too much white bread. And passing judgement on line-dancing cats and fire-eating grannies never was a proper occupation for a grown man. But there's something about him. Maybe it's the way he talks about his children...

'Piers Morgan or Ryan Gosling?'

Theodora always knows how to lift my mood.

'Oh come on,' I say. 'No contest! Marry Piers. Shag Ryan.'

Before I can so much as enquire, 'David Cameron or David Beckham?' Theodora takes charge of the remote control.

The television's back on.

But instead of American reality, I am confronted once again with the supersized reality of my mother. She's now surrounded by a bunch of ethnically balanced ten-year-olds, chanting a cheerful little song that rhymes the word 'mummy' with – in rapid succession – 'chummy', 'dummy' and 'tummy'.

A trumpet's final note fades into silence. Then Mum blinks directly into the camera and murmurs, 'Wasn't that lovely?' Blinks again. 'And, if you're interested in fostering or adopting any of these delightful singers, then please text—'

Theodora finally thumbs the channel changer button, and the image of my mother is replaced by a man who morphs from Elvis into Mick Jagger and then into someone who's either Russell Brand or Johnny Depp, before disappearing into a huge green transparent bubble and rolling himself off stage. Piers Morgan starts to laugh and, despite myself, so do I.

We've seen this episode before. But that doesn't stop us watching it again, and we work our way through the food – and a bit too much of the booze – in companionable silence. Then Theodora turns to me, her blue eyes brimming with sympathy, and asks quietly, 'Why do you let your mum get to you like that? When you come to think about it, she's only doing her job.'

Theodora's much more fun when she's burbling about her latest artistic creation, or explaining why she's broken up with the man she thought she was in love with a couple of weeks earlier. ('...And then he told me he wasn't going to wash his hair for a whole year, to make a *real* contribution to climate change.') But she's doing her best to help, and she deserves a proper answer. It's just that having a mother like mine is complicated.

'I don't know why she winds me up so badly,' I say.

What I don't add – because speaking the words out loud would be about as useful as stabbing myself in the thigh with the kebab skewer I just stripped bare – is that I am a terrible disappointment to my mother.

Mum could probably have won Miss World if ever she'd wanted to. The gawky kid in *Little Miss Sunshine* is more my style.

Not that looks are everything, but there's also the fact that my mum is one of the most accomplished women on the planet. I'd stake my life that by this time tomorrow, families from Cornwall to Caithness will be fighting one another to offer homes to those singing kids. Whereas I am just so awfully average. (OK, so unlike most people, I can lick my own elbow, but that's something Mum is unlikely to boast about to the President of the International Red Cross.)

'I'd better go and sort out my stuff for next week,' I tell Theodora. Before she can say anything else, I stand up, sweep the ironing into my arms, retreat to the bedroom and begin to stash a pile of clean tops into the drawer of a flea-bitten wardrobe that takes up almost as much space as my bed.

Oh. What's this? I had almost forgotten.

I sit down on the bed and start to read what I've taken from its hiding place.

'...and I hope my sacrifice will, in time, bring its own reward. At least now, with my conscience clear, I shall be able to sleep easy through the long, long nights...'

Hmm. That's best kept buried. I'd be mortified if anyone – even Theodora – were ever to find it. Maybe I should just dump it and be done.

But I realise I'm not quite ready to throw away my secret shame. So instead, I bury it deep under a mountain of socks.

Beth Jackson arrived home feeling tired and short-tempered. The discovery that her daughter hadn't bothered to send her a Mother's Day card did nothing to lift her mood.

Honestly, someone should have been supervising those children more closely. Instead, they'd been allowed to eat their weight in chocolate. With the inevitable result that one boy threw up all over her expensive silk shirt; at least it had happened off camera.

Beth scowled at her reflection in the ornate floor-to-ceiling mirror – it had been years since she'd worn anything from the Gap – and removed the skimpy white top lent to her by a production assistant. She put it with the rest of her clothes in a neat pile on the bed, then headed for the shower.

The powerful jets of hot water and the rich lather of her shower gel began to dissolve the stresses of a ten-hour working day. Beth combed conditioner through her long, lustrous hair and gave herself a quick body check – not bad for someone who had recently celebrated her fortieth birthday – while conducting her usual post-mortem on the latest edition of *At Home*. A good show, and hopefully some of those poor little orphans would eventually get fostered or adopted. Even the puker. It must be so awful, living in a grim home in Wolverhampton, with no one who truly loved you, come what may.

By the time she towelled herself dry and shrugged into her robe, there was less than an hour before the car would arrive to take her to tonight's film premiere. Never mind, when you were as experienced as Beth Jackson, that was plenty of time for hair styling and warpaint. Time enough as well to put Juliet's precious card back where it belonged. Beth padded barefoot across the huge room to an elegant white wardrobe that had once been owned by Coco Chanel and lifted a large wooden box from its place on the bottom shelf.

A last look – *'You are the prettyest mother in the world.'* Then Beth carefully restored the ancient sheet of cardboard to what she called her Treasure Chest. No Mother's Day card this year. But she consoled herself with an image of Juliet running home from school all those years ago, pushing the card into her hands, declaring it couldn't possibly wait until Sunday: 'Mummy, you need to have it right now!'

Juliet had always had such a sense of urgency. When Beth said she was going to need extra help with her maths homework, Juliet promptly phoned 999. Asked for Inspector Morse, if you please.

The Treasure Chest also contained a scrapbook. Beth Jackson's byline had begun appearing in newspapers soon after Juliet was born. She hadn't saved every piece she'd written. Only those that seemed to most vividly capture what it had been like to bring up an adorable and bright little girl who wasn't really all that much younger than you were.

Evening News, 22 April 198–

TEEN MUM VOWS TO PASS TEST WITH FLYING COLOURS

'Juliet's not my only contribution to society.
Just you wait and see!'

Her friends are revising for their GCSEs. But Islington schoolgirl Beth Jackson is facing an even stiffer examination: Motherhood. However, Beth is undaunted by the challenges that lie ahead. There's no mistaking her confidence as she announces, 'Yes, I'm only fifteen years old, no, I didn't mean to get pregnant, and why on earth would I be ashamed of my beautiful baby daughter?'

Little Juliet was born last week at the Royal Free Hospital in Hampstead.

'There's no way that we'll be living off benefits,' Beth declared, 'and we didn't do it just to get a council flat. I've known Juliet's father, Matthew, since he came to live in our street, when I was ten and he was twelve. He's put university on hold for a couple of years and got himself a job, and I'll be looking after my gorgeous baby, along with some weekend work and doing my A levels. I think it's great to be such a young mother. In a way, I'm having maternity leave before I start my career.'

Beth acknowledged her parents 'weren't entirely delighted' by the news they were to become grandparents. 'But they've come round to the idea, and they already love Juliet – especially the way she smells, which is a beautiful mix of baby lotion and slightly sour milk.'

Beth grimaced. She'd been so certain she knew all the answers. The years since had demonstrated why ignorance was such bliss. What in God's name would have happened to the three of them if the woman in the next bed on the maternity ward hadn't been married to a journalist? Her parents had been furious to see their family business all over the local rag, but it had turned out to be Beth's salvation.

The phone rang and she grabbed for it eagerly. 'Hi, Jeremy.' Not a trace of the disappointment she felt that the voice on the other end of the line didn't belong to

Juliet. 'Yes, we definitely need to talk about Tuesday's broadcast from Cairo. These poor wounded women. Tell me, are they in wheelchairs? Very important that we show how badly injured they are, but better not upset the teatime audience, so maybe shots of them in wheelchairs with upper limbs clearly intact. Oh, and while you're on the line…'

The next morning, things are looking up. For a start, I manage to get a seat on the tube. A small miracle when you're heading into the West End during the rush hour.

Mondays are my favourite day of the week. I'm at my most optimistic because nothing's had a chance to go wrong yet – especially now I've turned my back on the chocolate vending machine that lies in wait on the platform at Camden; when you've just grabbed an extra ten minutes in bed with your boyfriend instead of chewing your way through a high fibre breakfast, the advantages of avoiding eye contact with several hundred bars of Cadbury's Dairy Milk are self-explanatory.

It's a great omen – especially as today will probably turn out to be the best day of my year … maybe even the best day of my life (so far).

As we rattle our way into Mornington Crescent, I replay what Rob said to me last night, when he got back from visiting his parents. (Apart from 'Mum sends you her love', which made me feel sad again about my own Mother's Day.) OK, so he didn't actually say it as such – there was no, 'JJ, I love you more than anything in the world, and I want us to get married right away. I've already booked the church.' That's not Rob's style. You know those public school types. Articulate and opinionated about everything except their own emotions.

Where Rob's concerned, actions speak louder than words. I'll never forget how last year, when his boss was about to start chemotherapy and no one knew what to say, Rob came back from lunch sporting a shaven head in place of his blond slick back. I was so proud of him, even though he looked like a boiled egg.

Anyway, last night, Rob managed a little babble about the fact that if he spent many more nights sleeping over with me, then Theodora would probably start charging him rent. And that he was already paying more than enough for his own place, thank you very much, especially considering he's hardly ever in it. All in his diffident I-could-be-Hugh-Grant's-much-younger-brother way, but the message was clear.

And here's something else.

A couple of weeks ago, I overheard Rob making a phone call. We'd just come out of the Odeon Leicester Square, and the instant he switched his phone back on, it burst into life. (For some extraordinary reason, he's recently changed his ringtone to *Yes! We Have No Bananas!*) He pulls this apologetic face and says,

'Got to take this one, JJ.' So I back off a few paces and follow on behind him. It's not as though I'm eavesdropping or anything. I just have twenty-twenty hearing. And anyhow, I'm not paying too much attention until I hear my name mentioned.

'...JJ doesn't actually know, yet.' Rob shoots a furtive look over his shoulder, so I put him off the scent by slowing down to study a display of mysterious herbs and spices in the window of one of the Chinese restaurants on Charing Cross Road.

Irritatingly, I miss the next couple of exchanges.

'...but I'm so excited.' Rob's almost skipping along the street by the time I'm back within hearing distance. 'I just can't wait for this to happen.'

'What don't I know?' I ask him once the phone's back in his pocket.

'You still don't know the name of Tottenham's goalkeeper,' he teases.

'What's going to happen? Tell me! Who were you talking to?'

'Only Mum. She's looking forward to seeing you soon. And everything in good time.' Rob leads the way into the tube. 'I want everything to be a complete surprise,' he adds. 'You'll find out soon enough, I promise.'

I got a great big clue a couple of moments later.

You know those adverts they have running alongside the escalators on the tube? As we rode down towards the platform at Tottenham Court Road, I couldn't help but notice that most of them were for diamond rings. I saw Rob looking at them too. Then he whipped out his BlackBerry again and started tapping away. Making a note of the jeweller's website, I suspect.

At which point, I stopped trying to tease out answers from him. Better to let him do everything in his own time, and in his own way. Even so, I can't help but wonder if I'll be moving in with Rob, or if he'd rather we look for a new place of our own. I'll find out soon enough.

Tonight's the night.

I can't wait.

Chapter Two

Euston. Time to turn my thoughts to the working day.

I work for an advertising-slash-PR-slash-digital-media agency just off Leicester Square. It's called Cognita. I am the cog.

Actually, I'm a middleweight copywriter. I know it makes me sound a bit like a boxer, but that's vaguely appropriate, since I spend most of my life fighting to defend the English language. It's what comes of having a mother who's a journalist, a father who's a deputy headmaster, a half-decent education (which would have been entirely decent had I not been hell-bent on rebellion) plus the fact that I'm a Taurus – and we can be just a touch stubborn, especially when we're certain of our facts. Also, the only prize I've ever won in my life was for punctuation; that was the term our housemistress decided everyone deserved a prize for something.

Most of the time I love my job – it would be even better if there were some rule that stopped our clients from meddling – although advertising wasn't actually my first career choice.

I wanted to be a spy.

Probably because of all those James Bond movies I watched with Dad, in which I noticed that while the girls were beyond beautiful, they always died long before Sean/Roger/Pierce (my favourite, until he sang his way through *Mama Mia!*) or Daniel finally saved the world. I've also always yearned to travel to exotic places at someone else's expense.

So when I was in my last year at Bristol, I applied for a job with MI5. The first hurdle was easy. Just a questionnaire at mi5careers.gov.uk. I filled it in when I was meant to be deep into my dissertation, explaining that Charles Dickens wrote so many books not because he was work-obsessed, but because it was easier than entertaining his ten children, or trying to sort out his hideously complicated love life.

The questionnaire was great. Like something out of *Cosmopolitan*. They said you had twenty minutes to complete it, but I thought this was bound to be a test, so I whizzed through it in half the time.

Are you looking for a job where you can express your natural creativity?

'You mean,' I type, 'the kind of career where I instinctively realise the one-eyed Hungarian who's so keen to seduce me is merely the evil megalomaniac's chauffeur and has never even seen the blueprint to the nuclear reactor?' I think better of it, and hit the delete key.

YES.

Do you find it frustrating having to share team responsibility with others?

NO, I lie.

Are you good at keeping secrets?

I resist the temptation to type 'I have made a solemn vow not to answer this question' and bang in a *YES*.

Do you set yourself targets?

Like finishing my dissertation, working out what I really want to do with my life and making sure the tall boy with the floppy blond hair and green eyes who's in my tutorial group finally realises I exist? I think to myself, before adding another *YES*.

Do you finish all your work every day?

Great. An opportunity not to sound too perfect. *NOT ALWAYS*.

Do you enjoy challenges?

'Have you met my mother?' I ask Her Majesty's Secret Service. 'She has written to the University Pro Vice-Chancellor requesting that my class graduates in the morning, rather than the afternoon, as she has to be on a plane to some war region by five o'clock. Even worse, the Pro Vice-Chancellor has agreed, and is angling for a spot on television.' I delete my latest anxiety, and type *USUALLY*.

Thirty questions in all and, as I pressed the SEND button, I wondered if my phobia of blood, dentists and needles would prove to be too much of a handicap once I became a secret agent.

'What do you think?' I anxiously asked Theodora that evening. 'Will I be able to cope?'

'You'll be great, babes. So long as you shoot first and shut your eyes before the enemy body parts start to splatter.'

Next thing I knew, Theodora had told her friend Cassie, who told her friend Danny, who told his friend, the tall, green-eyed, floppy-haired boy. Who marched up to me at the end of our next tutorial and said, 'The name's Butcher. Rob Butcher.'

The warmth in his voice left me shaken *and* stirred, and I tried desperately to think of something witty to say. The best I could manage was, 'I've got an interview to be a desk officer next month. At an office near Goodge Street tube.'

'Now you've disclosed the location, I'm afraid I'll have to kill you.' Rob Butcher paused for dramatic effect. 'Or at the very least, take you to dinner.' Another pause, to gauge my reaction. 'We could discuss Charles Dickens's work ethic if you like? Or you could tell me if I'm making the right move by going into reality TV.'

'Which show?' When you spend your days absorbed in the Victorian underworld, mindless television is a great way to relax. It's still one of my guilty pleasures, even though I've joined the workforce.

'Not as a contestant.' He smiled at me, and my heart went *BOOM*. 'I'll be producing.'

By the time of my interview, I was three-quarters

in love with Rob Butcher. During those final few weeks of our uni lives, we spent almost every hour together. Instead of cramming for our finals, we studied one another.

Rob sailed through the Mummy Test with flying colours. (Unlike the first boy I ever took home to meet her, who brought along his CV and asked if she needed an intern.) As soon as I decently could, I did a bit of deliberate name-dropping and told Rob how Mum had managed to get my graduation ceremony rearranged to suit her schedule.

I braced myself for the flood of questions that usually follow the admission I'm Beth Jackson's daughter – the top three are whether I can get free tickets for the next big show at the O2 (no), if I can get hold one of Mum's handbags/recipes/autographed photos for an alleged charity auction (try asking her agent), and did I grow up in a house with a butler? (I wish) – and sat there waiting to see if Rob would turn out to be a groupie.

He said nothing for what seemed the longest time. 'Your mum's the reason it took me so long to pluck up the courage to talk to you,' he said at last. 'Knowing I wanted to work in TV, it seemed important to wait till I'd actually got a job.' Rob kissed me on the nose. 'I'm only interested in you because you've got great legs,' he assured me. 'Not because of who your mum is. Now tell me about your dad.'

In turn, I learned Rob has two older sisters. His mum's a former dancer, who enrolled him in ballet classes when he was too young to protest – 'Let me show you third position,' he teased, embracing me in a clinch that was definitely more *Kama Sutra* than *Swan Lake* – and his dad's a lawyer.

The first time I cooked Rob a meal, I discovered he's allergic to green peppers. This came as a huge relief, as no sooner had he declared 'Delicious!', than pearls of sweat began running down his face. When he started clutching his throat, I was convinced I'd committed murder by meatballs and sauce.

To celebrate Rob's recovery (he had to sit in a cold bath for thirty minutes to kill the fever), he took me on a paddle steamer to Lundy Island. Not the most idyllic place in the world, you might think – Lundy's a small lump of granite in the Bristol Channel – but it will always be paradise to me.

We arrived late one afternoon. Rob led the way down the wooden jetty and I felt as though we'd stepped back in time. We soon shook off the handful of other tourists and started to explore places with names like Beacon Hill, Battery Point, Earthquake and Devil's Slide, all of which were within a couple of miles of one another. When we reached the tip of the island, we ignored a NO ENTRY sign and walked towards an abandoned lighthouse.

'On a clear day, you can see Wales,' Rob whispered in my ear.

But I only had eyes for him.

Even though our romance was so new, I wondered how I'd ever managed without him. Finally, I knew what people meant when they talked about the missing piece of the puzzle. Rob and I were a perfect fit. An evening in his company was like a week with anyone else: there was never any danger we'd run out of conversation.

'I still can't believe we've been ignoring one another for three years,' I said after discovering we shared a secret passion for fish finger butties with a dash of Worcestershire sauce.

'Better make up for lost time,' he declared. 'Talking of which, we should be getting back. Don't want to miss the return ferry.'

We walked back towards the harbour, along a deserted track, chatting about the exams we would soon be taking. Until Rob said, 'Close your eyes.'

I did as he asked.

Keeping his arm confidently around my shoulder, Rob guided me about a hundred paces. 'You can look now,' he said.

There in front of us – slap bang in the middle of nowhere – stood a pretty cottage, encircled by a ring of pale granite bricks.

Rob produced a brass key from his pocket. He jogged

the few steps to the front door and did the honours. Then he ran back down the path, scooped me up in his arms and carried me across the threshold.

'Here we are.' Tenderly, he deposited me on the wooden floorboards of a sparsely furnished room. 'We both agree our student digs aren't exactly the most private places in the world. So I've rented the cottage for twenty-four hours, and I thought we might stay here tonight. Only if you want to,' he added, mistaking my amazed expression for a one of reluctance.

'But I didn't bring my toothbrush.'

'Don't worry about that.' Rob took me by the hand and led me through a couple of doors, into what turned out to be a well-stocked bathroom. 'I've taken the liberty of planning ahead with the rental company.'

'Um. You know what. I think I'll take a shower.' Translation: I need a few moments to compose myself.

When I emerged from the bathroom, I was greeted by another wonderful surprise. Everywhere I looked, candles were burning brightly, creating a delicious golden glow.

'One for every hour we've been together,' Rob announced shyly.

And while the candles burned low, we created a few fireworks of our own.

Anyway.

By the time I arrived in London a few days later, I

was definitely having second thoughts about being willing to die to protect my country, even if MI5 insisted on sending me to fight evil on a sun-drenched beach in Fiji, or entrusted me to outwit wickedness among the Inca ruins of Machu Picchu.

As it turned out, this didn't matter.

By the end of the interview, I'd learned two things: MI5 officers don't get sent abroad – that's MI6 – and my job search was only just beginning.

When the headmistressy woman with the iron-grey permanent wave asked me to confirm I'd discussed my application with no one apart from my family (um, they were just about the only people I *hadn't* told), I started to explain how my overwhelming desire to be a desk officer had helped spark a love affair, well, it was probably a love affair, even though it was still early days, but I was pretty sure I'd met The One, and *he* thought I'd make a great success out of any career I decided to follow. It wasn't until I realised my potential employer was trying not to laugh that I bit hard on my bottom lip and stopped short of confiding I wasn't so sure I wanted the job now that she'd explained I might be based in Sheffield or Glasgow, rather than London.

Theodora's fond of pointing out that I occasionally seize the wrong end of a stick, but even I realised I'd blown it completely when my interviewer got out from behind her desk, shook me firmly by the hand and said, 'I wish you luck, my dear. Whatever you decide to do.'

Four months and six interviews later (including a half-hearted attempt to train to become a lawyer, a job selling radio advertising, another where I'd have been the assistant to a Lib-Dem MP's assistant, and the memorable afternoon where four of us were shoved inside a windowless room and ordered to stay there until we'd decided among ourselves which candidate should be hired to become a trainee writer of greetings cards) I arrived for the first time at the Cognita offices.

I'd taken the same tube ride that's now my daily commute – along the Northern Line from Camden Town – more out of a sense of duty than with any real hope of anyone ever giving me a job I actually wanted to do. Mum had been right; no one wanted English graduates. I should have studied business or management.

A lurch of the tube ends my trip down memory lane. Here comes Leicester Square.

By the time I emerge from the underground, a light rain that's guaranteed to make my hair frizz is starting to fall, so I walk briskly towards the office.

I've been at Cognita for more than three years, but every time I think about how I finally got the job, I can't help but grin.

They gave me the sort of test that MI5 could have

used as a code-cracking exercise; a piece of paper with the following written on it:

THAT THAT IS IS THAT IS NOT IS NOT IS THAT IT IT IS

Chapter Three

Natasha doesn't even attempt to hide the newspaper from me. She just continues to smirk at a photo of my mother, who's pictured picking flowers with a toddler who appeared with her yesterday on TV. I sneak a look over Natasha's shoulder on the pretext of hanging up my jacket.

'They're saying your mum's being lined up for a guest spot on *The Simpsons*,' she informs me. 'She really is blessed with movie star looks, isn't she?'

'Don't believe everything you read in the papers.' I'm determined not to rise to the bait. Natasha never misses an opportunity to embarrass me and, any moment now, she'll find an excuse to make me spell the word 'prettiest', in case anyone within earshot missed the Mother's Day card I never created.

My tactic works.

Natasha closes the paper and turns to me. 'JJ,' she says in that imperious voice of hers, 'when will you have finished the VitalVitamins website update?'

Last Friday, as it happens. But Natasha's not to know that. Anyway, it's none of her business.

Natasha likes to think she's senior to me on account

of having started at Cognita a few months before I did. But the fact is, we're equals.

And rivals.

There's an opening for a new Creative Group Head and we've both applied for the promotion.

I'm the first to admit Natasha's better than I am at office politics – you know the type: claims she loves gardening just because our boss grows his own weed, and insists on elbowing her way into client meetings that aren't strictly her business, then proceeds to drown out every other viewpoint with a tidal wave of customer offer visions, client-focused strategies, feel-good factors, skill sets and big-picture thinking – but I honestly think the work I produce is no worse than hers. And given that everyone at Cognita has been living through a pay freeze, I really need this next major rung on the career ladder and the salary hike that comes with it.

'So how was your weekend, Tash?' I sidestep the question about my work and abbreviate her name because I know it annoys her.

'I spent most of it putting together final concepts for the Cliftons campaign.' Natasha manages to sound both put-upon and self-important. Then her face softens and she adds, 'I did have a lovely afternoon yesterday, though. I drove my mum out into the country and bought her lunch at a gorgeous place where they actually make their own wine. So eco-friendly. And wonderfully customer-centric.'

I sit down at my desk and prepare to check my emails. If I make a show of getting into work mode, perhaps Natasha will spare me further details.

But no, she's still talking. 'JJ, I keep meaning to say. You really must get into the habit of shutting down your computer when it's not in use. Especially at weekends. Do you have any idea how much energy you're wasting? I turned it off for you when I was in here on Saturday.'

I remember why I'm never going to be friends with Natasha, even though I'm obliged to spend at least thirty-five hours a week sitting opposite her in this just-larger-than-a-cupboard office we share. Roll on promotion, and a room of one's own.

While I'm waiting for my Mac to whirr its way through the start-up routine, I glance up at the poster on the wall above Natasha's head. Fifteen words in Times New Roman, each one three inches high, embossed on a slab of shiny whiteboard.

THAT THAT IS, IS. THAT THAT IS NOT, IS NOT. IS THAT IT? IT IS.

It's the word puzzle that got me hired. Me, and every other writer here. Devised by Silas Grove, who started Cognita back in the days before broadband, it's his final hurdle for potential new recruits.

I'd already fought my way through two interviews, and decided this was the job I definitely wanted. There was a buzz about the place. The list of clients looked exciting – a canny mix of entrepreneurial businesses ready to embrace bold, off-the-wall marketing, along with a couple of charities that couldn't afford any of the bigger agencies to do their fundraising for them, and a boring old bank that paid a fat monthly fee. I was also thrilled by idea of actually getting paid to write, because I adore playing with words and trying to put them in the right order. Also, it was getting harder and harder to resist my mother's, 'Darling, you only have to say the word, and I'll get them to hire you as a production assistant on *At Home*.'

When you've racked up £17,500 in student debt (over and above your official student loans), you're working nights behind a bar and your circle of friends have all started wearing business uniforms, the only thing worse than failing to be hired would be accepting a pity-job as one of my mother's minions.

So, the third interview.

I loved Silas from the moment he announced, 'Don't think I'm going to hire you just because you're Beth Jackson's daughter.'

'How do you know that?' I asked. Every so often, a stranger recognises me from childhood photos that have appeared in the papers – maybe it's time I got rid of my fringe – but Silas didn't seem the type to read the women's page. And Jackson's a common enough name.

'You'll spend the rest of your life wondering,' he said amiably.

Just in case this was some sort of double bluff, and the man in front of me was yet another member of Mum's fan club, I opened my mouth and this torrent of words came out about how I was determined to succeed and make it on my own despite my mother rather than because of her, that I already had some ideas about an advertising campaign for one of the agency's charities, that I would repay Silas's faith in me by working long and hard, that Charles Dickens was my role model and I hoped one day to write as well as he did, and that having a famous mother had already cost me my chance of serving my country by becoming a spy.

That last one was a lie, obviously, but I wanted Silas to realise that I shouldn't be punished just because of an accident of birth.

My potential new boss, meanwhile, had been expertly rolling a cigarette while I was banging on. (Even now, he takes absolutely no notice of the no-smoking-in-public-buildings rule, but since it's *his* building, we let it pass.)

'You certainly have a lot of words,' he observed laconically. 'Now choose three of the ones you've just spoken to persuade me to give you the job.'

'Faith. Hope. Charity,' I shot back.

He smiled through a cloud of dodgy-smelling cigarette smoke – I learned later that Silas is known in the
office as Skunk – and revealed two neat rows of surprisingly white, almost Hollywood teeth, encircled by the
ginger bristles of his beard. Then he started scribbling
on a piece of paper. Once finished, he lobbed it across
the desk, along with a chunky Mont Blanc rollerball,
and asked, 'Can you make sense of this?'

I looked at the words he'd written:

THAT THAT IS IS THAT IS NOT IS NOT IS THAT IT IT IS

Obvious.

Yet it seemed too easy.

Or was I missing something?

I could play the game, or take a gamble.

In our family, Mum's the one who takes risks – like
the time she insisted on broadcasting from Zimbabwe,
even though the press was banned – but it was Dad
who taught me how to trust my own judgement.

'No such thing as a certainty,' he'd remind me, as we
leaned against the rails of the paddock at Epsom examining the runners for the next race on Saturday
afternoons while Mum was doing one of her guest
spots on Britain's most popular radio talk show. 'But if

you've got an instinct for something, go with your hunch.'

I sensed Silas Grove would be impressed by something out of the ordinary. So instead of writing on the paper, I tossed the test back across the desk and paused until I had his full attention.

Then I said, 'It's never going to make sense. Not until you add two commas, three full stops and a question mark. Oh, and you've missed out a "THAT". Is that it?'

Silas didn't miss a beat. 'It is, indeed. My mistake!' he chuckled, re-examining the words. 'Oh, and how soon can you start?' he added matter-of-factly.

I was so gobsmacked, I meekly accepted the impossible-to-pay-back-your-debt starting salary Silas offered. But on the plus side, I accidentally swept the Mont Blanc into my handbag when I was leaving. A week later, on my first day of work, when I confessed I'd nicked my new boss's pen, he let me keep it.

Four years on, and now I know for sure that Skunk is a bit of a softie behind that well-trimmed beard of his. Even though he works us hard and I could pay off my debts faster by moving to another agency, he's a decent boss and I've learned a lot from him.

I glance at the watch Theodora gave me last Christmas; Salvador Dalí's moustache says it's eight minutes to ten. Across the room, Natasha is assembling a large bunch of papers.

'Chop chop, JJ. Don't want to be late.'

The Monday morning agency meeting is attended by all forty of us at Cognita. It's a general catch-up, where we review what's going on across the business, and work gets allocated for the week ahead. In addition, there are usually two big plates in the centre of the boardroom table, each one laden with a golden pile of fifteen still-warm almond croissants, so it doesn't do to be late. (Unless, of course you're Natasha, who says she has wheat issues, and is always one of the first to arrive so she can bag a seat that puts her as close as she can get to Skunk without actually sitting on his lap.)

The familiar ding-dong sound from my computer announces that a batch of emails has just downloaded to my in-box. Plenty of time to look them over before I walk down the corridor to take a gorgeous, crumbly croissant and my usual seat in the back row. 'You go ahead,' I mumble to Natasha's designer-clad back. 'See you there.'

I turn my full attention to the screen. A motley collection of messages, most of them spam – plus one from Bruno Lombardo, my client at VitalVitamins. There's also one from Theodora, with 'Shall I have a go at this?' in the subject line. Naturally, I open that first.

Turns out Theodora is thinking of entering some modern sculpture competition. There's a prize of

£50,000, and according to the link I follow, lots of prestige. I type, 'Go 4 it! See you tonight. Can't wait for Rob to make his Big Announcement! xxx' and hit the reply button.

I'm sure I can smell croissant drifting down the corridor, but I'll just check the client email first. Hopefully, it's thanking me for a job well done.

From: Bruno Lombardo <bruno@vitalvitamins.co.uk>
To: JJ Jackson <jj@cognita.com>
Subject: Website Update

I'm sure you've done your best on this, but I'm afraid it's just not up to your usual standard. In particular, there are some words in the various headlines that I'm not at all keen on. Please make the following amendments:

1. New – replace with the word INNOVATIVE
2. Science stuff – TECHNOLOGICAL FORMULATION
3. Natural – NON TOXIC
4. Largest selection – COMPREHENSIVE RANGE
5. Hot new products – SCIENTIFIC BREAKTHROUGHS
6. Dynamic diets – WEIGHT ISSUES?
7. 75% off – BIG SAVINGS
8. Prime of life – THE MATURE GENRATION

9. Best-sellers – POPULAR PRODUCTS (nice alliteration there, don't you think!)

In order to make the improved headlines more attention-grabbing, I would also like you to scatter plenty of exclamation marks around them. I'll leave it to you to decide exactly where to put them.

Hope you don't think I'm being difficult. Actually, these are my wife's suggestions, and I have to say I agree with her. Look forward to seeing the revised version. Please send asap.

BL

'Will you look at THIS?' I type to Rob. 'Not only am I blessed with a client who commands me to insert a spelling mistake (see No. 8), he's such a pussy... he's letting his battleaxe of a wife run his business now. As for the exclamation marks, you can guess where I want to stick them. What a wanker!(!) Hope your day's going better than mine. See you tonight. Love you xxx

I hit 'send'.

Something's not quite right.

Oh my God.

Chapter Four

OH MY GOD.

OH MY GOD.

OH MY GOD.

I've hit send.

And forgotten to hit the forward button first.

Which means—

I leap into the air and grab at a wire along the side of my Mac. Can I kill the internet connection before—

I can't.

Too late.

The jaunty little tune confirms that my email has arrived at its destination.

Bruno Lombardo's in-box.

I have just told one of Cognita's most important clients he's a wanker.

In writing.

My stomach is turning somersaults and I think I might be about to throw up. I reach for my mobile and call Rob. He picks up on the second ring. 'I've done something *terrible*,' I howl.

'What's up? Have you been in an accident? JJ, where are you? What's happened?'

I try to explain.

'You did *what*?'

'It's the sort of thing that could so easily happen to anyone,' Rob reassures me.

'Yes, but the last time I was this scared, cousin Tommy was trying to persuade me to cuddle his pet rat.'

'Sweetheart, I'm really sorry. I'd love to help you sort this out, but I'm not sure there's anything much either of us can do. Better hope they see the funny side of it. Look, I'm actually in a meeting right now. See you tonight, OK?' And with that, my boyfriend is gone.

So how do I dig myself out of this one?

A grovelling apology wouldn't go amiss. *Dear Bruno.* No, it's safer to go formal and call him Mr Lombardo. *As you will have gathered, I was upset by your comments.* Or maybe devastated will win me more sympathy. My mental composition is interrupted by a voice.

'JJ. We're waiting for you. Everyone's waiting for you. Come ON!' Natasha pokes her head round the door. She looks as cross as she sounds.

'I'm coming.'

I get up from my chair, still feeling shaky. Almost on autopilot, I check my email.

Oh crap.

From: Bruno Lombardo <bruno@vitalvitamins.co.uk>
To: JJ Jackson <jj@cognita.com>
Subject: Website Update

I don't think you meant to send this to me.

Thanks.
BL

You'd think my day couldn't get any worse.

It got worse.

By which I don't mean simply that the almond croissants were long scoffed by the time I crept into the meeting.

For a start, I'd never seen Skunk so angry. Bollocking didn't even begin to describe it. And of course, everyone in the agency knows what happened.

I'm a laughing stock.

And already an hour late for dinner.

Tonight was meant to be so special. Dinner with Rob, plus Danny – who's Rob's best friend if you don't count me – and Theodora.

'I'll treat us all to supper at El Paradiso,' Rob had announced a few days after that frustrating phone call with his mum where he told her there was something I didn't know, then refused to tell me what it was. 'We've got something to celebrate.'

'What?'

But Rob wouldn't say another word.

I'd stood on tiptoe to kiss him. So this was how we'd be telling our closest friends we'd decided to live together, and I might even have a diamond ring on my finger by the end of the evening. We've been together long enough now, and I don't want to end up being one of those girls who lets her relationship drift until the day her boyfriend sits her down and tells her he's met someone else. It's high time for the pair of us to take things to the next stage. And even though Theodora and I will miss one another like crazy, we'll still get together all the time.

In the meantime, Rob persists in being mysterious about tonight. Keeps telling me I have to be patient a bit longer, so I've given in gracefully; if he's so keen to do the alpha male thing, and make a public show of our declaration of togetherness, why spoil it for him?

But now the celebration – the happiest day of the year – is happening without me!

Here's what happened.

I arrived at the weekly meeting just in time to learn Natasha – bloody Natasha – had volunteered to devise a low carbon diet for Cognita. Words like 'best practice', 'value added', 'management information strategy', 'incremental revenue' and 'leading the line' engulfed me, while my own brain spat out some shorter words, including 'sacked', 'broke' and 'dole queue'.

Anyway, just as everyone was giving Natasha a lack-lustre ripple of applause, Skunk's PA, Carlotta, came into the room. She's the only person who doesn't have to attend the Monday meeting; someone needs to answer the phones.

Carlotta threw me a look, marched straight over to Skunk, whispered something in his ear, and then left. Was it my imagination, or did she give me another look on her way out? One of pity laced with a smirk.

Skunk consulted his BlackBerry for what seemed like an age. Then he looked up. At me.

'OK guys, that's it for today,' he said.

'But we haven't even started the—'

Skunk quelled Natasha's protest with a glare. 'I said that's it. Everyone back to work.'

I fled the room and headed for the loo. If I just sat quietly for five minutes I'd be able to get my act together and formulate some sort of a plan. But thirty seconds later, my mobile beeped a text alert. I pressed and clicked my way to the message: 'MY OFFICE. NOW.'

Like I said, Skunk delivered a royal bollocking. What made it worse was that he didn't shout. He did that thing he does in pitches ... dropped his voice almost to a whisper, so you have to strain to listen, and you end up hanging on his every word. He reminded me that Bruno Lombardo is a personal friend of his, that VitalVitamins had been one of the agency's first accounts and that it now earns us over four million pounds a year.

Oh, and guess what else?

Like the showman he is, my boss saved the best till last.

Mrs Lombardo – 'or battleaxe, as you prefer to call her' – turns out to be, um, Skunk's sister.

'So tell me, Juliet,' Skunk concluded. 'What would you do if you were me?'

Juliet? He'd never called me by my proper name before. He *was* going to fire me. Even worse, he was going to make me fire myself. I stood up and turned away from him. No way was I going to let him see me cry. 'I'll clear my desk,' I said, just about managing to keep my voice steady.

'You what?' Even in my misery, I could hear Skunk sounded astonished. 'Oh, come on,' he chivvied. 'You can do better than that!'

What did the man want? Compensation? Did he think I've got a trust fund?

'That that is, is. That that is not, is not. Is that it? It is!' Somehow, the words slipped out of my mouth before I could stop them. The thing is, they've become a private mantra, sort of.

I bit my bottom lip.

Hard.

I shot a quick look at Skunk. He was suddenly

enormously involved in the intricacies of his latest roll-up. His ginger beard was twitching, and his shoulders were shaking. I could just about handle his anger. But now it looked as if he was going to bloody laugh at me.

'Quickly, JJ,' Skunk said. 'Three ways to deal with the situation.'

'You could make me give a week's wages to StreetKidz.' I named one of our charity accounts. 'Or,' I added hastily, giving Skunk no time to fall in love with this foolishly expensive suggestion, 'put me in charge of organising the next agency away day. Better still—' I took a deep breath, because I knew I had arrived at the correct solution '—you could send me to VitalVitamins. In person. To apologise to Bruno. And your sister. His wife. Your sister, his wife, I mean.'

Skunk was determined to rub my nose in it. He insisted I go home first. 'I know we run a pretty relaxed dress code at Cognita. But you really should smarten yourself up. Generally, I mean. Not just because you're meeting a client. Do you actually own any other kind of shoes?'

OK, so I could never be a chick-lit heroine. I simply don't have it in me to go all orgasmic over a pair of high heels. That's Theodora's style, not mine. I love my Crocs too much.

Crocs have always been very Marmite. You either adore them, or you know all about that website where fashionistas waste their lives banging on about how horrid they are.

Take it from me, reports of their death have been greatly exaggerated. Crocs are more than just a trend. They're a way of life. As it so happens, on this occasion, I'd even been ahead of the curve. (An early adopter, as Natasha would say.) Mum gave me a pair she'd picked up at some PR junket at least six months before they first went into the shops.

As you can imagine, Mum wouldn't be seen dead in a pair of Crocs, which is presumably why she discarded them in my direction. I thought they were so ugly they were almost pretty, and once I actually put them on, it was as if they'd been custom-made. Bliss! Much better for your feet than heels. I tell you, it's no coincidence that seventeen per cent of the population of Iceland owns at least one pair.

People are always having a go at my shoes, but I don't care. I suppose they're part of my image. And Rob insists he likes Crocs. He even wears the pair I gave him for his birthday.

Occasionally.

I digress. Having decided Skunk's mean parting shot was unworthy of a response, I returned to the office to collect my bag, curtailed Natasha's attempt at interrogation with a, 'Sorry, can't stop now,' dashed back home, clambered into the green outfit I wore at cousin Anne's wedding – it tones well with my celery and white Sassari Crocs – and made my way to South Norwood.

For someone like me, who's lived their whole life north of the river, South Norwood is like being in a foreign country. Bulgaria, perhaps. It's a twenty-minute walk from the bus stop to the VitalVitamins factory. Or Mission Centre, as Bruno Lombardo prefers to call it, although just one look at the building – a grim combination of breeze blocks and cement – is enough to remind me why we never feature it on their website.

Bruno and Sister-of-Skunk kept me waiting in reception for almost three hours. Not because they're rude, or as some kind of punishment, but because I'd lacked the courage to call and say I was on my way, and they were out enjoying a long lunch. It was almost four o'clock by the time they returned.

Then Bruno pushes through the swing door looking his usual dapper self, with his cropped salt and pepper hair and year-round tan (I'm pretty sure it comes from one of the spray cans he sells on his site under the heading 'Body Beautiful!'), but the big surprise was his wife. For a start, Sister-of-Skunk is at least six feet tall, while Bruno is more Tom Cruise-sized. She looks nothing like her brother, either. I mean obviously she doesn't have a beard, but she's blonde to his ginger, and so far as I can tell, it's natural.

Bruno looks as me quizzically. We've met three or

four times, always at Cognita, so I realise that although he recognises me, he can't quite place me.

'JJ,' I begin. Even though I've had plenty of time to work out what I'm going to say, now that the moment is upon me, I'm terrified. 'From Cognita.'

'The one who called my husband a wanker.' Sister-of-Skunk is faster on the uptake. She's doing that same low-voice thing her brother does, although her words are loud enough for the receptionist to hear, and I notice her head bobs up from behind the magazine she's been reading all afternoon. 'I gather you weren't very keen on my improvements to your work.'

This is not going at all according to my plan. I had intended to start with a short speech about email being a great communication tool, but one that…

'Um, no, but.' I have talked myself into a standstill.

'Why are you here?' Bruno looks perplexed.

I thrust a bunch of wilted flowers into his hands. I bought them at London Bridge station, and they were meant for Sister-of-Skunk. But she looks like she prefers guns to roses.

'OUCH!' Bruno recoils from the bouquet as though it's harbouring a snake. He stamps his foot and waves his thumb in the air. 'Look what you've done!' And he waves a blood-splattered finger at me.

Blood!

My response is immediate.

There's a ringing in my ears. My skin goes hot and clammy. I can hear every beat of my heart. That makes it even worse. But this has happened before, and I know how to cope. If I can just get away from Bruno's bloody finger, I'll be fine. I reckon I have about ten seconds before I faint.

Fortunately, there's a door just to the right of the receptionist's desk. If I can make it in time, and have a bit of space ... I lurch towards my escape route. All you have to do is open the door, and shut it behind you, I instruct myself.

I do exactly that.

And find myself in a space the size of a broom cupboard.

As my eyes adjust to the darkness, I realise it *is* a broom cupboard. I'm surrounded by mops, toilet paper, kitchen towels and the like. I shuffle around and find myself nose to nose with a giant vat of bleach.

On the positive side, I am away from the blood, and no longer about to faint.

On the less positive side, Sister-of-Skunk is hammering on the door and yelling, 'What on earth do you think you're doing?'

'So how long did you spend in the cupboard?' Rob pours me another large glass of wine.

'And did you clean the floor by way of an apology?' Theodora giggles.

'More like they cleaned the floor with her!' Danny points at the pale green splodge on the left shoulder of my smartest green jacket. Or rather, what was my smartest green jacket until I rubbed up against that tub of bleach in the broom cupboard.

It feels as though everyone at El Paradiso has abandoned their own conversation in favour of listening to the story of my day.

My friends are eating for England, but I have no appetite and pick half-heartedly at the plate of honeyed chilli calamari that's been placed in front of me.

Still, I mustn't let a rubbish day at work spoil what's about to become an enchanted evening. Some day in the – very – distant future, when I tell our kids about the night Daddy declared he couldn't live without Mummy, my email cock-up will be forgotten, and the unfortunate episode in the cupboard will have been erased from my mind.

All I'll remember is what's going to happen any moment now.

I look around the table. Rob and Danny have moved on to reminisce about some boy called Brinkley, who they once locked in a cupboard at school, and I start to relax for the first time in hours. It's great to celebrate this wonderful moment with our best friends.

I feel Rob's hand on my knee. Even though he's still banging on about the hapless chap in the cupboard – now a hotshot banker who doesn't deserve his gigantic bonus – my boyfriend is letting me know he understands I've had a miserable time. The swirl of his fingers advancing towards my thigh is a promise of better things to come.

Across the table, Theodora and Danny are bickering; something about whether a digitally enhanced photo reproduced on canvas still counts as art. Since Danny comes from a family whose ancestors hang from the walls in faded oils and gilded frames, his views are predictable.

Danny and Rob have known each other even longer than I've been friends with Theodora. They went to the same prep school. And any artist who gets to paint Danny will have a field day. I mean, Rob's gorgeous, and I prefer blonds anyway (apart from Sister-of-Skunk), but Danny is movie-star handsome, with a mop of black curls, spectacularly full eyelashes that every woman I know would die for, and a permanent smile on his face. The fact that he's the second son of an earl – which makes him The Honourable Danny Houghton – doesn't do him any harm, either.

I pour myself another glass of wine and realise how lucky I am. I mean, work's important to me, and I want to be successful, but I'm so glad that when I wake up in the morning, I'm me. And not, say, Natasha. Cognita seems to be her whole life. Whereas I have the work–play thing in balance. And soon, I'll be living with Rob.

Who has removed my shoes and is firmly massaging my toes.

No. That can't be right.

Rob has both his hands around the wine list. And he's consulting with the waiter about champagne.

In which case…

I push back a few inches on my chair, so I can see beneath the tablecloth.

What the hell?

One Sassari Croc lies on the floor. In pieces. Its partner is wedged firmly between the teeth of a white furry creature. Which, upon closer examination, turns out to be a dog.

The animal sees me looking at it, and backs off, jaws still clamped around my Croc. Next thing, it's leapt onto Danny's lap, and is presenting him with the shoe as if it's a hunting trophy.

'Asbo! What have you got there?'

Blimey, Danny is crooning at the horrible thing as if it's a new girlfriend.

'Whose is it? Who's the Cinderella?' Now Danny is waving my mangled footwear in the air, and our table is once again the centre of attention.

'That'll be JJ's!' Rob and Theodora speak in unison.

'Sorry.' Danny is too engrossed in a game of tug of war with the dog and my Croc to sound sincere. The dog wins easily, jumps down from his master's lap and heads off towards the back of the restaurant and the kitchen.

'I really am sorry, JJ. Asbo's still settling in. She's a country dog, you know. Used to interesting smells and that.' Danny pauses, aware this isn't the most tactful thing to say.

Before I can ask what a dog's doing in a restaurant, two waiters are at our table. One of them is bearing Asbo, who has swapped the remnants of my shoe for a fat wedge of chorizo. He disappears with it underneath the table.

'Jack Russell, is it?' The waiter sounds as soppy as Danny. 'My mum and dad used to keep them. Full of character.'

'He's about ten months old and—' Before Danny can give us the damn dog's life story, the second waiter uncorks a bottle of champagne.

A satisfying pop. Four glasses are poured and distributed around the table. The waiters retreat, and the three of us turn and look expectantly at Rob.

'So the reason why we're all here tonight,' he begins. 'It's not every day that someone begins a new phase in their life. An important new phase, that will hopefully shape the whole of the rest of their life.'

Rob shoots me a smile. His eyes are glittering with excitement. I love him so much.

'There've been a few false starts, I know.'

That terrible row we had in Ibiza, he means. Why's he bringing that up?

'But it's important to take your time, explore a few options, and...'

Options? Is that a dig at my three ex-boyfriends?

'....both of us are convinced this is the right thing to do.' Rob gets to his feet and holds his champagne glass in the air.

To be honest, I was expecting something more romantic than this. And there's no sign of a ring. At this rate, he'll soon be muttering 'Whatever love means...' But no—

'Danny and I are going into business,' Rob announces. 'We've thought about it long and hard. And yes, I know it's a risk, but we really believe we can make a difference. We'll have to cut back on the champagne, but as we're going to be making healthy drinks ourselves, that won't be too great a hardship.' A wry smile. 'Let's make the most of this bottle, and drink to the success of our new venture.'

'To success.' I have no idea how I dredge the words from my mouth, but somehow I manage.

Starting a business?

That's the big secret?

I mean, I'm pleased for Rob.

But devastated for myself.

And how could I have got it so wrong?

I feel my face going bright red, and the champagne tastes like acid as it trickles down my throat.

Rob mustn't see me like this.

I put my glass down, mumble something about needing to get some air, and turn towards the door while the others are still clinking glasses.

I take only a single step before my bare feet land in something soft. And squelchy. And sticky. And smelly.

Asbo appears not to be house-trained.

Beth Jackson twisted the opal Matthew had given her the day Juliet was born. It had belonged to his grandmother and was the closest thing to an engagement ring he could conjure. On their tenth wedding anniversary, he'd offered to replace it with a diamond, but that was never going to happen. The opal was part of her now. Just as Juliet would always be part of her – even though the two of them seemed to be drifting further and further away from one another.

A crack that could all too easily widen into a chasm. Beth knew. She had interviewed so many people whose children seemed more of an abstract concept than living, breathing flesh and blood. Successful people with important jobs and busy lives, who found it more convenient to lavish money rather than time on their offspring. Each time she wondered how anyone could be daft enough to let their kids become such a low priority, but now she realised it could happen even if the parent wanted no such thing. Juliet seemed congenitally unable to plan ahead, and refused to be pinned down more than a day or two in advance. Still, Beth reminded herself, she was the adult. She needed to make more of an effort.

Beth picked up her phone. She had two missed calls from Theodora, but there was no answer when she tried to reply. As for Juliet, her daughter's phone went straight to voicemail. '*Hey, it's JJ. If you're part of the problem, hang up now. If you're part of the solution, leave a message.*'

Beth hesitated, then severed the connection.

Daily News, 8 September 199–

MY WEEK
TALES FROM THE HOME FRONT WITH TEENAGE MUM
BETH JACKSON

Write to the point

Even though Juliet has barely started school, she definitely knows what her As, Bs and – indeed – her Cs are for. On Tuesday, she came rushing home and thrust a piece of paper into my hand. It turns out to be her first ever composition. I reproduce it for you here in full, and exactly as written:

WHEN I AM OLD

'I have long hair and I am maried to a Prince. His name is Melvyn. We live in a new cassle near home. We are very very very happy.'

As regular readers know, Juliet's latest guinea pig happens to be called Melvyn. He's gentle, clean and easy to care for. All of which bodes very, very, very well for my darling daughter's future.

Beth sighed. She knew she should have tried harder – much harder – to get to know Rob. He seemed like a nice kid, Juliet was obviously serious about him and he might one day turn out to be her son-in-law.

Juliet getting married… Beth smiled at the thought of her daughter radiant in a long white dress, undoubtedly with those ugly shoes she persisted in wearing peeping out from under the hem. All in good time, and hopefully not too soon. Meanwhile, perhaps Juliet could bring Rob round for supper one night next week.

But no, that wasn't going to work. Beth knew without checking her diary she had commitments every evening for the next three weeks.

Chapter Five

Look, I think Rob's having one of those quarter-life crises I was reading about in last week's *Grazia*.

Here's the evidence:

- He's twenty-six years old.
- He's got a job most of us would kill for.
- He earns £40,000 a year.
- He rents this gorgeous apartment with a view of the Thames (you have to stand on a chair and squint to glimpse the river, but it's still the nicest flat of anyone I know).
- And – here's the clincher – perks of his job include two tickets for next month's Reality Awards of the Year Show, hosted by Piers Morgan – tickets he says he's given away to one of the interns.

'Now I know you're having me on! I thought you were hoping for a gong?' My voice is light-hearted, because I'm doing my best to hold it together. But inside, I'm dying. This was supposed to be *our* night. Rob was going to sweep me off my feet, not make me feel like a complete idiot who was obliged to walk home minus her shoes.

'I know you only love me for my Piers Morgan tickets.' Rob playfully tousles my hair. 'But I had to let them go.' A long pause. Then he adds, 'I resigned on Friday.'

You did what?

A stab of pain shoots through me.

We've been in a relationship for three years, so I could understand Rob forgetting to mention trivial things, like what he had in his sandwiches today (tuna, most likely). But not telling your partner you're planning to quit your *job*?

'Look, if I've screwed up by springing this on you, I'm sorry.' So much for my poker face. 'But I've been working really hard,' Rob continues, 'juggling two jobs. When I'm with you, all I want to do is relax and unwind. Not talk business.' He sounds contrite. 'Besides, I wanted to surprise you. In a good way. I was hoping you'd be really proud of me.'

'Of course I'm proud of you.' It's true. 'But I'm gutted you didn't confide in me. And to be honest, I'm worried for you. You've got to admit there's a lot to be said for a regular paycheck especially these days.'

'Shall we go to bed?'

Rob gives me what, in other circumstances, might pass for a seductive look.

I'm not wholly immune to his extraordinary green eyes.

But I'm still reeling from shock.

Rob shrugs, then walks out of the room and a moment later I hear water running in the bathroom. He never locks the door, so I follow him inside.

'I didn't mean you shouldn't be doing this,' I say. He's cleaning his teeth – literally foaming at the mouth – and as Rob always brushes for the full two minutes, I take advantage of his silence to try to explain why I'm so concerned. 'I thought you loved your job. That you were hugely ambitious. You've done so well. Now you're giving up on everything you've already achieved. And are you really sure about making Danny your business partner? I love him loads, but he's hardly Richard Branson. Part-time modelling suits him fine. Aren't you worried you'll ruin your friendship? Or end up doing all the work? And what did you tap into your BlackBerry that night when we were going down the escalator at Tottenham Court Road?'

Whoops.

I prepare to bite my bottom lip, but my runaway mouth is silenced by a bullet of spit hitting the wash-basin. A quick gargle. Rob looks quizzical, as he tries to remember. 'Oh yes, the Mayor's Office is offering grants to start-ups run by the under-thirties. I noticed a poster. I knew there was something I've been meaning to do. Thanks so much for reminding me, sweetheart.

I'll get on to it tomorrow.' He spits again, splattering threads of blue foam around the basin.

'Even so. Giving up your job's such a big step. Maybe this is something you could do on the side, until you're sure it's going to fly? I'm used to having a workaholic mother, so I know how to cope with a workaholic boyfriend. I'll take up a new hobby. Beekeeping or something.' That last bit comes out more sarcastically than I intended.

Rob looks me in the eyes. 'Actually, I think it's time you stopped being so negative.' He marches me back into the living room. 'Sit down,' he tells me.

'I'm sorry, I'm just tired. I was trying to be supportive.' It's long past midnight. 'Definitely time for bed. Some of us have to get up for work in the morning.' I make a stage yawn to show I'm joking.

'You've had your say.' Rob sits opposite me in the shabby armchair he inherited from his godfather. It's one of the few pieces of furniture he actually owns. 'Now it's my turn to tell you something.'

Last time Rob looked so serious, his mum was on the phone to tell him the cat's kidneys had packed up, and they'd had to have her put down.

'I know you think reality TV's a bundle of laughs,' Rob begins, 'but I'm sick of finding oddballs and show-offs who are desperate to appear in the latest freak show. I realised for sure the day I was finalising the cast for *Between a Rock and a Hard Place*.'

That's the programme where a bunch of unemployed hedge fund managers and investment bankers wrap themselves in animal skins, dine off raw meat, nettles, berries and twigs – serves them right – and insult one another while dwelling in caves somewhere off the west coast of Ireland for forty days and forty nights, hoping to win fame and a fraction of the fortunes they used to earn. Rob's first solo credit as a series producer, notable for becoming the first reality TV show where a candidate sued for unfair dismissal after he was voted off on day three.

'We both know my work's well paid,' Rob continues. 'But I hate sitting in meetings full of smug suits who specialise in mocking all the characters who are so desperate to fast-track themselves onto the celebrity D list that they'll do any ludicrous thing we ask them. It makes me feel dirty inside. And you know what's most frightening of all?' Rob looks genuinely scared. 'When I had my review, they told me I was in line for a five thousand pound pay rise.'

Like that's a *bad* thing?

'Unless I quit now, I'll be there for life. Trapped in a velvet rut and despising myself. This way, I'm my own boss. And I honestly think what Danny and I are going to do will make a difference. We're aiming to create new jobs, and make a name for ourselves. The economy needs us!'

Rob pauses for breath, while I digest what he's just

said. Before I can respond, he continues. 'Sorry, JJ. I don't mean to keep banging on about myself. What I wanted to say is that maybe instead of worrying so much about me, you should concentrate on your own life. Do you really want to sell someone else's vitamins forever? And be told where to stick your exclamation marks?' The corners of his mouth twitch for a split second. 'And what about your mother? That crack you made just now about her working so hard. What's wrong with hard work? I know advertising's just one long party—' Rob's expression tells me he doesn't really mean what he's just said '—but are you going to spend the rest of your life in your mum's shadow? You're worth so much more than that.

'I know she's a tough act to follow. And remember, I've seen the way random strangers grab you in the street and bang on about her programmes as though you're some long-lost relative. Hideous. So maybe it's time to show your mum you're every bit as capable as she is, and step into the spotlight on your own terms.'

'Um … are you forgetting mum works in television? That superficial industry you say you've had enough of. As for being recognised, it wouldn't happen so often if she'd only stop writing all those ludicrous stories about me. It's not as if I've even made it to the D list, either.'

'I know, I know.' Rob's voice softens. 'And I understand why you feel she's used you as cannon fodder for her career. But you're definitely top of my A list. Ever since I found out about the time you tried to make a Swiss chalet out of a box of Tampax. Not to mention the way you tried to smuggle that poison arrow bullfrog out of London Zoo in your pocket.'

'Mum and Dad told me I'd adopted him!' I quell Rob's mirth with a look. 'I thought I was allowed to bring him home. And it was a skyscraper, not a chalet. Anyway, how do you know about that?'

'My mum mentioned it,' he confesses.

'Thanks, love. You've proved my point. Everywhere I go, people think they know my life story, thanks to Mum's charming little fairy tales about me. Except they're not charming at all. They're an invasion of my privacy.'

'And probably your human rights as well.'

Rob thinks I exaggerate, but he doesn't know the half of it.

When you're obliged to grow up in the spotlight, there is no place to hide.

From the moment I went to school, kids wanted to be friends with me – or their parents encouraged them to be my best buddies – because of who my mum was rather than because of who I was.

I clench my teeth, remembering the time Mum was convinced the cleaning lady was stealing her underwear. It turned out two of the boys I'd invited to my birthday party had raided the bedrooms. But, of course, we didn't find that out until one of them was caught by his own mother, parading in *my* mother's bra and panties. And then the other boy (who I secretly liked) announced to our entire class of fourteen-year-olds that my training bra had an 'age eleven' label on the inside. I've never told anyone about that; not even Rob. I wrap my hands across my chest and hope he's finished.

But no, he's still going strong. 'Listen,' he says, 'the point I'm trying to make is that quite apart from the tales of your childhood, which only make me love you all the more, your mother's an excellent campaigning journalist. She uses television to change lives. In a good way. She's done it on her own terms, too. I'm not saying you should abandon advertising. But maybe it's time you thought about your career path, and where you want to be in five years from now. And, in the meantime, you should stop worrying what people in general – and your mum in particular – think about you.'

We sit and look silently at one another for what seems like a long time. Then Rob says, 'You're right. It's definitely time for bed.' He gets up, stretches and disappears into the bedroom.

He's offering me an olive branch. But I feel as if he's whacked me over the head with an oak tree.

Is this really what he thinks?

That I should get a new job because that's what he's decided to do? And that I shouldn't be irritated every time a stranger recognises my face and accosts me in the street with the words, 'So *you're* the girl who tried to cut the grass by setting fire to it when you were eight!' (I so did *not*. It was simply unfortunate that my experiment with dad's lighter proved so successful.)

'Are you coming?' Rob's voice from the bedroom.

Usually, I'd quip back, 'No, it's just the way I'm standing.' One of those silly, secret routines that cement a relationship. But I'm still thinking about what he said.

Rob appears in the doorway. 'If you're not coming to bed, maybe you'd like to look at this.' He advances towards me, clad only in the boxers I gave him on Valentine's Day, and drops a document into my lap.

It weighs at least as much as *Bleak House*.

I scrutinise the cover, which has 'Business Plan' written on it. Underneath these words – mysteriously – is a photo of a Jack Russell that looks suspiciously like Asbo.

'Danny and I have done our homework,' Rob says. 'We're going to make this work. I know it won't be easy, but I've always liked a challenge. That's why you're my girl.' He gives me a gentle hug, and retreats back towards the bedroom.

I'm too proud to follow. Even though I have to be at work in a few hours – and I'll have to go home first, since I can't appear in the office in yesterday's clothes, still smelling faintly of bleach and with only one Croc intact – I'll never get to sleep.

Make-up sex?

I toy with the idea.

But I'm still hurting.

I mooch into the kitchen and make a cup of mint tea. Then I pad back to the living room, and sprawl into the armchair, which is still warm from Rob's body. I pick up the business plan, scowl at the dog, take a sip of spearmint and start reading.

Documents like this are one of the occupational hazards of copywriting. You have to work your way through zillions of words that spell out all the stuff you need to know about a business – what it actually does, who its products and services are aimed at, how it fits into the marketplace, the state of the competition and lots more – and then crunch a ton of market intelligence into a few sentences that persuade people to buy whatever it is you're selling.

'Not bad,' I say to the empty room about thirty minutes later. Actually, the business plan is pretty damn good. For one thing, it's written in plain English as opposed to Natasha-speak, which means it's refreshingly short of out-of-the-box partnerships, integrated holistic networks and cross-media e-services.

But as for the business itself…

Maybe I'm being snitty because Rob's taken me so much by surprise, but the real truth is that I can't understand why on earth he wants to devote his life to this particular enterprise.

I mean, if Rob had announced that he and Danny intend to solve world poverty or invent an alternative to oil, I'd be first in the enthusiasm queue.

But chucking in your job to manufacture and flog fruit juices?

Fruit juices and smoothies.

I know I'm in the minority, but I think smoothies taste like chilled sick.

I take another look at the projected sales figures. I know these are always based largely on foolishly optimistic guesswork, but even if Rob only does half as well as he predicts, turning his back on television is going to make him rich.

There's only one thing wrong with the whole business plan.

And that's easily fixed.

I get a notebook and pen from my bag and start to scribble.

Ten minutes pass, and I'm more than halfway towards solving the problem. At least I would be, if Rob hadn't reappeared in the doorway. Clad only in pyjama bottoms, blond hair ruffled and rubbing his sleepy eyes, he looks irresistible yet vulnerable.

'What'cha doing?' he enquires.

'Saving your bacon.'

Before I can say any more, Rob has his arms around me and I'm nestled in his lap. 'I'm sorry I didn't tell you,' he whispers. 'I was scared you'd talk me out of it.'

After a leisurely kiss and make up – by the time we're finished it's starting to get light – Rob picks up the business plan from the floor. 'So what have we done wrong?' he asks.

'This.' I jab a finger at the picture of the dog on the cover. 'Your branding's not going to work.'

'But Danny and I spent hours going over names,' Rob protests.

'Look,' I say. 'You can't call a juice business The Dog's Bollocks. Trust me. You just can't.'

'But it's funny. It's clever. It's saying we're the best.'

'It's linking a particularly unhygienic piece of canine anatomy with a product you want people to put in their mouths,' I say firmly.

'You're only saying that because of what Asbo did to your shoe.' Rob is crestfallen. 'We want to use him on our labels. In an HMV post-ironic way.'

Every once in a while, my boyfriend comes across as a lovable twat.

'I'm only saying you need to rethink the name because I don't want you to lose your life savings.' Rob is putting thirty thousand pounds into the business. I was stunned when I saw this in the funding summary. Partly because I never realised he's got that much squirrelled away, but also because I can't help but think it would be enough for the deposit on a flat. 'Still, I'm not going to fight you over it. Call it The Dog's Bollocks if you want. Do I look like I'm bothered?'

'You look—' Rob adjusts his position and gives me a quick up-and-down '—as if you need to pull a sickie and spend the day in bed. With me.'

'Can't do that. I'm in enough trouble at work as it is.'

I'm also still chewing over what Rob said earlier, about me needing to take a look at my own life, rather than being a world authority on what he should be doing with his.

'I'd better shoot off home and get ready.' I reluctantly unwind myself from Rob's lap, and we both stand up.

'Are we OK?' Rob's question is another apology for not telling me about the business any sooner.

'So long as I don't have to say my boyfriend's The Dog's Bollocks whenever people ask me about you.'

'You mean you don't say that already?' Rob gives me a big kiss.

'Only in a post-ironic way.'

Rob goes back to bed, and I start to clear up my stuff. By rights, I should be sink-into-a-coma exhausted.

But my brain is still racing.

I read somewhere – *Grazia*, probably – that when we criticise people, what we're really doing is running away from our own faults, flaws and insecurities.

So what do I want as much as Rob wants to make this juice thing work?

*

Instead of going home, I fetch an A4 pad from the top of Rob's bureau, sit back down, and begin to record the facts of my life.

By the time it's broad daylight, I've spilled my guts. I sift through the spidery pages with a professional eye.

Hmm.

If I were a brand, I wouldn't even begin to know how to sell me.

There's nothing about me that makes me stand out from the crowd. I'm just another twenty-something London girl, being pulled along by the tide of life.

How come I don't want to save endangered species in an Amazonian jungle?

Or win an Olympic gold for table tennis.

I don't even yearn to speak Mandarin Chinese.

The fact is, my ambitions are ordinary. Bog standard. Even the one thing I don't dare to write down is something millions of other people have accomplished.

My secret ambition.

My skeleton in the closet.

'Some day,' I've said to Rob on a couple of occasions when we've both had a bit too much to drink, 'when I've got more time, I'll sort it all out. You'll see.' I think that's what he was prodding me about when he suggested I'm wasting my life adding superfluous exclamation marks to the VitalVitamins website.

If only we weren't always so busy at Cognita. Then

again, work is where I feel genuinely competent and where I'm judged by what I produce, not on who my mother is.

My mother.

I have to do something about my mother.

Or at least I have to do something about the way I feel about her.

This is the thing.

My mum is an amazing woman.

I mean, when you say 'pregnant at fifteen', you think of someone living off benefits in a tower block with a stud through her nose, a tattoo on her ankle and a chip on her shoulder.

Not *my* mum!

Beth Jackson might have made an initial mistake – I've gone through my whole life knowing I shouldn't really be here – but she also made a stunning recovery.

When I was fifteen, all I had to worry about was whether I was always going to be too tall, and if I'd be allowed to pack a tent and go to Glastonbury with Theodora.

Unlike my mum: she was juggling nappies, sleepless nights and ceaseless whispering behind her back. She had this unquenchable drive to succeed. Prove to everyone who'd ever mumbled the word 'abortion' that she was not only up to the responsibilities of motherhood, but also completely capable of carving out a career.

I can't count the number of times I've heard Dad boast that Mum collected straight As in English, French and Geography, along with the Young Journalist of the Year award, all in the month I learned to walk without holding on to anything.

Fast-forward a few years…

By the time Mum was in her mid-twenties – more or less the age I am now – she was making appearances on the BBC, a bubbly, confident spokeswoman for Generation X, while continuing to entertain readers of the *Daily News* with regular updates of my juvenile transgressions. And, of course, she was blissed out with Dad, celebrating the fact he'd recently finished his teacher training.

Whereas Rob and I…

Are you jealous of your own mother? I confront the question I've written.

Well…

I wouldn't have wanted to bring me up, that's for sure.

But here's a home truth: Mum and I are so close in age, I feel as if she's my competitor rather than my mother.

Anything I can do, she's already done.

Better.

She is Wonder Woman.

And I'm such a loser.

Deep in debt.

Working at an agency no one's ever heard of.

Unable to get my boyfriend to commit.

A real disappointment to my mother. No wonder she doesn't want to spend time with me. Mum's got life all worked out, whereas I just muddle along from one mini-drama to the next. If life is a journey, I definitely have no sense of direction.

My only ambitions – I consult my written summary – are:

- To live with Rob.
- Stay at Cognita and get promoted.
- Make my mum proud of me.

Not to mention that other thing I'm too superstitious (or too cowardly) to put in writing.

The way things are going, I've got as much chance of achieving any of my goals as I do of saving a rainforest, collecting an Olympic gold, or ordering sweet and sour chicken in the local language next time I happen to be in Beijing.

You know what?

It's not my boyfriend who's having the quarter-life crisis.

It's me.

Chapter Six

That that is…

…doesn't have to be.

Or to put it another way: Welcome to the New Improved JJ Jackson!

Amazing how something so small as rewriting my mantra can make such a huge difference.

It's been three weeks since that sleepless night when even my modest ambitions seemed beyond me. Since then, I've been fighting back against my underachieving life and everything's back on an even keel, which goes to show that once you change your behaviour, different things begin to happen.

True, I've barely seen anything of Rob, but that's only to be expected now he's in full-on business start-up mode. My new Supportive Girlfriend Policy consists of leaving him to his own devices.

I don't want to seem needy. I've got my own life to lead, and it won't take long before Rob realises he's not seeing enough of me. At least, that's what Theodora and I believe.

Thank God for best friends.

Theodora was as shocked as I was when it turned

out we were celebrating a business launch instead of a Rob-and-me launch, although that was probably because I'd done such a good job of convincing her – and myself – it was about to happen.

'Don't worry, babes,' she told me last night. 'You and Rob belong together. Just give it a bit more time.'

Talking of time, Theodora seems to be spending every spare minute holed up inside her room. I accused her of having a mystery lover tied to the bed, but she insists she's immersed in a new artistic project.

As usual, she won't tell me what it's about. I begged her to give me a clue, but the only words I could prise out of her were 'pride and prejudice'.

'Something to do with Jane Austen, then?' But my fishing expedition produced nothing more than laughter.

So far as work goes, I'm living up to my ambitions: keeping my head down, using plenty of exclamation marks every time I go near the VitalVitamins website, sending regular have-you-thought-about-improving-sales-by-doing-this? emails to Bruno Lombardo, and turning into a deaf mute every time Natasha tries to lure me into discussing our respective chances of promotion.

I've also been spending at least three nights a week working on the Goal That Dare Not Speak Its Name – pumping flesh and blood into that skeleton of mine – and I'm thrilled with the results.

But best of all, my mum.

The more I think about our dodgy relationship, the more I realise I've been waiting for her to make some grand gesture. Something that declares she yearns to be closer to me.

And now I've had this eureka moment.

Why don't I take the initiative?

Do something out of the ordinary.

Something that will make her realise I am a shining example of the sophisticated young woman I aspire to become.

In short, a belated Mother's Day treat.

'What do you think?' I consulted Dad over soup and sandwiches when we met for one of our regular lunches.

'Great idea. I know Mum was really disappointed she had to work that day. And she's bound to appreciate something out of the ordinary.'

My dad, ever the diplomat, determined to keep the peace between the two women in his life.

I briefly considered inviting Mum to join me for a trip on the London Eye, which I keep meaning to try, but thought better of it: too public, and Mum would be standing there signing autographs instead of admiring the view.

Next, I worked my way through the theatre listings. I was halfway to booking tickets for *Richard III* before I admitted I actually wanted to see *The Book of Mormon*, which is definitely not a 'mummy show', and besides, going to the theatre isn't really an intimate mother–daughter bonding experience.

I reluctantly ruled out zorbing because (a) it's too expensive, (b) it probably didn't count as poised and (c) I could already hear my mother saying, 'Juliet, let me see if I've got this right. You're suggesting we strap ourselves inside a giant hamster ball and then let someone propel us down a hill?'

There was also the chocolate-making course that would prompt her to tell me about all the latest diets, the vineyard tasting tour that was, alas, a hundred miles out of London, and something called Wet and Wild that is definitely not for mothers and daughters.

A zillion internet hits later, and I've finally come up with the perfect gift: A Ladies' Pampering Experience.

In an ideal world, I'd love to take Mum to some place really swish. Somewhere like Canyon Ranch in Arizona, where you spend a whole week being coddled and cosseted and come out glowing like a goddess. I spent a happy half-hour on their website, picturing myself on the Life Enhancement Program, picking and choosing from an enormous list of activities – I keep meaning to learn yoga – and noting that a peanut butter and banana sandwich was classified as a healthy breakfast option.

But my daydream came to a crashing end when I looked at their rates. Four nights in a single room is more than I earn in a month.

Undaunted, I checked out places closer to home. But having seen – almost felt – Canyon Ranch, they seemed like second best. And still way beyond my budget. As a last resort I typed 'Cheap Spa London' into Google, and solved my problem in 0.21 seconds.

I found somewhere not only geographically convenient for us both, but also on special offer as a buy-one-get-one-free, which meant I could just about afford it. And even if it is a cheap and cheerful version, at ninety-five quid for half a day, it's the most expensive present I've ever given anyone other than Rob.

(Well the lingerie was for me.

But he got to see me in it.

And out of it.)

The thought of my bank balance makes me walk faster from West Hampstead tube. Probably just a vain attempt to shake off my debts, but I do need to get a move on. This place is much further from the station than it looked on the map, and I don't want to get off to a bad start by being late. Mum's always so punctual I'm convinced we have at least one German ancestor lurking inside our family tree.

It feels strange not to be at work on a Friday, but this was the only slot Mum could manage before Whitsun – her PA's already rearranged twice with me – so I've officially taken the morning off. By the time I get back to the office, I'll be healthy, glowing and every inch a creative group head. What was it Napoleon's wife once said to him when he was having a bit of a meltdown? 'Walk like a general, talk like a general, dress like a general, *et voil*à … you will *be* a general.' She probably didn't say it in a mixture of French and English, but you see where I'm coming from.

Ah, here's Mum!

Emerging from the back of a chauffeured black BMW that's parked insouciantly on double yellows. Blimey, she looks like she's just come *out* of a spa. I sprint the final few metres to greet her.

'So this is Kilburn.' My mother sounds like Scott discovering a particularly chilly bit of the Antarctic. But there's a smile that goes all the way to her eyes, and melts my instinctive defensiveness. We hug, genuinely pleased to see one another. Then she holds me at arms' length, gives me a quick once-over, and nods almost imperceptibly. I feel I've passed the first test of the day.

Just as well, because the Beau de Jour day spa is not as I remember it from the internet.

It's wedged between a hardware shop and a furniture store that looks like it hasn't ordered new stock in my lifetime. Then there's the logo, which I don't remember seeing at all: a pneumatic female silhouette, wrapped around a cartoon palm tree that's planted on an angry orange sun. Or is that blob supposed to be a sand dune? Also, the spa's windows are shrouded in heavy metal shutters. I know beauty products can be expensive, but this seems unnecessarily secure.

'Shall we go in, then?' Is it my imagination, or is that the tone of voice Mum used when she did that special report from Basra?

She leads the way.

The Beau de Jour reception area looks more like a doctor's waiting room than the gateway to a morning of opulent relaxation. I fumble in my bag for the vouchers they sent me, but before I find them, the receptionist looks up from her crossword puzzle and greets us. 'Booked in on the BOGOF, aren't you, my loves?'

She's a podgy, middle-aged woman with bright pink hair and chipped nail varnish. 'Such good value, isn't it?' She'd never get a job at Canyon Ranch. 'Follow me,' she says as she gets out from behind her desk.

We trudge Indian file through a warren of dingy corridors. 'I'll leave you girls in the changing room. Robes and everything are inside.' Ms Pink hands over a pair of locker keys. 'Your schedule and options are there, too. Call me on the house phone when you've decided what you want.'

'That's very efficient. Thank you,' Mum says.

The changing room turns out to be slightly less spartan than its surroundings. Which is to say it's clean, and smells faintly of pine. New Age music plays in the background.

It takes me a few moments to realise I'm listening to a version of Beethoven's Fifth. On pan pipes. Recorded on location at Niagara Falls.

Mum's already examining the treatments menu with the same fierce concentration she usually reserves for production notes. I grab a robe and scarper for the nearest changing cubicle.

'So are you keeping well, darling? Dad's been soldiering along with a bit of a cold, poor love. I almost suggested he came along and rested himself up in the steam room. How's Rob? I managed to get hold of a DVD of that cave dweller thing he did. Very funny. Won't be long before I'm asking him for a job. Such a talented boy. Everything all right at work? I've been frantically busy. As usual. You'll never believe who I met the other week. Madonna! Her kids seemed really sweet, and so well behaved. She showed me this special yoga position that's meant to be terribly good for the back. Written any good ads lately? This is terribly kind of you, by the way. So thoughtful. I'm only sorry we couldn't manage to meet on Mother's Day, but you know how it is. Dad's always telling me I work too hard, but that's just the way I am. Love me or leave me, I always say. We're hoping to get away for a long weekend some time next month. Dad keeps saying we should go to back to Venice before it sinks. Did you know he's joined the Green Party, by the way? Hilarious. He'll be sticking solar panels on the roof next, and have me worrying about my carbon footprint. Actually, I think the whole carbon footprint business is one big con. We had this guy on the show the other afternoon. Proper charlatan. I asked him, "If we can't trust British Airways to get our luggage safely from London to New York, why on earth would we believe they're going to plant trees or whatever with this money they're asking us for?" and next thing, he went off on a rant and blamed me, personally, for all the environmental woes on the planet. Mind you, we've had this off-the-record briefing about a hush-hush Government working party that's already mapping out climate change disaster scenarios. Even if the temperature rises only a couple of degrees, we're all in the shit.'

Did I mention that my mother is a human wall of sound?

That's not the same as saying she doesn't listen. But I find it's often easiest just to let the words run over me like a lukewarm shower, while I interject the odd 'Yes', 'No', and 'Really?' to prove I'm keeping up.

When I emerge from the changing cubicle, Mum's stripped off and is on the phone. Even at forty, she could still grace page three of any tabloid, although you're more likely to find her towards the front of *Vanity Fair*, styled and adorned by this month's hot designer, with her four-figure fee going to one of her deserving causes. I could have sworn Mum's waist is smaller than mine, but today she's looking just a shade rounded. Or maybe I've finally lost weight.

'...We'll take the restore, refresh and relax options, thank you. To incorporate the tropical fruit saltbox scrub and the hot stone body massage. What do you mean the heater thermostat's not working? Why not? OK then, the aromatherapy massage with an extra fifteen minutes, since we can't get what we wanted. That's fair. And coffee in the Roman Room to begin. One double espresso. One cappuccino.'

Mum puts down the phone and shrugs her way into a swimsuit, followed by the towelling robe provided by the spa – which if it's anything like mine, is far from the luxurious embrace I'd been expecting. Ever since I booked, I've been anticipating the sheer indulgence of being snuggled inside a fluffy cloud. But this feels more like being attacked by a swarm of thirsty mosquitoes.

Confession.

I have never actually been to a spa before. So I am secretly relieved Mum's taking charge. And even more relieved I have made the correct choice, by changing into a swimsuit, rather than the clean underwear inside my sports bag. Guess that means we're beginning with a dip in the pool.

We make our way to the Roman Room. It's in the basement, which means more dim, unheated corridors, plus a couple of flights of concrete stairs. 'I somehow don't think this place is in the *Good Spa Guide*,' Mum remarks as we prepare for the official start of our Ladies' Pampering Experience.

'Sorry, Mum, but—'

'Oh, I didn't mean it as a criticism, darling. No need to apologise. This is all very sweet of you, Juliet. Let's treat it as an adventure.' She opens the door to reveal the Roman Room in all its subterranean splendour.

Having lowered our expectations, we are unsurprised to find ourselves in a medium-sized bunker that is thankfully the warmest place we have encountered so far. The ceilings are low, illuminated by fluorescent tubes, and supported by pillars that look as though they belong in a Sainsbury's car park rather than this supposedly Greco-Roman bathing chamber. Three of the walls are tiled in baby blue, while the fourth sports a mural depicting half a dozen life-sized men and women, all of them middle-aged and naked, and doing dodgy things that involve birch twigs and buckets of water. I hastily avert my eyes.

Then sneak another look.

Mum, meanwhile, is picking her way through a grove of plastic palm trees. They lead to a semicircle of sunbeds surrounding a Jacuzzi that's marginally bigger than the paddling pool I had when I was a child.

Our coffees have already arrived, which displays some reassuring efficiency, and, to my delight, the beverages are accompanied by some decidedly un-spa-like chocolate biscuits. I'm busy wondering whether I can snaffle Mum's as well as my own, when she nudges me.

'Over there,' she whispers.

First of all, I think Mum's pointing out the plaster statue of an enormously well-endowed man skulking in the alcove, but she's drawing my attention to the fact that we are not alone in the Roman Room. There's someone in the Jacuzzi. To be more precise, there's a big, fat, bald bloke with a walrus moustache climbing out of the water. He's not wearing swimming trunks. Or even clean underwear. I bite hard into my chocolate finger, step backwards, and wonder if I have time to escape to the security of the palm trees. Too late.

'Morning, ladies.' Naked bald bloke gives us a leer. 'Overdressed, aren't we?'

At moments like this I'm enormously grateful for Mum's sharp wit and ability to put people in their rightful place. Which in this case, I imagine, is behind bars. But to my surprise, she treats him to one of her best 'hello and welcome' television smiles and says, 'Sorry, it's our first time here. We weren't aware of the dress code. Undress code, I should say. Darling—' she turns towards me '—what a lovely surprise. You didn't tell me this is a nudist spa.'

Mum points a highly polished pink fingernail towards a sticker on the wall. It's got illustrations of swimming costumes decorated with big black crosses running through them.

Oh crap.

I was expecting a cheap and cheerful version of Canyon Ranch. Instead, I've brought my mum to a place that's one step up from a massage parlour.

Bloody internet.

Bloody copywriters who exaggerate the facts.

Bloody fool that I am, trying to impress my mum.

'Nice to see some new, um, faces here.' Naked bald bloke shakes himself dry like a Labrador, oblivious to his wobbly bits. Unlike his head, the rest of him is covered in tufts of grizzled hair. I pull my itchy robe tighter. 'Don't I know you?' he says to Mum.

'I don't think so.'

'You're definitely familiar.'

'I've just got one of those faces.'

I've heard Mum go through this routine hundreds of times when she's spotted in public. Even so, I have to admire her poise. You'd think we were in Selfridges.

'No, I do know you.' Naked bald bloke is more persistent than most. 'You're that lady off the telly.' And before Mum can deny it, he adds triumphantly, 'Fiona Bruce!'

Mum shoots him a smile. 'You have to promise not to tell,' she stage-whispers. And before she can say another word, naked bald bloke is thankfully climbing into his tent of a robe, and scuttling towards the door, presumably to spread the word that a real live A-list celebrity is about to get her kit off in the Roman Room.

'Fiona will kill me if this ever gets out!' giggles my mother. I laugh with her, but I know what's going to happen next, and my heart sinks.

'Darling, I'm so sorry,' Mum says.

'I know. I understand. My fault entirely.'

'I just can't take the risk.'

We stand there, assessing the likelihood of headlines announcing Fiona Bruce has been discovered in a nudist day spa in Kilburn, enjoying a buy-one-get-one-free session with her young lesbian lover.

'At least he didn't have his camera phone.' I do my best to sound more cheerful than I feel. But we both know the paparazzi will be on their way.

'Look, there's no need for you to leave too,' Mum tells me. More of a command than a suggestion.

Since I've already made such a magnificent screw-up of this special occasion, I don't have the nerve to disagree. 'If anyone asks questions, or if I see any reporters, I'll tell them it was Jeremy Paxman,' I offer weakly.

Ten minutes later, Mum is on her way to the office, while I'm face down on a massage table being assaulted by a heavy-handed woman – Romanian, I think – whose only sentence of English appears to be 'YOU LIKE IT HARD'. I shudder to think where she's been going for her language lessons. Actually, I shudder in pain as she descends on me again, this time zoning in on my shoulders.

Whatever she's doing feels more like a floor scrub than a fruit scrub. Or is this supposed to be my aroma-therapy massage? Either way, I am being systematically beaten up. Also, there's a faint aroma of chip oil coming from my spine. It all goes to show that my decision to avoid spas – in the same way that I make it a policy to steer clear of doctors and dentists – has been vindi-cated. I mean, what is the point of being prodded and poked by white-coated strangers? I know they're full of good intentions, but I'm convinced they do more harm than good. At this rate, they'll be taking me back to the office on a stretcher.

'I DO NOT LIKE IT HARD!' I howl.

But this seems only to encourage my assailant, who shifts the towels around in order to pummel my shoul-ders more efficiently.

Will this torture never end? I'll tell them whatever they want to know. Yes, it was Beth Jackson down there in the Roman Room. I'll even confess to being her gay groupie if it will only get me out of here. I hear a voice that sounds strangely like my own.

Groaning.

Then sighing.

Then nothing.

I open my eyes and Ms Pink Hair is in the room, helping me back into my robe and offering me a glass of water. 'Am I dead?' I ask.

'No, dear.' She helps me off the massage table. 'But

Svetlana tells me you were beautifully relaxed. Now take this, please. You need to rehydrate yourself.'

The fizzy water she gives me tastes as good as champagne, and it's having the same impact. I'm decidedly light-headed. And, um, good. Actually, I feel great. I run a finger tentatively across my neck and shoulders. Beautifully soft. And not a whiff of chip oil.

I float my way back to the changing room, explaining to Ms Pink Hair that I will forgo the other treatments. 'Enough is as good as a feast,' I say, before realising one of Mum's favourite sayings is coming out of my mouth.

There's a surprise waiting for me when I open my locker and am reunited with my clothes. Nestled in among my jeans is a box about the size of one of those old Rubik's cubes. Except this is definitely something for grown-ups.

The box is a muted shade of ebony that whispers: *'What's inside me is precious and expensive.'* It weighs promisingly in my hands as I examine it further. A silver-embossed logo on the top flap is obscured by a yellow Post-it note, adorned by Mum's handwriting.

'For you, darling,' it reads. 'Something that will improve your life. I guarantee it! xxx'

I carefully stash my unexpected gift in the sports bag – it looks far too good to be opened – while I remain half-dressed and still in a bit of a daze. I'll enjoy whatever it is later on, when I'm feeling less humiliated.

It's a lovely gesture, of course, but today was meant to be about showing Mum I'm capable of giving *her* a wonderful treat. I assume she was going to give me this beautifully wrapped package to say thank you, but in the circumstances, it feels more like a consolation prize.

So much for glamour.

So much for sophistication.

I offer a little prayer – better make that a big prayer – that our mother–daughter bonding experience won't feature in Mum's next broadcast to the nation.

When I arrive back at the Beau de Jour reception, Ms Pink Hair is back behind the desk. 'You might want to slip out the back way, dear.' Her lips barely move. 'Photographers.'

I walk in the direction she's indicating, and she adds, 'I've always been a big fan of that Natasha Kaplinsky. Always looked so lovely in all those sequins. Is she getting in shape for a new project?'

Miss Pink leans closer and adds, 'If the two of you fancy a return visit, we have a special ladies' night every other Thursday. Very special. After hours. Discreet.' The receptionist gives me a lascivious wink.

I flee.

Chapter Seven

Friday afternoons at Cognita are usually pretty relaxed. Either the week has been a success, in which case long lunches are followed by the five o'clock appearance of the drinks trolley and we do the team-bonding thing. Or the week has been a disaster, in which case, ditto.

But not today.

By the time I arrive in the office, just after three, everyone's milling around and there's a definite buzz in the air. Is it my imagination or are people looking at me as I walk from the water cooler to my desk? What have I done now?

I won't have to wait long to find out.

Even before I've hung my jacket on the back of the chair, Natasha is by my side. 'Skunk wants to see you in fifteen minutes.'

'Any idea why?'

'Not sure. Did you have a nice time at the spa?'

'Lovely, thanks.' If only you knew.

Instead of getting on with her latest customer-interfacing win-win viral ping what-have-you, Natasha is still perched on the edge of my desk.

'How's your low carbon diet thing coming along?'

I'm not particularly interested, but I can't think of anything better to say, and I don't want to be rude.

Natasha launches into an enthusiastic exposition of designated teams, scope of assessment and SMART goals. Followed by a whole bunch of sources, resources and recourses. All of which, apparently, will culminate in one of her renowned Death by PowerPoint presentations coming to a screen near me in the near future.

I surreptitiously download my emails, while Natasha continues to position Cognita at the forefront of corporate environmental stewardship. How come neither Rob nor Bruno Lombardo have responded to my messages? I dive into my out-box to make certain I haven't inadvertently been telling Rob how to increase market share by targeting silver surfers with calcium and glucosamine (!), while advising Bruno on the finer points of guerrilla product tastings at the Electric Ballroom. Nope, the correct emails have gone to the relevant men in my life.

Natasha has stopped babbling and is looking expectantly at me. Presumably it's my turn to say something.

'Yes?' I mean it as a question, but Natasha takes it as an affirmative.

'Well, I'm glad I can count on you,' she says. 'Oh, and good luck with Skunk.'

I'm not sure which remark should give me greater

cause for concern. But at the mention of my boss's name, I stand up and prepare to discover why he wants face time with me.

When I arrive outside his office, the door is shut. I peer through the glass and see him deep in conversation, pacing up and down with his phone in one hand, an obese roll-up in the other, and a thin cloud of smoke hovering above his head, almost like a halo.

'You want a coffee?' Carlotta asks.

If Skunk's PA is offering me a drink, something's definitely up. While she fusses around with milk and sugar, I try to work out what's about to happen.

It's the promotion. Has to be. Why else would we be having a scheduled, private conversation? Which means…

Either I am about to become a creative group head.

Or I am not.

Before I can think this through any further, Skunk's off the phone and ushering me inside. 'You know why you're here?' he asks.

'I think so.' I'm starting to feel confident. He must have noticed I've been getting into work a bit earlier and staying quite a lot later. And, since he doesn't know my extra hours are because I've discovered a quiet office is the ideal place to work on my Secret Goal, he's putting this down to my incredible loyalty and ambition.

'I thought it only decent to tell you first.'

There are two words in that sentence that I don't like. The ones sandwiched between 'it' and 'to'.

'And now you tell me—' Skunk smokes and definitely inhales '—three reasons why you're not quite ready to be a group head.'

Is this a trick? Quickly. Think. 'You're asking the wrong question,' I declare. Before Skunk can correct me, I continue, 'What you need are three reasons why I'd make a fantastic group head. And they are…'

My mind's gone blank.

'Yes, JJ?'

'One…' I'm playing for time, and we both know it. 'Actually, one, two and three all add up to the same thing…'

'Six?'

'Tell me why you're giving the promotion to Natasha.'

'No need to bite your bottom lip quite so hard. Don't want you bleeding on the carpet. Definitely don't want that. Not from what I hear.' A cruel little chuckle. 'Calm down and drink your coffee.'

I take a gulp, as instructed.

'As it happens, you're entirely correct. I made an unfair demand on you. But only because in our business clients do that all the time. As, indeed, do bosses. You did well, trying to turn it around. Even though the follow-through didn't quite come off.'

I'm paying close attention. Where's Skunk going with this?

'You still need to learn that, ultimately, our clients get the advertising they deserve. Look.' He swivels the screen of his iMac towards me, and I'm confronted with the VitalVitamins home page. 'Complete mess, isn't it?' Before I can respond, he continues, 'Do you know how many exclamation marks there are on this page?'

'Twenty-three.'

'I must have missed two.' Skunk laughs for real. 'How many should there be?'

'Two. Maximum. Here.' I point. 'And another at the end of that headline. Debatably.'

'Agreed. And yet…'

'Yes?'

'Virginia just called.'

Sister-of-Skunk.

'She tells me they're about to announce record profits. And yes – I'll say it before you beat me to it – with fewer exclamation marks, their figures might have been higher still. But, even so, we have to accept that our clients are in the driving seat. If they insist on superfluous screamers, then let them remain ignorant of the fact that what really matters are the words, and that punctuation marks are actually supposed to be signposts.'

Interesting. But I still don't get what this is all about.

'Give me three reasons why Natasha deserves promotion,' he demands.

'She sucks up to clients more than I do. She's well dressed. And, oh, I don't know. She cares about the planet. Except if she really cared, she wouldn't waste so much paper on her bloody memos. And don't you wish she'd stop going for broke in the bullshit bingo stakes?'

My outburst is rewarded with the merest hint of a beard twitch. 'If Natasha spoke plain English more often and you managed to speak it less frequently, I'd be a happy man,' Skunk informs me. A glance at his watch. 'Look, JJ. Let's cut to the chase. You and Natasha are rivals for the group head vacancy. The fact is, I've decided not to fill it.'

What? 'How come?'

'You youngsters are far too preoccupied with job titles. It's what you do that's important. Not what's written on your business card.'

This isn't the right moment to tell Skunk no one has ever asked me to produce a business card.

'So here's the thing. I'm putting the decision on hold for six months. Let's see who's contributed most to the agency by then.'

'Contributed to the bottom line, you mean?'

'Good question. But financial success can't be measured individually. You know the old saying, there's no "I" in team.'

'But there is a "me".'

Skunk decides to overlook my observation, which

is generous. 'Although, talking of money…'

This sounds promising. I take a casual sip of cold coffee.

'I'm putting you on Podolski.'

I shudder.

In the creative department, Podolski is our least favourite client. The account no one wants to work on. Martyn, who used to be in charge of it, resigned last week – a clear case of cause and defect.

'Why me?' Translation: *Why me???*

'Because I have faith in you. Podolski's our biggest revenue generator. You'll find they're receptive to good ideas and intelligent writing.'

'But they're a bank.' A boring old bank that's set up a bunch of branches over here to woo Polish immigrants. With a head of marketing who speaks seven languages, and – reputedly – has no sense of humour in any of them.

'Glad you know which business sector they're in. Good start.'

'Does this mean I'm off VitalVitamins?' Might as well try to retrieve something from the situation.

'No, JJ. It means you're accepting greater responsibility and an increased workload. We all have to do our bit to deliver maximum value, especially these days.' Skunk looks meaningfully at me. 'You'll be the lead writer. I'm also putting you in charge of Ravi. He'll help you out.'

Ravi is our department's newest recruit. Started in January, and hasn't quite got the idea of work yet. Bit of a party boy. I haven't had much to do with him, but at least this is a step in the right direction.

You could almost look on it as being group head. Two's a group. Technically.

Skunk fiddles with his jumbo cigarette papers and tobacco pouch. I take this as my cue that our meeting's over and stand up.

'Two more things.' Skunk stops me in my tracks. 'Merit rise. Extra five hundred a year. And—' Skunk rubs his upper lip in a meaningful way.

It takes me a second to catch on.

Have I really been sporting a cappuccino moustache for our entire meeting?

'Send Natasha in, will you?'

Our business is concluded and my boss returns to his roll-up.

Back at my desk, I'm leafing through the Podolski Bible, which is to say I'm turning the pages of a large scrapbook to examine the adverts and mailshots we've produced on behalf of our clients.

The Poles take money seriously. No cartoon frogs sitting on lily pads dreaming about second homes in Spain – or even first homes in Stoke Newington. No perky horses waving their hooves in the air as they frolic in the fields. And definitely no images of happy customers messing about on a beach and laughing all the way to the bank.

No, no, no.

Podolski believes in numbers. Lots of them. Along with grainy pictures of hard-working people who pause from their grim labours just long enough to save every penny – in contrast to our frivolous British habit of spending whatever we earn – or send their earnings safely home to family in Warsaw and beyond.

As for the copy… I scowl at a bunch of sentences that contain very few vowels. The trouble with Podolski is that everything we write gets translated into Polish.

With one eye on my career, it's good to have a Pan-European account under my belt. But why can't I have a sexy bit of Pan-Europe, like Paris, or Rome? Oh God, will they make me go to Warsaw?

I log onto the Podolski website – it must be the only place on the net that's entirely in black and white – and discover their headquarters are in Krakow. I'm nervously Googling the weather over there, when I sense someone standing behind me.

'Are you going to teach me everything you know?' Evidently, Ravi has heard we're going to be working together.

'Tell me about Podolski.'

Ravi grimaces. 'It can wait until next week. I just came to let you know we're all about to congratulate Natasha.'

My stomach does a flip-flop.

'Birthday.' Ravi answers my unspoken question.

'Thank God for that. I mean – I'll catch up with you in a minute.'

My new protégé wanders towards the drinks trolley, while I breathe an unworthy sigh of relief. I really did think for one moment that Natasha had somehow talked Skunk into promoting her.

The phone rings and Rob's name appears on the screen. 'Hello you,' I say. 'What time are we meeting? I checked times for the film and—'

'Really sorry,' Rob cuts me short. 'I'm not going to be able to make it. We've just had an extra order come in. Big one. But we have to deliver by eleven, so I need to stay here and juice. Catch you later, OK?'

Even before I can volunteer to help, Rob's hung up. I'm still trying to decide whether to call back when Natasha reappears. We exchange a look.

'Bloody Skunk.' She scowls. 'Typically indecisive old man. All that dope's turned his brain to marshmallow.'

Blimey. Natasha has definitely taken on board Skunk's desire that she should speak everyday English more often. 'I've been tasked with writing the new agency brochure,' she continues. 'Poisoned chalice, or what?'

'Podolski.'

She pulls a sympathetic face. Then she looks expectantly at me. 'You've forgotten. Haven't you?'

'Of course not. Happy birthday, Natasha.'

'I mean you've forgotten our bet. From last year.'

'What makes you think that?' What's she on about?

'So where is it?'

'It's… It's…' I've got it.

Natasha's birthday is a couple of weeks before mine. Last year, she presented me with a scented candle that was almost good enough to eat. Embarrassed at having got her nothing, I promised to reciprocate next time round. And – it's coming back to me – she bet me fifty quid I'd forget. Or was it dinner at Gordon Ramsay's I promised? Forgotten that, too. Along with her wretched present.

A costly mistake.

Unless…

I hesitate. There *is* a way out of this. Not an ideal way. Not as good as Natasha dismissing our stupid bet, as any normal person would. My solution demands sacrifice. But the alternatives – cold hard cash, or an expensive evening facing Natasha across a tablecloth loaded with knives – are far worse.

Reluctantly, I scrabble beneath my desk and unzip my sports bag. I dig around, pushing aside my clammy swimsuit, until my fingers close in over the beautiful package Mum left for me in the changing room at the Beau de bloody Jour spa for naked show-offs.

I hesitate. Then fumble in the bag to remove Mum's

Post-it note with the promise that her gift will change my life.

Is it wicked of me to give whatever it is to Natasha?

Part of me tries to justify what I'm about to do by thinking I don't really deserve it anyway. Not after messing up the way I did. The other – bigger – part of me thinks I can still thank Mum, and she'll be none the wiser.

'How can you imagine I'd forget something so important?' I gloat. 'Here it is!' I produce the beautiful, glossy black package with a conjurer's flourish, and place it in Natasha's hands with a wave of regret, and a sudden, terrible conviction that Mum has given me a precious piece of jewellery that I will be expected to wear on special family occasions.

'Why, JJ!' Natasha is gratifyingly lost for words as she makes short work of the packaging. I bask in the glow of generosity. Besides, it's too late to snatch it back and make a reservation at Ramsay's.

'It's…' Natasha discards the packaging on my desk, and holds up what looks like a mother-of-pearl container. It shimmers in the afternoon light.

'It's…' Natasha seems lost for words. Hurry up, woman! I'm so desperate to see what Mum's chosen for me, I want to wrench the pot out of her fingers.

'It's…' Natasha turns the object around in her hand. Then she looks up from her birthday present to me.

'Do you love it? I spent hours searching for something really special. It is your birthday, after all.'

'It's…'

Wow! Mum's gift is so magnificent, Natasha looks as though she is about to burst into tears.

She finally recovers her powers of speech and asks, 'JJ, why have you given me a tub of wrinkle cream?'

Chapter Eight

What's going on?

At this rate, I'm actually going to *need* wrinkle cream – (in fact, it turned out to be anti-wrinkle cream, but that's beside the point) – because it looks like I'm going to carry on crying till I've solved the world's water crisis.

All I want is to make the best of myself. I'm not unrealistic, so I know I'm never going to get talent spotted by any of those model scouts who prowl Topshop in Oxford Circus, but I thought that at least I have good skin. Apparently not. My own mother thinks I'm ageing badly.

I blow my nose and relive the moment when Natasha opened the package and looked at me in such bewilderment. No point pretending she's a proper friend, but if I'd wanted to find the most insulting gift I could, wrinkle cream would have come second only to 'feminine deodorant'. As it was, Natasha's stricken face made me feel deeply ashamed, and the best I could manage was, 'I'm so sorry, there's been a mistake.' With that, I grabbed my jacket and sprinted from the agency.

I was halfway down Tottenham Court Road when Ravi phoned. He meant to console me, saying he'd read the blurb that came with the jar, and it was – at least – expensive anti-wrinkle cream, developed in a secret laboratory near Tokyo and containing a proprietary blend of thirty-three active ingredients including ginger, oolong tea extracts, wheat protein and – yuk – bovine stem cells, but it didn't really help.

By the time I got home (I walked all the way to Camden almost in a trance, alternating my thoughts between the horror of what I had done to Natasha and the hurt of what Mum had done to me) I was in such a state that Theodora thought I'd been sacked. Or that Rob had dumped me.

'It's nothing like that,' I mumbled. 'I'll be fine.'

Fortunately, Theodora was on her way out, and I convinced her she didn't need to babysit me. Once she was gone, I gave in to my feelings and started to sob.

Morning now, and I lie on my back in bed thinking about all the times I've disappointed Mum. High on the list comes my failure even to apply for Oxford or Cambridge. Then there's the fact I still smoke at least ten cigarettes a week. And my peculiar inability to pass the driving test despite six attempts. I was doing so well last time, my full licence was a formality, until I was obliged to veer towards the pavement in order to avoid a couple of pigeons. A fresh waterfall of tears, as I remember how Mum happened to mention this when she appeared on *Top Gear*.

You know what it's like when you start crying. Some people say it's irrigation for the soul, but in my experience, one sad thought leads to another, and even though you know you're getting things out of proportion, you somehow can't seem to stop yourself from spinning round in ever-decreasing circles. I muffle the sound of my sobs by playing Amy Winehouse over and over, and stay put in the bedroom until gone eleven, when hunger forces me out.

Theodora is lying in wait. 'Whatever's happened, you have to promise me one thing,' she demands.

'Bot?' I sniffle.

'You'll never play that bloody CD again.'

I manage a wan smile.

Theodora's great. She brings me scrambled eggs on toast, followed by a family-sized bag of Revels for dessert. And a choice of red wine or Grey Goose.

Looks after me with unconditional acceptance.

No questions asked. As though she were my... I'm not going to finish that sentence.

But I'll tell you one thing.

Friends are the new family.

Theodora and I are going clubbing. She insists. Thankfully, it will be dark, and too noisy to talk.

I emerge from my bedroom in my Saturday best.

'What do you think?' I give her a twirl. 'Do I still look as if I've been crying?'

'Take off the sunglasses, and I'll let you know, babes.' Theodora giggles. 'Or shall I get you a guide dog? How about that horrible mutt of Danny's? I hear he tried to pee into a vat of freshly squeezed orange juice this afternoon. Now that really *would* have been the dog's bollocks.'

Thank God for Theodora. I'd been wondering if I'd ever laugh again. 'Who told you that?'

'Rob. He called me because your mobile was off.'

'And?' I remove my sunglasses.

'I wasn't sure what to say. In case you'd had a huge fight. Or something?' Theodora looks me in the swollen eyes. 'In the mood to spill any beans yet?'

'Thought you wanted to go clubbing.'

'I only suggested clubbing because I know you hate it. I thought you'd say no way, and then we could stay in and talk about whatever it is that's upset you so much. Last time I was this worried about you was when you nearly got expelled.'

We grin in unison at our shared memory of my thwarted attempt to sell the school on eBay – '...complete with eighty-four attractive sixth-formers of various shapes and sizes, healthy revenue from hugely expensive school fees, plus ample playing fields that are ripe for redevelopment...'

I suppose that little escapade was the first piece of

sales copy I ever wrote. Even though the bidding reached £753,000 before someone sneaked, our alma mater was none too pleased. Mind you, Mum and Dad thought it was hilarious…

'It's my mum,' I finally tell Theodora.

'Oh my God. Is she ill?'

By the time my tale of woe is complete, a fresh cascade of tears is threatening my cheeks. Any more of this and I'll be dehydrated.

'I know I've defended your mum in the past –' Theodora fetches me a box of tissues '– but you're right. It's a mean thing to have done. Tactless, at the very least, and you don't deserve to be treated like that.' She pauses. 'Not quite up there with bombing Iraq, but definitely on a par with getting hammered with bank charges just because I went overdrawn for half an hour. More wine?'

By the time the bottle is three-quarters empty, Theodora is no longer so keen to hit town. We've shifted into the living room, the iPod's on shuffle, I'm starting to feel like myself again, and we're having a proper catch-up.

'So if you think the Beau de Jour spa's embarrassing, it's got nothing on what happened to Pete.' Theodora's friend Pete is a photographer who's been to supper a couple of times. 'He's been having terrible trouble with his teeth, and needed a root fixed.' I wince at the thought. 'He managed to get an emergency appointment on Saturday, and then rushed off to do a wedding, drugged to the eyeballs. Didn't realise anything was wrong till his phone started singing the *Star Wars* theme halfway through the service and an irate bridegroom told him he'd gone to the wrong church!'

'Pete really fancies you.'

Theodora shrugs. 'You can tell a lot about a man from the quality of his ringtone. Besides, I don't have time for men at the moment.'

'And my man doesn't have time for me.' That's something else I was thinking about while I was secluded in the bedroom.

'Yes, the new business seems to be taking over Rob's life,' Theodora sympathises. 'And you were so convinced he was going to ask you to move in with him.'

'Let's just say that in the past few weeks, his ringtone's gone from *Yes! We Have No Bananas!* to *Strawberry Fields Forever*, via *Raspberry Beret* and *Orange Wedge*. Anyway…' Time to change the subject. 'Tell me about your new work of art. *Pride and Prejudice*, wasn't it? How's it coming together?'

'Oh, you know. I've been doing sketches.'

'Of Jane Austen?'

Theodora shrugs. 'I'm trying to work out how to show something some people just can't see. Even when it's usually starting them in the face.' She pulls herself up from the futon and tops up my glass. 'Babes, I've been meaning to talk to you about—' Before she can finish the sentence, Theodora's own phone leaps to life.

A straightforward ringtone.

She checks out the caller display. 'This might take a while. It's to do with the work. I'll take it in the other room.'

Twenty minutes pass, and Theodora's still not back. I'm going to have an early night. My last waking thought is wondering what I'm going to do about my mother. Maybe the answer will come to me in a dream.

Until it does, I'd better avoid her.

I pull open the curtains just before ten the following morning. It's hard to be miserable when the sun's shining so unexpectedly. It feels almost like a Sunday in summer, even though we're still only in April.

A quick peek in the mirror reveals I don't look a day over twenty-four. Maybe a good bout of tears every once in a while is good for the complexion.

PLEASE, GOD, LET ME STOP THINKING ABOUT WRINKLE CREAM.

I never gave the wretched gunk so much as a thought in my entire life until Friday, but now I'm obsessed with the stuff.

I need a distraction.

Rob doesn't need much persuading when I call with my suggestion. 'I still haven't thanked you properly for thinking up such a brilliant name for the business,' he says. 'And, I'm already at Danny's. Come over about three.'

I hang up before he can ask why I've been so elusive since Friday, and dash to our local deli, a couple of streets away. Even by Camden standards the prices are high, but the food is delicious. I pick out smoked salmon, a thick triangle of melt-in-the-mouth Brie, bread that's still satisfyingly warm from the oven and studded with crunchy, good-for-you grains, plus two large handfuls of black grapes, a couple of delicious dinky crème brûlées – no make that three – and a few plump green olives.

Back home, I mess about online for a while, then nip into the shower and slather myself in my favourite orange-scented gel. I change into my newest pair of skinny jeans, topped by a jade silk shirt that Rob hasn't seen before. It's also time to baptise my latest pair of Crocs: with their cool blue cameo pattern and rugged look, they're perfect for climbing to the top of Primrose Hill for a Sunday afternoon picnic. A few squirts of my favourite perfume and I'm good to go.

'Are you sure you don't want to come? There's easily enough food for three,' I say to Theodora. She's sitting at the kitchen table, working her way through one of the tabloids.

'Not this afternoon. But what time will you be back?'

'Dunno. Why?'

'There's something I really need to talk to you about.'

More about my mother, I suspect. Theodora's looking shifty, the way she always does when she's gagging to give me good advice I'm not yet ready to hear.

'Look forward to it.' A mental note to stay over at Rob's tonight. 'Laters!'

Ten minutes later I'm threading my way through Camden Market – stuffed with German tourists on the hunt for magic mushrooms – when I realise I don't have a spare set of work clothes at Rob's.

Funny how the brain works.

One thought leads to another.

All these months, I've been expecting Rob to ask me to move in with him: waiting with more patience than I knew I possessed, and foolishly thinking he was going to make a big song and dance about it. But the fact is, he has other priorities.

Like pineapples.

And ice cubes.

And a never-ending pile of paperwork.

That's not the same thing as him *not* wanting us to be together under one roof. Rob's problem is that he thinks he needs to be a fruit juice tycoon before making a formal commitment. So he'll be thrilled when I tell him that doesn't matter at all – and I'll be helping to reduce the pressure I know he's under.

There's no one in the world I'd rather be with than Rob, and I know he feels the same way. We're ready to take our relationship to the next level. So instead of behaving like I'm in the eighteenth century and waiting for him to sort it out, it's high time to make it happen.

As I approach the footbridge into Primrose Hill, I grab my phone from my bag and speed-dial Theodora. 'Guess what?'

I'm too excited to give her a chance to reply. 'I'm going to tell Rob we should be living together! This playing hard to get, it's just a game.' A guilty thought occurs to me. 'That is ... provided you don't mind me moving out. Every time we've discussed it, you've said you'll be fine. But I have to be sure you mean it.'

'Of course I'll be OK! And Rob's bound to say yes. This is *such* good news!'

I walk up the path to Danny's place. The property that belongs to Danny's family trust, I should say. It's all to do with death duties and inheritance tax. The sort of stuff the seriously rich – and seriously titled – lose sleep over, instead of wondering like the rest of us if their council tax direct debit is about to bounce. Hideously complicated, but the bottom line is that Danny gets to live rent free in a two-bedroomed flat that's close to the park and was bought by his great-grand-earl or someone for about eighty quid, back when Queen Victoria was a girl.

My finger's on the doorbell, but there's no need to

press. A series of sharp little barks that rise to a growling crescendo signals my arrival.

Rob answers the door, with Asbo in hot pursuit. The creature seems to have doubled in size since last time I saw him. I do a quick sidestep to make sure he can't get anywhere near my new shoes and give Rob a huge hug.

'You look great.' He runs an appreciative finger along my silk-clad arm and my whole body starts to tingle. 'Come on in, I'll be ready in a sec.'

I follow Rob along the hallway, and notice his tennis racket is propped in a corner, surrounded by three or four carrier bags. I'm thinking Danny must be out, but when I reach the kitchen, he's shovelling peaches into what looks like a giant food processor. He looks up and realises I'm there.

'JJ, great to see you.' He fetches a glass and pours me a generous helping of juice.

I take a sip. 'Delicious!' It tastes completely different from the stuff that comes in supermarket cartons. Three gulps and I'm holding out my glass for more. Maybe Rob and Danny *can* conquer the world. The juice world, at any rate. Maybe we'll end up living in Mayfair. With a holiday home in France. Maybe—

Danny interrupts my daydream. 'Take a seat,' he says. He gestures to a corner of the kitchen, where Asbo is curled up in old armchair, guarding a couple of peach pits. The chair is brown leather and looks almost identical to Rob's favourite piece of furniture. 'Just push him out of the way. I know I spoil him.' Danny is beaming, and obviously still besotted.

'Was he an impulse purchase?' Since Asbo seems to be a permanent fixture, I'd better show some interest.

'Last time I was home he was involved in a bit of a fracas with a neighbour's peacock,' Danny confesses. 'Poor little thing needed to make a fresh start. Dad started calling him Asbo, and the name seems to have stuck. He was called Rufus until then. It wasn't really his fault with the peacock...' Thankfully, before Danny can describe the dog's crime in detail, Rob reappears.

'Ready to go?' he asks.

Asbo is paying altogether too much attention to the picnic basket for my liking, so we make a hasty exit.

I've been coming to Primrose Hill since I was in my pram, and it remains one of my favourite places. Mum and Dad used to bring me here at weekends. They'd spend hours pushing me on the swings, or making sure I didn't come to grief on the climbing frame – and explaining every once in a while that actually I was their daughter, not a younger sister.

'...And you're not listening to a single word I'm saying. Are you?' Rob gives me a friendly nudge in the ribs. I beam up at him. This is a day we'll remember – and treasure – for the rest of our lives. The day I gave fate a shove and convinced Rob we're ready to start building our first home together.

As if he can read my mind, Rob pulls me closer to him. 'Everyone thinks our company name is fantastic,' he announces.

The Dog's Bollocks has been thankfully strangled at birth, and my boyfriend is now the CEO and chief bottle washer of a firm called – drum roll – FruityFul.

'So how's business?' I lay out our picnic fare on paper plates while he brings me up to date.

FruityFul is off to a flying start.

Six contracts with gyms and health clubs. A night-club in South Kensington. A couple of West End delis. All within the space of a few weeks. Rob has even managed to sign up his former employers. 'Mind you, I get a few funny looks when I show up with the deliveries. The CEO reckons I'm having a nervous breakdown, and that if they humour me, I'll come crawling back.'

'So are you making a fortune?'

Rob pulls a face. 'Losing one, more like it. The start-up costs are a lot more than we expected. You wouldn't believe how much we're being charged for plastic bottles. We're looking for greener alternatives, of course, but those are even more expensive.'

My boyfriend draws breath to continue, but since I can be lectured on the necessity to save the planet any time I want by Natasha – supposing she ever speaks to me again – I interrupt. 'Have an olive!' I pop it into his mouth and fix him with what I hope is an irresistible smile.

Blimey, he must have swallowed it whole, because he's started a new sentence while I'm still mentally rearranging the words *live*, *darling*, *let's* and *together*.

'The thing is, JJ,' Rob takes my hand, 'I need to make some sacrifices for the next few months.'

My stomach takes an ominous lurch, the way it always does when I'm confronted with bad news.

'We want to grow as fast as we can, and that means taking on some staff. I'm meant to be running the business, and I can't do that properly if I'm spending ten hours a day pressing fruit.'

I'm scared to make eye contact with Rob, so I look down at our entwined hands; his are stained orange – like he's gone ballistic with Fake Bake, or developed a three-hundred-a-day habit.

'So…' Rob pauses. 'I've managed to sublet my flat for the next six months, and—'

And it all makes horrible sense.

The tennis racket in the hall. The armchair in the kitchen.

'You're moving in with Danny!' I manage to choke the panic that's shooting from my chest to my throat before it can escape into the fresh air.

'I love it when you finish my sentences.' Rob kisses

me softly on the lips. 'The best thing about it,' he continues, 'is that I'll be living closer to you. No more tube treks.'

The remainder of our picnic passes in a haze. Rob doesn't notice I've not eaten, and he hasn't asked a single question about what's happening in my life, which is just as well, all things considered, but hardly the point.

At least I didn't make a complete fool out of myself. Theodora and I will be able to have a giggle about it when I get home.

It's not as if Rob doesn't love me.

It's just that the time was wrong.

Oh crap.

The one good thing about this picnic is that I haven't been thinking about Mum.

Until now.

Beth never forgot the day she was discharged from the Royal Free, cradling her newborn daughter. Matthew was a few minutes late, and a nurse mistook Beth's impatience for anxiety. 'Don't worry, my sweet,' the nurse told her. 'Life will get easier as you grow older.'

It had seemed like a prophecy. A blessing that had kept her safe for almost a quarter of a century.

Until now.

Beth was supposed to be prepping tomorrow's interview with a diet doctor who was convinced raw tomatoes, hard-boiled eggs and nettle tea were the only ingredients you needed to look great in this season's bikini. She planned to call it the 'You're An Idiot Diet' once the cameras were rolling, but for now, she sat alone and unobserved in a café not far from home, feeling God – or someone – had torn up the script for the rest of her life and presented her with an entirely different storyline.

All those plans she had made with Matthew. Learning to tango next Christmas in Buenos Aires. Running the London Marathon together. The retirement home they were planning to buy in Cornwall in another five or ten years. How strange to think none of these would now be happening.

Unless…

No, never.

Beth Jackson already knew she had no choice except to follow her heart.

Daily News, 8 September 199–

MY WEEK

TALES FROM THE HOME FRONT WITH BETH JACKSON
She's leaving home…

Like most mums, I sometimes daydream about how my life will change when Juliet leaves home. On the plus side, I won't have to clean up after she and seven friends have spent a boisterous afternoon finger-painting and making chocolate brownies. But then again, how empty our home will feel without her.

Saturday afternoon, I had a rehearsal for what's in store. Juliet brought home a less-than-perfect school report, and when Matthew and I sat her down for a chat, she responded by flouncing upstairs, uttering several words I'm afraid she has learned from us – along with a couple of others I fondly imagined she hadn't yet encountered. Ten minutes later, my darling daughter stomped back into the room, clutching her new Jacqueline Wilson book, a bowl that contained her terrapin, Moses, and a tent. 'That's it. I'm leaving home. Serves you both right,' she spat.

Perhaps Matthew and I shouldn't have fallen about laughing, because, a few moments later, we heard the front door slam and Juliet was gone. I shadowed her all the way to Hampstead Heath, then hid in the bushes for two hours, watching over her while she pitched her tent – eventually – and sat inside, happily turning the pages of her book. Thankfully, by the time it was getting dark, she'd packed up and was heading for home. I sprinted, and managed to arrive a couple of minutes ahead of her.

'I've only come back because I finished my book. And because I knew you would miss me,' Juliet told me when I answered the door to her.

'You're absolutely right.' I resisted the temptation to gather her in my arms and forbade her to leave home till she's thirty.

If her school gave marks for independence, Juliet would definitely get an A*.

Usually she fell asleep the moment her head hit the pillow. Tonight was different. She listened to the steady rhythm of her husband's breathing, but it offered no comfort.

Matthew had no idea his world was about to be turned upside down. How would he respond when she broke the news? Maybe he'd try to talk her out of it. More likely, he'd do what he always did when he was under pressure: retreat to the snooker table and spend thirty minutes whacking balls around while he processed the information.

Then there was Juliet.

Her reaction was more predictable.

She would almost certainly hate her mother forever.

Have you ever wondered why my parents called me Juliet?

It's one of the few things Mum's had the good grace not to explain to her fan club.

The truth is, I'm named after a song by a bunch of ancient rockers called Dire Straits. They had this big love anthem that was Mum and Dad's special song when I was, um, conceived, and the chorus bangs on and on about Romeo and Juliet's poor timing.

At least I wasn't a boy.

Rob pulls me back to the present day on Primrose Hill with a crème brûlée-flavoured kiss. Then I notice him sneak a glance at his watch.

Before he can say anything, I ask, 'Ready to feed the ducks?' It's one of our rituals. After a picnic, we wander across the road to the lake in Regent's Park and cast our leftover bread upon the waters.

Not today.

'I'd love to.' Rob sounds like he means it. 'But I'm already going to be up until gone midnight sorting next week's logistics. Really sorry, sweetheart.'

Midnight? So there's our Sunday night tradition down the drain as well, and most likely flushed away forever now Rob and Danny will be sleeping on opposite sides of a bedroom wall.

'Off you go then, Fruityful.' I manage a smile – no point in us both being miserable – but it hits me that Rob's got a lot in common with Mum so far as work–life balance is concerned.

What does that say about me?

It's too difficult a question to ask, let alone answer. 'I'm going to head over to the park anyway,' I say. 'Can't let the ducks starve.'

'You're such an angel for putting up with me. I'll make it all worthwhile. Promise.' Rob pulls me close and runs a finger down the length of my spine. For a moment I think he's about to weaken.

But no.

We walk down the hill together hand in hand, and go our separate ways with a casual hug and see-you-soons.

By the time I get to the lake, I'm relieved that at least I didn't make a complete tit of myself by inviting Rob to live with me, only to have him turn me down flat. I sit on a bench, watching three ducks making a beeline for the bread. Then I open my bag and take out the rectangular yellow card I've taken to carrying with me, wherever I go.

My Magic Wish List.

OK, I admit it, I stole the idea from an old magazine article about one of the Spice Girls. Geri, I think it was. Before she was famous, she wrote down her goals and ambitions. Two years later, she had everything she'd wanted – superstardom, money, a mansion with a swimming pool, kisses from Prince Charles – except she wasn't married to Robbie Williams, which, if you ask me, was probably a bonus.

My own Magic Wish List is far more modest, yet the goal of making my mother proud of me seems way out of reach, especially given recent events. On a more positive note, I'm still convinced I'll be living with my own Robbie in much less than two years, even though he's at Danny's for now. And my promotion prospects are alive and well. Maybe they'll be a stepping stone to an ad agency people have actually heard of.

Ironically, I've made the most progress with my Secret Goal. I've managed to write it down now, but I'm still too superstitious – too chicken – even to tell

Rob I've taken his words to heart and I'm getting on with it.

I take out my pen and hesitate.

Give up on Mum, and concentrate on the other three goals? No, crossing out one of my goals would make the Magic Wish List look untidy. I put the card back into my bag, take a last look at the ducks, and head for home.

By the time I'm back in Camden, the light is fading fast and the temperature's dropped by five degrees. I'm looking forward to a revitalising brew of fresh mint tea, accompanied by whatever Sunday night rubbish is on TV.

Home.

Can't wait to tell Theodora what happened.

As I round the corner, I open my bag to look for the keys.

This is weird.

The front door's open.

Isn't that my bed propped up sidewise against the corridor wall? And my bookcase in the street?

Look, there's a white van parked outside, doors half open.

We're being burgled!

'What the hell—' I advance on the white van, and jerk open the double doors at the back. Empty.

What next?

I weigh the options.

Dial 999?

Grab my copy of *Great Expectations* – it's a hardback – and use it as a weapon when I burst in through the front door?

What if Theodora's inside and tied to a chair?

Before I can shout 'Help!' my best friend appears in the doorway.

My relief evaporates when I notice she's carrying two bin bags, both of them bulging with shirts, jumpers and dresses. Clothes that were hanging neatly in my wardrobe, the last time I saw them.

'Can I give you a hand with those?' I don't mean the words to be as cutting as they sound, but all the business with Rob's things being out of place at Danny's, it's like starring in a personal version of *Groundhog Day*.

'Babes!' Theodora drops both bags. 'I can explain.'

This doesn't sound good.

'Just … just wait there a moment, will you?'

Theodora disappears back inside, while I continue to play guessing games with myself.

Obvious, really.

Theodora must have had someone else lined up to take over my room. Probably sounded them out a while ago when we were both so certain I'd soon be living with Rob. Whoever she – he? – is, they've definitely wasted no time.

Still, once I explain I'm not going anywhere, we'll move my stuff straight back in. Strange about the bed being moved out of the room. Was this person intending to sleep in a hammock? Or a hideously uncomfortable futon? I'm remembering a happy evening that involved me and Rob and a futon, when Theodora returns, accompanied by a burly bloke dressed in grey combats that are at least two sizes too small and a sweaty black vest I can smell from here.

He turns to Theodora and says, 'Sorry about the mix-up. But if you need any more of the stuff, just let us know. Hang on a moment and I'll find you a discount card.'

This makes as much sense as Mandarin Chinese. Theodora's following the man out to his van, but I'm freezing cold, so I leave them to it and go indoors. In the corridor that leads to our flat, I squeeze past the bed, noticing most of my possessions – iPod, laptop, phone charger, bedside light, clock, candles and so forth – are stashed in a cardboard box beside it. Is this really happening? Almost as if I'm sleepwalking, I successfully negotiate the obstacles, only to be ambushed by my bedside table, which is loitering just the other side of our door.

'Bugger.' I rub my leg, hoping it won't bruise, and continue towards my bedroom door, which is shut. 'Hello,' I call, in case someone's inside.

No reply.

I tap the door lightly with my knuckles.
Still no reply.
I open my bedroom door.
Oh my God.

Chapter Nine

OH MY GOD.

OH MY GOD.

OH MY GOD.

For a moment, it's as though I've been papped. Someone's snatched my photo, using a flash, and I can't see for a few seconds because my eyes need time to readjust. In the meanwhile, I hallucinate strange shapes.

Everywhere I look, I see bags. Not the sort of bags any girl would be pleased to see – hot new designs from Mark Jacobs, Coach, and Fendi – but bags that appear to have come from British Columbia. At least, that's what they have written on them. Actually, these things look more like sacks than bags. Oblong. Made of waxy, reinforced, bright yellow paper.

They're everywhere.

EVERYWHERE.

When I say everywhere, I mean these sacks are stacked neatly in rows that begin at the far end of my bedroom and stretch all the way to the door, covering every available inch of floor space.

More sacks have been stacked on top of the first lot of sacks.

Then another layer's been added – the way you do if you're making dauphinoise potatoes – and so on, until the final bunch of sacks sits waist-high.

I blink.

My eyesight is normal.

There is no sign that I ever inhabited this room.

Instead, the sacks are still there.

EVERYWHERE.

'Three hundred and thirty-six of them. We carried them in from the van, one by one.' Theodora places a tentative hand on my shoulder. 'They weigh eighty pounds. Each.'

'Isn't that about the same as Sarah Jessica Parker?'

'Felt more like Big!' Theodora sort of giggles.

I turn around. 'What the fuck is going on?' I enquire.

'It's sand.'

'Sand?'

'Sand from a place called Harrison Hot Springs. In Canada.'

'What's it doing in my bedroom?'

'It wasn't meant to come till next week.'

'What's it doing in my bedroom?'

'You're moving out.'

'I'm not.'

'Yes, you are.' Theodora speaks slowly, as though she is puzzled. 'To live with Rob. Remember? You phoned me a few hours ago.'

'No, I'm not.'

'Oh.'

'And even if I were – which I'm not – why are you replacing me with three hundred and thirty-six bags of sand?'

'Fancy a drink?'

Theodora has finally said something that makes sense.

We retrace our steps, manoeuvring past the table and the bed. I pause to grab a sweatshirt from one of the bin bags, and we sprint down to our local, the Crown and Goose. Theodora gets a round in while I compose myself.

'So how come you've turned my bedroom into the Gobi Desert?' Having got over the initial shock, I'm intrigued.

'Remember that sculpture competition I told you about?' Theodora puts a glass of plonk in front of me.

'Of course. *Pride and Prejudice*. What about it?'

'It's open to anyone who's never had a public exhibition before. Which narrows it down to a few million of us. I'm through to the final stages.'

'Fantastic! What did you have to do?'

'A detailed written proposal, plus preliminary sketches.'

'So what happens next?' I answer my own question. 'You're doing a sand sculpture.'

'Yes. The theme of the competition's "transience" – here today, gone tomorrow. How something wonderful can shift and change. Sand was the obvious choice for what I want to achieve.' Theodora's eyes sparkle as she begins to talk about her project. 'I mean, I don't think I'll win or anything. But even if I come third, I'll get ten grand. Just as well!'

'How come?'

'Well, the sand itself was only about twenty quid a ton. But the shipping cost me a fortune.'

'What's wrong with Homebase?'

'All sand is not the same,' Theodora confides. 'The stuff you get on the beach gets rolled around with the tide, and won't stick together the way I need it to. My sand's dredged from a freshwater lake in British Colombia, and it's much finer, so I'll be able to carve it exactly the way I want – at least eight feet high – without the whole lot collapsing on me.'

Silence between us for a few moments. Then Theodora says, 'When I first told you about the competition, you were so certain Rob was going to ask you to move in with him. I've been trying to pluck up the courage to tell you, since I got through the first round, but I bottled it. I'm really, really sorry. When you phoned today to tell me you were going to pop the question – as it were – it was like the answer to a prayer. What's happened, anyway?' She is suddenly anxious on my behalf.

'Never mind right now. You couldn't rent a studio? Even for a couple of months?'

'I need to *live* with the sand, JJ. That's just the way it works. Not to mention the cost. And, to be brutally honest, I need to be on my own while I'm working.'

'Yes, but…' I'm sure there's an alternative solution, although I haven't worked out what it is yet.

'I'll send the sand back,' Theodora says quietly.

'Don't be silly. This is your big chance. It's just … where am I going to live?'

Over another round of drinks, we discuss my options. They're not great. It's not that I'm JJ-no-mates or anything like that. But I've lost touch with so many of my friends from uni, even the ones who live in London. That's what comes of being a couple, I suppose.

Ten minutes later, we've established that (a) I am too old to sleep on floors – even if we could think of someone with a spare floor, (b) we don't know anyone who could lend me a room for the next few weeks, (c) even to get a random room from a stranger means I'll need to get my hands on several hundred quid, for the advance rent and a deposit, and (d) turning up at Danny's and begging to share the spare room with Rob is not the proper way to achieve my Magic Wish List goal.

'I could pawn something,' Theodora volunteers. 'Not sure I've got anything that's valuable enough, though. Maybe Rob—'

'No. There's only one thing for it.' Option (e). 'I'll do it outside, though. Too noisy in here.' I take my mobile from my bag, and hit the speed-dial as I walk towards the pavement.

Dad answers after a couple of rings. 'Hello, darling,' he says. 'Nice surprise.'

'Bit of a problem,' I blurt out.

'What's wrong?' He sounds worried.

'Nothing nine hundred pounds can't solve.' I try to sound jaunty, like it's no big deal.

'Juliet, are you in trouble?'

'Yes,' I say. Then I realise what he means. 'Not that sort of trouble.' I give him the short version of Theodora, the sand and my predicament. 'And I'll pay it back eventually, I promise.'

If I'd been thinking clearly in the first place, I'd have anticipated Dad's response.

'I'll put you onto Mum,' he announces. 'Hang on a moment.'

Eeek.

I can't explain that Mum and I are no longer on speaking terms. Especially as Mum's not aware that so far as she's concerned I have taken a vow of silence.

A vow I am now obliged to break.

'Juliet,' my mother begins, 'I'm sorry to hear there's an issue with your flat. But do you really think a handout is the ideal solution?'

Um, yes. 'I'll pay it back,' I say.

'But you still have your student debt?'

'Yes.'

'How much have you got left? Eight thousand or so, wasn't it? And how much are the monthly repayments?'

Mum's behaving as though she's under the heat of studio lights grilling the Chancellor of the Exchequer about the national deficit. I'm getting a lecture on living beyond my means … the importance of having a regular savings plan … the possibility of me getting a second job … something about her lending me two hundred quid when I was eighteen that I apparently never paid back … and there's more.

Much more.

Mum is doing that wall of sound thing again.

So far as I'm concerned, the good old Bank of Mum and Dad might just as well be an underground vault in Switzerland.

Without a key.

You know what?

Sometimes, I hate my mother.

'…blah, blah, blah. Blah, blah, blah. Blah, BLAH, so when shall we expect you?'

'Pardon?'

'I said I'll get your old bedroom ready.'

I yank the phone away from my ear and stare at it in disbelief. But it doesn't prevent me from hearing Mum's next words.

'You're coming back home to live with us,' she says. 'And I think you should stay until you're debt free.'

Book Two
That that is not . . .

Chapter Ten

The room is smaller than I remembered. And full of stuff I'd forgotten about. I'm surprised Mum hasn't turned it into a yoga studio slash shoe closet. Instead, it's been preserved as a museum of childhood.

My childhood.

Midnight-black walls. A galaxy of glow-in-the-dark stars spread across a lime-green ceiling. Above the chest of drawers, a poster of the Hanson Brothers. (Whatever happened to them?) A prehistoric computer that weighs more than one of Theodora's sandbags gathers dust on the wooden desk beneath the window. And on the far wall, a clutch of swimming certificates, arranged in a shape that looks alarmingly like a Swastika.

I was sixteen when I abandoned this room in favour of a larger space in the newly converted loft, which is now Dad's study.

When I arrived last week, accompanied by my worldly goods, Mum said, 'I'm sure you wouldn't want to sleep in the guest room. Far too impersonal, and I like to keep it free, just in case. You'll be nice and cosy in your old bedroom. It's so lovely to have you home again.'

I traipsed up the stairs behind Mum, feeling about ten years old.

And today is my twenty-fifth birthday.

Even though I definitely won't be here for long, I'm still mortified.

- Twenty-five years old.
- Living with my mum and dad.
- Sleeping in a pink metal frame bed.
- A *single* pink metal frame bed.
- A single pink metal frame bed topped with an official Kylie Minogue bedspread.

If this was happening to someone – anyone – else, I'd be laughing.

I'm meant to be getting ready for dinner. Mum and Dad's treat.

'Wherever you'd like to go. Gordon's new place is getting rave reviews, especially the beef that's hacked off the side of a holy Japanese cow and Fedexed to London overnight. They turn it into hamburger, served with *pied bleu* mushrooms plucked from the earth at twilight in the forests of France by professional hunters, then shipped into Battersea heliport, greeted by Securicor, and rushed to the West End to be sautéed in Alpine mountain butter blended with just a hint of organic parsley.' Mum should have been a scriptwriter for *Monty Python*. 'Or how about that new place in

Primrose Hill? The maître d' is good enough to eat, and the asparagus and truffle risotto is to die for. Chinese, maybe? You've always liked crispy fried duck. Remember when you were little, and you asked Ken Ho for his crispy fried dick?' I swear I'll kill my mother if she ever reminds me or anyone else about that again. 'And what about that time we took you to St Malo and you insisted on steak tartare, well done? I know … we could push the boat out and see if I can get a reservation for the Lecture Room, at Sketch. I'm told they do this fabulous starter of spider crab, milk-fed veal and caviar. Or there's always the River Room…'

On Planet Beth, the credit crunch has always been an abstract concept.

I've chosen a place in Soho that Rob and I always enjoy. The table's booked for eight o'clock, so if I'm quick, there's still time for a shower.

But even with the solid glass cubicle door closed tight behind me, the hot water jets that beat down on my head are insufficient to silence the steamy sound of giggling that floats across the landing. Followed by a shushing noise.

Not again. Please. Not again. And besides, they should be getting ready, too. The taxi's due in a few minutes.

In the three weeks I've been back home, I've grown aware that my parents have, um, how can I put this…? They enjoy a vigorous love life.

They're never in the kitchen when I get back from work. Or watching television, like normal parents. Instead, the house seems mysteriously deserted. When they eventually come downstairs, Dad's a bit red in the face and Mum's readjusting her clothing. Even when we're all in the same room, they're always touching one another. Almost like teenagers. And definitely more touchy-feely than Rob and I.

Not that I'm keeping score.

Especially when *our* score is a big, fat zero.

At the restaurant, the three of us have been making polite conversation for almost forty-five minutes.

Topics covered so far include my quest for promotion ('If I could only get my hands on a new account with an intelligent, open-minded client, I'd show everyone what I'm really capable of'), Dad's options for career advancement ('I love my job, so why would I want to switch schools to gain a headship?') and Mum's rejection of global domination ('My agent wants to put me up for a new BBC series comparing childhood in Britain, China, India and Japan. Great concept. I'm sure I'm right for it, too. But far too much travel involved').

Mum shoots a coquettish look at Dad. Who reaches for her hand. I'm feeling like a gooseberry at my own birthday party.

Rob's phoned twice.

First to say he was on his way.

Then to apologise he'd been delayed.

'He'll be here soon.' Dad's noticed I'm checking my watch again. As he says the words, my boyfriend finally arrives.

The kiss Rob gives me tastes of cranberries. 'I'm *so* sorry,' he says. 'Danny and I got locked into a meeting to figure out whether we need to register for VAT. We're growing so fast, but it's all a bit random at the moment. We're too busy getting business to sort out our own paperwork.'

Before I can say hello – before Rob can even wish me happy birthday – Mum's off and running. 'The VAT threshold is about seventy-nine thousand pounds. Or has it gone up? Such a pity the zero-rated supplies category doesn't extend to drink as well as food. Then again, maybe you should consider registering on a voluntary basis to reclaim the tax on your inputs. You'll also find VAT registration increases your credibility with potential clients. Oh, and do make sure you choose the cash accounting scheme, in case you get any bad debts.'

My mother's knowledge of VAT would be sufficiently enthralling to make me fall face down in my food, except the snacks that kept us going until Rob arrived have been cleared away. Mum really is remarkable. She knows everything.

Towards the front of the restaurant, a loud conversation's going on. Heads are starting to swivel.

'Yes, I know it's not fresh. That's what I'm telling *you*.' The words are spat out by a guy of about my age, who seems to be on a date with his size-zero girlfriend and seeking to impress. 'Katie thinks it's made from concentrate.' Size-zero confirms the allegation with a nod and a hair flick. 'It might even have added sugar.' He makes this sound worse than hemlock.

I feel sorry for the waiter, being told off for something that's not his fault. Ah, he's about to be rescued.

'Is there a problem, sir?' A woman in a black trouser suit glides up alongside the waiter. She gestures towards the offending glass of orange juice and listens patiently while the disgruntled diner has another rant about the sub-standard beverage. When he's finished, she says, 'Awfully sorry. You're absolutely correct. This isn't fresh. We've been let down by our usual supplier. Perhaps I can offer you a bottle of wine by way of apology. On the house, of course.'

The offer is accepted without hesitation. 'No worries about sugar and carbs after all,' I observe, turning to Rob.

But my boyfriend is no longer sitting next to me.

He's dashed off in pursuit of the woman in the black suit. I rise from my chair to find out what's going on, but Mum gently pulls me back. 'Better not to interfere,' she tells me. 'He's smelled a business opportunity. Leave him to go after it.'

If only the business opportunity weren't quite so stunning.

The woman in the obviously expensive tailored black suit has an oval face framed by tendrils of auburn, shoulder-length hair. She's almost as tall as Rob's six foot two. And drinking in his every word. I watch the pair of them disappear through a set of swing doors.

Dad's giving me one of his sympathetic smiles. 'Will you order for Rob?'

I hadn't noticed the waiter hovering at our table.

'Sure.' I take a final look at the menu. I've already decided on sea bass for myself and I'm sorely tempted to order the Cajun curry for Rob, because I know he won't like it. Luckily for him, I am a supportive girl-friend, and not a mean one, so by the time he returns, a rack of lamb is sitting reproachfully in a puddle of rosemary jus along with a herbed potato cake, flanked by Rob's untouched place setting.

Even Mum and Dad are embarrassed on my behalf, which only makes it worse.

'I'll make it up to you, JJ. I swear.' My boy-friend sounds suitably apologetic as he slides into his seat.

Before I can think of a gracious – or witty – response, Rob continues. 'I never realised, but this place is part of a group of fourteen restaurants and bars across London. Sonja's already placed an order for juice. And with a bit of luck, FruityFul will soon be supplying fresh ingredients for the cocktail mixes as well. Isn't that wonderful?'

Sonja. Her name is Sonja.

Rob's shovelling down his lukewarm dinner. 'Mm, this is good,' he says.

Mum evidently knows more about cocktail mixes than the head barman at the Savoy (she had him on her show last month), which surprises none of us. '...great opportunity to diversify. Fresh fruit slices, of course. And how about freezing mint leaves, lemon peel and orange bits into ice cubes? You could sell maraschino cherries, olives and fresh, edible flowers as add-ons, too.'

Dad and I exchange glances across the wall of sound.

I wonder what it's like to be my dad. Content to let Mum do more than enough talking for the pair of them. Happy in his own skin. Satisfied by teaching English to a bunch of fifteen-year-olds. Relentlessly proud of Mum's every achievement – and mine – and never seeming even the slightest bothered that she earns, I don't know, at least a hundred times more than he does. Does he ever get jealous when Mum's in the papers, arm in arm with someone like Sting, as she was last week, or is he at peace with the fact that it's just a business opportunity?

Sonja. Her name is Sonja.

I listen with one ear to Mum's anecdote about how

some footballer had the garden fountain at a stately home adapted to spout a giant stream of champagne cocktail for his wedding guests, while thinking of inappropriate rhymes with the name Sonja. The best I can think of is Good-on-ya, which isn't particularly helpful.

Here she is back at our table, armed with dessert menus. But now it's Mum's turn to be looking at her watch. 'I think not,' she says to Sonja. 'Early start tomorrow.'

'Of course, I understand.' Is that a hint of Swedish in Sonja's accent? She turns to Rob and says, 'So I will be ready at three o'clock, yes?' Addressing the rest of us, she adds, 'So kind of Robert to offer to take me to the market at Spitalfields so that I can source some Meyer lemons. They're so hard to come by at the moment. Well worth missing a night's sleep for!'

Robert?

I'm the only person who ever calls him that.

'Robert definitely needs his beauty sleep.' I place my hand on his and feel his fingers stiffen in response. 'He's been working so hard. But don't worry. I'll make sure he's up on time.' Before anyone can point out that Rob and I won't even fit into the single, pink metal frame bed decked with an image of Kylie in scratchy polyester I continue, 'Thank you so much for the business opportunity. We're all very excited.'

Mum gives me the slightest nod of approval. So

quick I almost missed it. Either that or she's starting to fall asleep at the table.

Have I overlooked some rule that says once you're twenty-five, no one has to give you a birthday present? All I've had is a card from Mum and Dad (with the message 'Don't just count your years, make your years count' in Mum's neat handwriting) and an e-card from Theodora, in which a pair of animated penguins promised me a 'birthday surprise worth waiting for'.

But what about Rob?

Did he give my present to Sonja-Be-Gone-With -Yer?

A knock on my bedroom door.

Followed by my mother, while I'm still trying to decide whether to answer, 'Come in!' or 'I'm almost asleep.'

I'm at an immediate disadvantage: a brushed-cotton nightie decorated with a border of dancing teddy bears is no match for the designer dress Mum wore to dinner.

'Darling, you disappeared so quickly,' she says. 'You didn't think we'd let you go to sleep without your birthday presents?' Exactly what I *had* thought. But I try to look as if I'd been expecting her to appear laden with gifts – even though she's empty-handed. 'Dad's making tea downstairs.'

I grab my robe and join my parents in their kitchen, which is roughly the size of Theodora's entire flat. I'd give anything to be back there now. This whole living-back-at-home business makes me feel so inadequate.

'Do you still take three sugars?' Dad enquires.

'Just the one.' This is a lie, but I want to seem as if my palate – unlike the rest of me – has matured.

'For you.' Dad has a mug of tea in one hand and a hefty, brightly wrapped package in the other. 'No prizes for guessing what's inside.' Dad and I exchange grins. He almost always buys me books, and then borrows them back as soon as I've finished them. I unwrap the gift and smile at his latest selection. Great choices, including four newly published thrillers – in hardback – plus three books about advertising, and a just-published biography of Charles Dickens.

'That's lovely. Thanks.' I give him a hug.

'And the envelope,' Mum prompts.

I hadn't noticed the envelope.

It's the wrong shape to be a birthday card. Eagerly, I open it and find myself staring at what looks like some sort of a bank receipt.

Yay!

There's my name.

And a figure of £2,600. Which has evidently been paid into my account.

'That's incredibly generous.' I give Mum a big kiss.

My brain's gone into overdrive. Not only can I move out and find somewhere to stay till Theodora's finished sculpting her sand, but there's also enough for a holiday, rejoining the gym, and several more pairs of Crocs, including the new Celeste Suede model which is a limited edition in a dramatic colour combination of chocolate and plum.

'I'm so glad you approve,' says Mum. 'Dad and I had a long talk. We almost gave you the money to spend on whatever you wanted, but—'

What?

'—arranging to have it paid directly to those dreadful people who should never have lent to you in the first place will save you paying even more in interest. As well as help you clear the debt more quickly.'

I take another look at the bank receipt thingee.

It's actually an acknowledgement of receipt of £2,600 in respect of the bills I ran up having a good time – educating myself, I mean – at uni.

'That's very kind of you both.' I'm trying not to sound like a spoiled brat, but now I know how contestants feel when they blow one of the big money questions on *Who Wants To Be A Millionaire?*

Definitely time for bed. When I get back upstairs I notice a blue light flashing at the side of my mobile.

A text from Rob: 'Idiot! 4got 2 give u ur prez. See u soon.'

Followed by my favourite smiley – the one with horns.

I call his number, but the phone goes straight to voicemail.

By the time it gets to 3am, I am hunched over my laptop, learning more than I ever wanted to know about Meyer lemons.

Was it selfish to have been so thrilled when Juliet found herself homeless? Yes, of course she could have lent her daughter enough for a short-term let; it amounted to no more than loose change. But Juliet did need to learn that money (especially other people's money) wasn't the answer to every problem in life.

Beth changed the configuration of the packets of flour, sugar, pasta and dried kidney beans – the cleaning service never got the kitchen cupboards the way she wanted them – thinking perhaps she was being harsh. Matthew never had such doubts. He'd been saying for a while that he knew Juliet was bothered by her mountain of debt. Though to be fair, it had been her idea to use the birthday as a timely excuse to help make a dent in it.

Or was that just so much bullshit? Was that why Matthew had long since gone to bed while she was puttering around in the kitchen telling herself she was a good mother when she was nothing of the sort?

No, not entirely. She tossed a past-its-sell-by-date can of lentil soup into a bin bag. The truth was that the prospect of having her little girl at home again – even reluctantly at home, due to a financial crisis – had been too good to resist. Fate offering the two of them some quality time.

An out-of-the-blue chance to enjoy the lull before the storm Beth knew she would soon be obliged to unleash.

Daily News, 4 July 199–

MY WEEK

TALES FROM THE HOME FRONT WITH BETH JACKSON
The sweet smell of success

Juliet is learning to knit. To be more precise, she is engaged in a fight to the death with two pointed cylinders of plastic and several balls of bright blue three-ply.

What she lacks in skill is more than compensated for by grim determination. Night after night, for more than three weeks, she's been knitting and purling up a storm – instruction book by her side – the moment her homework's finished. And every time I ask what she's making, she looks solemnly at me and says, 'It's a secret.'

This morning, I was presented with the secret. It turns out to be my birthday present. A scarf. As knitting goes, it's not quite up there with Kaffe Fassett – Juliet's first production is big on holes and ragged edges – but every stitch has been created with love and care.

'I can't afford that perfume I know you like,' she informed me, 'so I made you this, instead. Isn't it great!' And with that, Juliet unwound the scarf from my neck, threw it around her own, and gave me a twirl. 'Promise you'll wear it next time you're on television?'

Look out for me on Thursday!

Beth placed her wooden Treasure Chest on the dressing table by the window and fumbled in the semi-darkness until she found the squishy package she was looking for. There it was, carefully wrapped in tissue paper now yellowed with the passing of the years.

Every family had its secrets. If only hers was as simple as a scarf.

Chapter Eleven

Mum and I had words the other night.

She stuck her head round my door to say it was gone midnight. And I should turn the light off because I had work in the morning.

Unfortunately, she caught me smoking a cigarette, and treated me to a lecture about what it was doing to my lungs. I'm sure she was deliberately graphic because she knew it would make me feel queasy.

(I haven't smoked since.)

Since then, we've been like ships that pass in the night.

Mum is busy, busy, busy.

We were supposed to go shopping together last weekend, but something came up – nothing new about that – and she blew me out.

Whenever that happens, I am five years old again. Mum was meant to be the parent helper on an end-of-term trip to the Tower of London. She let everyone down at the last minute because someone at work was off sick, and our treat got called off because it was far too late to get a replacement. By way of alternative entertainment we got a lecture from the nit nurse. From now on, whenever Mum lets me down and wants to reschedule I'm going to make out I'm even busier than she is.

Busy keeping out of her way.

I yearn for the days when I could put the key in my own front door and do whatever I wanted in my own space without being watched or told off. So this afternoon, it feels like a small victory to know I'm about to have the house – the whole house – to myself.

Bruno Lombardo, my VitalVitamins client, has cancelled the meeting we were scheduled to have with almost no notice, so Skunk said I could knock off early.

I'll go straight to my bedroom and get out of these work clothes. Then maybe I'll watch a DVD.

That's strange.

As I climb the stairs, I hear Mum's voice coming from my room.

Must have left the TV on this morning, and I'm back just in time for the last few minutes of today's edition of *At Home*.

I open the door.

And there is my mother.

Except she's not on television.

She's sitting at my desk.

With a television camera pointing at her.

She looks at me.

Doesn't miss a beat.

'...and talking of the boomerang generation, what a

wonderful surprise. My own Juliet. Darling, you're live on the air. I was just saying how much fun it is having you back under my roof. Despite the circumstances. Our last caller explained how angry he is that even though he graduated last year with a decent degree from Nottingham, he can't get a job – any job – no matter how hard he tries. So he's back living at home, and deep in debt because of his student loans. You can empathise with that, I know.'

Kill me now.

A second camera that's been squeezed into the room pans from my awful pink bed to my stricken face. Like a deer in the headlights, I watch it zone in on me.

Mum continues undaunted. 'Yes, the look on your face says it all. Student debt is a terrible burden. It begs the very real question, should we encourage so many of our children to go to university? Much better surely to bring back apprenticeships. Especially for the less academic. As for the rising cost of fees, it's nothing short of a scandal. And then there are all the youngsters who are back with Mum and Dad because they can't afford to buy a place of their own. Juliet, darling, do you see yourself in danger of falling into that category? Isn't your dream to live with Rob in a home of your own?'

My dream is to be anywhere on earth – with or without Rob – other than in this room.

Mum waits until she realises I'm not going to answer. Then turns her head and says direct to camera, 'Juliet's boyfriend is *such* a lovely young man. Recently started his own business. FruityFul, it's called. Wonderful juices and smoothies. I know it's going to be hugely successful, but until then, there's no way anyone is going to give him a mortgage. And, of course, Juliet's in so deep with her student debt she can't even begin to think about saving for a deposit. And these are good kids I'm talking about. Hard workers, the pair of them. We're in danger of betraying an entire generation.'

I am pretty sure the viewers of *At Home* are being treated to a full-on view of my Kylie Minogue bedspread while Mum concludes, 'Anyway, that's all we've got time for this afternoon. Except to say that one of the advantages of having my little girl back home is that I'm determined to help her kick her filthy smoking habit. In fact, darling, if you're willing to swear here and now that you'll never touch another cigarette, I'll pay for you to have your teeth whitened. What do you have to say?'

Never in my life have I yearned so deeply for a cigarette.

And a blindfold.

And a gun.

'Sawyer from *Lost* or Sylar from *Heroes*?' Theodora asks.

'Hmm.' I ponder the question while admiring a

jogger who's definitely got the right kind of legs to go with those skimpy green shorts he's wearing. The tan looks real as well. 'Tough call.'

'Go with your gut feeling.' Theodora takes our game very seriously.

'OK. Shag Sawyer. Preferably under a palm tree. And marry Sylar, even though he's a serial killer. Do you think I have a thing for bad boys?' I pause. 'Actually, I think I could have a thing for just about anyone at the moment. I'm so celibate it's only a matter of time before I qualify as a born-again virgin. I even caught myself wondering about Skunk the other morning.' That stops Theodora in her tracks. 'We were stuck in a very long meeting,' I add in self-defence.

'You've *got* to dump that Kylie bedspread!' Theodora feels my nun-like predicament is mostly her fault.

I'm still too traumatised to have told her (or anyone else) my bedspread was featured on national television the day before yesterday. Mum's away filming in Rome, most likely telling the Pope about my yellow teeth, and I'm trying to pretend the 'My little girl is home' broadcast was something I dreamed.

That might work.

Until it shows up on YouTube.

'Can we stop running now?' I plead to Theodora.

We'd been intending to take part in a bums-and-tums session at Fitness First. But Theodora persuaded me to hop on the tube and go jogging along the Thames instead. It's great to have lighter evenings again.

'We've barely managed ten thousand steps.' Theodora checks the pedometer that's clipped to her waistband. 'Come on, race you to the London Eye!'

That's at least another ten thousand steps.

Theodora doesn't wait for my agreement, she just sprints effortlessly away. I adjust my backpack and force myself to follow. I'm so out of condition. Give me horizontal jogging any day. Or even bums and tums, followed by chocolate and crisps.

By the time I reach the Eye, I'm sweating buckets and thinking it's going to take an ambulance rather than an Oyster card to get me home. Theodora's nowhere in sight. Ah, here she comes.

'Catch!' She lobs a plastic bottle in my direction.

I pluck it out of the air, whip off the top, and soak up the litre of water as if I'm one of the neglected pot plants on my office desk.

'Ready?'

'For what?' How much further is she going to make me run?

'Ready for your birthday present!' Theodora produces two tickets and announces, 'I'm taking you on the Eye. I know you've always wanted to try it. Sorry it's taken me two weeks to get my act together.'

A moment later, I step inside one of the glass capsules – they're much bigger than they look from the top of Primrose Hill – and we're off.

'Wow! We've got this all to ourselves. How'd you manage that?'

'Told them you've got chicken pox.'

The Eye begins to climb and we're presented with a view of the treetops. Even though it feels we're barely moving, the scenery soon starts to change.

'What a great surprise,' I say.

'Sorry it's so late. But I've been up to my eyes in the sand.'

"How's it going?"

'Oh, you know. I'm trying to sort out the pride from the prejudice. Look! Post Office Tower. Over there!' Then Theodora confides, 'It's more difficult than I thought. I've tried adding sugar to the sand to give the mix more body, but all that did was attract a swarm of ants. And I gouged a chunk out of my thigh while I was experimenting with a cheese grater.' I immediately avert my eyes from the wound, although Theodora knows better than to show me. 'I'm about to start the tamping. Building the foundations,' she explains in response to my quizzical look. 'Can't decide whether to use salt water, or good old London tap. And I'm going to change the whole shape of the structure, which means drawing up a new set of sketches.' Despite the tale of woe, she sounds upbeat.

'So what's it going to look like when you're done?'

'Everything in good time, babes. You'll find out soon enough. Is that Battersea Power Station?'

'Only if it's been moved to the wrong side of the river.' I walk across the capsule for an aerial view of South London. 'I think that's Battersea. Just to the left.' Behind me, I hear a soft popping noise. Theodora's uncorking a half-bottle of champagne and has produced a couple of flutes. She hands me a glass of fizz and says, 'Happy belated birthday. Make a wish!'

We clink glasses and I find myself wishing Theodora wins the competition. But I'm not allowed to tell her or it'll never come true, so I do my best to look inscrutable.

'You planned this all along, then?' I gesture at the champagne bottle.

Theodora nods. 'I was worried the glasses would break while we were jogging. But I thought you deserved a present that actually *did* something.' A reference to Rob's belated birthday gift.

We turn away from the Houses of Parliament, far below, and look at one another. 'He means well,' I say softly.

'Be honest. Wouldn't you rather Rob had whisked you off to Venice for the weekend?'

'Yes, of course! But you never know. This could turn out to be the most valuable present anyone ever gives me.'

For a moment I forget the glorious tableau of London, spread out far beneath me. Instead, my eyes are filled with Rob's earnest expression when I found him sitting in reception at lunchtime on the day after my birthday.

My first thought was that something was wrong because he never turns up anywhere unannounced. But the way he kissed me the moment the lift doors swished shut told me otherwise. (Shame Cognita's only on the third floor.)

We sat down on a bench in Soho Square. 'About last night…' he began.

Followed by a sort-of apology for hijacking my birthday dinner into a business meeting.

Followed by a gleeful account of how the dawn search for Meyer lemons resulted in a firm order for daily deliveries of orange juice – with and without bits – to the restaurant.

Followed by Rob rummaging around in the back pocket of his jeans and producing a brown envelope. 'Happy birthday, sweetheart.' I catch a whiff of pineapple as he places it in my hands.

Déjà vu all over again.

I pull out of piece of paper wondering if Rob has joined forces with Mum and Dad to pay off my debts.

And discover I own ten per cent of FruityFul.

'I talked it over with Danny,' Rob explains. 'He's cool about me giving you a share of my half of the company. I want you to know how grateful I am for all your support. I'll have our accountant sort it out properly. As soon as we get a proper accountant.'

'So does this make me your permanent sleeping partner?'

Rob sidesteps my innuendo and assures me I have voting rights. And I'm welcome to help out with marketing from now on. 'Or you can develop a head-ache and spend the afternoon helping us squeeze oranges,' he suggests.

'Is that code for something?' I ask hopefully. But Rob's puzzled expression confirmed that liquidising oranges was the only thing on *his* one-track mind.

'You've gone awfully quiet.' Theodora's voice makes me jump.

'Sorry, sorry, sorry,' I apologise. 'I was thinking about Rob's present instead of enjoying this lovely gift from you.'

'And?'

'And I reckon that as soon as we get down to earth, you should take a night off from the sand, and have supper with me at that new burger place on Inverness Street. My treat.'

Theodora grins. 'Is that the one I was reading about in the *Camden New Journal*? Where the waiters sing "Happy Birthday" and give you a free ice-cream sundae with sparklers in it?'

'Do they?'

Theodora's not fooled by my innocent response. 'One

of the good things about being a grown-up,' she declares, 'is that we can eat as many ice-cream sundaes as we want. No one can stop us.'

Chapter Twelve

Trouble on the tube this morning, and I'm twenty minutes late for work.

The first thing I notice when I get into the office is a cluster of my colleagues gathered around Natasha's computer.

Laughing.

I stow my backpack under my desk, hang my jacket on the back of the chair and join the group to find out what's so funny. Maybe it's Natasha's first draft of the agency brochure.

Nope. It's a video. I crane my head above Ravi's shoulder to get a better look. There's this woman, thirty-something, with shoulder-length black hair and crazy popping eyes. Armed with a pair of pinking shears and sitting at a kitchen table, surrounded by slivers of blue plastic. Every time she whittles away at the diminishing – and somehow vaguely familiar – wedge of plastic that's lodged in her non-cutting hand she cackles manically.

'In just a few moments,' she says, sweeping her bounty into what looks like one of Rob's smoothie blenders, 'we'll strike a blow for environmental sanity, and give these hideous little babies the fate they deserve.'

Another wave of laughter from my workmates as the blender's turned on.

'What is it?' I ask.

Everyone jumps, and Natasha swivels round from the computer. 'Ah, JJ,' she says. 'Didn't realise you were here.' She presses a button and the screen goes to sleep.

'What's going on?'

'Nothing much,' Ravi says. 'Just a YouTube video.'

'About?'

'Um … recycling.'

Someone sniggers.

'Come on,' I insist. 'Show me.'

Everyone's looking at Natasha – who has barely spoken to me since the Wrinkle Cream Incident. (Is it my imagination, or is her skin looking particularly soft and smooth today?)

'It's part of my low carbon diet initiative,' she begins. 'Tightening the corporate belt. Remember?'

I nod my head, puzzled. What's that got to do with blue plastic pieces being churned around in a liquidiser? Is Natasha going to make us drink them?

'We're switching to low energy light bulbs. Obviously. That'll cut our CO_2 emissions by over two tonnes. I'm recommending we buy power strips for all the computers. So many people ignore my request to turn them off when they go to lunch.' Natasha shoots me a baleful look. 'I'm also investigating a paperless, electronic meeting system. And I've told Skunk I'm happy to counsel our clients about their carbon footprints.'

A couple of sniggers. I still don't get it. Something to do with making our clients environmentally anorexic?

'Talking of footprints,' Natasha continues, 'I conducted some desk research into shoes. *Your* shoes...'

Everyone chortles. You'd think we were on a night out at the Comedy Club. Before I can defend my beloved Crocs, Natasha declares, 'Over two hundred million pairs of those hideous apologies for shoes that you persist in wearing have been sold. They're not biodegradable, so that's an awful lot of landfill.'

Just as I am about to protest that Crocs has an army of celebrity fans that includes Michelle Obama, Ben Affleck and the Beckham children, and that some of their designs, like the raspberry Jayna model I'm wearing today, look almost like conventional shoes, only more comfortable, Natasha jabs at her keyboard and her computer monitor returns to life.

'While I was doing my research, I came across this fascinating video. Thought I'd share it with the team. Unfortunately, you were late, JJ. But never mind, I'm sure everyone would like to see it again.'

A couple of my colleagues decide instead to slink back to their desks.

Which means I've got a clear view of the pop-eyed crazy woman.

Sitting at her table, she reaches for a blue Croc Beach Clog and produces those pinking shears.

OUCH!

She separates the uppers from the sole with a few deft snips that suggest she's done this before.

EUW!

They've speeded up the camera, and now she's reducing the strap to blue matchsticks.

EEK!

This shouldn't be allowed. I turn up my toes inside my own scarlet-and-black Crocs. It feels like a personal assault.

WOOOOOAH!

We're back to the bit I've already seen. Croc cuttings swept into a blender. Crazy woman looking smug.

The video ends. Natasha – and everyone else – looks expectantly at me.

'So what do you do with your old shoes?' I do my best to sound as if we're having a casual, water-cooler conversation.

'I usually donate them to Oxfam. King's Road branch,' Natasha informs me. 'Are you asking for my cast-offs? It would be a pleasure. For me. And everyone else.'

It's a relief to get into my meeting with Podolski. My client, Feliks Butynski – Feliks Unpronounceable, as we call him – is already in the Cognita boardroom, unfurling his usual array of spreadsheets and marketing data.

'*Dzien dobry*,' I greet him. (It's pronounced *jean dough bree* and I memorised it by imagining a cheese sandwich stuffed inside the pocket of my DKNYs.)

'Good morning, JJ.' Feliks is in his late thirties – at a guess – and has an impeccable English accent. Most of the time, he sounds even posher than Danny. 'And Ravi. Are you well?'

'*Tak.*' Ravi nods, and I know he's thinking about Tic Tacs. We exchange conspiratorial glances.

About the only thing I have in common with Feliks Unpronounceable is that we share a mutual dislike of peppering advertising copy with exclamation marks.

His idea of fun is working his way through the British Museum, exhibit by exhibit. I learned this a couple of weeks ago, when I asked him if he'd done anything interesting at the weekend. A simple 'No' would have been enough, but Feliks started rambling on about the three hundred and thirty thousand objects on display in the Middle Eastern department.

I was afraid he was about to tell me about them. One by one. So I cut him short. 'My mum took me to see the Elgin Marbles when I was about ten.' I did my best to sound enthusiastic. (Or key into his vibe, as Natasha would say.) 'Huge disappointment. Did you know they're just a bunch of statues?' For a second,

Feliks looked blank, then laughed, as though I'd told him a really good joke.

Since then, we've both stuck to business.

Feliks is already frowning at his spreadsheets. 'I have identified a big problem,' he announces.

'Let's think of it as an opportunity,' Ravi responds.

'No. It is a problem.'

'Tell us,' I encourage.

'Two problems. Firstly, the English banks are beginning to compete for our Polish customers. We have lost market share for two consecutive months.' Feliks jabs at the numbers on his spreadsheet with his index finger. 'Your banks know Polish people are a good credit risk, so they offer them lower fees and bribes to open accounts. Movie tickets, and the like.'

I remember Rob once summed up Polish cinema as: 'Boy meets tractor. Boy falls in love with tractor. Boy loses tractor. The end.' But this isn't the right moment to mind-share (another of Natasha's favourite expressions).

Feliks continues, 'Then we have the problem of thrift.'

This grabs my attention. 'Why's thrift a problem? It's a good thing, surely?'

My client looks at me as though I am a simpleton. 'JJ, how do you think banks get rich? Not by encouraging people to save. Banks need people to spend. To spend money they don't have.'

'Like student loans, you mean?'

A nod of approval. 'Yes, and loans for cars, holidays, internet-ready televisions, cosmetic surgery, weddings and other luxuries. All the things you English people believe you're entitled to the moment you decide you want them, no matter what is happening with the balance of payments, the fiscal outlook or even GDP. Live for the day, isn't that what you say? It's very different in Poland. We believe in saving, rather than overdrafts and borrowing. We wait until we can afford things.'

'And that's bad for the bank, right?'

Ravi, Feliks and I spend the next hour brainstorming the problem of rival banks muscling in on Podolski's market share. At the end of which, our three best ideas are:

- Persuade Podolski customers to get into debt by offering borrowers free flights home – or tickets to the States if they borrow enough.
- Promote loans to customers who are setting up businesses in England.
- Encourage Polish immigrants to send their kids to private school – develop a school fees loan package.

'Not bad. Not bad at all,' Feliks says, but he still looks bothered.

'Shall we keep going?' I suggest.

'No. It's not that.' A long pause. 'I feel bad about this. About encouraging my people to break with tradition, and spend money they haven't earned. Stupid, I know. But head office in Krakow is insisting.'

I have a flash of inspiration. 'Let's steal some market share of our own.' I lunge for the Magic Marker and add an extra idea to our list:

- Convince customers from English banks to switch to Podolski and borrow money for business and pleasure.

Feliks looks at me with new respect. He nods twice and says, '*Tak! Tak! Tak!*'

I treat myself to an extra-sugar Starbucks for lunch, and spend the afternoon working on ideas to tempt the English into debt with money from Poland. In fact, I'm wondering whether I could persuade Podolski to lend me enough to clear my debts – with a bit to spare, so I can take somewhere on a short-term let, until Theodora's finished her sculpting, and swept all that sand from my bedroom. Maybe I can even convince Feliks it's my professional duty to 'live the brand' – as Natasha would say, if we were on speaking terms – and negotiate an exceptionally good rate of interest.

Like zero.

*

Almost the end of the day.

I catch a whiff of something in the air. Closely followed by Skunk, sucking hard on one of his vile roll-ups.

Natasha launches into one of her leading-edge lateral-thinking conversations about the necessity for our clients to reduce their CO_2 activities.

'Another time,' Skunk tells her. 'Although I have to say, I don't think suggesting the chairman of a FTSE 350 company sets an example to his staff by swapping his limo for a Boris bike is going to get out of first gear.'

And then our boss turns to me and says, 'There's a new client I'd like you to meet. He's in my office now.'

You know how it is when you meet someone for the first time and you know – you just know – they're going to be important to you?

That's what happens when I'm introduced to Freddie Ford.

The moment I walk into the room, while Skunk is still telling me his name and what he does, there's this ... how do I explain ... this jolt of recognition that passes between us. As though we're old friends, ready to resume a conversation that started long ago.

We settle ourselves around the big table at the back of Skunk's office, and I give him a sneaky once-over, only to feel horribly self-conscious when a pair of fierce, intelligent eyes zone in on my own. Freddie

Ford's gaze is so intense I feel he's reading my mind.

'I expect you're wondering what I'm doing here.'

Blimey. He *does* know what I'm thinking. 'Um, yes,' I manage. 'Our clients tend to work for banks and charities. We've never had a publisher before.'

Especially not one whose voice is rich as a bar of melted chocolate shot through with rum. I censor the thought before I can add whipped cream to the recipe.

Freddie's tongue darts along his bottom lip. His chin, I notice, is heart-shaped and his mouth a sort of Cupid's bow, floating in the middle of a ring of designer stubble.

'Let me explain,' he says.

I pick up my pen, ready to make notes.

'First of all, I've chosen Cognita because of you.'

That's weird. He's looking at me, rather than my boss. This time, I return his gaze. Wow! That's the most awesome hair I've ever seen on a man. Rock star hair. Styled and groomed to perfection. If I were a hairdresser, I'd probably pay *him* for the pleasure of running my fingers through those thick chestnut locks. Perhaps just a tad too long for a man who looks about the same age as my dad. But who can blame him?

I'm surprised this Freddie Ford isn't representing a shampoo company.

On giant billboards.

All over the world.

Um, what was it he was saying about me?

'I've trawled through dozens of agency websites and

their online portfolios,' Freddie's explaining. 'The good, the bad and the acts of downright digital crime. Cognita's work stands out from the crowd. I loved the StreetKidz site so much I made a donation. After which I happened to meet the CEO at a fundraiser, and she gave me your name. Along with a glowing recommendation.'

I look up from my doodle of a question mark that's been struck by a bolt of lightning. Before I can ask, *Is it a website for your own business?* my new client continues, 'And no, I'm not here to promote myself. Not as such. I want you to launch one of my authors on the world stage. I'm wildly enthusiastic about his book, and, happily, he's signed a contract that gives me global rights across all media. I think we're in with a realistic chance of a film deal once we've made a few headlines, built up a fan base, sold plenty of books and put Ford International Publishing well and truly on the map. That's where you come in. This is such an important book for me that I've decided to outsource the marketing.'

'What's the author's name?'

'Nikk Fryer. That's Nikk with a double k, I'm afraid. His book's called *The Elephant in the Room*.'

'An ironic reference?'

Freddy Ford rewards me with a grin that makes him look five years younger. 'No, there really is an elephant. Not to mention a room. But I'll start with the elephant.

Asian. Born in Bangalore and destined for a life of logging, until she crossed paths with a gang of poachers who wanted to turn her tusks into billiard balls. Fortunately, a British electronics tycoon who was out there setting up a factory made the gangsters an offer they couldn't refuse, and next thing you know, the elephant's got a name – Jasmine – plus a pet passport, and she's living in a private zoo in Bridlington.'

Freddie interrupts his narrative and pulls a Murray Mint from the pocket of his jacket. Followed by another that he lobs towards me. Then he resumes. 'So now let me tell you about Nikk Fryer. Our author. Having failed as an actor, an architect and an artist, he decided to hit the other end of the alphabet and try zoo-keeping. No prizes for guessing which zoo. Five years ago, Nikk notices Jasmine scratching around in the dirt with her trunk, and he has a brainwave. Gets together some canvas, paints and a long-handled brush and encourages Jasmine to express her creativity. Which she does. Rather successfully. Turns out Jasmine is the Picasso of elephants. I'll show you her work later, but take it from me, she's really good. By the time we get to the middle of the book, the electronics tycoon has unfortunately suffered a fatal heart attack, Jasmine's been shipped to San Diego and Nikk is unemployed but in possession of forty paintings. He borrows fifty thousand pounds, holds discreet art exhibitions in Beijing, Moscow and Tokyo – where the new money is – and comes back with half a million pounds in his back pocket. Then finally, Nikk tells us how he uses his fortune to set up a sanctuary in Goa for abused elephants, and teaches them all to paint as part of their rehabilitation. But he never forgets Jasmine and, as the book concludes, he rescues her from the Americans and installs her in the sanctuary as Head of Art. Oh, and he falls in love with a former Miss India who runs a yoga centre just along the coast, and she teaches him the joy of tantric sex, which – coincidentally – involves an elephant position. Which might perhaps be too much information for animal lovers of a sensitive disposition, although I must say it makes for a fascinating read.'

My mind's racing even before Freddie completes his polished summary. We'll go heavy on Jasmine's masterpieces, of course. Accompanied by praise from an eminent artist. Tracey Emin? Links to all the social networking sites are essential – Nikk-with-two-ks had better start blogging and tweeting his heart out – so I can arrange for a tame journalist or two to 'discover' Jasmine's amazing talent. Then we'll need a video trailer explaining what the book's about. Hopefully Freddie can supply me with footage of Jasmine doing her thing. How about a competition to win an original work of art? And a 'Talented Pets' section to get people involved in the site, and let us have their email address so we can mail them in the future. And what if—

Before I can share my ideas with Freddie – who am I kidding, before I can try my hardest to impress Freddie – he slides a piece of paper across the desk. 'Here are my initial thoughts for the website,' he says. 'What do you reckon?'

I eyeball a list of headings that includes 'Author Biography', 'Future Works', 'Media Centre' and 'FAQ'. And bite my lip.

The first time you disagree with a client is always an important moment. You have to sure of your ground. The conversation that follows tends to set a benchmark for the rest of the relationship. 'Hmm … interesting.' I suck hard on my Murray Mint.

Skunk is studying the piece of paper. Just as he clears his throat, I add, 'They're not exactly original headings, are they?'

'Should they be?'

'Do you want Nikk Doublekay to be like every other author?'

'Would that be a bad thing?'

'If you want a copycat site, why would you bother with Cognita?'

'You're saying my input's unwelcome?'

'Do you tell your authors what to write?'

'Do you want me to say yes?'

'Do you want me to pretend your headings are helpful when they're not?'

'Are you telling me they're crap?'

'Anyway,' I ask, ' what about the people who'll swear Jasmine didn't do the paintings?'

'Are you suggesting my author's elephant is a fraud?'

'Isn't it a possibility?'

'You might think that, but I couldn't possibly comment. Could I?'

'I've heard that line somewhere before. Haven't I?'

'What do you like to read?' Freddie asks.

'Is this the bit where I say authors like Nikk Doublekay?'

'Are you always this confrontational?'

'How much of this book is for real?'

'Would you two like a cup of tea?'

We both turn to look at Skunk. I'd completely forgotten he was in the room. Freddie seems equally surprised to hear a voice that's not mine.

'Do I take sugar?' Freddie asks me.

We laugh in unison.

Skunk darts from the room, roll-up in hand.

Freddie produces another pair of Murray Mints. 'Was that some sort of a test?' he enquires.

'On your part? Or mine?'

'That's two questions. Unfair!'

We suck our sweets in companionable silence for a few moments. Then Freddie says softly, 'We're going to get along just fine. Aren't we?'

'Yes,' I say.

'Sorry about the headings stunt.' Freddie grins. 'If

you'd said they were OK, I'd have had to think twice about working with you.'

'So tell me more about this book.' I pick up my pen again. 'Whereabouts would I find it in the bookshop?'

'Hopefully, right at the front. In a bloody great pile. In the window, too. Depends on the budget.'

'Budget?'

'Books don't get into the shop window by accident. Literary merit is a lot less important than money. Publishers have to pay to get their books into pole position. I'm taking a big risk here, but something tells me I'm onto a winner.' Freddie cups his perfect chin in his hands and asks, 'Do you spend much time in bookshops?'

'I am to bookshops what other women are to shoe shops.' For some reason, I hope Freddie doesn't judge me solely by my Crocs.

'Then you've probably noticed stories about animals are hugely popular.'

'So would you call this a biography? Or a memoir?'

'There's a whole new category called Animal Lit that's opened up lately. Started with dogs and horses and getting more exotic every month.'

'My friend Theodora was in floods of tears by the time she got to the end of *Marley and Me*.'

By the time the illegal smell of skunk drifts back into the room, accompanied by its owner carrying two mugs of lukewarm tea, Freddie is educating me about publishing trends. 'It's the feel-good stuff that's selling well,' he's saying. 'Heart-warming stories that enchant the reader and lift the soul. As for the animals, they're really not new at all – think back to *The Jungle Book*. Or *Animal Farm*.'

Just as I am about to say something tremendously intelligent about Winnie the Pooh, Freddie looks at his watch. 'Shit,' he says. 'Afraid I'll have to skip the tea. I'm meant to be at a book launch. Half an hour ago.' He stands up and asks me, 'Are you doing anything tonight?'

Well, yes, as it happens. I'm meeting Rob for a drink. We'll spend an hour – perhaps two – talking about pomegranate smoothies, the texture of mangoes and the potential to blend the two with a half-litre of fat-free yoghurt. I'll drink a bit too much wine, then try to persuade him to let me stay over with him. He'll tell me, kindly but firmly, that he still has work to do, an early start in the morning and Danny next door in the other bedroom. Then—

'No,' I say. 'I've got no plans for the evening.'

Freddie Ford reaches into a brown, calf-leather brief-case, and pulls out a thick sheaf of A4. About four hundred pages. 'This is Nikk Doublekay's manuscript.' He places it gently in my hands. 'Enjoy!'

After I've pocketed Freddie's business card and exchanged goodbyes with a sort of hug that pulls me close enough to inhale his cologne – a heady scent that reminds me of churches and choirboys – I call Rob to explain it will have to be a *very* quick drink. 'Work to do,' I explain, amused I'm stealing his favourite line.

That evening, Dad's out so Mum and I have supper together. Even though I still feel violated by her 'My little girl is home' broadcast, I've been pretending it didn't bother me. Perhaps that's why the two of us have a short but intense argument about the best way to cut a cucumber (she favours wafer-thin circles, whereas I reckon chopped matchsticks are not only far crunchier, but also look better in a salad), after which I go upstairs and start reading *The Elephant in the Room*.

By the time I've learned Jasmine sleeps standing up, her favourite colour is blue, her preferred medium is acrylics and her trunk is insured for seven million pounds, I've discovered it's an unexpectedly good story. Even the art bits have a ring of truth to them, especially once I discover Jasmine is by no means the first elephant to lift a brush.

By the time I've digested Doublekay's detailed descriptions of tantric sex by way of a blow-by-blow account of his first time with the former Miss India that goes on for three chapters, it's way past my bedtime.

Can two people really *do that?*

Before I can discover whether the elephant position has a happy ending or concludes in an operating theatre,

I'm almost asleep, a page of manuscript still in my hand.

Despite Natasha's assault on my footwear, it's been a great day.

Chapter Thirteen

Good old Danny's first cousin's stepsister! She got married this afternoon, necessitating D's attendance at a posh society wedding. So Rob and I have some space to ourselves for the first time in … far too long. I close my eyes in the split second before our lips collide.

A hungry kiss that declares: *I've been waiting so long*. But in my heart, I know I'm not genuinely lost in the moment. A small part of my brain is regretting I over-dosed on a family-sized bag of Revels instead of lunch, and I'm pretty sure they've been digested only as far as my thighs.

'That's definitely not tantric,' I protest as Rob moves in for the kill. 'Let's try this.'

I begin to explain how we need to lie face to face with our arms around each other before synchronising our breathing. That'll take us to first base in the two-becomes-one tantric experience.

'Are you sure this is essential?' Rob asks. 'We couldn't just—'

I shush him by brushing a tantric fingertip across his lips. 'I want it to be romantic. Something we'll always remember. Like Lundy.'

'Wasn't that the point of all those candles in the bathroom? You sure we put them all out?'

Before he can get up and do a fire drill, I whisper, 'Let's try this.' We'll skip the breathing bit and I'll show Rob what aural sex is all about.

Gently, I begin to massage his right ear with my fingertips, working my way along the outer rim until I get to the spot where it joins his head. I do this a few times until he grunts. I interpret this as a signal to continue and slowly prod the middle of his inner ear with the tip of my tongue.

When the former Miss India did this same thing to Doublekay, he writhed with unspeakable pleasure. Rob, however, flings me out of the way, sits bolt upright and announces, 'That's horrible. Makes me think I've got tinnitus.'

'Oh.'

'Let me try something instead.' Rob gets out of bed and returns with an uncorked bottle of champagne in his hand. Next thing I know, he sploshes a generous glug across my back, spreads it around with the palms of his hands, and begins to lick it off.

This is more like it. Very tantric!

'Your turn now,' I whisper.

Rob and I reverse our positions.

After a while he says, 'I think you should finish the bottle. On your front.'

The champagne fizzes against my thighs.

Mmmmmmm.

Rob comes up for air. 'If I swear my soul is now joined firmly with yours,' he says, 'do you think we could, you know…'

Seeing as how it's occurred to me that tantric sex is a bit like yoga – great idea in principle, but actually a lot less fun than, say, rollerblading or hang-gliding – it would be hypocritical to object.

Afterwards, we snuggle up together and I begin to give Rob a potted history of my week. I'm just starting to tell him about Nikk Doublekay, his book and my new client, Freddie Ford, when he interrupts.

'JJ, I know you're a genius, but how can you do that and talk at the same time?'

'Do what?'

'Use your tongue to—' Rob throws back the duvet. 'GET OFF!' His voice is a full octave higher than usual.

Asbo stares unblinkingly back at us both, unperturbed by Rob's howl of protest.

I notice one set of the dog's eyelashes is white, the other brown. 'I thought he was in the kitchen,' I manage, before dissolving into helpless laughter.

It's the first time I've felt an ounce of sympathy for the little villain. He's got his head crooked to one side, front paws balanced on Rob's knees, and looks for all the world as though human flesh wouldn't melt in his mouth. 'He's only trying to be affectionate.'

Asbo takes my words for encouragement. Before

either of us can say 'good dog' – or even 'bad dog' – he wags his tail, advances up the Egyptian cotton, and carves out a Jack Russell-shaped space between the two of us. A happy sigh, then he shuts his eyes and relaxes into instant sleep.

Rob strokes Asbo's wiry white fur. 'Suppose I'd better take a tantric shower,' he says ruefully. 'Join me?'

And we both tiptoe out of the bed, letting the sleeping dog lie.

Over a supper of lamb chops with aubergine, Rob says to me, 'This is the first time in weeks I've felt properly relaxed.'

'First time in weeks you haven't been preoccupied with pineapples.' I keep my voice light so he knows I'm kidding.

'Sorry, sweetheart. Am I turning into a work bore?'

'No … not exactly … it's just—'

'That's a yes! And you're absolutely right. Danny and I went to a school reunion the other day. We thought it would be good for networking. But everyone else in our year seems to have gone into the City or politics. Apart from the one who's in prison – and he *used* to be in politics. Soon as we started talking about FruityFul, the old crowd melted away. Treated us like losers, and went back to discussing their third homes and fourth cars. Even our old enemy, Brian Brinkley, who used to be such a dork, looked down his nose at me when I told him about the business. He still bangs on about how we locked him in that cupboard, too.' Rob grins. 'Still, if anyone had told me a year ago they'd actually rehearsed what to say to their old classmates about summer fruits and supply sources, I'd have thought their life was very sad indeed.' His tone of voice suggests exactly the opposite. 'So tell me more about this new client of yours.'

I give Rob a synopsis of *The Elephant in the Room* – nowhere near as poker-faced as the one Freddie gave me – and by the time I get to the Head of Art promotion, Rob's snorting with laughter. 'You really have to advertise this tosh?'

'It's no worse than that stuff I wrote about the miniature replicas of the England World Cup winners. In porcelain,' I protest. 'You know I've always felt guilty for shifting over half a million quid's worth of three-inch statuettes in a single weekend. Especially when Dad told me Bobby Charlton never had that much hair.'

'Is the client as bad as the bloke from Podolski?'

'Hopefully not.'

'Publisher, is he?'

I've done my research into Ford International Publishing, and I start to tell Rob about Freddie's business. It's obviously successful, with a list that covers everything from celebrity biographies and cookery to music and cricket. Fiction, too.

But I can tell Rob's not really listening. The moment I pause he says, 'I met an interesting new client this week. At least I thought she was going to be a client, but turns out not.'

'What happened?'

'Danny has this friend of a friend who's the juice buyer for Fortnum's. We found her on Facebook and I fixed up a meeting. We were getting on like a house on fire, but then she said she's leaving at the end of the month. Giving up her career to train as an opera singer in Paris. Following her dream. You have to admire someone like that, don't you?'

I realise Rob's subconsciously talking about himself. Abandoning the prestigious job in favour of doing the thing you most want to do. Which in my boyfriend's case is building a business.

Whereas in mine…

'Rob, have you ever pictured me starving in a garret?' I keep my voice casual, but my stomach's in knots.

'Is it really that hideous, living with your parents?' He's sympathetic, but missing the point. 'I feel so bad I can't come up with the cash to help you get a place of your own. How long will it be before Theodora's finished the sculpture?'

'What I meant was—'

'With a bit of luck, your shares in FruityFul will come good. It's my way of saying thanks for all your support.'

'No! I mean yes. I understand about the shares. But I'm not talking about being stuck at home. Garrets. You know…' I'm going to have to prompt him. 'Who lives in a garret?'

My boyfriend continues to look as blank as the next page of my manuscript, which has grown by over a hundred pages in the couple of months since I took it from the back of the wardrobe in my old bedroom and blew off the dust.

Finally.

The goal that dare not speak its name has found its voice.

Rob's not the only one who's living the dream. I've been paying quiet attention to my own ambitions. Getting this story of mine out of my head – where it's lived for at least five years – and onto paper. Working at it on evenings and weekends while Rob's been so busy.

'Garrets… Oh, you mean writers,' Rob says. I watch him join up the dots. 'You mean *you* want to be a writer, JJ? That's what you used to say at uni. I remember. I suppose every English student says that at some time or another. I'm sure you'll get there, one day. I started a book once. About a paramedic who part-timed it as a vampire. It was pretty good, actually. Did I ever show it to you?'

'Not that I remember.'

'He was called Dara de Vere. Lived in Clifton. In a

penthouse, as opposed to a garret. If only I had time to finish it, I'm sure it would be a best-seller.' My boyfriend is sporting a nostalgic smile.

And I'm biting on my bottom lip.

Later on, towards midnight, we're watching Sky Sports. 'You don't mind, do you?' Rob says. His question is clearly rhetorical, but he softens the blow by cuddling up next to me on the couch.

Someone in a white shirt aims his head at the ball, and misses an open goal.

'You see that!' Rob gestures at the telly. 'Even Asbo could have scored from there!'

At the sound of his name, the dog crosses the room and leaps up to join us. Grown men chasing after a ball is more his line of country than mine. A man in a red shirt thwacks the ball into the back of the net and Rob informs Asbo the ref needs a guide dog. My eyes remain fixed on the screen, but my mind is elsewhere.

I'm lost in a delicious daydream that involves Freddie Ford buying my book and presenting me with a fat cheque that gets me out from under Mum and Dad and Kylie. The more I think about it, the more I'm sure he could help me become a real writer, rather than just someone who churns out words to sell vitamins and performing elephants. Not to mention getting people into debt to please Podolski.

I honestly think what I'm writing is good.

And if someone like Nikk Doublekay can get a deal, then why not me too?

'Ouch!' I sit up smartly. Rob has flicked a small silver coin in my lap.

'Twenty pence for them,' he's saying. 'Inflation.'

'Oh, I was just thinking…' Rob's still got one eye on the game, so this isn't the ideal moment for a serious talk about the rest of my life. 'I was thinking about something that happened at work the other day.'

'Tell me,' he says. 'We're playing so badly. I need a distraction.'

I relate the story of the 'Crocs in a Blender' video.

'That Natasha, she's such a cow,' Rob declares, and I know why I adore him.

'But do you think I should stop wearing my Crocs? Buy different shoes?'

'What, pander to Natasha? Good God no! Take no notice and concentrate on getting your promotion. That's what you want, isn't it?'

'I need to come up with a good campaign for Podolski,' I say. 'Actually, you're the ideal person to ask. They're trying to fight back against British banks making moves on their customers. How can I get businesses over here to borrow money from them?'

Rob stares at me as though he's a four-year-old being asked if he believes in Father Christmas. 'You've just given me a really good idea,' he says. 'Two really good ideas.'

'What are they?'

By way of an answer, he brushes his fingers against my ear, and produces a twenty pence piece between his fingers. 'It's like magic,' he murmurs. 'Not only have you just told me how I'm going to get enough money to take FruityFul to the next level, you've also explained exactly how I'm going to do it. I really, really love you JJ. Let's go back to bed.'

It had seemed like a good idea at the time: all three Godfather films, back to back, at the Finchley Phoenix. Matthew loved Al Pacino almost as much as he loved his wife, which was why Beth had agreed to accompany him to the Saturday screening marathon. Old movies – especially those about olive oil and gangsters – weren't her thing.

She was nonetheless immediately enthralled by the story of a man who was prepared to sacrifice his soul for the well-being of his family. During the second film, when Al Pacino's wife tried to leave him, taking the children with her, she held her breath. This wasn't going to turn out well: when parents got divorced, it was always the children who paid the heaviest price.

Some time in the early hours, when Pacino told his son, 'All families have bad memories,' Beth shifted uncomfortably in her seat. Her mind began playing a parallel movie.

She was sixteen years old. Juliet was teething and had been wailing for hours. Matthew had decamped to his parents to study in peace, and Beth tried everything to comfort her baby. She fed Juliet frozen slivers of banana. Failed to distract her with a favourite stuffed toy. Gently rubbed her gums with vanilla extract, which seemed only to make things worse. Now Beth was crying louder than her baby. They'd been right. This was never going to work out. Having a baby at fifteen was going to ruin her life. Having a baby *was* ruining her life.

Too proud to go to her parents – or Matthew's parents – and ask for the help she needed, Beth strapped Juliet into the pram and pushed her towards the door of social services. 'I don't want my daughter any more,' she was going to say. 'I don't love her. I'm too young to be doing this. I want my life back.' She was still trying to work out how she would explain Juliet's disappearance to Matthew when she realised their child had stopped screaming. Juliet was asleep, lying on her back, arms outstretched, her tiny fists clenched into their yellow mittens, but otherwise calm and serene. She had never looked more adorable. Even at the risk of waking her, Beth gently lifted the baby out of the pram and hugged her tightly, oblivious to the stares from curious bystanders. Of course she would never abandon her daughter. Everything was going to be fine. Just as soon as she caught up with her sleep.

Beth forced herself back to *The Godfather: Part III*. On an opera house staircase, a daughter was taking a bullet that was intended for her parent. And even though Al Pacino was richer than God, he could not buy forgiveness.

Daily News, 3 May 199–

MY WEEK

TALES FROM THE HOME FRONT WITH BETH JACKSON
Why am I here – and not there?

It's the question every working mother dreads. I don't mean the one where your daughter asks you where babies come from. (Which reminds me, when she was four, Juliet informed me babies come from Tesco, because she'd seen people taking them around the aisles on their trolleys. And please could she have a sister when we went shopping on Saturday.)

No, the question I was hoping she'd never ask was: 'Mum, why are you always working?'

So many possible answers. And none of them correct in Juliet's beautiful blue eyes. She wants me to be a Proper Mummy. Someone who does the school run ten times a week, cooks three perfect meals a day – ideally chocolate, fish fingers and ice-cream sundae – and stays at home in-between, occupying herself with tasks like gardening, dusting and dress-making.

Don't get me wrong. I'm not, for one moment, criticising home-makers. But I'm still in my twenties, so what kind of an example would I be to my darling daughter if I never worked at all? And the honest truth is I'd die of boredom. Working makes me a better person. And, I believe, a better mother.

Even so, what do I tell Juliet when she's begging me to take her to school? I know she adores Heike, our wonderful mother's help. Nevertheless, I'm feeling guilty just sitting here writing this. Should I be baking cup cakes? Or telling my boss to ensure urgent stories occur before three o'clock sharp, because I need to leave then, to look after my daughter?

Let me know what you think.

Once Juliet's baby teeth were safely through, and she had located an affordable childminder who was only two years older than herself, Beth talked her way into a freelance job on the *Daily News*. It soon became a full-time position. She told herself (and Matthew agreed) that happy parents meant happy children – although her joy was tarnished when the childminder reported how Juliet chuckled with delight the day she blew a giant bubble by breathing on a plastic wand. If only she could have seen it.

'Mum, why are you always working?' Even at twenty-five, Juliet occasionally asked the same question. And always with the familiar hint of accusation. Did a desire to do her job, and live up to the responsibilities that came hand in hand with fame, make Beth a terrible person? Or just a terrible mother?

She turned the page of her cuttings scrapbook, trying not to think about the shameful way she always pretended – sometimes even to herself – she had been forced to give in to Juliet's wish to join Theodora at boarding school for her AS levels. The reality was the minute Juliet suggested the possibility, Beth jumped at it. With her daughter gone from Monday to Friday, she had felt liberated. It was fantastic that she and Matthew could finally behave like other couples in their early thirties. Make plans on the spur of the moment. Go clubbing. Enjoy leisurely meals at increasingly expensive restaurants. And make up for it by spoiling Juliet a little more than was good for her on weekends.

How much spoiling could you do when your daughter was twenty-five? And what was she making up for this time? The answers were – respectively – not much and her own guilty conscience.

She'd asked Juliet to go to the cinema with them that Saturday evening but was told her daughter had plans with Rob. Fair enough. And it wasn't unusual that Juliet was still out when they arrived home. No point waiting up according to Matthew, and of course he was right, but after tossing and turning for what seemed like hours, she crept out of bed to check Juliet's room, just in case she'd come in so quietly Beth hadn't heard.

The bed was still empty.

A dozen gruesome headlines flashed through Beth's mind in pulsating neon. This was what happened when you'd been a lousy mother. You lost what you had never sufficiently cherished. Beth sat on Juliet's bed, as though somehow that would bring the two of them closer.

Juliet was out there somewhere. Scared. Or broken. Or...

Beth hugged Juliet's pillow, inhaling its faint scent. So much for the big job. And the plump bank account. They added up to a big fat zero when you were powerless to protect your beloved daughter.

Mum's on my case even before I get my key out of the lock.

'Where have you been?' She wags an accusing finger in my direction.

'At Rob's.' What's the big deal?

'You didn't tell me you were staying out all night.'

I stare at my mother in disbelief. Surely she doesn't expect me to ask permission for a sleepover. Any moment now, she'll be saying–

'This place isn't a hotel, you know.'

It's the moment when a good bit of lip-biting wouldn't go amiss. But I'm still cross I didn't stand up a bit more for myself last night and make it plain to Rob that his student scribbles bear no comparison to the novel I'm writing.

So instead, I say, 'You're absolutely right, Mum. This place feels much more like a prison than anything else. Believe me, I don't want to be here, any more than you want the inconvenience of having me under your roof. I'm just counting the days till I get my life back. I'm very, very sorry I didn't tell you in advance that I was planning to spend the night with Rob. Oh, and I think you meant to say an hotel.'

I know I sound like a precocious twelve-year-old, so I eyeball the hallway's highly polished floorboards, and brace myself for mum's verbal retort. *Juliet, how dare you speak to me like that. I will not tolerate insolence.*

But it's not happening.

Instead, silence.

I look at Mum. She's crying.

'Mum … I'm so sorry. I didn't mean …' My voice trails off. I've hardly ever seen my mum cry. When Grandpa died, of course. And once on screen when she was reporting from an orphanage in India. Theodora and I watched the piece over and over on video and were never quite sure if her weeping was genuine or for the camera. But there's no doubt about these tears. They're very real indeed, trickling in a pair down Mum's cheek.

'I stayed awake all night, worrying about you,' she finally manages. 'I know we were out when you left, but you didn't even leave a note. Then it got to 3 am, so I called your mobile. Rob's too. But both went straight to voicemail. That made me think you might have had an accident. By five o'clock, I was calling the hospitals. Imagining the worst. Dad told me you'd be fine, but I just couldn't help myself.'

My hands go automatically to my bag, and I fish out my mobile. Hadn't bothered to turn it on. I do so now and the Nokia tune is followed by a rapid succession of beeps as my messages arrive.

'I'm sorry I snapped at you,' Mum says. 'It's just that I was so relieved you're safe.'

'Um, do you want me to make you a cup of coffee?' This is so wrong. Mum apologising to me when – let's face it – I've just behaved like a brat. Like *Invasion of the Body Snatchers*. Except my mother has been invaded by something vulnerable and benign.

'I'm not drinking coffee at the moment.' Mum manages the ghost of a smile. 'But make one for yourself and I'll join you in a moment.'

As I head for the kitchen, her voice follows me. More forceful, this time. 'And you're correct. I did mean to say *an* hotel.'

While the kettle's boiling, I check my messages. Four from Mum. In which she shoots up the emotional Richter scale: concerned ... cross ... angry ... hysterical. And in-between, one from Theodora, who wants to know if we're having lunch together.

Mum reappears in the kitchen. 'You really shouldn't talk to me like that, you know. Dad and I are only trying to help. Offering you a place to stay while you sort yourself out financially. And it's not as though we expect much of you in return, Juliet. No one's expecting you to do any housework, or even your own washing. I know it's not ideal for you. But you'll just have to make the best of it. And a little common courtesy wouldn't go amiss.'

That's better. Mum sounds like her usual self. No trace of the tears. 'Sorry,' I say. 'Um, how's work?' I venture. Asking Mum about her job is always a safe bet.

'I'm having a huge row with Jeremy.' She sighs. 'My producer. The wretched man is obsessed with make-overs. Obsessed. He's had me making over bathrooms, breakfasts, hairstyles, hemlines, window boxes, relationships and loaves of bread. And that was just last week. After Friday's show, I really let him have it. Told him it's not what our viewers want. Not what the show's about. Let's aim higher, I said. I'm gagging to do an investigation into all these ridiculous jobs that are still advertised in the *Guardian*, even now. Did you know, darling, you can earn forty-seven thousand pounds a year as a borough council engagement officer, where your duties, apparently, include best practice with client groups and other stakeholders. Ridiculous, when you consider they can't manage to empty the bins more than once in a blue moon. Then there's the one for a healthy workplace officer. Officer for workplace health, I think they meant to say. You get to advise businesses serving the public on healthy eating. Not restaurants, mark you, just businesses. Oh, and you need a post-graduate diploma. Or preferably a PhD. Then there's my personal favourite – somewhere in Scotland they're recruiting an outreach officer whose job is to deliver significant carbon savings across the community. You get thirty-two thousand pounds a year *plus a car* for that one. Makes you wonder which public sector jobs they *did* cut!'

Mum strides across the kitchen with a pair of scissors in her hands and proceeds to decapitate a bunch of hapless green foliage that's been growing harmlessly in a plastic tray on the windowsill. I'm pretty sure she's thinking of Jeremy while she snips. Meanwhile, I am thinking ignoble thoughts about exchanging Cognita for the security of becoming a well-paid jobsworth who engages with stakeholders.

My mother continues. 'But bloody Jeremy. He wants me pinned to that damn sofa, discussing made-over leftovers with the likes of Jamie Oliver and Gordon Ramsay. It's so insulting to the viewers. I want a couple of researchers to go undercover and at least interview for these rubbish jobs to find out if they're as much a waste of our money as I suspect.' Mum has lined up the green stuff next to a stainless steel juicer, and is now peeling and slicing raw beetroot, in a surprisingly professional manner. As though she has been taught by Gordon Ramsay himself, which she probably has. I take a reassuring sip of coffee. 'Then finally I'd like to lure a few of these so-called public servants into the studio for a debate with some council tax payers. Or clients as they are undoubtedly called. I think that would make for some extremely interesting engagement. Don't you? I'm having a double shot of wheatgrass with a beetroot and mint chaser. Packed with vitamins. Join me?'

Even Rob doesn't expect this of me! And when did Mum become so über-healthy? She must be worried about approaching middle age. 'So I'd love to hear what you've been up to at Cognita.'

I know I wasn't paying full attention, but did Mum just ask about my work? When's the last time that happened? Even as I think it, I know I'm being unfair. Since I've been back at home, she's always asking about my work. Just like she used to enquire how I got on at school. Makes me feel I'm ten years old again.

'My little girl is home.'

Usually when Mum employs Gestapo tactics, I respond with a muttered 'OK' but as I'm still feeling ashamed of my outburst in the hallway I decide to make more of an effort and I'm halfway through telling her about how Podolski and I plan to lead British business into bigger borrowing when Dad ambles into the kitchen. He's wearing Sunday clothes, jeans and rugby shirt, plus designer stubble that reminds me for a moment of Freddie Ford.

'I was thinking we might all go out to lunch,' Dad says. 'Nip across to that pub we like in St John's Wood and treat ourselves to a proper roast.'

Before I can say anything Mum answers. 'That sounds lovely,' she says. 'But you've forgotten. I'm doing radio this afternoon. Standing in for Chris Evans. At least I won't have to talk about makeovers.' She rolls her eyes in my direction then glances at her watch. 'Better go and get ready.' She pauses at the kitchen door and says, 'I really enjoyed hearing about Podolski, Juliet.'

In the end, I text Theodora to say I can't make lunch, and Dad and I take ourselves off to the pub for roast beef with all the trimmings. He keeps me entertained with stories of bureaucracy at school – the bursar makes teachers sign four separate forms every time they need to stock up on stationery, which probably explains why paper rationing is about to be introduced – and I give him an upbeat version of the Crocs-in-a-liquidiser episode.

To which he responds, 'Darling, I won't pretend to be a fan of your footwear—' he nods towards my Sabbath choice of Crocs in Cayman Lime '—but if this happened at school, I bet you fifty quid the injured member of staff would make a complaint of workplace bullying. And receive enough compensation to buy herself half a dozen pairs of Jimmy Choos.' Dad smiles the smile he used to give me when I fell over and cut my knee, or grazed my elbow. 'However, since you live in the real world of advertising – if that's not a contradiction in terms – I rather think you have to turn the other cheek and hit Natasha where it really hurts. Make sure you get that promotion. And be true to yourself.'

Back at home, an hour or so later, I am in my bedroom, trying to add to my novel. Instead, I catch myself gazing into the eyes of the cutest Hanson brother, wondering how come I find it so much easier to confide in Dad rather than Mum.

It's ironic when you think about it. Mum and I both communicate for a living. Between us, we know most of the words in the dictionary. And yet … I try to think about the last time we had a truly, madly, deeply meaningful conversation.

You know the kind of thing. We're lounging on a big bed, high with plumped-up pillows, and Mum's giving me a manicure (I peek at my scissor-cut, unvarnished nails) while we exchange our inner feelings on topics like… I pause… Sex? God no! Big shudder. Mum's sex life is so much more lively than my own. And besides, it involves Dad!

Fashion? Even when I was young, I never let Mum dress me. Always insisted on choosing my own clothes. And every time she dragged me towards the party dresses, I insisted on jeans.

Work then? While I'm willing to give Mum edited highlights of what goes on at Cognita, I'm determined not to ask her for advice. She'll only give it to me, and that would somehow feel like cheating.

The writing muse seems to have deserted me, so I get up from my desk and turn on the radio. I rarely bother to tune in to Mum's broadcasts, but perhaps if I catch this afternoon's show, it will bring us closer together.

I find the correct station and settle back to listen. Just in time to hear my mother announce to four million listeners in England, Scotland, Wales and Northern Ireland – plus a vast internet audience scattered across the globe, and including remote parts of Africa, where the computers run on solar power – '…so there I was at four o'clock this morning, convinced Juliet was lying dead in a ditch. Or on life support in some unknown hospital, with no ID. I know they say that when you're dying, your whole life flashes before you. But what happened to me in the early hours of this morning was that Juliet's life was running in my mind like a movie. I saw it all. From the moment I held her in my arms as a beautiful newborn baby, untouched by life, her first steps, when she collided with the piano – I've always thought that's why she sings out of tune by the way – the time she went on her very first date, aged thirteen – he was called James Duggan and Juliet announced afterwards that he kissed like a vacuum cleaner, which was rather too much information, don't you think? Then when James dumped her, Juliet decided to be a lesbian, and tried kissing her best friend, Theodora. That cured her. Instantly, I might add. I was remembering how relieved Matt and I were when Juliet brought her current boyfriend, Rob, home to meet us. Lovely young man. Last night, I pictured the two of them together and thought perhaps they'd been out late on the streets and got themselves mugged. Or an accident in the car. My only consolation was that the pair of them had died together. So when Juliet waltzed in through the front door this morning, not a care in the world, and treating the place for all the world as though it were an hotel, I was unimaginably relieved to discover that my daughter is simply a dirty stop-out...'

So what else is new?

Chapter Fourteen

Theodora and I are clutching one another for support. I'm laughing so hard it's only a matter of time before I crack my ribs. Even Rob – who keeps telling us off for making Danny's job more difficult – is struggling to maintain a poker face.

Our hilarity is quelled by a beanpole of a man called Eric, who is one of Rob's former colleagues. 'Let's take a twenty-minute break,' Eric says. 'Then go again. Someone take the kids to the park for a runaround.'

Eric is famous for the edgy videos he's shot with every rock band you ever heard of. He's not much older than us, yet he arrived in a chauffeur-driven Aston Martin, accompanied by enough camera equipment to make a movie. Which is more or less what we're doing here.

Everything's happened so fast.

It's been less than a month since Rob and Danny arranged to meet Feliks Unpronounceable, my client from Podolski.

I was horrified when I discovered the directors of FruityFul were taking my name in vain and volunteering to help the bank out of its thrifty customer predicament. Apparently, Rob's opening gambit was, 'We're here to borrow money from you. Lots of money.'

No kidding.

One week and three meetings later – the final one in Krakow, with Mr Podolski himself – my boyfriend and his business partner were in hock to the tune of what feels like the national debt of Poland. It's not, of course. But even so, a loan of three hundred thousand pounds definitely puts my student debts into perspective.

'Aren't you scared?' I asked Rob, once I'd got over the shock. (And after flowers from Feliks, accompanied by a sweet note that thanked me for persuading Rob to rush into the arms of his beckoning bank.)

'It's only money.' Rob managed to sound nonchalant. That lasted for about five seconds before he continued, 'I still can't believe our luck. And it's all down to you, JJ. Danny and I had already been laughed out of every bank in the high street. They all said their lending criteria had totally changed, and to come back in a couple of years when we had more of a track record. The truth is, they're only willing to lend serious money when you've proved you don't need any help. Whereas Podolski ... they understand the entrepreneurial mindset. Now we're taking FruityFul in a different direction, the original revenue predictions in our business plan seem like loose change. We'd been thinking too small.'

Even though Rob and Danny might pretend

otherwise, it wasn't charm alone that got them the money. Danny's put his home on the line – he had a huge battle with his family trust before they agreed – and the final meeting went on for six hours before Mr Podolski was convinced.

The clincher was when Rob declared he was happy to live on a hundred pounds a week and spend every penny of his life savings on equipment and marketing, instead of using it to subsidise himself and Danny, until FruityFul was turning a profit. *Tak!*

And that is how Danny himself comes to be standing before us.

Clad in a magician's outfit.

I am responsible for this, too.

'The moment you told me about watching a pair of Crocs being destroyed,' Rob said, 'I had a vision. Honestly, JJ, that's the only way to describe it. I saw the future. We're operating in such a competitive market. Getting a small brand like ours into the super-markets was always going to be a hard slog. So we need to take a different route. And you can barely open a newspaper without reading about childhood obesity. Fat kids on rubbish diets. Eating themselves literally to death. FruityFul's going to change all that.'

About that magician's outfit…

In transforming FruityFul, the first thing Danny has transformed is himself. He has morphed into a character called The Wiz. By this time next week, The Wiz will be appearing on computer screens everywhere. All thanks to the magic of viral marketing.

Did I mention, by the way, that FruityFul is the latest name on Cognita's client list?

It's why I'm here today, 'assisting' with the filming. (Natasha tried to grab the account for herself, saying it was unethical, unprofessional and unfair that Rob and I should work together. Rob, however, told Skunk he'd be uncomfortable doing business with Natasha because he didn't like her shoes. And Skunk told me I was getting an immediate bonus payment of five hundred quid for showing initiative.)

FruityFul is going to make a big splash in the national newspapers as well. And the really good news is that all the media space will be paid for by Podolski!

I've convinced everyone to let me put together an advert that tells the world how FruityFul is on the fast track to success, thanks to the faith shown in them by their bank. I've come up with a great line for the campaign I'm going to work up – *Podolski: Helping British Businesses Grow Faster* – and once today's filming is over, we've got a stills photographer arriving for the press shots. I've secretly briefed him to get a few pictures of me and Rob together. I am, after all, a five per cent shareholder in a business that's definitely going places. And this is my very first perk.

Across the room, one of Eric's tribe of assistants is refreshing Danny's make-up. Even though he's not my type, I can see why Danny is never short of admirers. To complete his magician look – it consists of black trousers, white shirt, the red and black Dennis the Menace-style waistcoat he wore as an Eton sixth-former, and a silly pointy hat – he's sporting this amazing cloak.

On the outside it's a traditional black model. But whenever Danny does a twirl, it opens to reveal a violet silk lining, studded with a riot of appliqué oranges, apples, strawberries, bananas, cherries, grapes, cranberries, passion fruits, pineapples and even a pomegranate or two. Knocked up in Savile Row by the family tailor at a cost that would buy you the freedom of Primark, it leaves Joseph and his Amazing Technicolor Dreamcoat for dead.

'Hold still, won't you!' The make-up girl giggles. She's dusting Danny's dark curls with silver glitter, running her long fingers through his glossy hair. The pair of them are loving every moment.

The stylist, meanwhile, is checking out the set. Danny's kitchen, as it used to be known. That's had a radical makeover, as well. A bunch of brawny builders arrived and ripped out a dozen perfectly good oak cabinets, replacing them with a vision in stainless steel. 'We need to come across as cutting edge,' Rob explained. 'A touch of the laboratory almost. Modern to the point of clinical.'

The vast metal cabinets that now line the walls

remind me of those drawers you see in American cop shows – the ones that swish open when weeping relatives are taken to view the bodies of their recently departed. Not that there's so much as a saucepan inside them: the entire kitchen is even more of an illusion than the magic Danny is about to produce.

Even though I work in advertising, I was shocked when the stylist set to work with her bag of tricks. 'So hard to make fruit look good on film,' she confided. 'The heat from the arc lights makes everything go brown even faster than usual.' With that, she whipped out a can of spray deodorant and attacked a bunch of grapes. 'Perfect!' She stood back to admire the frosty veneer she had just created. And that was just the start. I watched her brushing pineapple slices with vegetable oil – 'Makes them glisten so beautifully!' – polishing apples with what looked suspiciously like furniture wax, and misting mangoes with a fine spray of glycerine – 'for that just-picked look'.

Then there are the oranges, stacked high in six silver bins that are grouped around the stainless steel and granite workstation where Danny is about to strut his stuff. The fruits appear to be packed in ice, but the truth is, every cube is made of resin. ('Frozen water simply won't do. Can't have those oranges sitting in slush.') The fake cubes were Fedexed overnight from New York at a cost of twenty quid each. And there are at least two hundred of them.

They were accompanied across the Atlantic by a selection of the most mouth-watering raspberries, blue-berries and blackcurrants I've ever seen. Individual, perfect fruits. Just looking at them precisely arranged on Danny's work surface (Eric's art director fiddled for ten minutes to make them appear casually scattered) makes me want to reach out and pop one – or two – into my mouth. But since they are sculpted from nature's finest bone china, I manage to restrain myself.

The dozen children who have been recruited to take part in FruityFul's first video collection file back into the kitchen. Theodora, Rob and I are banished to the furthest corner. Eric says, 'Places everybody, please.' An expectant hush descends. Then, 'Three ... two ... one ... And rolling.'

A nod from Eric and the children troop towards Danny. 'We're off to see The Wiz!' they sing. 'We know he is the biz!' These kids would never make it even to the back row of the chorus in a West End musical. The cute blonde girl is tone deaf. And possibly a bari-tone. (Or a boy?) But that's the intention. Rob and Danny have recruited real kids, off the streets of Camden – with their parents' permission, of course – rather than opting for stage school brats.

We also had a long debate before agreeing Danny should become the public face of FruityFul. 'A fun advertising campaign is one thing,' I'd argued. 'But you don't see the CEO of Marks and Spencer or Toshiba togged up in fancy dress to appear in their corporate ads, do you?' At one stage, we toyed with the idea of inviting Piers Morgan to star as The Wiz. But Danny's a lot prettier. And a whole lot less expensive.

'Besides,' Rob insisted, 'we're *not* Marks and Spencer. Or Toshiba. That's the difference. We're a fresh young start-up. New and different. The point of all this publicity is to persuade schools to invest in a FruityFul franchise. We're going to sell complete packages. Everything from signs, menus and blenders to boxes of frozen fruits and sachets of ready-to-mix smoothie combinations.'

Before Rob could continue, Danny expanded on FruityFul's new mission. 'If a school can't afford a franchise, we'll give them a free starter pack so they can raise enough cash to buy one. We'll produce back-up material that shows kids how to run their own business, and while they're at it, they'll learn about diet, nutrition and turning a profit. We're hitting all the right buttons with the adults. But to engage the kids, we need to show them it's more fun than the usual classroom stuff. So provided the videos are memorable, and make them laugh, we'll have them going to their teachers and demanding a FruityFul franchise. Pester power. Isn't that what you advertising professionals call it?'

To think I once doubted Danny's passion for anything other than girls and a good time. I jabbed a finger towards him, and in my best Lord Sugar voice, announced, 'You're hired!'

Rob squeezes my hand, pulling me back into the present. The cameras are still rolling, and the tallest of the boys steps up onto the raised platform where Danny's workstation is situated. Solemnly, the lad hands over a red football shirt with the word 'WALCOTT' written on the back. He looks as if he's about to burst into tears.

While Danny examines the garment – raising his eyebrows and pulling comedy faces – another boy appears. He tugs at Danny's cloak, gestures towards the shirt and asks, 'Will it wiz?'

Danny stares directly into the camera lens and lights up the entire room with a smile. A quick swirl of his cloak. Then he scrunches up the shirt and stuffs it unceremoniously into the industrial-sized blender in front of him.

'Walter. Fetch me water!' Danny commands. A nerdy-looking boy, with an unfortunate haircut, who has been contracted to act as The Wiz's unglamorous assistant, hands over a pitcher. Danny covers the shirt in liquid and solemnly screws the blender's lid into position.

Before anything else can happen, Eric shouts, 'CUT!' and the cameras stop. 'That was great,' Eric says. 'Everyone's doing really well. And now for *my* next trick…' He smirks. 'And even though my old mum

warned me never to work with children or animals—'
a theatrical pause '—bring on the dog!'

A chorus of ahhhhhhs as Annette, the animal
wrangler who has been training Asbo for the past ten
days, appears and leads her charge towards Danny's
workstation.

Asbo is dressed to match Danny. Which is to say
the dog is wearing a leather collar that sparkles with
suspiciously real diamond chips (Danny refuses to say
whether or not they're genuine, which makes me fear
they are) and a canine cloak, also run up in Savile Row,
which features an interesting combination of dog bones
and bananas. Asbo was also going to wear a matching
miniature pointy hat, but that idea bit the dust when
he shook it from his head, gave it a good chewing and
then cocked his leg over the remains.

I think he was trying to say, *Don't push your luck.*

Danny and Asbo appear to be deep in conversation.
I can't hear what they're whispering to one another.
But the dog is looking at its master with steadfast
devotion. Until eventually Danny says to Eric, 'OK,
let's give it a try.'

'This is never going to work,' I whisper to Rob.
'Never in a million years.' Rob places a finger over my
lips to shush me.

'Three ... two ... one ... And rolling.'

The film set returns to life.

For his first trick – set in motion by an off-camera

hand signal from Danny – Asbo marches confidently up a short flight of stainless steel steps that has been built into the side of The Wiz's workstation. He arrives at his carefully rehearsed destination with a jaunty tail thump, and I realise I'm rooting for the little blighter to succeed.

Eric nods at the blonde, baritone girl-boy, who steps forwards and yells, 'Go, Toto, GO!' (We all agreed that since FruityFul will be dealing with educational establishments, Asbo's name was not ideal, but he only recognises something that sounds more or less like his own.)

On command, Asbo scampers back down his staircase and heads for the kitchen door, where he pauses, cocks his head to one side and stares at Danny. As if to say, *This is so dull. And how come all these people are in our house? C'mon. Let's go to the park.*

'CUT!' Eric shrugs. 'Let's go again.'

Eight failures later, and it's looking as if we'll have to resort to Plan B.

'Let's try one last thing before we give up,' Danny suggests.

He leaves the room, returning a few moments later with a cup in his hand. Armed with a soft brush borrowed from his new best friend, Trish the make-up girl, Danny returns to his workstation, dips the brush into the cup, and coats the blender in a thin, liquid film.

'Three … two … one … And rolling.'

Asbo climbs the silvery steps with renewed enthusiasm. This time, the moment he hears, 'Go, Toto, GO!' he places one front paw on the worktop. He looks for a split second at Danny, who gives a tiny nod. Then with his other paw, Asbo firmly pats the blender's 'on' button.

Exactly as he is supposed to!

I barely manage to stifle a cheer.

The cameras continue to roll, and everything happens exactly as we wrote it in the script:

- The blender springs to life.
- Its blades begin to make mincemeat of the football shirt.
- The kids start chanting 'Gee Wiz! Hit or mizz?'
- The kitchen plunges briefly into darkness.
- After which, a spotlight illuminates Danny's workstation.
- Danny swirls his cloak and taps the top of the blender three times with his magic wand.
- Danny presses the magic wand's secret button.
- A flurry of gold and silver stars shoot into the air.
- A couple of the boys take oranges from the silver bins and begin to juggle.

The one piece of improvisation comes courtesy of Asbo. Having started the blender, he's been trained to remain in shot at the top of the steps, while the machine's whirring blades turn the soccer shirt and water into a blood-like pulp.

But instead of retreating from the blender, Asbo advances upon it.

And embraces it.

With his tongue.

He licks the blender's plastic surface as though it were a juicy morsel of flesh. Which in a manner of speaking – as we discover five minutes later, when everyone has finished laughing, Asbo has stopped licking, and Eric has managed to choke out the word, 'CUT!' – it is.

'I used chicken stock to coat the blender,' Danny confesses. 'Just a pinch. I thought the smell of it might tempt Asbo to do the business with the "on" button. Get him up close to it, so he'd remember what he'd been taught.'

'Never mind,' Eric says. 'What we've got here is brilliant. Ten-minute break everybody. Then we'll shoot the final sequence.'

The last part of the video is plain sailing. Danny pours a tall glass of football shirt, and hands it to the boy whose garment has been destroyed. He looks at it in horror and says, 'It's got no vitamins. I know it tastes bad without taking a sip. It's just not FruityFul.'

'It's a wrap!' Eric punches the air in jubilation. He's still got to direct his way through a further three videos, where The Wiz and his team will blend Walter the unglamorous assistant's homework, then a girlie selection of make-up, and finally a prehistoric computer – at least ten years old – which has to be dismembered with power tools before it goes into the blender. And once it's been reduced to fine powder, our director will get cracking on the second set of videos, where The Wiz conjures up delicious, nutritious fruit-based recipes, all of which will be pronounced as Great Big Hitz with the kids.

It's a big job – even supposing Asbo behaves himself – and Eric's got only three days to get it all finished. Then the post-production people take over. They'll add the 'Will it Wiz?' titles, plus a Disneyesque soundtrack, and a subtitle that says: 'Don't try this at home'.

While all that's happening, I'll be putting the final touches to my FruityFul launch strategy: setting up Facebook groups, YouTube links and Twitter feeds for the video distribution, writing the case study ad for Podolski, and then starting to prepare the materials Rob and Danny will need to start selling FruityFul franchises into schools and youth clubs. It's one hell of a lot of work – especially as I haven't quite finished the Doublekay website – so I'm probably going to have to give up sleeping.

Theodora taps me on the shoulder. 'I'd better be getting back to work,' she says.

'How's the sand?'

My friend pulls a face. 'Interesting,' she manages. 'Some days I feel I might actually be the artist my mother always told me I was. But most of the time I think I'm just a kid messing around in a sandpit. And that I ought to get a proper job.'

'Like this, you mean?' I nod at the stainless steel kitchen illusion.

'What are you two laughing at?' Rob appears by my side. 'Fancy a quick walk while we're waiting for the photographer to arrive? It's hot in here.'

We walk Theodora to the corner of the street. Then Rob and I continue into the park. 'Are you pleased with the way it's turned out?' I ask.

'Thrilled.' Rob's positively glowing. 'In fact, let's walk down to Camden. I want to buy you a new pair of Crocs. To celebrate.'

'So, in a manner of speaking,' I say, 'FruityFul's success will be all down to Natasha.'

We grin. Then Rob says, 'When you told me about that video where the Crocs were destroyed, it reminded me about a blender company in America that's been running spoof videos. I've been in touch with them and we're probably going to offer their machines in the franchise package. They've been hugely helpful with advice about making sure a professional video looks home-made.'

'That that is not, is not,' I remark.

Rob gets the joke. Apart from Skunk, he's the only

person in the world who would. Another reason why I love him.

'Now I'll tell you something funny,' Rob says. 'The first joke I ever learned. It's kind of relevant.'

I look expectantly at my boyfriend. Who asks me, 'What's red and green and goes round and round?' A pause. 'Kermit.' Another pause. 'In a liquidiser.'

I pull a face. The shoe shops in Chalk Farm Road are in sight, and I'm walking faster.

'What's the first joke you remember?' Rob asks.

'Why did the koala bear fall out of the tree?'

'Tell me!'

'It was dead.'

From: James Duggan <james.duggan@gmail.com>
To: JJ Jackson <jj@hotmail.com>
Subject: Remember Me?

Hi JJ,

I am trying various combinations of your name and internet addresses and hope a message will get through. Four years ago, I married my lovely Lydia. We have a beautiful daughter, and expect our second child in August. Family is the most important thing in my life, even more so than my job. (I am a Senior Private Sector Adviser in the Policy & Research Division, based in Whitehall.) I don't have much time to listen to the radio, but we happened to be in the car last Sunday, and tuned in for Chris Evans. Unfortunately, he had been replaced by Beth Jackson. I say 'unfortunately', because just as I was about to tell Lydia that Mrs Jackson used to live in the same street as my parents, I heard my name being taken in vain. Very much in vain, I might add. JJ, I know you were madly in love with me and were heartbroken when I broke up with you. However, Lydia and I think it is very unkind of you to have pretended to your mother that I 'kiss like a vacuum cleaner'. Lydia assures me I do not. I hope you are well, and I would appreciate it if you could get your mother to apologise next time she appears on the radio. Best regards, James.

Poor Lydia.

I finish wincing, and forward the message to my mother. In a red font I write above the email: 'BE GREAT IF YOU FEEL LIKE APOLOGISING TO POOR JAMES.'

Then I press 'send'.

I deal quickly with the other emails that are lying in wait. Then sneak a glance at my new Adara Crocs. They're bronze, with a small heel and a criss-cross strap. Perfect for summer, always supposing we get one this year.

I've got a ton of work on. Making FruityFul famous is at the top of my To Do list. But maybe I should spend half an hour road-testing the Doublekay website first, to make sure I don't embarrass myself when I present it to Freddie Ford tomorrow. Feliks is already asking how the 'Podolski: Helping British Businesses Grow Faster' campaign is progressing. It's still inside my head, but I've promised he'll have something to see by the end of the week. As for my novel, it's been more than a week since I was able to work on it, and I'm feeling frustrated because I'm sure that if I could just concentrate on my story and nothing else for the next month, I'd be pretty close to typing 'The End'.

To work.

Better get on with it, or I'll be here all night.

I have every intention of clicking diligently on my FruityFul folder, but at the moment of decision, I type James Duggan's name into Google. The top hits include a professor of law and a boy who plays tennis in Barcelona. His other doppelgangers include a Roman Catholic bishop from Chicago and a professional wrestler.

I try, 'James Duggan senior private sector adviser policy research division'. There he is! No mention of the teenager who taught me how not to kiss, but I discover he is on a pay scale that rises to £66,873 a year. Funded by my taxes. And those of several other people. Talk about the gravy train. This is exactly the sort of stuff Mum was ranting on about the other week and, for once, I agree with her.

James Duggan's on-screen biography declares that

he is dedicating his life to fighting world poverty. His job appears to involve persuading businesses to expand into transitional countries. Whatever they are. In a low carbon, sustainable kind of way. Of course.

What was it Bruno Lombardo once said to me? It's at least two years ago since we had the conversation, not long after I was put on the VitalVitamins account, but I still remember what we discussed. 'JJ,' he said, 'for the time being, I'm content to remain a UK business. But I'm keeping an eye on Europe. It's not so much places like Italy and France that interest me. I think the real money's to be made in the old Commie countries.'

Even though he's by no means my favourite client, Bruno, to his credit, never pussyfoots around with words like 'transitional' when he's got Eastern Europe in his sights. And how much carbon can you get through, making pills, potions and lotions?

I reach for the phone, punch in the numbers, and ask the switchboard man at VitalVitamins to put me through to Bruno.

'Hello.'

I recognise the unmistakable quiet-yet-deadly voice of Sister-of-Skunk. I'm tempted to hang up and try again later, but instead, I ask for Bruno.

'You're the girl who fainted in our store cupboard, aren't you?' Despite the words, Sister-of-Skunk sounds pleasant enough. 'What do you want with my husband?'

'Oh, it was just an idea I had about expanding your business.'

'Really? That sounds interesting. Tell me more.'

So I do. I figure it will be quicker to talk than to put it all down in an email.

Forty-five minutes later, Sister-of-Skunk and I are still deep in conversation. Bruno has been summoned from wherever he was hiding, and we're having a conference call.

Thirty minutes after that, Feliks Unpronounceable is on the line as well. '*Tak*,' he's saying. '*Tak!*'

In principle, he adds, Podolski would be delighted to fund the expansion of VitalVitamins into Hungary, Romania and Poland. In fact, he has an uncle near Gdansk who owns land that might prove ideal for a low-emissions production plant. Tying up the deal will most likely necessitate a visit to Krakow, since the required borrowings are likely to be in the region of five million pounds. But this is exactly the kind of project Podolski is eager to support.

We all hang up our phones, and I wonder how long it will take Sister-of-Skunk to tell her brother – my boss – about my latest initiative.

My chances of promotion are beginning to look good.

Chapter Fifteen

'Fancy a Murray Mint?' Freddie Ford nods towards the open packet he's placed on the boardroom table, next to a pristine yellow notepad.

'You want to be sure I can't talk?'

'I'm all ears!'

Actually, Freddie is all choirboy aftershave, along with fashionably distressed denims, a white cotton shirt with a granddad collar and a green cashmere jacket that would look far too effeminate on any other man – Rob, say – but somehow suits him perfectly. Freddie's cloud of freshly shampooed chestnut hair seems to have acquired a few mahogany highlights around the crown, making it even more magnificent than before.

I force myself to think about business. 'As you know,' I begin, 'the purpose of the Doublekay website is five-fold. We're going to drum up book trade buzz, spark press and TV coverage, get film scouts interested, make sure you're the toast of the Frankfurt Book Fair, and see to it that *The Elephant in the Room* is a UK bestseller.' I pause to check my computer is linked to the widget that will make the web pages I'm about to show

Freddie appear on the meeting room's giant screen.

'Hang on.' Freddie half raises his hand.

That rich chocolate voice of his reminds me I haven't had breakfast. Or anything to eat since yesterday lunch-time, unless you count the pair of stale energy bars I found hiding at the back of the Cognita fridge. 'Are you not sitting comfortably?' I enquire.

'I'm absolutely fine. But you're not going to force-feed me a formal presentation, are you?'

'You don't want to see the website?'

'Of course I want to see it. Look, JJ, I know about agency etiquette and all that. But since it's just you and me here, there's no need for the big show. I'd rather get my hands on the website, fiddle around with it, and then ask questions. If that's all right with you?'

A small part of me is disappointed. At two o'clock this morning, while Mum and Dad were sleeping across the hallway, I was still wide awake, rehearsing a couple of spontaneous jokes to work into my presentation. Now they'll be wasted.

But Freddie is already taking off his jacket, and moving towards my end of the big table. He slides into the seat next to mine, and touches my forearm by way of an apology. 'You don't mind, do you?'

A low current of electricity pulses through my body. Must be hunger. Nerves, even. I've poured my heart and soul into this website, and I'll be gutted if Freddie finds fault with it.

He reaches across the desk and pulls my laptop in front of him. 'Mmm. I like the look of this.' A nod of approval at the home page.

I've summed up the concept with an in-your-face visual featuring Jasmine at work on one of her masterpieces, assisted by Doublekay, an array of brightly coloured giant paint pots and a headline that poses the question: 'Is Jasmine the most talented elephant in the world?'

Freddie clicks a button. 'Hello, I'm Nikk Fryer,' says the man himself. 'Welcome to my website.' Doublekay does a good job of reading my script. His voice is a bit nasal, but the diction's clear enough, and the potted history of how his journey has taken him from the dole queue to elephant art facilitator and humanitarian sounds enthusiastic. We'll do a video version later, once there's some TV footage to play with.

'Love it,' Freddie mumbles. He shifts slightly in his seat. 'That's inspired. Well done, JJ!' Freddie's discovered my link to a company that turns elephant poo into writing paper. Even Natasha was obliged to be impressed when I mentioned elelphant dung contains so much fibre, it's ideal for high-class stationery – and the company that makes it donates a portion of their profits to saving trees.

Freddie spends another ten minutes clicking buttons and making appreciative noises. Even though it's always good to bask in the glow of client approval, with nothing better to do than suck on my third Murray Mint, I'm feeling a bit redundant.

'Now what's this?' Freddie asks.

Oh crap.

While I've been sitting here daydreaming, Freddie's been roaming around my computer. I can see at a glance that he's found my manuscript. The pages I've been longing for him to read are right in front of him.

I have a split second to make a decision.

'It's nothing,' I say. 'Just a few notes from an old project.' I leap from my seat, pluck my laptop from the desk and close the lid. 'Are we done?'

I can see Freddie's a touch nonplussed, and I wonder what he managed to read before I confiscated the computer. An uncomfortable silence fills the room – broken eventually by the unmistakable rumbling of a stomach.

'Is that me or you?' Freddie asks. Without waiting for an answer, he continues, 'I should take you out for celebration lunch to say thank you for all your hard work. Come on, get your coat.'

There's a taxi parked on the double yellow line outside Cognita, and Freddie ushers me inside.

Where's he taking me? I'm having hungry hallucinations of the Savoy, maybe even the Groucho Club. Isn't that where publishers do their business? But the cab pulls up a few minutes later in St James's

Square, a London backwater that manages to be posh yet dull.

And without a single restaurant in sight.

Freddie pays the driver. He notices my puzzled expression and says, 'Lunch can wait a while, can't it? Especially as it's not even twelve o'clock. Besides, I've had a better idea.' With that, he pulls me smoothly out of the path of a cyclist who's going far too fast. Another whiff of that gorgeous aftershave. I'm desperate to ask what it is so I can buy some for Rob, but it feels too personal a question.

We stand together on the pavement. It's one of the first decent days we've had this summer. But what am I doing here? I'm beginning to feel my client has kidnapped me.

'See that building over there?' Freddie nods in its direction. 'That was General Eisenhower's headquarters during World War Two. And over there's where William Pitt used to live.'

What is this? A history lesson?

'This way.' Freddie beckons towards a grey stone building nestled in the corner of the square. It's narrow and tall. Obediently, I follow him up a short flight of steps. Before I can ask, 'Where are you taking me?' he's pushed open the building's front door and ushered me inside.

I feel as though I've walked onto another film set. Costume drama. Everything is so old. In a good way.

We're standing in some sort of vestibule. Very high ceilings, and flooded with light.

I'm still getting my bearings when a man comes walking towards us. 'Hello, Mr Ford.' His greeting is warm, and he shakes hands with Freddie. 'Good to see you again,' he says.

'You, too, Thomas,' Freddie replies. He turns to me and says, 'This is JJ. JJ Jackson.'

'Welcome to the London Library, young lady,' Thomas says to me.

Immediately, I feel at home. Even before I could walk, Mum used to take me to the library in Camden. (Apparently we both had junior member tickets.)

'You told me you liked books,' Freddie says.

'And you've got a good memory.' As soon as I say it, I feel foolish. The man's a publisher, so of course he's going to remember when someone says they like books. Mind you, I also told him I liked lunch, so with luck this is just a fleeting visit.

Freddie signs his name in some sort of register. 'Let me give you a tour,' he says.

We walk up a grand flight of stairs, panelled in oak or something similar, passing assorted dead people whose portraits hang from the walls. Perhaps there's a snack bar upstairs, like they have in Waterstones. I feel I ought to say something. Show some enthusiasm. 'I never knew there was a library here,' I blurt out.

'Been here since eighteen forty-five.' When Freddie

smiles he's very attractive. In a wolfish kind of a way that I'm sure appeals to lots of women. 'This is actually the world's largest independent private library. I'm a trustee. I help them out with a bit of fundraising from time to time.'

Everywhere I look, I see books. Hundreds of them. Thousands of them. Hundreds of thousands of them.

'Over a million books in stock.' Freddie's doing that mind-reading thing again. It's hugely disconcerting. Then again, if I focus on a plate of fish and chips. Or lasagne…

'And fifteen miles of shelving spread across all six floors. Enough to stretch from here to Hampton Court.'

We've already climbed more stairs than they make you do at Camden tube station when the lift's broken and I'm feeling slightly out of breath. Maybe Freddie's noticed, because he rests a hand lightly on my shoulder and says, 'Let's sit over there.'

We settle down in a red-carpeted corner of the London Library. Freddie shifts a comfortable armchair that's definitely a lot older than I am – older than he is even – so he's facing directly opposite me. Whichever way I look, the walls are lined with books from floor to ceiling. Books of all shapes and sizes, dressed in a rainbow of bindings. 'I had an instinct you'd like this place,' Freddie says.

Perhaps I'm not so bothered about lunch after all. I could sit and listen to his chocolate voice all day. It's like sinking into a warm bath. With bubbles. Although I'm still not sure why we're here.

'You'll have to forgive me,' Freddie says. 'It's been a tough week and I feel somewhat frazzled. This is my refuge. It's served generations of readers and writers. I come here when I can, to remind myself why I'm in the business of books. Anyway –' Freddie shifts in the chair '– enough about me. Tell me about you, JJ.'

'What would you like to know?' About the couple of pages of my manuscript you saw on the computer?

But Freddie's mind-reading talent has evidently deserted him. He continues to look expectantly at me. 'Well,' he muses. 'How did you get into copywriting?'

'Not much else you can do with a degree in English. Is there?'

'Ever thought about a career in publishing?' Freddie shrugs. 'Got my two-two at Exeter. You?'

'Bristol. Two-one. More luck than hard work.'

'You say that. But I know how much you've put into the Doublekay website, so I probably don't believe you. What did you do for your dissertation?'

'Dickens.'

'*Really?*' Freddie sounds a million times more excited by this piece of information than my tutor ever did. He jumps out of the armchair. 'This way,' he instructs. 'I've got something to show you.'

I follow him along corridors. Up and down flights of stairs. More corridors. This place is a rabbit warren.

We must have passed at least two miles of shelves by now. Enough to stretch to Brixton.

Freddie leads me down a narrow, book-lined aisle. 'Here we are.' I notice the pride in his voice. 'Come and sit next to me.' He drops to his haunches and pats the carpet. I hesitate then do as I'm asked. 'This place was founded by a man called Thomas Carlyle,' Freddie says. 'Have you heard of him?'

'Thomas Carlyle. Victorian. Scottish. Philosopher. Historian. Writer. Oh, and he spent a few months as a maths teacher in Kirkcaldy.' Just because I read *Heat*, it doesn't mean I've forgotten everything I learned at uni. I bite my lip.

'Maths? I didn't know that.' Freddie smiles, and I instantly forgive him for underestimating me. 'What you might not know is that our friend Mr Carlyle had a big falling out with the British Museum Library, because they wouldn't let him take their books home. So he got together with a few of his fellow writers and set up this place. Some of the early members included Henry James, H. G. Wells, and Kipling.'

This is quite good stuff, but I wish he hadn't mentioned Kipling. A vision of cherry cake, so clear in my mind's eye I can almost taste the sugary icing, is making it hard to concentrate.

'...and I'm sure you're familiar with Carlyle's writing on the French Revolution.' Freddie pauses and stands up. 'So by the time Dickens was fiddling around with

A Tale of Two Cities, he had come across Carlyle – the rumour is they met for the first time right here, in the London Library. Dickens mentioned he was having problems with the descriptions and Carlyle lent him two cartloads of his own research material. Had it taken across town by horse.'

I'm sitting cross-legged on the floor, looking up at Freddie, who's leaning casually against a bookshelf. He's telling me how even Dickens got stuck with his stories every once in a while, and I'm hanging on his every word. It's almost like being back at school, except this time I'm paying attention.

'But enough of me rattling on.' Freddie delves into the bookshelf. 'This is what I wanted to show you.' He plucks an ancient folio from its neighbours, brushes off its light coating of dust, sits back down next to me and pushes the volume into my hands. 'Take a look.'

It's been a long time since these yellowed pages have seen daylight. I scrutinise them, until I realise what they are. 'Really?' I ask Freddie.

'What do you think?'

'That you might be teasing me?'

'Why would I do that?'

'Isn't it too valuable to be on public display like this?'

'You're not going to set fire to it, are you?'

I abandon our verbal ping-pong to take a closer look at the history I'm holding in my hands. Thomas Carlyle's manuscript pages. His take on the French

Revolution. Thoughts and observations that Dickens worked into one of his best-selling novels.

'The handwriting's difficult to read. Maybe Carlyle should have been a doctor?' Freddie sounds tentative, as though he wants to be sure he's not intruding on my inspection, and even though the comment is light-hearted there's a note of reverence in his words.

'Not many crossings-out though. I don't know how he and Dickens managed without computers. When I'm writing my story, I'm continually slashing sentences and shifting paragraphs around. Thank God for cut and paste.'

'Your story? Your copywriting, you mean?'

'Um. No. My story. Is what I mean.'

'So you *have* been holding out on me. You never told me you're a writer. A real writer, I mean. Tell me.' Freddie's voice is soft and beguiling.

I take a deep breath, and begin. 'It's the story of—'

My sentence is interrupted when Freddie's phone butts in with an undignified version of 'Colonel Hathi's March' from *Jungle Book Singalong*. He fishes it from his pocket. 'Whoops!' He swiftly quells the ringtone, glances at the caller display panel and gets to his feet. 'I'll get shot for having this on in here. Breaking the sacred vow of silence.'

'Stripped of your trusteeship, at least.'

'I'll need to find out what they want, I'm afraid. Let's go.'

When we reach St James's Square, we are greeted by a vicious downpour.

'Typical barbecue weather,' Freddie laughs. He ducks back inside the library and emerges with a huge blue-and-white umbrella. 'Quickly, or you'll get soaked.' He pulls me towards him, snuggles me casually against his shoulder, and sets about returning the call. Something urgent about newspaper serial rights. Freddie mentions the name of a really famous actress-turned-writer, then I hear him say he'll be back in the office within fifteen minutes.

'Walk me to the kerb,' he says. A taxi appears immediately, and Freddie hands me the umbrella. 'Give this back next time we meet.' I'm treated to a dazzling smile as he gets inside the cab. As it's about to pull away, he winds down the window and shouts, 'Really sorry about lunch. I'll make it up to you, I promise. Oh, and send me your manuscript. By email, please.'

With that, Freddie Ford disappears.

And I go in search of the nearest branch of Nando's.

She couldn't remember the last time she had shopped for her own clothes: far more convenient to let a stylist make the selections, then mix and match from amongst the gifts and samples that were sent to the studios by fashion designers begging her to wear their latest creations. But Beth could hardly have instructed someone else to make these particular purchases.

Dressed as far down as she could manage – jeans and a baggy beige jacket – she worked her way methodically through the Knightsbridge store. Approaching the till with her new lingerie, she whipped a pair of extra-large Sophia Loren sunglasses from her bag, and put them on for extra protection.

Great. The assistant was wrapping her purchases without even a flicker of recognition. Now all she needed was an evening dress or two, and perhaps a swimsuit.

Then she would be ready for her new life.

Daily News, 7 October 200–

MY WEEK

TALES FROM THE HOME FRONT WITH BETH JACKSON
Mind the age gap

I have to get used to it. Or as Matthew so wisely advises me, keep calm and carry on. After all, does a seven-year age gap between two people really matter? In theory, no.

What a difference it makes though, when one of them is your daughter! I'm as liberal as the next mother. But then again, Juliet isn't quite sixteen. And the new man in her life, I discovered last week, has just turned twenty-three.

They met last month at a rock concert. JJ assures me it's love.

'I don't care what it is,' I told her, 'make sure he has you home by eleven. Or you're grounded. Forever.'

My daughter shot me a grade one disdainful look, tossed her beautiful hair and treated me to a muttered farewell.

Fast-forward three hours. Matthew and I were watching *News at Ten*. At least Matthew appeared to be watching. I was remembering what he and I used to get up to when we were Juliet's age...

A slam of the front door announced Juliet's premature return. She went straight up to her bedroom. We heard sobbing. I abandoned Trevor McDonald, took the stairs two at a time and rushed to comfort my daughter.

'What did he do to you, Juliet?'

My daughter managed a faint smile. 'He took me to this nightclub,' she began.

So far, so bad.

'I wanted to seem sophisticated. So when he asked me what I wanted to drink, I said I'd like a Molotov cocktail. Once he'd finished laughing, he told me I was very sweet. Then he asked me how old I was.'

'Didn't he know already?'

My daughter flushed. 'I might have given him the idea I was eighteen,' she muttered.

I went to the kitchen to fix her a mug of hot chocolate. Then kissed Matthew for giving me such excellent advice about keeping mum. Is it so very wrong of me to be relieved that Juliet's romantic fireworks have turned out to be no more than a damp squib?

Matthew mustn't discover her new clothes. Instead of hanging them in her wardrobe, Beth took the packages from their green tissue wrapping paper and stashed them in an old suitcase.

She saved the new bras until last. They – more than any of her other purchases – symbolised the emotional tsunami that would soon engulf them all.

Even now, Beth still wasn't sure if she was struggling to the shore. Or drowning. Was she simply pretending, as Juliet had pretended all those years ago, to be someone other than her true self?

'Keep calm, and carry on,' Beth whispered, foolishly aware there was no one at home to overhear her words.

She carried the suitcase downstairs and placed it at the back of the family junk cupboard, tucked away behind an old rowing machine that had outlasted Matthew's plan to combat a hint of middle-aged spread. And wondered for the first time if they would sell the house.

She couldn't imagine living anywhere else.

Not even for love.

Chapter Sixteen

'I'll have to cancel,' I wail. 'Say I've got a migraine, or something.'

Theodora ignores my protest, and continues to search the abyss that is my wardrobe. 'How about this?' She plucks a blue gypsy skirt from the rail, gives it the once-over, then adds, 'Maybe not.'

My bedroom looks like a minor tornado has swept through it. My Kylie Minogue bedspread is buried beneath a heap of shirts, skirts and dresses. Stuff that should be donated to a charity shop, so Theodora informs me. 'The trouble with you,' she announces, 'is that you're stuck in a clothing rut. You've got plenty of office gear—' she gestures at the dark suits that are still in the wardrobe '—and your casual stuff's OK. But you've got nothing really sophisticated.'

'That's because I never go anywhere dressy.'

And because I never feel completely comfortable when I'm in a proper girlie dress. I think it's because when I was in my teens, I was photographed a few times with Mum. She, of course, was dazzling. Whereas I couldn't help but make comparisons between myself and a sack of potatoes.

'So are you going to be famous, JJ?' Theodora discards another skirt – floral, and more suited to the beach than any place else – onto Kylie's tomb. 'Wouldn't it be great if you turned out to be even better known than your mum?'

'I'd hate that. And besides, writers don't get recognised. That's one of the good things. With a bit of luck, Freddie Ford can make me rich. Or at least less poor. But I'm never going to be a celebrity.'

'Not unless you turn out to be J. K. Rowling. Or the *Fifty Shades* woman. And I'll be able to say I knew you when!'

I throw a torn pair of tights at Theodora. 'Look,' I say, 'Freddie hasn't promised to publish my book. It's not even finished yet.'

'But he's taking you to dinner. At a really fancy restaurant. He wouldn't do that unless he loves what you've written.'

I nod. Freddie's invitation arrived in my in-box two weeks after I sent him the manuscript. I lost count of the number of times I checked my email while he kept me waiting. Every time his name appeared in the 'From' column, I got nervous. There was no telling whether this was *the* message because – annoyingly – Freddie always leaves the subject line blank. He sent me eight messages about last-minute changes and updates to Doublekay's website (now successfully launched) until, at last, the one I'd been losing sleep over appeared.

'Read your script,' it said. 'We should talk. How about Ella's, Old Compton Street, next Thursday. 8 pm? Let me know if you're free. Fxx.'

Ella's is so achingly trendy it's almost impossible to get a reservation. Even Mum hasn't been there yet. Three Michelin stars. A chef who's fond of telling the media, 'My work is theatre!' And, on occasion, a forty-one course tasting menu.

It took me an hour to work out how to reply to Freddie's email.

So glad you love my book.

Nobody likes a big-head.

Could we make it the Friday?

What am I – crazy?

Always a pleasure to talk to you.

True. But too forward.

What's the name of that aftershave you wear?

Delete.

On my next draft, I wrote three hundred words confessing I have no idea how to finish my story – or at least, I have four possible endings, but none of them really work – and perhaps Freddie would be kind enough to make some publishy suggestions when we met. But that just made me sound indecisive.

I sat glaring at my freshly blank computer screen. This simple exercise was turning out to be much harder than writing a novel. I squandered a further thirty minutes pondering the significance of the two kisses after Freddie's initial. He'd never done that before. Usually, all I get is 'Cheers'. (I respond with 'Best'.)

- Then I typed: *I'll be there. JJ x.*
- Another keystroke – *I'll be there. JJ xx.* More balanced: two initials deserve to be followed by a pair of kisses.
- I deleted the two xxs. Keep it businesslike.
- Then finally: *I'll be there. Best, JJ x.* The middle finger of my left hand remained hovering above the x key a moment longer, until I managed to clutch my mouse, and click the 'Send' button.

So in four-and-a-half hours, I'll be sitting across the table from Freddie at Ella's. Which would come as a big surprise to Rob.

I meant to give him the good news the other night, but we were sitting around the kitchen table with Danny until well after eleven discussing the FruityFul franchise information packs I'm about to write, and it didn't feel like a good time to divert our attention.

Now I'm thinking it's worth waiting a bit longer, just so I can see the stunned – proud – look on Rob's face when I tell him my book is going to be published.

And just wait till I tell Mum and Dad!

Theodora is looking at her watch. 'We still have time to cab it down to Selfridges and pick you out a frock,' she suggests. 'But we'll have to shift.'

'You sure this won't do?' I pick the black skirt, white shirt and scarlet waistcoat I'd been planning to wear tonight from the rubble of fabric on my bed.

'Absolutely not. Far too businesslike – especially if you happen to be an Alpine milkmaid. If you're going to be a writer, you need to look gorgeous. Have you seen those author photos on the backs of book jackets?'

I've been rifling through the books at Waterstones all week – and feeling hugely intimidated – but I'm too embarrassed to admit it.

'Not that you're not gorgeous, of course,' Theodora reassures me. 'But you need to look the part. You need to shimmer, babes. Good job you got me over to help with the make-up. C'mon, let's hit Oxford Street. We'll have you looking like an A-list celeb in no time. Why are you looking like that? We'll find something great for a hundred quid. Hundred and fifty, tops. I can always put it on my credit card. Probably.'

'No, it's not that.' Theodora's talk of celebrity has given me an idea. 'We don't need to go to Selfridges. And even though I really, really appreciate your offer, we won't need your credit card. Follow me!'

With that, I lead the way out of my bedroom…

…And into Mum and Dad's.

As luck would have it, my parents will be at some charity event tonight, so there's no danger of them coming home and catching us. We go into Mum's dressing room, a large alcove off the bedroom itself, and Theodora opens the door of one of the wardrobes. 'Wow! Your mum has a walk-in closet just for her shoes.' I am underwhelmed by this piece of information, although I notice each pair of shoes – I rapidly count to sixty – sits in a box of clear plastic, and is neatly labelled.

Typical Mum.

I'm starting to worry that I am two inches taller than she is. And at least half a stone heavier.

'This is much better than Selfridges.' Theodora holds a whisper of black fabric up against herself and looks into the full-length mirror. 'Remind me to be nicer to your mother in future.' She laughs, and returns to her mission. 'Try this.'

She pushes an almost weightless dress into my hands. It's the same shade of violet as Danny's magician cloak, and I think it's made of chiffon. I take a closer look. The U-shaped neckline will suit me. But the hemline is something else – a frill of flamenco ruffles.

'That's *so* not me!' I hand the dress back to Theodora.

'Just try it on.' Before I have time to shake my head, she adds, 'Humour me.'

'Keep looking.' I unzip the dress. 'I don't think I'm even going to be able to squeeze into it.'

'Let me help you. Hold up your hair.' I do as I'm told and Theodora locks me snugly inside Mum's dress. Wordlessly, she tugs me towards the mirror.

Blimey. Is that me? If we'd been in Selfridges

– anywhere – I would never in a million years have tried on this dress.

My mistake.

I don't just look good in it.

I look great in it.

Fits me like a glove.

Makes me curve in all the right places.

'My artist's eye.' Theodora has every reason to be smug. 'I knew it would be perfect for you.'

'The hemline's not too high?'

'You should show off your legs more often, babes. They're one of your best features. And I'd give anything to have hair like yours.' My tumble of split ends and frizz? Before I can acknowledge the compliment, Theodora continues, 'Now what about shoes?'

'I've got those sorted. Let me go fetch them.' I return to my own bedroom, collect my brand-new shoes and walk back across the hallway. 'What do you think? They'll go with the dress, won't they?'

Theodora stares hard at my latest purchase. 'These might look good on Eddie Izzard.' I hear the doubt in her voice. 'But not you, babes. They're not so much fashion crime as fashion weapons of mass destruction.'

Dejected, I take another look at my latest pair of Crocs.

The Cyprus model.

I thought it would be witty to go dressed for dinner

in a pair of my favourite shoes. Especially as not many people know Crocs make shoes with three-inch heels.

I've never noticed anyone wearing the Cyprus. They're a classic combination of black and silver (I'd hesitated over a pair in red, but decided they made a bit too much of a statement), and I've been trying to teach myself how to walk in them every night for the last week.

Theodora shakes her head. 'Much as I adore you, you're a paid-up member of the sartorially challenged.' She sighs. 'Let's just hope you and your mum are the same shoe size.' With that, she disappears back into the shoe closet. I hear some hmming and ha-ing, then Theodora comes back with her choices. The first pair is at least a size too small. 'Try these,' she says.

The second choice is fashioned from metallic grained leather with an open toe and a T-strap. It has a Versace logo. And heels that are definitely more than three inches tall. I finish putting them both on, then try to work out how to stand up. 'I can't wear these,' I tell Theodora. 'It feels like I'm on stilts.'

'Fantastic!' Theodora appears not to have heard a word I'm saying. 'Come and take a look.'

I totter towards the mirror. Again, Theodora is correct. The shoes and the dress go perfectly together. Now all I have to do is learn to walk without toppling over. I take a single, hesitant step.

'You really haven't got a clue, have you, babes?' Theodora's voice is kinder than her words.

'You know how some people are illiterate, just because they missed out on being taught to read?' I say. 'Well, that's me with shoes and make-up. Mum never stopped me from trying to experiment, but the moment she wanted to *show* me, I turned off. Same sort of thing as when she gave me driving lessons.'

We exchange a look, remembering the occasion when Mum and I plus a white Fiat Uno all ended up in a weed-strewn duck pond that I mistook for a patch of grass while attempting to execute a three-point turn in what was supposed to be the safety of a rural car park.

That one made the ten o'clock news.

'It's never too late!' Theodora declares. 'Up you get.' She extends her hand towards me. 'Let's show you how to put your sexiest foot forward.'

Before I can remind my friend that I am also a miserable failure at ice dancing and rollerblading, she has me standing upright again.

I totter a few steps.

'You're making the classic beginner mistakes,' Theodora says. 'Wobbly ankles, stiff knees and tense thighs. Don't worry, it's not rocket science. Just remember, heel first. Then toes.'

I try again. Heel, toes. Heel, toes, Heel, toes. So that's what I've been doing wrong! No more plopping my foot down all in one go. This is like learning to walk, all over again.

Heel, toes. Heel, toes.

'Keep your chin up,' Theodora coaches. 'Pretend your whole head is being pulled up by a single hair on the crown of your head. Excellent, JJ! Chin up, neck long, shoulders back, chest out, and swing your hips a bit more. Now practise changing direction. Walk, stop, pivot, walk.'

Walk, stop, pivot, walk.

I really am getting the hang of it now. I turn left, then right, then right again. 'But what about stairs?' I ask. All the time I was secretly practising in the Crocs – how cumbersome they seem, compared to their Versace counterparts – I was worrying about getting up and down steps.

'Nothing to it,' Theodora reassures me. 'When you're going down, sidestep, nice and slowly. And when you go upstairs, just take the treads on the balls of your feet, so the heels don't make contact at all.'

I heel-toe my way confidently out of the bedroom and swagger towards the stairs. They're pretty steep, but at least they're carpeted. Carefully, I sidestep my way down, keeping a hand on the banister for reassurance. Getting back up again is much easier.

'Amazing! This is beginning to feel like a life-changing moment.' I successfully execute another diva stride across the bedroom floor.

Theodora looks thoughtful. 'Time you got yourself in the shower,' she tells me. 'Then we'll do your hair and make-up.'

I take off the dress and the shoes. Might as well use Mum and Dad's state-of-the-art wet room, which is closer, and much more fun, than my own pink-tiled bathroom.

Ten minutes later, I emerge from my ablutions, clad in the sort of robe you steal from posh hotels – Mum probably had it given to her by an honoured proprietor – and a blanket of warming steam.

Theodora is sitting at Mum's dressing table, picking her way through a well-organised maze of bottles, jars, phials, tubs and mysterious containers that I'm not even sure how to open. From time to time, she makes an envious sigh.

I'm more confident when it comes to perfume – all you have to do is aim it at yourself – so I make my way towards the smellies. They're arranged in order of height on a glass shelf, next to one of the floor-to-ceiling mirrors that reflects the king-sized-plus wrought iron bed. I shudder at a mental image that has no business being in my head, and reach for a bottle.

The first present Rob ever gave me – unless you count the pint of lager we shared in the uni bar on our first date – was a bottle of perfume. Pleasures, it was called. I fell in love with the scent the moment I felt it on my wrist. And when Rob confessed he'd asked his mum what to buy, I fell in love with him as well. It's still my signature scent.

But perhaps tonight it's time for a change. Not this bottle, though. Far too floral. Rapidly, I reject a further four options. Maybe I'll opt for good old Pleasures after all.

A large bottle in the middle of the back row catches my eye.

Ornate, almost carved from a slab of glass.

Expensive-looking, and masculine.

One of dad's, I imagine.

I remove the glass stopper, and inhale.

Ooooh!

Choirboy aftershave.

The smell of Freddie Ford!

Obviously, I can't go out with Freddie wearing an identical scent. But at least now I know what to buy for Rob. I make a note of the name, decide I'll stick with my familiar Pleasures after all, and put the bottle back where I found it.

Theodora asks for a second time whether I'm ready for my nails and make-up, and I sit down at the dressing table in Mum's chair. Theodora spins it round – 'Pretend you're a judge on *The Voice*, babes!' – so I can't look in the mirror while she sets to work.

By the time she has finished using my face as her canvas, there is nothing familiar about my features.

'What have you done?'

'I think you mean "Thank you, Theodora."'

'It just looks so ... so ...'

'So much more glamorous than usual?'

'So much less like me.'

'Look, babes. I know you've never tried false eyelashes before, but trust me. I cut them in half, and only used them on the outer edge of your eyes. Windows of the soul and all that. All I've done is to accentuate another of your best features.'

'I don't look like a tarantula then?'

'You look very feminine. Mind you...' Theodora stops in mid-thought.

'Mind you what?'

'I was just thinking. You certainly seem to have this Freddie Ford caught up in some sort of a web. Either that, or he's the spider. Which would make you the fly.'

I spin round from the mirror and face Theodora. 'It's not like that at all,' I protest. 'My relationship with Freddie is purely professional. He's a client, that's all. Actually, that's not all, at all. I think that after tonight he's going to be my publisher. So that makes him even more important to my career than he was before.'

'At all, at all,' Theodora muses.

I'm in mid-laugh, when she adds, 'So you don't fancy him then? Not at all, at all?'

The thing about having a best friend like Theodora is that we both know immediately when a flip remark has a serious question lurking inside it. But she's barking up the wrong tree.

'Oh, come on. He's really old. Over forty. Probably even older than Piers Morgan. But I can see from the way he's worked with me on the Doublekay website that he's very good at his job – based on the fact that he was sensible enough to let me get on with mine. His list is full of authors people have heard of. He's even got two novels up for prizes. And it's all strictly professional. He never talks about his personal life. Just seems to be married to his BlackBerry. In the beginning, I thought he might be gay – you know, well groomed and very touchy-feely – but now I reckon he's been on a course in body language. Can't imagine he hears the word "no" all that often. And, Theodora, the best thing about him is that he's so interested in me. Really listens when I speak. It's as though, when I'm with him, I'm a better version of myself. Does that make sense?'

Theodora remains silent for what seems like an extraordinarily long time. Then she looks me square in my tarantula eyes.

'Rob Butcher?' she asks me. 'Or Freddie Ford?'

Heel, toes. Heel, toes. I'm doing my best to follow Theodora's last-minute instructions about trying to make my footprints form a single line, as though I were on a tightrope.

I'm here in Soho five minutes early, checking out my reflection in the window of an Aston Martin, illegally parked outside Ella's. I sense Freddie Ford's presence in the moment before his fingertips land on my shoulders, and I pivot on my heels to face him.

'Wow!' is all he says.

'Thank you.' I inhale a glorious whiff of Choirboy, and allow Freddie to lead the way inside.

'We'll be starting off in the cocktail bar. Piña colada?'

I'm not sure whether Freddie's teasing me. 'Surprise me,' I say.

'I certainly intend to. And quite possibly myself.' With that, my future publisher strides towards the bar, leaving me to heel-toes my way to a corner table.

Freddie is obviously a regular here. I watch him bantering with the barman, and nodding at a couple of other people, one of whom looks remarkably like the Chancellor of the Exchequer. It feels good to be sitting down. How *do* women wear heels like this for hours on end?

While Freddie sorts the drinks, I take in my surroundings. Elegant yet understated. Decorated with shiny people who share a sense of entitlement. And yes, that *is* the incumbent of No. 11 Downing Street, sitting about six feet away from me. I feel a thrill of excitement, even though I know it's not cool to do so.

Freddie returns and presents me with a piña colada. Complete with a cherry and a paper umbrella. While

I practise sipping without leaving lipstick marks on the glass, he brings me up to speed with Doublekay. The website's attracting attention, and a bunch of film producers have already been in touch. He drops two Oscar-famous names then continues, 'Everyone's praising the website and I think you're going to find other publishing people beating a path to Cognita's door.'

What does that mean? Is it Freddie's way of telling me not to give up the day job? Surely not. He could have told me that by email, or over a quick lunch. I know he's paying me a compliment, but it's not what I want to hear.

Before I can ask, a stunning woman walks into the room. She's about thirty-five and dressed to the nines. She navigates her route to the centre of the bar by tapping on chairs, tables and couches with the white cane held lightly in her right hand.

'Welcome, everybody.' The woman has an American accent. 'My name is Naomi, and I am your hostess this evening. And yes, I *am* blind. Visually challenged, if you prefer. Call it whatever you like, but the bottom line is that I can't see. If you've ever wondered what it's like to be blind ... well, you're about to find out.'

What's going on? Around me, people are smiling. No one – and that includes Freddie – seems startled by what they've just heard.

'So let's get our Opaque Evening underway,' Naomi

continues. 'And thank you everyone for supporting the Talking Books charity tonight. So very worthwhile. Your guides will be here in just a moment. Please have your bags, phones and any luminous watches ready to be put into the secure lockers. Then you'll be making your way into the dining room.'

Everyone begins to follow Naomi's instructions. Except me. I look at Freddie with a question mark written all over my face.

'Play along, JJ, there's a good sport. I've spent six months trying to persuade the chef here to partner with Helen Mirren on a cookery-as-theatre book, so it's important I show my face. In a manner of speaking.'

'Yes, but I don't understand…'

'We're about to experience something called blind dining. Dining in the dark,' Freddie says. 'I think it's the most interesting concept ever to come out of Switzerland. Unless you count the cuckoo clock, which, personally, I don't. Ella does it every six months, and I managed to grab the last reservation this time round.'

Blind *what*? You mean I spent a whole afternoon getting ready for you to take me out to dinner. Agonising over what to wear. Learning how to walk all over again. And you'd already decided that looking at me, and eye contact and all that stuff was unnecessary? 'Freddie,' I say, 'it sounds intriguing.'

'That's my girl.'

Girl?

I hear my mother's voice: *My little girl is back home.*

I know Freddie's old. But I'm twenty-five. Too old to be called a girl. At least in the dark, he won't see me biting my lip.

Freddie shepherds me to the door, and I hand over my phone and bag – Mum's bag, actually – as instructed. Freddie relinquishes his iPhone, hesitates a moment, then fishes a BlackBerry from his trouser pocket, and gives that in as well. Behind us, I can hear the Chancellor of the Exchequer insisting he is constitutionally forbidden to be parted from his instruments of mobile communication. And Naomi responding charmingly that she personally will run the economy in his absence. Freddie and I exchange conspiratorial smiles, and I know we're both thinking she should answer the C of E's phone on a permanent basis.

Maybe this won't be so bad, after all.

'Right, everyone.' Naomi claps her hands. 'You need to form a train. Single file, please. Put your hand on the shoulder of the person in front. Then we'll proceed to the dining salon. Your guide will greet you, and make sure you get safely to the table. Enjoy your evening.'

As she finishes speaking, the lights are dimmed, and then turned off. In the half-light, I can still make out the shapes of the people around me. We organise ourselves into a single line. My hand is on the shoulder of a woman an inch or two shorter than me, and a moment later I feel Freddie's fingers drumming a marching tune on my violet chiffon. Next thing I know, unseen hands brush against my hair, something is placed over my head and a silky blindfold touches my eyelids.

Before I can ask 'Is Christian Grey the guest of honour?', we're on the move. Heel, toes.

We're on the move. Heel, toes. Heel, toes. Heel, toes. Wait till I tell Theodora I actually have two people ready to save me if I fall off my shoes!

Thirty or forty heel-toes later, I thrust my way through a blackout curtain.

Oh my God.

Chapter Seventeen

OH MY GOD.

OH MY GOD.

OH MY GOD.

I can't see a thing.

This is nothing like the darkness you get when you wake up too early in the morning. This is beyond black. I have stepped into the colour of death.

I am blind.

Instinctively, I pivot back on my heel, and blunder into Freddie's arms. But before either of us can say a word, I feel a hand on the nape of my neck.

Then a voice says, 'You're feeling claustrophobic, aren't you?'

I appear to have lost not only my sight, but also my ability to speak. All I can manage is a nod, although, as I make the gesture, I realise there's no point.

'My name is William,' the voice continues. 'I'm your guide for the evening.' William smells faintly of soap. His accent is Ant and Dec, although older, with a good, deep voice. Reassuring. 'Comes as a bit of a shock, doesn't it? The darkness. Party of two, isn't it? You and the gentleman.'

'That's us,' Freddie says. 'I'm Freddie, by the way. And the lady's called JJ.'

'Lovely to meet you both. JJ, if you just put your hand on my arm and, Freddie, you keep hold of JJ's hand, nice and tight, then I'll lead you to your table. Step this way.'

Even though my heel-toes technique is improving with every step, I feel enormously vulnerable. William could be about to lead me into a deep pit filled with snakes and I'd be none the wiser until the ground disappeared from underneath me. Or perhaps we're heading for a hospital reception desk. (I can see the point of going blindfolded to hospital.)

That's better, I'm starting to relax. 'How come *you* know where you're going?' I ask. 'Are you wearing night goggles?'

'No, JJ.' William laughs, and behind me, Freddie does, too. 'I'm blind.' William pauses. 'Just like you. Except I've been blind since birth. If I could suddenly see, I'm sure I'd freak out a bit, too. You can hear the bells, can't you?'

Now William mentions it, I can. Soft chimes, bouncing around in the darkness. 'Every guide wears a bell,' William explains. 'Mine's round my neck. It's so we avoid bumping into one another when we come and go with the food. We're going to turn left here.' I pivot in the direction of William's moving arm. 'Now make a right, and we're at the table. I'll pull out your chair, and help you into it, shall I?'

'Please.'

'And Freddie, I recommend you sit next to JJ, rather than across the table. You'll both find it easier to communicate.'

Once we're seated, William runs through what he refers to as the rules of engagement. 'If you need me at the table,' he says, 'just call out my name. Same if you need the bathroom. Otherwise you never know who you might bump into.'

I smile into the darkness. This is absurd, but I'm not frightened any more. Besides, I can kick off my high heels – they've started to pinch like crazy – and no one will be any the wiser.

William tells us he'll be back soon with our starters. 'Before I go, may I fill your glasses? What would you like?'

'I'll have a large whatever's nearest,' Freddie says.

'Me too!'

'That would be two glasses of white then.'

We hear William doing the honours. Liquid glugging into glasses. A cold, long-stemmed glass placed into my hand. 'I'll leave you to settle in,' William says. His bell clatters as he walks away from our table.

'Cheers.' Freddie's voice is coming from my left. 'Shall we attempt to clink glasses? Or is that too dangerous?'

'Much too risky,' I declare.

My eyes have adjusted to the darkness.

And I am still blind.

I think we've been seated with our backs to a wall. Cautiously, I stretch out the hand that's not clutching a wine glass to check. Correct. Embossed wallpaper. That's the tablecloth in front of me. Thick linen. And most probably white. Mind you, it could also be green with yellow spots on it. I have no way of knowing, but giggle inwardly at the thought.

The dining room is quiet. Almost silent, apart from the footsteps of our guides – a description that seems much more appropriate for them than waiters – and their bells.

'What do you think of the wine?'

'I'd forgotten I'm meant to drink it. I was just thinking—'

Before I can finish the sentence, my voice is drowned in a wave of laughter, rolling towards us from the far corner of the dining salon.

'Indeed you have a point.' I recognise the Chancellor's voice. 'At Westminster, they do like to keep us in the dark,' he booms. 'And working amongst civil servants means I've grown accustomed to being spoon-fed with dodgy offerings.'

Everyone in the room bursts out laughing. It's as though we're really at the theatre.

'I'm so sorry.' This time, the Chancellor lowers his

voice to a stage whisper. 'I appear to have egg on my face.'

One or two people actually applaud.

'Well, that's broken the ice,' Freddie says softly. 'JJ, you still haven't tried your wine.'

'How do you know that?'

'X-ray eyes.' For a second, I believe him.

William is heading back towards our table – I've noticed each guide's bell sounds different – and his arrival is followed by the clunk of cutlery on china. 'You'll probably need this.' He hands me a napkin. 'Best use it as a bib.'

Clumsily, I tie it round my neck (it doesn't matter what I look like, and I'm hoping to get away without a dry-cleaning bill for Mum's dress) and I think Freddie's following suit.

'I've topped up your glasses,' William says. 'They're sitting in front of you, at about ten o'clock. You both have individual starters. And your silverware is on either side of the plate. Enjoy!'

'Mmmm!' Freddie sounds like a Bisto kid. 'I love cheese. At least, I'm pretty sure that's what it is. What have you got, JJ?'

Since no one can see what I'm doing, I stick a cautious finger into my plate, and then raise it to my mouth. Hmm. Cold. Textured. Something sticky on top. Plus a hint of nail polish.

Freddie's correct. He definitely does have cheese

– I'm aware of its musky aroma. But my starter isn't yielding any clues. This is like a Bushtucker Trial. So long as no one's expecting me to eat anything that started life in a jungle or a rainforest…

I grope my way to a fork. 'Bon appetit!' I dig in, and lift the food to my mouth. 'Meat. Cold meat. Chewy, cold meat. But not unpleasant. I can taste garlic. And pepper. And something green.'

'I reckon you've got steak tartare.'

The moment Freddie says it, the food in my mouth makes sense.

'You sure you haven't done this before? How's the cheese?'

'Delicious. Sheep's, I think. Or possibly goat. And it appears to be sitting on a bed of beetroot chunks. Would you like to try some?'

'That's a bit adventurous, isn't it?'

'I'm going to cheat and use my fingers to load it onto a fork. Here we go…are you ready?' Freddie leans in towards me. 'Talk to me…I need to find your mouth.'

Before I can say, 'I've never liked beetroot,' something is pressing against my cheek. Goat or sheep, I presume. I put down my own fork, and reach out to redirect Freddie's. My hand lands on his wrist, and he allows me to guide the food to the right place.

A kaleidoscope of flavours turns in my mouth. Big surprise. I do like beetroot, after all. And is that a sliver of walnut? The cheese is deliciously warm, and I suspect the dressing has a hint of Tabasco.

I return the favour, keeping my hand rock steady while I picture Freddie's Cupid-bow mouth opening … closing … chewing …

More wine, with Freddie doing the honours this time.

'It's so quiet in here.' I whisper, not wanting to intrude on our fellow diners.

'Yet curiously intimate, wouldn't you say?'

Freddie's choice of words reminds me what Theodora said.

Rob Butcher?

Or Freddie Ford?

I'm still struggling for a non-committal response, when Freddie touches my wrist. And says, 'So tell me about you.'

'In terms of my writing ambitions, you mean?' This is certainly going to be a story to dine out on. How my publisher and I planned my career while blind dining on raw meat and sheep's cheese – which might have come from a goat – with the Chancellor of the Exchequer.

'No, I mean tell me about you.'

'Oh. What do you want to know?'

One of the great things about my relationship – association – with Freddie Ford is that he hasn't got a clue who my mother is.

I want it to stay that way.

To make it as a writer because I'm good.

Not because I'm Beth Jackson's daughter.

If I let that particular cat out of the bag, everything will change.

Freddie will change.

He'll treat me differently.

People always do.

In Freddie's case…well, he's used to dealing with people as famous as Mum, so he won't go all ingratiating and obsequious. Or try to be my new best friend. But I bet he'll revise whatever he's planning to say about my book. No matter how much he likes it, he'll absolutely adore it if he finds out who my Mum is.

'I've never heard you so quiet for so long.' Freddie interrupts my mental processing. 'Let me ask you a question. It's been on my mind for some time. What kind of parents call their daughter by a pair of initials?'

Dangerous territory already. I contemplate the deliberate spilling of white wine, but decide to keep that in reserve. 'It's not what's written on my birth certificate.'

'That's a relief. What *is* your name?'

'Juliet. My name is Juliet.'

'Juliet!' Freddie's decibel count has risen, and I'm sure heads are swivelling in our direction. 'You mean your parents gave you the most romantic name in the history of English literature, and you've reduced it to *initials*?' He sounds genuinely scandalised.

I'm tempted to bring him back down to earth by pointing out the prosaic truth – that I'm named after a pop song. Instead, I quip, 'But what's in a name?'

Freddie's response is instant. And word perfect. '"That which we call a rose by any other name would smell as sweet",' he says.

'Like the way the fishing industry has rebranded pilchards, you mean?'

'Excuse me? Oh, I get it. I love the way your mind works. Absolutely love it. Tell me about the fishing industry and pilchards.'

'They call them Cornish herring now. And sales have tripled.'

'How on earth do you know that?'

'I probably read it in *Marketing Week*. Or overheard it on the tube.'

'Juliet.' Freddie swirls my name in his throat. 'That's what I'll call you from now on, if you don't mind. Or even if you do. As for your parents, well they've definitely gone up in my estimation. If you're reluctant to talk about you, shall we chat about them?'

I am saved by the bell.

William is back at our table, clearing away the dishes. But once he's departed, Freddie repeats the question.

There is only one thing for it.

I take a deep breath.

And tell him, 'I'm an orphan.'

Even despite the darkness, I can tell Freddie is taken aback.

It's a good job neither of us can see my face.

'I'm so sorry,' he murmurs.

By the time our main course arrives, I am deep into my fictional misery memoir. It turns out I'm the daughter of a chartered surveyor father and an ex-model mother who ran a pet shop.

Both deceased, obviously.

Car crash on a rainy road in Wales.

No other vehicle involved.

Mechanical defect.

Eight or nine years ago, I forget when, exactly. Freddie's right, I've probably blanked it from my memory. On the positive side, I was left an inheritance sufficiently large to see me through uni, and purchase a small flat in North London.

I am beginning to horrify myself at the ease with which one falsehood tumbles from my mouth followed immediately by another. Having explained that I am now too scared even to apply for a driving licence, and just as I begin to describe the court case against the negligent motor manufacturers – I'm wondering how much compensation to award myself for the tragic deaths of both parents – William manages to interrupt for long enough to advise that the plates are very hot and our wine glasses are very full.

'And I'm very sorry for your loss, JJ,' he adds.

Shame ripples through me, and after William has retreated, I tell Freddie, 'I really don't want to talk about this any more.'

'Of course. It must be very difficult for you. Maybe I should adopt you.'

I struggle for an appropriate response – that's surely a joke – and happily, Freddie appears to mistake my silence for pain. 'Let's concentrate on our main course, instead,' he says. 'Have you worked out what's on your plate?'

My sense of smell, heightened since we were plunged into darkness, has already identified that my main course is as fishy as the tale I've been telling Freddie. I investigate with my fingertips.

Before I can be sure what I'm going to eat next, a bell rings.

Not one that signals an oncoming waiter.

This is several million times louder.

I hear a voice saying, 'Ladies and gentlemen, I'm afraid there's been a small incident in the kitchen. Would you kindly all remove your blindfolds, and proceed back into the main salon. There's no cause for concern, but if we could all move quickly. The fire brigade are on their way.'

I don't need telling twice.

I pull the cloth from my eyes just as the main lights are switched on. It takes me a few seconds to get used to being able to see again.

I focus on a table near a window, and wonder if I am hallucinating.

Oh my God.

Chapter Eighteen

OH MY GOD.
OH MY GOD.
OH MY GOD.

I'm still shaking at the thought of what almost happened. To my dying day, I'll never know how I managed to get out of that place in time, high heels in one hand, Freddie in the other.

I literally pulled my publisher-in-waiting from the dining room into the safety of the street, and around the first three corners I could find.

'Slow down,' Freddie pleaded. I ignored him. Until eventually he dragged me into a doorway, put a steadying hand on each of my shoulders and said, 'I think you're overreacting, Juliet. Someone probably set a tea towel alight and they evacuated us all as a precaution. It was hardly *Towering Inferno* in there.'

'No.'

It was far worse than that.

When the lights came up, I saw Mum and Dad.

Sitting alongside the Chancellor of the Exchequer.

So this was the charity do they were attending tonight. They must have arrived late and been ushered in after everyone else had been seated. For which I am truly grateful.

While Freddie's busy at the bar, I imagine what would have happened if my getaway had failed.

- Possibility One: My mother recognising not only me, but also the dress and shoes I've stolen from her wardrobe.
- Possibility Two: Freddie discovering I've spent most of the evening telling him a pack of lies.
- Possibility Three: In which I am denounced as a liar clad in stolen clothes.

It was a narrow escape, but at least the premature end of dinner means I finally get to see inside the Groucho Club. Freddie's brought me here to discuss the real business of the evening.

Some time soon, I'll need to explain to him that, um, I'm not exactly an orphan. Perhaps I can make him believe I was experimenting with improvised, on-the-spot fiction. Anyway, it can wait till I find out how much he's going to offer to publish my novel.

No sign of anyone famous tonight... I just have to pray my parents don't show up. I've got a feeling Mum's let her membership lapse, but I'm keeping a wary eye on the door, and I've earmarked a table across the room that I can duck under, if necessary.

'So tell me, Juliet, how much do you know about

the way publishing works?' Freddie places two glasses of wine on the table and settles alongside me on the squishy couch.

'Not much,' I say. 'I was about to investigate literary agents, but then I met you.'

'I can introduce you to a few agents,' Freddie says. 'Always a good idea for a writer to use one. If it weren't for agents, we publishers would be inundated with hundreds of manuscripts every week.' From the way he says it, I realise this would be a bad thing. 'But I have to admit, I made an exception in your case. You've worked so hard on Doublekay. And besides, I'm rarely accused of missing an opportunity.'

'And have you found one?' I hope I sound a lot braver than I feel.

'Well, for a start, I read everything you sent me. Including, I might add, the list of ways in which you say you would like to murder someone called Sister-of-Skunk.'

'That wasn't meant to be there! It's just that sometimes when I get stuck, I doodle on the page with words. I must have forgotten to delete it.'

'For what it's worth, I thought your idea about crucifying the unfortunate lady with metal spears shaped like exclamation marks was the best. I also liked the one about tampering with a go-cart. I'm sure she deserves her terrible fate, but remind me never to cross you, won't you, Juliet?'

'I promise.'

'Now then, let's cut to the chase.'

I taste my heart in my mouth.

'I love your opening sentence: "It was a dark and stormy night." Even a more experienced writer would hesitate before pulling that one out of the bag.'

Fancy a publisher not recognising dramatic irony.

'And now I know more about your own life, especially the tragic loss of your parents—' Freddie makes direct eye contact as he says this, although his expression is unreadable '—I feel I understand more about what you've written. They say stories choose their authors you know, rather than the other way round.'

'That's interesting.' What does he mean?

'If I were a gambling man,' Freddie continues, 'which incidentally, I am, I'd bet fifty quid you started writing this story while you were still at uni. Or just after you left.'

'Isn't that called hedging your bets?'

'Sort of. But I'm right, aren't I?'

'Is it important?'

'Um…'

In all the hours I've spent with Freddie, this is the first time I've heard him hesitate.

'Juliet, you're not going to like what I'm about to say.'

'I'm sure every author has to accept constructive criticism.' Oh crap.

'Well, for a start, I was surprised you'd chosen to write historical fiction. For some reason, I was expecting a comedy.' Freddie hears my mouth open to protest, but cuts me short. 'Yes, I know there are a couple of funny scenes. The one where Elisse steals her mistress's wig and sells it to pay for Christmas dinner...'

The highlight of Act One, he means; a poignant moment that highlights my theme of sacrifice.

'....and the chapter where Elisse offers to swap places with her long-lost cousin and go to jail is thrillingly reminiscent of *A Tale of Two Cities*. That is, if we overlook the fact that your heroine is eager to get herself behind bars only because she's enamoured of the defence lawyer, and reckons he'll need to visit her on a daily basis if she's on death row.'

Every story needs a spark of sexual excitement. How come Freddie doesn't realise that?

'I'm sure you mean to show her as noble and resourceful. But the fact remains that even though she's an orphan, she comes across as a bit of a spoiled baby. That can be fixed. I'm more concerned that you appear to have misappropriated plot lines from *Oliver Twist*, *The Old Curiosity Shop*, *David Copperfield* and *Great Expectations*. I know you studied Dickens, but—'

Maybe I've had too much to drink.

But this is just cruel. And you know what?

I've had enough of keeping mum – as it were – every time someone drops bad news in my lap.

Pretending it doesn't affect me.

I try so hard to be the perfect girlfriend. Making sure I don't come across as needy. When actually I *do* need more of Rob than I've been getting lately.

I do my best to rise above office politics and Natasha's ongoing niggling (productive conflict, she had the temerity to call it, when I told her to back off).

And of course I've never – ever – properly sat down with Mum and filled her in on the teasing I've put up with all my life, thanks to the captivating anecdotes she rips from the pages of my life. Instead, I've taught myself to pretend to her it's just water off a duck's back. I didn't even take her to task for her 'My little girl is home!' bedroom invasion. Just acted as if it didn't matter.

But it did.

And so does this.

'Let me just make sure I'm following you.' For some reason, my voice is absolutely calm. 'You appear to be accusing me of stealing the complete works of Dickens. Have I got that right?'

'Juliet, just listen a moment—'

'No, Freddie. You listen to me. Until the start of this evening, I really liked you. You've been an excellent client, and Doublekay was an interesting project. It was very kind of you to read my rubbish story. Especially since you're obviously such a hot target for every wannabe who ever picked up a pen or turned on a computer, or cherished the thought that perhaps one day they'd end up on the shelves of a bookstore, instead of queuing up at the tills. The bit I don't get is this.' I gesture around the room. 'Why didn't you just send me an email to say what I'd written was unsuitable? Especially bearing in mind that I didn't pester you to read what I'd written in the first place. You asked me. Remember?'

I'm proud of the fact that I've managed to say all that without raising my voice once, although I did notice a slight slur when I said 'shelves'.

'Juliet, you're overreacting. And I'm eager to avoid appearing on your next doodling death list.'

'It's really not that important.' If Freddie thinks he can win me back with his sense of humour he'd better hire one of his own, best-selling comic authors.

'Do you think you could just do that thing you do – the lip-biting thing – and let me get a word in?'

I scowl. And bite my lip in an exaggerated fashion.

'Thank you. As usual, you're absolutely correct. I didn't bring you here to tell you your writing's no good. As I said, I read every word you sent, all the way through to the premature end of your story.'

I am desperate to say *thank you very much*, but manage to restrain myself.

Which is just as well, because Freddie continues,

'You realise, of course, I can tell if a writer has talent within the first six sentences. And that was rather the point of this evening. I want to tell you I believe you're going to be a very good writer, one day. You've got a lot to learn, and your technique's all over the place, but that will improve with experience. If I was too brutal calling attention to your reworking of Mr Dickens, I apologise. But this is a brutal business you're looking to get into, Juliet. Only the fittest – perhaps more accurately, the most persistent – survive. And before I invest any of my professional energy in you, I needed to discover if you're in this for the long haul, or whether dabbling in fiction is just a passing fancy. I rather think you've answered the question. So the real issue is where we go from here. What are we going to do with you, Juliet? And I think I'd better pipe down now. I'm frightened you're going to burst.'

Even though I've been given permission to speak, I don't know what to say.

'I'm sorry I didn't let you finish what you wanted to say,' I manage.

Freddie treats me to a smile bright enough to power the Blackpool Illuminations.

'So how do I salvage my book?'

'I'd be curious to see a version where you change the story,' he muses. 'Maybe totally. And also the characters. Oh, and how would you feel about an ending that's radically different from the one you've been contemplating?'

'That bad, huh?'

'Maybe you should look on it as your apprenticeship.'

'Actually, I'm relieved I don't have to think of an ending.'

'I'll drink to that! A toast to your future success?'

I've drunk far more than I would usually, even on a weekend. But the evening's been such an emotional roller coaster.

By the time Freddie returns with two glasses of champagne I have regained most of my composure.

'To success!' Freddie utters the toast and stares directly into my eyes as our glasses touch. 'And to the future,' he adds softly. 'I'm eager to see what you do next, and I'll be happy to introduce you to a few literary agents in due course.'

We spend the next twenty minutes or so chit-chatting. I'm relieved to think that by the time I get home, Mum and Dad will be asleep. I've already taken the precaution of texting Mum to tell her I'm working late, and she's not to worry.

Freddie stifles the merest hint of a yawn, which I interpret as a signal that our evening is over.

'So where do we go from here?'

'We'll talk again soon. Until then, I return to Canary Wharf. And you, Juliet?'

'Hampstead.'

'Ideal place for a writer to live. I often think it's the default occupation for the NW3 postcode.'

While Freddie's settling the bar bill, I climb into my Versace footwear. With difficulty. All the booze has gone to my head.

Heel, toes. Heel, toes. Heel, toeshhh.

I command myself to focus on walking.

We make our way back down towards the street. I trail a few steps behind Freddie, grateful he can't see how unsteady I am on my spikes. Thankfully, there's a rail for me to cling to when I feel myself falter.

We walk out into the refreshing night air.

'We're most likely to get cabs on Charing Cross Road,' Freddie says. Then he adds, 'Despite our little misunderstanding, I've really enjoyed myself this evening. You're very good company. And I want you to think carefully about what we've said. I'm pretty sure you've got what it takes to get published.'

Heel, toes.

Heel, toes.

Heel, whoooooops.

Someone has put a pothole in the middle of Dean Street.

I am going ... going...

Freddie grabs me by the waist, a split second before the back of my head splatters onto a paving stone.

We must look like that Rhett-and-Scarlett pose from *Gone With The Wind*.

I wait for Freddie to pull me back to my treacherous feet.

Oh my God.

Chapter Nineteen

OH MY GOD.

OH MY GOD.

OH MY GOD.

Freddie Ford tried to kiss me!

It was awful.

I swear I did nothing to encourage him.

First I was on my heels.

Then I was in his arms.

My face against his face.

Next thing you know he's coming on to me.

We were as close to a kiss as you can be without kissing.

Stupid man.

Stupid old man.

Stupid old man with his oldest-swinger-in-town haircut.

Stupid old man with his oldest-swinger-in-town haircut and inappropriate religious smell.

But then again, he's an important publisher.

Maybe I should forgive him.

Or pretend it never happened.

Maybe I imagined it.

What was it he said after he'd made sure I was steady on my feet again?

Something along the lines of, 'Juliet, you've had a bit too much to drink. And I never mix business with pleasure.'

The cheek of it!

Trying to blame me.

For something that didn't quite happen.

But almost did.

Freddie managed to whistle up a taxi out of nowhere. He opened the door and helped me inside. 'I'll call you soon, Juliet.' And then he had the nerve to give me a fatherly peck on the cheek. 'Oh, and you'll need this,' he added.

I finally uncurl my fingers to see what Freddie has pushed into my hand. If he's given me money for the ride home, I'm never going to speak to him again.

A yellow street lamp on Tottenham Court Road reveals Freddie hasn't insulted me with a twenty-pound note.

If only he had.

Nestled in the palm of my hand is a single tarantula eyelash.

Chapter Twenty

The office is buzzing with rumours that Skunk has received a police caution for smoking illegal substances in Soho Square. I find myself defending him, probably because I've just finished my latest performance review, and he said he's been hearing flattering things about me from VitalVitamins and Podolski. 'You're becoming a real asset to Cognita,' Skunk told me. 'Keep it up.' I smiled all the way back to my desk, my mood enhanced by the glorious June weather.

Even the prospect of Feliks Unpronounceable's imminent arrival can do nothing to spoil my day. I'm becoming almost fond of him. And at least today we don't have to talk business. We're celebrating his promotion.

He insists it's due – at least in part – to the splendid advertising he and I have been creating. So he's taking me out for coffee and Polish apple cake.

Natasha, meanwhile, is talking to herself. '...future-forward design ... businesses that catalyse sustainable resource management ... high touch low tech ... determine client focus...' She's preparing to impress

Skunk with her low carbon diet crusade and her draft copy and design for the agency brochure.

We both know these performance reviews are anything other than routine. Our glorious leader is making up his mind which one of us will triumph in the Creative Group Head stakes.

Even though I'm doing OK, I mustn't get too confident. Especially now Natasha's informed me her suit is made entirely of recycled plastic bottles. I got a bit lost when she was banging on about how they get milled into flakes, then granulated into pellets. And if I'm being strictly honest, the fabric definitely *feels* as though it ought to be holding liquid rather than posing as a fashion item. Still, full marks to Natasha for living up to her beliefs.

Natasha treats me to an absent-minded scowl, then gathers a sheaf of papers. I'm about to wish her luck when she mutters, 'See you on Tuesday then. It's all right for some, I suppose. Oh, and I hope you've paid the voluntary flight tax to make up for all those carbon emissions you're about to unleash.'

That would be Natasha's way of saying she hopes I have a fantastic time in New York.

New York, New York.

This time tomorrow, I'll be climbing the Empire State Building. Or hanging out in Greenwich Village. A carriage ride in Central Park. Maybe even oysters at Grand Central Station.

There's only one problem.

Freddie Ford.

He's left me two voicemails (friendly but formal) requesting a couple of additions to the Doublekay website. Plus an email (no xxs) this morning, asking when the aforementioned updates will be ready. From which I deduce he's decided to forget about our close encounter.

If only I could manage to do the same.

Obviously I'll never wear high heels again: God invented Crocs for a reason.

But that's hardly the point.

The harder I try not to think about what did – or didn't – happen, the more I obsess about it.

Logically, I have nothing to feel guilty about.

In fact, I'm proud I stood up for myself when Freddie told me my book isn't good enough, even though it turned out I was premature to go in with all guns blazing.

A ringing phone interrupts my recriminations.

Feliks is waiting for me in reception.

I shut down my computer – Natasha will be pleased at least about that – and grab my weekend bag. I've got another two hours before I need to board the Heathrow Express. Plenty of time to chew the fat with Feliks, and so long as I restrain him to a single cup of coffee, I'll still have time for a pre-flight airport shopping binge.

Ten minutes later, I feel like I'm already abroad. Feliks has shepherded me into a cobbled mews just a few streets from the office, with a whitewashed café tucked into the far corner. We've been awarded the only outside table. I'm surrounded by two dozen pots of lush red geraniums and a faint smell of vanilla tobacco, watching a leisurely procession of passers-by in various states of summer undress. Feliks – clad as always in his double-breasted business suit, collar and tie – is locked in rapid-fire Polish banter with a middle-aged woman who's laughing at whatever he just said.

Much better. I can feel the sun charming the tension from my body. I'm not going to waste another moment of this precious weekend thinking about Freddie bloody Ford. He is officially banished from my brain.

The waitress reappears bearing two giant plates of apple cake swimming in lakes of cream. She treats me to a beaming smile and a single word of Polish that probably means 'Enjoy!' seemingly oblivious to the fact that this kind of comfort food would be more suited to a cold November evening.

Still, duty calls, and I pick up my spoon. 'Congratulations on your promotion,' I say to Feliks. 'I'm sure it's richly deserved and you'd have got it anyway, without our "Helping British Businesses Grow Faster" campaign.'

Feliks shakes his head, whilst simultaneously manoeuvring a dainty piece of cake into his mouth.

'*Nie*. I must respectfully disagree. Thanks to your advertising, we're getting sixty business enquiries a day. We're taking on extra staff just to process the applications. Everyone at Podolski thinks I am a super-star. But it was all your idea in the first place. And for that, I am forever grateful.'

The timely arrival of the waitress with my coffee spares my blushes.

'So how is FruityFul?' Feliks asks.

'The Wiz videos are doing hugely well on YouTube. Almost as many hits as the sneezing dwarf from Pretoria.'

'I love your videos! Every time I see that sweet little dog switch on the blender with his paw, it makes me laugh.'

I laugh, too. 'That sweet little dog chewed his way through an entire consignment of banana smoothie labels last week. You know what they say about Jack Russells – thugs in white clown suits. If I had anything to do with it, he'd be banished from the kitchen. But I have to hand it to him. He's getting almost as much fan mail as Danny. We've set him up with his own email address, and take it in turns to reply on his behalf.'

'And the sales? How are they doing?'

'The graph's going like that.' I raise a finger to the sky. 'I mean, it's still relatively small-time, but the figures are way ahead of the new business plan. Amazing when you think about it, how this successful enterprise is being run out of someone's kitchen in Primrose Hill. Rob's trying to concentrate on the franchise side, but we've got to keep existing customers happy because that's where the ready money is. So the kitchen's on the go twenty-four-seven.'

Feliks nods his approval. Then, before I can intervene, he waves at the waitress and orders more coffee. Goodbye, shopping time at Heathrow.

'Don't you have to get back to the office soon?' Maybe I can appeal to my client's work ethic.

'On a lovely day like this?' Feliks raises a bushy eyebrow. 'Besides, I was at my desk just before five o'clock this morning. So I'm more or less finished for the day. I can always catch up over the weekend.'

I'm wondering how to tactfully explain that I really must be off as soon as I've gulped down the coffee, when our waitress arrives, carrying two glasses shaped like goldfish bowls, and almost as big. She places one in front of me, full to the brim with ice cubes floating in pale-pink liquid. Then she nudges Feliks with her free hand and says something that makes him turn the same colour as our drinks.

'I know I promised you coffee, but I thought we should celebrate with something stronger,' he says. 'It's like a strawberry daiquiri, only with Polish vodka. And I am very sorry, but the waitress is mistaking our business meeting for a seduction. My apologies.' Feliks looks so abject you'd have to have a heart of stone not to laugh.

I take a long gulp of my strawberry cocktail, and crunch an ice cube. Not bad. At this rate, I'll have to revise my opinion of Polish cuisine. 'Are you going on holiday this year?'

'Absolutely. Trekking in South America. I'm away for all of September, which is the longest holiday I've had since I was a schoolboy. And, as it happens, I am also visiting Belgium next weekend.'

You could never mistake Feliks for a beach boy. He's one hundred per cent culture vulture, so Belgium makes sense. 'Rob and I went to Bruges last Christmas,' I say.

'Which museums and galleries do you recommend?'

Since our sightseeing consisted of an all-you-can-drink brewery tour followed by a chocolate-tasting expedition, I'm wondering how to let Feliks down lightly. Then I remember. 'There's one place you might find interesting.' Translation: *On our way to the brewery, we took a wrong turn.* 'The hospital museum.' *Where I fainted on the spot as soon as I realised what I was looking at.*

Soon, I am telling my client the whole story. 'The first exhibit was a collection of ancient medicine vessels. I thought they were beer bottles,' I confess.

'Easily done.' Feliks shoots me a sympathetic look.

'Then there was this big oil painting full of nuns. I

assumed they must have done the brewing at one time. You know, like those monks in Spain who make liquor.'

'*Tak.*' Feliks nods.

'I noticed some of the sisters were holding knives, and that the aprons they wore over their habits had red streaks, but I didn't think much of it. Rob had gone to ask someone where we were supposed to go for the beer sampling, so I wandered off on my own.'

I shudder at the memory of what happened next. 'I rounded a corner, and there was this larger-than-life oil painting of someone being disembowelled. Even a picture of something like that turns my stomach to water, although I've never understood why. Anyway, I'm walking away as fast as I can, trying to process what I've just seen. I mean, I was pretty sure it wasn't just some ancient hangover cure. There was a glass cabinet ahead, and I thought that if I could lean on it for a moment or two, I'd feel better. The trouble was—' I feel foolish, even as I say it '—the cabinet held the museum's prize collection of medieval surgical instruments. All helpfully labelled in English, explaining the hideous things they were used for. That was it. I crashed to the floor and was carted off to a real hospital in a Belgian ambulance. And when the doctor brandished her stethoscope and tried to admit me for overnight observation, I fainted all over again. Rob had to sign five different forms before they'd let me out.'

'You've certainly made me want to visit the museum.'"

I can't tell if Feliks is joking, but I suspect not. 'Tell them a museum about hospitals should smell of disinfectant, if only to warn off medical phobics like me.'

'I promise. And if it's any consolation, JJ, you're not the only one who has suffered embarrassment on holiday.'

Feliks launches into a detailed account of how he was taken away by security guards who might – or might not – have been Mossad when he arrived at Tel Aviv airport with a full set of passport stamps from Jordan, Lebanon and Syria in his passport. 'I enjoy visiting ancient civilisations, but those immigration officers were not especially civilised to me,' he says. 'I understand their reasons, of course. But there was no need for them to point their guns. I hardly look like a terrorist. Do I?'

Feliks has noticed I'm no longer listening. He lost me at the word 'passport'. I'm rummaging around in my bag like a crazy woman trying to dig her way out of a collapsed building. Keys ... phone ... credit cards ... no passport. Paperback of *The Girl Who Kicked the Hornet's Nest* to read on the plane ... three crumpled tissues ... hairbrush that should definitely never be allowed out in public ... two losing lottery tickets ... three snack-sized packets of Maltesers ... still no passport. Expired gym membership card ... four black pens ... one million dollar bill (Zimbabwe) ... lipgloss ... Oyster card ... yep, definitely no passport.

That's everything, spilled out into the sunshine. Including a gaping void where my passport should be. Along with a mental picture of the precious document left out last night in the kitchen next to the kettle, so I could put it safely in my bag when I made my morning cup of coffee. Which would have worked perfectly, had I not overslept and left the house in a whirlwind of panic.

'Feliks, I've got to dash!' I tell him. 'Rob's taking me to New York for the weekend. Our first holiday since Bruges, and— '

'And you've forgotten your passport. But you know where you left it?' Feliks is calmly stuffing my belongings back into my bag while he talks. I notice him hesitate over one of the tissues, then he spears it neatly with the end of one of my pens and it disappears from sight.

I nod gratefully.

'We'll catch up next week,' he says. 'Have a fantastic time. I suspect you will not be visiting the Guggenheim. Or even the Brooklyn Museum, which holds a special place in my heart. Just so long as you stay out of the hospitals.' Feliks hands me my bag and I decide he's just become my favourite client.

I wave him goodbye and leg it towards Tottenham Court Road tube. I'm in luck as a train arrives immediately, and I make it back to Hampstead in record time. Thank goodness I realised I had no passport *before* we were standing in line at Heathrow. That really would have been a disaster. As I arrive at our front door, I'm wondering whether I would have insisted Rob went to New York without me.

I turn my key in the lock. All I have to do is go straight to the kitchen, grab my passport and head straight out again, and so long as the Northern Line continues to co-operate, I'll be boarding the Heathrow Express only half an hour later than I originally intended, and no harm done.

But there's something not quite right in the kitchen.

It takes me a few moments to work out what it is.

Ah, I know.

Mum was doing something on breakfast TV this morning, and Dad had made his usual early start, too. As for me, I dashed into the kitchen, took one look at the clock and realised I hadn't even got time to boil the kettle, grabbed an apple and went on my way. So I was the last one out of the house. And when I left, there was definitely no heap of picnic leftovers – isn't that the remains of a lobster? – tossed carelessly next to the sink.

Maybe we've been visited by discerning burglars.

I tiptoe across to the kettle, pick up my passport and stash it in my bag.

Something else.

The door that leads from the kitchen to the garden and the pool is slightly ajar.

Should I scarper with my passport?

Or find out if we really have been robbed?

I feel my heart thumping in my chest as I slip out of my Crocs and pad on bare feet to the kitchen door.

I open it a fraction further and squint into the sunlight.

No.

That can't be right.

I must be seeing things.

Softly, I shut the door.

I can smell the lobster corpse.

It's making me feel sick.

I take a deep breath and calm myself.

Then open the door and look again.

The scene remains the same.

Like something out of *Homes of the Rich and Famous*.

Across the way from a perfectly manicured lawn, the sun beats down on the crystal clear water of an Olympic-sized pool. Under the shade of a red and white striped umbrella, stretched out on a teak sun lounger, a woman is lying on her front. Her bikini bottom is the size of a postage stamp. Her bikini top is nowhere in sight. A man with an admirable six-pack is straddling the supine figure. He places a hand on the woman's naked shoulder, and says something that makes her laugh.

Unable to look away, I watch the man pick up a

bottle of suntan lotion from the poolside table. He makes a big show of rubbing the oil between the palms of his hands, then begins to massage the woman's bare back. Broad, confident strokes. More laughter. The woman says something. I can't hear the words, but the man replies with a kiss that he buries deep into the nape of the woman's neck. Then he strides to the edge of the pool and executes a flawless swallow dive that barely ripples the water.

At Home With Beth Jackson.

And her companion.

Freddie Ford.

There was a first for everything. And today, Beth thought, she had been making up for whatever was the opposite of a misspent youth. She paid scant attention to illness, except when occasional tonsillitis left her unable to talk to the viewers of *At Home*. As for sickies and duvet days, they were pathetic excuses made by irresponsible wastrels.

But when Freddie called – *'It's going to be the hottest day of the year. Let's hang out together!'* – moments after bloody Jeremy had texted with details of that afternoon's makeover (woodworm-ravaged furniture was to be given a fashionably distressed look) – Beth broke the habit of a lifetime, and texted back to Jeremy with the unfortunate news of her sudden laryngitis.

Freddie arrived within the hour, bearing gourmet

seafood and tantalising gossip about the latest scandals in publishing.

The afternoon passed in a haze of bliss, and only later – after Freddie had kissed her goodbye and she was making herself look respectable ahead of Matthew's return from work – did Beth begin to feel guilty.

Daily News, 31 August 200–

MY WEEK

TALES FROM THE HOME FRONT WITH BETH JACKSON
Careful where you put it!

The recent postal strikes – apologies if you have contacted me lately but have yet to receive a reply – remind me of something Juliet did when she was six years old.

It was the occasion of her first customer complaint.

My darling daughter had bought a jigsaw puzzle with her pocket money. Three hundred pieces. At least, that's how many there should have been. But after many hours of hard work, it emerged two were missing.

The shopkeeper blamed the manufacturer, and refused to give Juliet a refund. She came marching home, stomped up to her bedroom and bashed out a letter. I wasn't allowed to see it, but she promised it was polite, so I gave her a stamp and helped her find the address of the puzzle-making company.

Days passed and no reply.

Indignant now on my daughter's behalf, I resolved to get

justice. And yes, I know that if my name weren't Beth Jackson, it's unlikely that we'd have immediately been sent a parcel with twenty new puzzles.

Juliet and I agreed fifteen jigsaws should go to the local charity shop. On our way there, she pointed to a blue rubbish bin on the corner of the street and asked: 'Do you have any letters to post?'

It turned out my daughter's new friend Theodora – who used to live in America – had insisted postboxes are blue. So the letter of complaint had ended up in the bin rather than the box.

As someone who only last week put her groceries in the oven instead of the fridge, all I will say is that anyone can make a mistake. And that Juliet and Theodora still laugh about theirs, all these years later.

Beth's father had been fond of telling people, 'Make every mistake in the book, but make it only once.' She wondered what he would have to say about her life if he were still alive.

There were small mistakes, like forgetting to renew her parking permit, that barely mattered. But the big mistakes – errors of judgement with lifelong repercussions – were so much harder to forgive. Already feeling guilty about her stolen hours with Freddie, Beth wondered how her father would respond if she could sit down with him now, and confess that her career no longer seemed like the most important thing in her life.

Was it so very wrong to imagine a fresh start? A new life, where love came first – and was all that mattered?

I don't remember getting to the airport. Numb doesn't even begin to describe the way I feel. I held it together until I was on the Heathrow Express, but after that it all dissolved into a kaleidoscope of tears and images I wish I'd never seen, against a soundtrack of dreadful thoughts and imaginary conversations.

My mother.

Freddie Ford.

The saintly Beth Jackson.

The powerful independent publisher.

Voted Wife of the Year three times. Or was it four?

My client who sucks Murray Mints.

'Mum, how could you?'

My client who sucks.

'I mean, how could *you?'*

The way he caressed her body with the suntan oil.

'How long has this been going on?'

Freddie Ford is right up with there with that creep of an MP who tried to seduce a mother and her daughter. Or was it two daughters?

Is pretending I was never there an option?

Oh shit. I told him I was an orphan.

'Where did you meet him?'

Well, he lied, too.

And then he kissed my mother.

'Are you feeling all right, young lady?' There's a hand on my shoulder and I look into the face of the man who clipped my ticket when I boarded the train. 'I was just checking before we go back the other way,' he tells me. 'Everyone else got off ten minutes ago. Nervous flyer, are we?'

I stare wordlessly at him, manage a nod of thanks, gather my belongings and follow the signs to Terminal Five.

Rob and I have arranged to meet by the bank of machines where you check yourself in, but there's no sign of him, even though I'm the one who's now running late.

That bastard. He knew who I was, all the time. Just played along with me. Like a fox, teasing a chicken. And how come he turned up at Cognita in the first place? I can work that one out with a single guess…

How could he?

How could she?

How could they?

I open my bag in search of a crumpled tissue. The message alert light is flashing on my phone. Rob, most likely, telling me I'm waiting in the wrong place.

But no, I have a missed call from Theodora.

I catch sight of myself in the reflection of a plate glass window. Not a pretty picture. More dragged-through-a-hedge-backwards than poised young traveller jetting off to New York for the weekend with the man she adores. Better make myself presentable before Rob arrives.

Chapter Twenty-One

The restroom is a short walk away. Inside, there's a cluster of already-immaculate women staring at themselves while checking out one another in the wall-to-wall mirrors. I beat a hasty retreat into the nearest cubicle and lock the door safely behind me.

Refuge.

I sit down on the loo, fully clothed, and ponder my next move.

What did he say that made her laugh?

'How many times have you brought him to the house, Mum?'

His oily hands on her body.

'Is he the first? Or have there been others?'

I take out my phone and dial Theodora, who picks up on the first ring.

'Hi, babes,' she greets me. 'You at the airport?'

'Yes.'

We've been playing telephone tag for three days, and Theodora gets straight to the point. 'I've been gagging to share my good news,' she tells me. 'Guess what? Tuesday morning, I'm hard at it on my sculpture when the doorbell rings. Three of the competition judges are standing on the doorstep, saying they want to have a work-in-progress meeting. I told them they couldn't come in. No one's allowed to see what I'm doing till it's done. Not even you. But they turned out to be very persuasive.'

'How do you mean?'

'They said that based on the preliminaries, I'm one of the strongest candidates. And they wanted to see if my piece was living up to its promise. With a view to featuring it – and me – on a TV documentary about upcoming young British artists.'

'That's fantastic! So you let them in?' For a moment I forget why I called Theodora.

'You bet!'

'And?'

'Well, they didn't give too much away. But I think they liked what they saw. They asked me if it would be feasible to transport the piece from the flat into a gallery space.'

'But that's impossible! Wouldn't it just collapse?'

'Put it this way,' Theodora seems undaunted, 'I thought the prize was going to be decided on photographs. If they'd said at the beginning that the winners would end up in a gallery, I'd have done something else entirely. But, as it is, I think I've worked out a way of getting the sculpture through the front door. I'm pretty sure I can carve it into sections – like a piece of meat – and then put the slices back together again. I'm going to experiment while you're away. Talking of which, are you excited? I know I was only tiny when we moved back to England from America, but I still remember my dad taking me to Yankee Stadium. Those hot dogs ... they were almost as tall as I was. Babes? Are you there? You're awfully quiet.'

'I've got some news, too.' My voice quavers.

'What's the matter? You sound dreadful. What's wrong?'

'I know why Mum bought that aftershave for Dad.'

'You what? Is that some sort of a riddle?'

'Remember when you were helping me to get ready for the ... the meeting I had with Freddie Ford? I was in Mum and Dad's bathroom, and I noticed a bottle of that stuff that smells like incense. You know, the aftershave Freddie always wears...' I trail off into miserable silence.

'You're making no sense. Start at the beginning.'

So I do. The whole story. Everything from the moment I realised I'd forgotten my passport, to the lobster leftovers, the lack of a bikini top and the dive into the pool. I omit nothing, including the fantasy that, with luck, Freddie hit his head on the blue tiles at the bottom and never came up for air.

'Wow,' Theodora says when I've finished. 'How awful. Your mum having an affair. And with someone you know. Someone you like.'

'Liked,' I say hollowly. I bring Theodora up to speed

on the final moments of my evening with Freddie. 'The truth is, I'm honestly not sure what happened. I think he was coming on to me, but I suppose it's possible I fell off those bloody high heels. The only thing I know for certain is that I still feel ashamed. You were right, Theodora. I did have a bit of a crush on Freddie, but the moment I ended up in his arms, I was well and truly cured. All I could think of was Rob, and how I don't deserve to have him love me.'

'That's just daft. And we don't have time to discuss it now. Go and have a lovely weekend with him.' Theodora pauses, and I hear the hesitation in her voice. 'But JJ. About your mum's affair. Don't you think you ought to tell your dad? And sooner rather than later?'

Theodora has said the unsayable. Voiced the dilemma that's been on my mind all along.

Does Dad have a right to know Mum's cheating on him?

It's a no-brainer.

Of course Dad has to know. Mum's playing him for a fool, and the truth will break his heart. But imagine if he found out the way I did. By coming home unexpectedly and catching them at it.

'Shouldn't I wait till I get back?' I ask Theodora. 'Calling him seems so brutal.'

'There's no good way to do it. Face to face might be even worse. At least if your dad's somewhere private, no one will see him cry.'

Her words make me want to sob. 'Are you sure?'

'I honestly think it'll be better for him. On the phone.'

'God only knows how I'm going to tell him.'

'Just explain it the way you did to me. Start with the passport, then tell him what you saw in the garden, and let him join up the dots.'

'I'll ring you back if I have time.' I hang up and sit staring at my phone. This next call is going to be the hardest one I've ever made. And what should I do if it goes straight to voicemail?

Dad, there's something I have to tell you. But before I do, I want you to know how much I love you.' I'm still rehearsing how to begin when my phone starts ringing.

'JJ, where *are* you?' Rob sounds worried. 'You're cutting it really fine. Tell me you're on the train at least.'

'I'll be with you in five minutes. Promise. By the check-in machines, right?' I end the call before he can ask me any more questions.

I've been sitting on the loo so long, one of my legs is starting to feel numb. Time to stand up. And maybe I should find some other place for my next phone call: it feels undignified to be telling Dad something so life-changing while I'm in an airport toilet.

I know. There was a secluded corner behind the bureau de change. I can do it from there. I turn around in the cubicle. Better flush before I leave, in case someone's waiting on the other side of the door. I've been gripping the phone so hard, I've got pins and needles in my fingers.

WOOSH.

The automatic flush of the toilet startles me.

PLOP.

What

Is

My

Phone

Doing

At

The

Bottom

Of

The

Toilet?

I stare at my mobile, nestled in its watery grave. Then I plunge my hand into the pan and fish it out. I dry it off with the cleanest of the crumpled tissues, then buff it with a losing lottery ticket.

I press the power key more from habit than optimism.

The phone is as dead as my parents' marriage.

I tell myself this is the universe's way of telling me not to make that call to Dad, and hurry to meet Rob.

My boyfriend has a face like thunder. 'I was beginning to think you'd stood me up,' he scolds me.

'Sorry. I dropped my phone down the loo.' I hold it out in evidence.

'You what?' At least I've melted his bad mood. 'How did you manage that?'

'Accident. Sorry I'm late.'

'I've already done our boarding passes. We just have to check in the luggage and we're on our way. Excited?'

I put my ruined phone into my bag, and resolve to make the most of our weekend. New York is a place I've wanted to visit all my life and Rob's an angel for treating me to such an extravagant getaway. He's insisting on paying for everything. Says he wants to thank me for not giving him a hard time about all the hours he's devoted to FruityFul, and make up for the fact that we don't have as much quality time together as we used to. We're also celebrating the first two FruityFul franchise deals.

I owe it to Rob to keep my troubles – Mum and Dad's troubles – to myself for the next seventy-two hours. And I suppose it's also a way of giving Dad three more days of happiness.

I watch my case disappear into the black void of baggage handling.

'You'd better make tracks,' an airline official tells us. 'Another few minutes and I'll be closing the desk. No hanging around in the duty free. Straight to the departure gate, please.'

Rob and I spend the next forty-five minutes shuffling our way towards the head of the security point.

So much for a relaxed start to our trip. 'We're going to miss the plane,' I fret. 'Do you think we should say something to get ourselves to the front of the queue?'

'Don't worry,' Rob reassures me. 'Everyone's in the same situation. Our luggage will already be on board, so the plane can't take off without us.'

Eventually, the authorities are satisfied we are nothing more sinister than a young couple taking a weekend break. Or at least, once Rob has taken off his belt and the machines have finally stopped bleeping at its heavy silver buckle, we are finally permitted to make our way to the departure lounge.

'Look, our flight's on last call.' Rob gestures at the flight information board. 'Race you!'

We arrive, out of breath, in time to join the last few passengers boarding the plane. Inside the cabin, I settle myself into the window seat while Rob stows our carry-ons into an overhead locker.

'New York, here we come.' Rob settles into his seat. 'Let's see what they're showing on the in-flight movies.' He reaches for the glossy magazine tucked into the back of the next seat.

I pull out my copy of *The Girl Who Kicked the Hornet's Nest*, and begin to read. The story is compelling, and soon I'm lost in a world of Swedish treachery, violence and – unfortunately for me – a detailed account of life-saving brain surgery. It's only when Rob nudges me that I realise we're still on the tarmac.

'We should have taken off thirty-five minutes ago.' He sounds concerned. 'Wonder what the problem is.'

In answer to his query, the plane's intercom crackles into life. 'Ladies and gentlemen,' says a female voice. 'On behalf of the captain and crew, I would like to apologise for the delay. The hold-up is due to an air traffic control issue. We hope to be on our way soon, and I'll update you with further information as soon as I am able.'

Rob and I groan in unison, along with two hundred other passengers.

'Save the book for the flight.' Rob pulls it gently from my hands. 'Tell me about your day so far. How come you were so late?'

To tell?

Or not to tell?

There's really no question. I only have to think about the way Rob has bruised my feelings by holding stuff back from me to be certain about what I have to do.

'It's my parents,' I begin. Speaking softly, to ensure Rob is the only person who can hear, I tell him the whole story.

'And now we're stuck here going nowhere, and I'm thinking this is another sign from the universe. Telling me I should find out what's going on between Mum and Freddie, instead of putting it off until we get back.

But I can't do that, because we're going to New York, and I know how much you're looking forward to it.'

'Thank God you *didn't* phone your dad!' Rob is so emphatic, heads begin to turn in our direction. 'It's your mum you need to speak to. Not your dad!'

'But—'

'But nothing, sweetheart.' Rob can see I'm holding back tears, and his tone softens. 'Look, this is a million times more important than New York. We've got the rest of our lives to go there. I'm going to get us off the plane so we can sort it all out.' Without giving me any chance to disagree, he presses the armrest button to summon a steward.

'Sir?' The steward looks as irritated as he sounds.

'I'm afraid something's come up, and we need to get off the plane.'

'Have you been using your phone?' The official is accusatory. 'That's not permitted.'

'Didn't you hear me?' Rob stands up. 'This is an emergency. Kindly allow us to disembark.'

'No chance.' The steward drops all pretence of politeness. 'Just because there's a hold-up, everyone's wanting to go back into the departure lounge. Take it from me, that's not going to happen.' And with that, he puts his hand on Rob's shoulder, and pushes him back into his seat.

'Get your hands off me!' Rob snaps. 'I want to speak to the captain. As I say, this is an emergency.'

'I don't see any emergency. *Sir.*' The steward's final word is dripping with sarcasm. 'And I think you'll find the captain is somewhat preoccupied at present.'

'He's not going to let you off the plane,' says a woman sitting across the aisle. Heads are turning in our direction, eager to see what the mini-drama is all about. 'Once the baggage is in the hold,' the woman continues, 'the only way they'll let you off is if you die. Or have a heart attack, at least.'

'There's always air rage,' jokes another passenger.

'Is that right?' Rob says slowly. 'Is that right?' he asks the steward.

'Sir, you're making a fool of yourself. Sit down.'

'Air rage. That's when a passenger goes out of control. Hits someone. Isn't it?' Rob turns to the man who suggested it.

'Yes,' he confirms. 'I was on a flight from Dubai the other week, and someone was a bit the worse for wear. Took a swing at the steward, and was arrested as soon as we touched down.'

'So if I were to hit someone,' Rob addresses our steward, 'you'd let us off the plane.'

'Don't be ridiculous.' The steward takes a few steps back from Rob. 'You don't want to get yourself arrested.'

'Will that get us off the plane?'

'And straight into police custody. Health and safety. You're verging on threatening behaviour as it is.'

This is getting out of hand. But before I can

intervene, Rob is out of his seat and standing in the aisle. 'I need a volunteer,' he says calmly. 'My girlfriend has an emergency to deal with. And, as you've heard, I've been told the only way we can disembark to deal with it is if I hit someone. Ridiculous, I know. But perhaps one of you is able to help.'

The man who mentioned air rage in the first place is on his feet. 'Just let them off the plane,' he tells the steward.

'Against the rules.'

The man turns back to Rob. *Be gentle with me*, he mouths.

As punch-ups go, it makes that fracas between Hugh Grant and Colin Firth look like the World Heavyweight Championship.

'Thank you so much,' Rob says. Then he plants his unclenched fist in the other man's chest and gives him a firm push backwards.

The 'victim' falls to the ground in an exaggerated fashion.

By now, half the passengers are laughing and the rest are pretending not to notice what's going on.

'THAT'S IT!' Our steward has been joined by a couple of reinforcements. 'I warned you, sir. I shall now perform a citizen's arrest on you.'

A pair of handcuffs is produced and Rob's wrists are shackled behind his back. Accompanied by the trio of airline officials and a low chorus of disapproval, he is frogmarched down the aisle of the plane, towards the cabin doors.

'Which of these bags are yours?' Rob's accomplice, none the worse for his experience, takes charge. 'Better take them and get off the plane before they close the doors again. Here's my phone number.' He presses a business card into my hand. 'Tell your young man I shan't be pressing charges. And whatever it is that's so important, I hope you sort it out.'

Gratefully, I follow Rob off the plane.

Chapter Twenty-Two

'Rob? What is it? What's happened?'

Mum sounds really worried.

'It's me. And I'm fine.' Although, of course, I am not. 'I'm just using Rob's mobile. I wanted to—'

'Darling! How lovely of you to call. How *is* New York? Are you having fun? I remember last time I was there. Do make sure you go to that wonderful bakery down in the Village. The cupcakes are to die for. Wonderful colours. Especially the orange ones. They taste like raw sunshine. All natural ingredients, too. Hang on, though…' Mum's voice trails off, and I can tell she has worked out it's the middle of the night in America.

'Um, we didn't actually make it as far as JFK.'

'Why on earth not? Some problem with the plane?'

'I'll explain when I see you. What are you up to this morning?'

'Juliet. What's going on? Where *are* you?'

My mother has switched to her commander-in-chief voice. I have no intention of telling her I've just finished a triple latte breakfast in Hampstead High Street. It's more prudent to launch a counter-offensive. 'Are you at home?' I demand.

'Yes, but— '

'And is Dad with you?'

'Yes, but— '

'Then I'll meet you at Highgate Ponds in half an hour.'

Before Mum can say another word, I end the call and turn off Rob's phone for good measure, before handing it back to its owner.

For a man who's spent the best part of ten hours in a cell, my boyfriend looks surprisingly perky. I think he's still cruising on adrenaline. We're both a bit shell-shocked by what's happened. I'd imagined he might get a rap over the knuckles for getting us off the plane like that, or at worst an on-the-spot fine like they give binge drinkers. But it turns out the police take 'undesirable passenger behaviour' very seriously.

Duty solicitors.

Statements.

Crown Prosecution Service.

There's still a possibility Rob will be charged with assault, although right now, after more than twenty-four hours without sleep, we feel more like victims than criminals.

Rob touches my arm and says, 'Do you want me to come with you?'

'You've already been heroic. And you're absolutely

right that I have to talk to Mum rather than Dad. Thank God I never made that call! But I need to do this on my own. I think you should go and get some rest. I'll call you when I'm done.'

'Or at least you would if you had a phone!' Rob reminds me. 'I'll be in Primrose Hill. Come on over whenever you're ready.'

I part company with Rob at the tube, then turn towards Heath Street. The ponds aren't far away, but with every step I take, I feel my stomach twisting in knots. Even though I know what I'm going to say – I had plenty of time to work that out while I was propping up the coffee machine at Heathrow police station – I'm scared.

It's one thing to be angry in the abstract (I spent most of the night raging inwardly at my mother) but now I'm only a few minutes away from confronting her, the whole idea is about as appealing as a kidney transplant. I distract myself by wondering whether I would insist on avoiding a life-saving operation if given the option. More people die in hospitals than anywhere else, so when you come to think about it my reservations are entirely logical.

GULP.

Fifty metres ahead of me, standing exactly where I was planning to lie in wait, is my mother.

How did she get here ahead of me? I'm ten minutes early as it is.

Witchcraft is the only explanation.

Even though the sun is beating down, Mum is wearing a black wrap and an expression to match. I take a deep breath, then march towards her with the calm resignation of someone who's about to be burned at the stake. I approach the Women's Pond – and a timeworn wooden sign that declares NO MEN, BOYS OR DOGS BEYOND THIS POINT – with a final rehearsal of my opening line.

'*So how long have you known Freddie Ford?*'

I'll look Mum straight in the eye as I ask.

Catch her completely off guard.

Her face, rather than her reply, will answer my question.

Hang about … it's not supposed to happen like this.

Mum is walking – running – towards me, and now I'm wrapped tightly in her arms, so tight I can't break free, and she's saying – sobbing, almost – 'Juliet. Darling. Now I understand why you're not in New York! But what on earth happened? Was it a panic attack? Please don't think I'm angry with you. I just want to know you're OK.'

Angry? Why would Mum be angry with *me*?

I manage to wriggle out of her embrace, but before I can say anything, Mum hands me a newspaper.

Red top.

Today's date.

Front page.

That's weird.

A photo of someone who looks so like me we could be sisters. A kindly looking man, older, is handing her a small travel bag. A motley crew of seated people surround them. They could be in a railway carriage, or—

Or—

Oh crap.

The headline says it all.

I'M A CELEBRITY'S DAUGHTER. GET ME OUT OF HERE.

When … how … who?

'Juliet, I'm sure none of this is true. What they're saying about you having a temper tantrum because the flight was delayed. I know you'd never behave like that. But I don't understand all this cloak and dagger business. What are we doing here?' Mum gestures towards the grass and the ponds. 'Why didn't you come home? Come to that, where have you been all night? And could you please confirm that Rob has *not* been arrested for fighting in the aisles with a software tycoon of some description. I've already got one of my lawyers onto that one, don't you worry. Also I believe this damn rag is in breach of copyright for reproducing one of my articles – one about patience being a virtue, would you believe – without permission. I'll have them for that, if it's the last thing I do. And we'll make sure they print a full apology to you. Damages, too. Don't you worry, darling. We'll have it all sorted out in time for tomorrow's edition. In fact, the *Sunday Times* has already been on, asking me to do a piece of my own, setting the record straight. Would you like that?'

'Mum. People are *staring* at us.' It's not strictly true, but at least it's a way of getting her to pause between sentences.

'Oh. Well, we don't want any more photographs, do we? Come on, let me take you home. I still don't understand why you made me come here.'

'Mum. I need to talk to you. Privately.' I fold the newspaper in half and stick it in the nearest bin. 'Come on, let's go for a walk.' I walk purposefully along the path that leads away from the ponds, hoping she will follow.

The great thing about this little corner of London is that even though it's only twenty minutes from Trafalgar Square, you could easily be in the country. Which makes it perfect for a clandestine conversation.

And my mother's confession of adultery.

By the time we get to the wooded area on the fringes of Highgate there's no one in sight and no risk of us being overheard. It's like being in a mini-forest. I wait for Mum to catch up – she's been walking a few paces behind me the whole time, as if unsure whether or not to humour me – then I look her straight in the eye and prepare to ask, '*So how long have you known Freddie Ford?*'

'Juliet, I've had more than enough of this hiking

expedition.' Mum is red in the face, and sounds cross. 'As it so happens, I've been wanting to have a talk with you, too. But I'm not taking another step until you tell me what happened on the damn plane.'

'How long have you…' My voice begins to wobble. 'How long have you… I couldn't go to New York because of you and Freddie Ford. I saw you. Together. Yesterday.'

Mum's expression is blurred by my tears. But her voice is calm, clear and faintly puzzled. 'Saw us? What do you mean, darling?'

'I saw him slathering you in suntan oil. If you really want to know.'

Silence.

The sound of children laughing in the distance.

Finally, my mother says, 'You mean you came home yesterday afternoon?'

'I forgot my passport.'

'And you saw Freddie and me in the garden?'

I nod.

'That was—' Mum is choosing her words carefully '—unfortunate. I was going to tell you everything in good time, of course. Look, let's sit down.' Mum drapes an arm around me and leads me to a bench further along the path. I can feel her taking charge of the situation, but I'm too tired to resist.

'What I don't understand—' Mum's arm is still wrapped around my shoulder '—is why this couldn't have waited until Monday. I know how much you wanted to go to New York.'

'How could I possibly go off for the weekend knowing you're having an affair with Freddie Ford? What about Dad? Does he know?' My final question is no more than a whisper.

My life is about to change.

All our lives are about to change.

'An *affair*?'

Mum sounds horrified. If I hadn't seen her and Freddie with my own eyes, I'd believe every lie she's about to tell me.

'Juliet. Freddie and I have known one another for years. We met at some ghastly awards ceremony. He keeps pestering me to write my autobiography, but I'm much too young for that. I thought you were upset because you realised I sent him to do business with you at Cognita. An affair? With Freddie? Why on earth would you think that?'

'So all your friends massage oil into you, do they?'

'I had no idea you were so prudish, darling.'

'What would Dad say?'

'You're welcome to ask him yourself.'

For the first time I have doubts. 'But you both seemed so—' Mum doesn't wait for me to say how comfortable…how intimate…she and Freddie seemed to be.

In fact, she seems to have decided our conversation has been satisfactorily concluded.

She stands up and smiles at me. 'Let's stroll back and stop at the café,' she suggests. 'Ice cream and cake. Like we used to. When you were small.'

'We used to come here a lot, didn't we?'

'Almost every day. Until… well, before you started school. Which seems like only yesterday to me. You'll always be my little girl, even when you're fifty years old. You know that, don't you, darling? And no one's ever too old for toffee ice cream and Black Forest gateau. Not even me! Look, I'm really sorry your weekend's been ruined. And I have to say I'm touched you went to such lengths to get off the plane, although I'm not quite sure now how to handle the press fallout. Perhaps better to say nothing at all.'

If Mum says I can ask Dad about Freddie, she must be telling the truth. They're friends. Just good friends. Nothing more.

Which begs another question: *Why do I always think the worst of my mother?*

Although I have just accused her of infidelity, she's taken it in her stride, without a word of reproach. If anything, she's faintly amused by my blunder, even offering to buy me a consolation ice cream, as though I were five years old. Even better, it seems she is not about to tell readers of the *Sunday Times* that I am a prude who incited her boyfriend to get arrested in order to rush home and brand her mother a harlot. Which is generous, and probably more than I deserve.

'You always loved that sign. It was one of the first things you ever learned to read.' Mum has been talking non-stop while we walk back, and it's comforting that some things never change.

"NO MEN, BOYS OR DOGS BEYOND THIS POINT," I recite, remembering it was Mum who taught me to swim – and read – all those years ago.

Today, the Women's Pond is a sea of female flesh.

'No men!' Mum makes a theatrical show of scrutinising the swimmers.

'No boys!' I follow suit.

'NO DOGS!' We giggle our punchline in harmony.

Then Mum says softly, 'You don't remember, do you?'

'Remember what?'

'Why we stopped coming here?'

I shake my head.

'It was horrible.' Mum shivers visibly, despite the heat. 'I turned my back for a second. I swear that was all. Somehow, you managed to get yourself into the water, fully clothed. You were three years old. It was March. Too cold for anyone to be swimming. For the first few moments, I thought you were playing hide and seek. I shouted your name, expecting you to appear from behind one of the trees. Then I realised…call it a mother's instinct…I knew you were in the water. By the time I spotted you, you were standing on tiptoe. Over there.' Mum points to a clump of reeds a couple of metres from the edge of the pond. 'I yelled at you to stand absolutely still. Like a statue. For once in your life, thank God, you obeyed me. I can still see the look on your face as you realised you couldn't get back to safety on your own. I leaped in and dragged you out. Another few seconds…it doesn't bear thinking about.' Mum hugs her tummy with both hands, as the absolutely stricken memory of terror floods through her body.

I rush to her side and put my own arms around her. 'I never knew,' I say.

'Of course not,' she says, sounding more like my mother with every word. 'I made sure you forgot all about it. We started going to Primrose Hill instead. And that summer I booked us places on the mother-and-child course at the Gospel Oak Lido. You were fine. I was terrified!'

'I remember. You wrote about it. But…but you never said anything about any of this.'

'Well, of course not. I tried to pretend to myself it had never happened.'

'No funny story about how I wandered off into the water and you came rushing to the rescue?'

'It wasn't funny at all, Juliet. You could have died. Now can we please talk about something else.'

We have arrived at the café with immaculate timing. A table is about to become vacant, and Mum hovers like a purposeful seagull. She times her swoop to perfection, then says to the waitress, 'Can I get a large portion of Black Forest gateau, please. With an equally large helping of cream.'

Impressed that Mum is openly defying the rules of every known diet – unless Lose Seven Pounds in Seven Days by Eating Your Weight in Black Forest Gateau with Whipped Cream is about to make its debut – I order a triple scoop of toffee ice cream with butterscotch sauce. Grown-up food can wait until tomorrow.

'So how come you sent Freddie to Cognita?' I ask.

'I know you'll find this hard to believe, my darling, but I was actually trying to help you.' Mum's voice is sad, rather than sarcastic. 'I know how much the promotion means to you, so I was trying to help you get an advantage. It's how business works. You've got to use your contacts. But I knew that if I'd been straight with you, you'd have found a thousand reasons to say no.'

Mum's absolutely correct. 'No good deed goes unpunished,' I manage. 'And I've done a good job for Freddie.'

'I know. He's been singing your praises.'

Has he?

'What's he been saying?' Let's hope Mum thinks I'm fishing for compliments, rather than information.

'Well, I've seen the website of course. Excellent. And there's been so much interest in that elephant, Freddie's in his element. Preparing to auction the American rights, but I expect you know that. Now I've got a question for you...' Mum seems strangely hesitant.

Oh crap. Here it comes. She wants to know why I told Freddie I'm an orphan. Even though it felt like a good idea at the time, I can feel myself flushing with shame.

'Why have you never told me you want to be an author?'

Thank God.

'Mum, I *have* told you. Or at least I've told you loads of times, I want to succeed because I'm me. Rather than because of who you happen to be.'

'That's not the same thing at all. And you know it. Has it never occurred to you that the reason *I've* succeeded is all because of *you*, Juliet?" Mum sounds exasperated. As though she were telling me to close the sitting room door for the thousandth time. But this is a lecture that's new to me. 'Do you think when I was starting out that anyone would have been interested in what I had to say if it hadn't been for you? Without you, I'd have been just another youngster trying to elbow her way into the media. As it was, the pram in the hallway made me unique. Not that we had much of a hallway. All I wanted was to be a good mother and give you the best of everything, so when I realised writing lovely little stories about our life together was going to pay far more than anything else I could do, I took their money and felt grateful. It meant Dad could follow his passion, and do teacher training. We could buy a washing machine for all the nappies. And the whole thing just snowballed from there. Took on a life of its own. I'm not going to pretend I don't enjoy what I do. I love it. Mostly. But it hasn't always been easy. In my business, saying no when you're offered work is a high risk strategy. Sometimes, I feel like a hamster on a treadmill, with a bunch of rats just waiting to nip my ankles if I forget to pedal. A very well-paid hamster, but that's not my point. You have no idea how jealous I was when you and Theodora had your gap year. I felt like I was watching a play I could never be part of. Here. If you're not going to eat that, I will!' Mum scoops a melting mound of toffee ice cream from my plate.

'Look, what I'm trying to say is I'm sorry if you think I haven't always been around for you enough. But as you get older, darling, you'll realise more and more that life is about making the compromises that seem right at the time. And the sacrifices. I remember years ago, I was meant to go with you and your class to the Tower of London. I was so excited about it, because I'd never been there either. Then the news editor offered me an extra shift, and I knew if I said I couldn't do it because of my daughter, I'd never be taken seriously. Thank goodness it's easier for women today. But don't let anyone tell you success is easy. One of the prices I've paid for mine is that I have a daughter who spoils her beauty by biting her bottom lip whenever she's pissed off with me. A daughter who won't let me help her. Which, actually, I greatly admire. And anyway, you're a million times better at business than I would ever be. But the point is, even though being a stupid teenager who happened to have a baby helped get me started in my career, if I hadn't been any good at journalism, and if I hadn't worked hard, I wouldn't have got anywhere. I can open doors for you, Juliet – or at least I could, if you'd let me – but in the end, you'll stand or fall because of you. Not because of me.'

Blimey.

Who is this person in my mother's body? Continuing to filch my ice cream.

Everything she says makes perfect sense.

For once in my life, I'm lost for words.

Unlike my mother.

'Juliet, I've been waiting for the right moment to apologise to you for that broadcast I did from your bedroom. I still feel dreadful about it. It was one of those last-minute things. I'd been telling everyone at work how delighted I was that my little girl was home, then next thing I know, there's a report out about how many grown-up children are moving back in with their parents. And Jeremy's setting up that afternoon's edition of *At Home* from *our* home. Bloody liberty. But they'd have thought I was a diva if I'd said no. Then by the time I arrived, the camera crew was set up in your bedroom, and we were too close to transmission to object. I suppose I hoped you'd never find out. But when you walked in on us, I was so horrified I just couldn't make myself shut up.'

'You should have bitten your lip,' I tell her.

And in that same moment, I forgive her.

Then I say, 'I do want to write books. Fiction. But Freddie says what I've written so far isn't good enough.'

'He didn't tell me that. In fact, he refused to say anything at all about what you've been up to. Said he'd be breaking a professional confidence. That must mean you're good.'

'Honestly?'

'Honestly, Juliet. Look, let's go back home and see what Dad's up to, shall we? You can ask him about Freddie. If you want to.'

'One other thing. How come Dad and Freddie have the same taste in aftershave?' I say it with a smile.

Mum grins straight back at me. 'A two-for-one offer that I simply couldn't resist. Such a heavenly scent, don't you think?'

Chapter Twenty-Three

Ravi has just told me that when Natasha invited me to take a bite of the reality sandwich at this morning's brainstorm, she was actually trying to rubbish my idea. (That would explain why there had been no food anywhere in sight.) We're about to have a sneer about wrong-siding the demographic, when my shiny new iPhone beeps.

A text from Rob: 'Need 2 c u urgent. X.'

Good to know my boyfriend can't live without me, even if I disapprove of his text-speak. 'Is Danny out tonight then? X x x,' I text back.

'Emergency.'

When I call Rob, his phone goes straight to voice-mail. Then, while I ponder my next move, another text arrives: 'On way 2 office. See u outside in 20. X.'

It's already five o'clock, so I quickly reply to a couple of emails that have been sitting in my in-box since yesterday, then grab my stuff and tell Ravi I'm knocking off a bit early.

I loiter in reception, imagining the possibilities. Hopefully, it's some unexpected good news that Rob can't wait to share. Did he buy a lottery ticket on

Saturday? But when I review the three texts, the word 'Emergency' leaps out from amongst all the others on the screen.

What kind of emergency? It's hard – impossible – to think of a good one. A few minutes later, when I see Rob walking towards the plate glass doors of Cognita, my fears are confirmed. That's definitely not the swagger of a lottery winner.

I rush outside to meet him. 'What is it? What's happened?'

Rob's face is grey. He grabs my hand and says, 'I need a drink. It'll be better if we're both sitting down.'

I manage to find us a table at the back of one of the bars on Wardour Street. Rob comes back from the bar, pushes a drink towards me and produces a folded piece of paper from his pocket. 'Take a look,' he says.

Immediately, I recognise the Podolski logo and the letterhead. But the words that follow might as well be written in Polish – or Serbo-Croat – for all the sense they make.

Sirs,

From time to time we review the account status of our valued customers.

In respect of your business FruityFul and with reference to your outstanding debt of £300,000, I must inform you we have recently revised your credit limit in line with the circumstances.

I am therefore pleased to request that you return your
account to a positive balance within the next thirty days.
Assuring you of our best services at all times.
Kindest regards.

The letter is signed by someone who appears to be
called Mr Squiggle.

'They can't do that!' I protest. 'Why would they?'

'When the letter came, Danny and I thought it was
a joke. We phoned our branch and discovered it's not.
They want their money back. And most of it's been
spent. We're finished, JJ. Ruined.' Rob drains his glass
and strides to the bar for a refill.

I take another look at the letter. It has to be a mistake.
A typical bank glitch. Unless— My stomach lurches
as though I'm in a fast-descending elevator.

OH MY GOD.

Two weeks ago. When I was sitting with a different
glass in my hand at a café less than five minutes from
here, entertaining Feliks Unpronounceable.

OH MY GOD.

Wasn't I laughing about Asbo's playful kitchen
antics? And prattling on about New York.

OH MY GOD.

But I was only making conversation! And all the
while, Feliks was sitting there politely paying attention,
tak-ing away, and making a mental note of every indis-
creet word I uttered.

Forget that we never got to New York; my client must have remembered Rob promised he was willing to live on a hundred quid a week.

Rob comes back from the bar. I take a deep breath. 'I think I know why this is happening,' I confess.

It would have been better if Rob had shouted at me.

Dumped me, even.

Instead, after he got over the shock – 'You told him Asbo was in the kitchen? And that we're living the high life in New York?' – he couldn't have been kinder. Just one of those things, he said.

According to the small print in the contract he and Danny signed with Podolski, the bank is within its rights to call in the loan on thirty days' notice.

Twenty five days from now…

Danny's attitude has been equally charitable. 'We'll find a way out of this, somehow,' he told me. 'We'd never have got this far without your help in the first place, JJ. So it's unfair to blame you now.'

But it *is* my fault.

At least tonight, I'll be able to forget about it for a while. I'm on my way to see Theodora.

'Come to the flat, babes!' she invited me. 'I've got something to show you – and I think you're going to like it!'

Which can only mean one thing.

Her sand sculpture is finally finished, and I'm about

to discover what *Pride and Prejudice* actually looks like.

It seems like ages since I lived with Theodora. How long has it been? I do a quick calculation. May … June …July…August…the summer seems to have passed so fast.

Theodora greets me with a big hug. 'I've made us supper,' she says. 'Hope you're hungry.'

'Starving. But you're going to let me view the master-piece first? That's why I'm here, right?'

Theodora gives me a half-smile. 'If you insist, you can go check out your bedroom. I think you'll like what you see.'

I need no further invitation.

I sprint from the lounge and fling open the bedroom door.

Bloody hell.

'What on earth have you done?' I squeal.

Theodora saunters into the room. 'Please don't tell me you're disappointed. I'll be gutted. I've been working really hard.'

Too true.

The room has had a makeover worthy of Mum's producer, Jeremy.

New curtains. A pretty dressing table with an oval mirror in an ornate frame. An elegant lamp in one corner. A bed covered with a gorgeous maroon velvet throw. And the smell of fresh paint lingering in the air, complemented by the scent of recently varnished floorboards.

'Where is it?'

'Your Banksy print? Couldn't find it anywhere. I was hoping it's at your mum and dad's.'

'Don't tease me! What have you done with your bloody sculpture? It's…it's like one of those tricks where the lady vanishes or turns a rabbit into a turtle dove…no, that's not right, is it?'

'You mean my sculpture?' Theodora shrugs. She's loving every moment of my confusion. 'Gone.'

'Gone where?'

'Gone to some gallery in Shoreditch. More like a concrete bunker to be honest. It's not exactly Cork Street. Even so. I've made it into the final three of the competition, babes.'

I let out a whoop of joy. 'Fantastic! I'm so thrilled for you.'

We celebrate Theodora's success with Prosecco, and mushroom risotto.

'So how *did* you manage to get the sculpture out of the house without the whole thing collapsing?' I ask her.

'I spent three days online looking for advice, but every site I clicked on said it couldn't be done. I was almost ready to give up, but then I came across a guy in Vermont who's been sand sculpting for years. He's called Noah…'

I recognise a familiar – faraway – look on Theodora's face. 'So tell me about Noah?' I prompt.

'We exchanged emails. Then started Skyping. And yes, he's really fit. But I haven't got time for anything like that right now. Noah reckoned it was almost impossible to move the piece.'

'So how did you manage it? Did he send good vibrations all the way from America, or what?'

'For a start, all sand is not created equal,' Theodora says. 'Remember, I bought top-notch stuff in the first place. It's all about how well the grains are held together by the water.' She launches into a technical explanation that includes the words 'surface tension', 'bonding agents' and 'initial compacting'. I pretend I'm following and wait patiently until she switches back into English. 'And then we did a huge diagram to work out how to carve the piece into sections. Two hundred and eleven of them. All numbered and protected in a double layer of bubble wrap.'

'Sounds exhausting.'

'You have no idea! And I was doing most of the work in the middle of the night, so Noah could supervise me over the webcam.'

'Yes, I meant to say I like your new haircut!'

A grin of acknowledgement. Then Theodora continues, 'A specialist art team from Pickfords came and crated up the individual slabs of sand. Shifted everything in the middle of the night, so they wouldn't have to keep stopping and starting with the traffic. They even plotted a special route to avoid sleeping policemen. I was so worried I'd never get the whole thing back together again. Like Humpty Dumpty. But in the end it was easier than I thought, especially once I'd built a new foundation platform. Bit like bricklaying.'

'So am I ever going to see this famous work of art?' I demand. 'I've waited so long to see what *Pride and Prejudice* is all about.'

'All in good time.' Theodora pauses to roll a crispy duck pancake. You can tell she's an artist. Her pancake has dainty fronds of spring onions dangling at either end, and looks like it belongs in a cookery book. Mine is already dripping plum sauce from its innards and bulging like a girl whose dress is a size too small. 'You'll actually be one of the first people to see my sculpture,' Theodora continues. 'There's going to be a special unveiling.'

'When?'

'In about three weeks' time. The details are still a bit vague. They're talking about filming your reaction when you see it for the first time. As part of the documentary they're making. Would that be all right?'

'I'd love to! Just tell me when.'

'They should have had their cameras rolling just now.' Theodora smirks. 'The look on your face was priceless!'

'I still don't understand why you're being so secretive about this sculpture,' I complain. 'Won't you even give me a clue what it's all about? I won't tell anyone, I promise.'

'I've had to sign a contract with the organisers. They're big on confidentiality. And the filming thing is a big deal. Not to mention the fifty thousand pound prize. Talking of money ...' Theodora hesitates. I know what she's going to say next. The subject is permanently at the front of my mind.

'It's hopeless.' I sigh. 'Worse than hopeless. Remember Danny signed over the deeds to his home. And Rob pledged his life savings...'

'It's a disgrace,' Theodora declares. 'What can we do?'

'If only I knew. I've sent Feliks a whole bunch of texts and emails. He's on holiday somewhere in South America. No one in the bank's marketing department knows where, exactly. Or at least that's what they say. And because the loan was approved in Poland, the London branch doesn't have a clue what's going on. They just keep saying the letter is correct and they look forward to receiving the damn funds.'

'If I win this competition, you can borrow my prize money for as long as you need,' Theodora offers. But we both know it's not enough.

'Anyway.' My friend tactfully changes the subject. 'How soon do you fancy moving back in? And do you approve of what I've done to your room?'

'It looks great. But—' I concentrate on my second helping of Theodora's delicious risotto to give myself a moment to think. 'Mum said I had to stay at home until I'm out of debt.'

'Since when did you take any notice of what your mum says?'

'Look. I'm thinking of asking her to intervene with FruityFul. The boys haven't said anything to their parents yet. Mostly because Danny thinks his dad might actually kill him, seeing as how he's only the younger son, rather than the heir. But Mum being famous and all that ... if she starts asking questions, or threatens to write about a foreign bank that encouraged British businesses to borrow then goes and pulls the rug from underneath them... Well, they might change their mind, don't you think?'

'It's worth a try.' Then Theodora shoots me a glance and adds, 'You seem to be getting on better with your mum these days.'

'Ever since I accused her of shagging Freddie Ford you mean?'

'What's the score with Freddie anyway?'

'He just flogged German rights to *The Elephant in the Room* for a million quid.'

'Wow! But that's not what I meant.'

'So now Cognita is in charge of all Doublekay's ongoing digital marketing. Ravi's going to do the content under my supervision. It'll earn the agency fifteen grand a month for the next six months.'

'Wow! But that's not what I meant either.'

'Me and Freddie, you mean?'

'Yep.' Theodora isn't going to let me off the hook.

'I made Mum swear she wouldn't tell Freddie. So that spared my blushes. He came into the agency with Doublekay, and that was fine. I'm going into his office next week for a chat about my writing.'

'Well, that's good. Maybe he can advance you a million quid, too.'

'Three hundred thousand would be more than enough. But seriously—'

I am interrupted by my phone ringing. I check to see who's calling, and am greeted by a photo of my mother spooning cereal into her mouth. A candid shot that makes her look less intimidating.

'Hi, Mum.'

'Darling. We were wondering what time to expect you home.'

'It's not even nine o'clock yet.' Theodora's right. I need to move out as soon as possible.

'We seem to have been chasing one another all week,' she says.

'I was thinking about staying over at Theodora's.'

'Juliet. I need to talk to you. We both do. Your father and I.' Mum sounds nervous, yet firm. 'Would it be too much trouble for you to come home right away?'

'Now, you mean?'

'That's what I thought I just said.'

'What's up?'

'As I say. We need to talk to you.'

I examine my conscience all the way to Hampstead. At least Mum didn't say it was an emergency. But she sounded serious. What have I done? I know my room's a bit messy, but surely that doesn't merit summoning me home for a bollocking. Maybe someone's ill. Or Mum's found out about FruityFul and my part in their meltdown.

Dad appears while I'm still putting my key in the front door. He's got a big smile on his face. At least my parents are not about to break bad news.

'What's going on?'

'Mum's in the living room. Go say hello.'

Mum is curled into a corner of the couch, watching one of the rolling news channels. As usual, the pictures are accompanied by her personal commentary. 'I don't know how that man has the gall to think anyone's going to vote for him ever again. Come to that, how did he ever get elected in the first place? I blame apathy and the abolition of the eleven plus. Hello, darling.' My mother pauses long enough to kiss me. 'Thanks for coming home. Tell me, do you think it's right that people can be threatened with prison for helping their loved ones to die?'

Oh my God.

Then I realise Mum is still commentating on a news story.

'As for him—' she scowls in the direction of the presenter '—I heard on the grapevine that he's demanding a two hundred per cent increase on his contract *and* he wants the money to be paid into an account in Monaco. The cheek of it. Mind you, these all-news stations. Everything's so flashy, fast and superficial. If God rolled up to create heaven and earth again, they'd turn it into a thirty-second sound bite wedged between the weather and the sports news. Or get David Blaine to explain how it's done.'

Dad comes into the room and turns off the television. 'Having one of your rants again, darling?' He sits down next to Mum and rests his hand on her knee.

From my armchair, I notice the smile that passes between my parents. If Rob and I are still so happy after more than thirty – yes, thirty! – years together, we'll be doing well. Always supposing Rob and I survive the next few weeks… No matter what he says, he's always going to blame me for ruining FruityFul.

'You're looking very thoughtful,' says Dad. 'Everything OK?'

'Yes.' This isn't the moment to share my woes. 'I think so. You tell me. What have I done wrong?'

Silence hangs in the room for what seems like a long time. I'm starting to feel uncomfortable when

Mum picks up a dainty package from the coffee table. 'For you,' she says.

The gift is almost weightless in my hand.

'What's this in aid of?'

'Open it and see.' Dad's got a dopey watermelon grin on his face. What *is* going on?

Carefully, I unfurl a sliver of metallic ribbon, then split the elegant white wrapping paper with my finger. I'm still none the wiser, because whatever I'm being given is hidden inside a layer of tissue paper.

Finally, I examine what I've been given.

A baby bib.

A pristine, white baby bib.

A pristine, white baby bib with the words 'I love my big sister' printed across it in red letters.

How weird is th—

NO WAY.

Even without looking up, I can feel my parents studying me like birds of prey.

I can't take my eyes off the bib.

By which I mean it seems safest to let Mum or Dad say something first. After all, I could be entirely wrong.

It wouldn't be the first time.

But which part of big sister am I not understanding?

I feel the urge to laugh, and realise I am on the verge of hysteria.

Then Mum is on her knees in front of me. She takes

my hands in her own, and squeezes them gently, compelling me to look at her. 'We've spent weeks wondering how to tell you,' she says. 'You're allowed to be surprised, but we're hoping you'll get used to the idea.'

'How on earth did this happen?' Even as the words escape, I realise how ridiculous they are. I lean forwards and give Mum a hug, unsure whether I'm about to give in to the laughter or dissolve into tears.

Dad says, 'Come and sit down over here. Both of you.'

Next thing, I am wedged firmly between my parents. Dad aims a kiss at my cheek, in the manner of someone touching an unexploded bomb.

'You don't look pregnant.' My brain is working again. 'Have you only just found out?'

'Actually I'm quite a long way along. Twenty-seven weeks. Just into the final trimester. I'm due at the end of November.'

'But you don't have a bump.'

'Oh, but I do! I'm just lucky tunics and flowy tops are back in fashion this summer. And I've taken to carrying a notebook in front of my tummy. It was the same with you – I only got really huge in the final few weeks. But there's a bump all right. Take a look!' Mum gets up, lifts a layer of Aztec printed silk, and stands proudly before me.

She's right. Her waist has been sucked into a

ballooning belly. Not massive. But pregnant. Definitely pregnant.

'So have you told them at work?'

'We haven't told anyone except you. Although I think one of my producers suspects. I noticed him eyeing me up the other day, so I said something about putting on weight and he got terribly embarrassed. Serve him right! I'll be back in a minute, darling.' Mum heads for the door. 'I'm at that stage where I have to go to the loo every ten minutes, and Vishnu is always especially active in the evenings.'

'Vishnu? You're kidding?' Maybe this whole conversation is an elaborate practical joke.

'Don't panic,' Dad says. 'Only a nickname. Vishnu was a Hindu goddess with eight limbs, and this baby's a real acrobat, kicking, somersaulting and trampolining on your mother's bladder all hours of the day and night. I started calling him Wayne, as in Rooney. But your mother put an immediate stop to that.'

'Him? It's a boy, then?'

'That's my instinct, although we decided not to find out in advance. It'll be a surprise.'

I hesitate. 'The whole thing must have come as something of a surprise?'

'No kidding!' Mum answers my question on her way back to the couch. 'My first thought was that I was having an early menopause. Or bloating from my wheat allergy. After all...' She glances at Dad, then continues,

'Actually, darling, we always wanted more children. I was pregnant a couple of times when you were small. Miscarriages. And then nothing. That's another reason why we've kept the news to ourselves for so long.'

'Oh.' I had no idea.

'So would you like to feel the baby kick?' Mum invites me.

'I'm not sure.' I am absolutely certain I don't want to feel a baby in the womb. Far too medical. I'm not even sure I'll be able to look at a scan without feeling icky. Before I can politely decline, Mum takes my hand and plants it on her tummy.

But Wayne Vishnu is taking a rest. I sit still for what feels like a long time, and the butterflies in *my* tummy gradually subside. Dad disappears into the kitchen to make us all tea – 'Unless you'd prefer anything stronger, Juliet?' – and Mum and I sit in companionable silence.

My thoughts, however, are in top gear.

Is this good news? Or bad? A miscarriage. How horrible. Poor Mum. I wonder how old I was when it happened. Was it ever in the papers? That would have been awful. If – when – I have children, they'll be only a few years younger than their uncle or aunt. What a modern family we are...

I want it to be a boy. Or maybe it'd be cool to have a baby sister. I could take her ice-skating. Although I don't know how to skate. We could learn together.

Maybe ping-pong would be a safer pastime. Or finger-painting. At least I'll be able to read to her. Maybe I'll even start writing children's stories. And I've never been to EuroDisney.

'Oooooh!' It's as if an electric current has passed through my body. 'I felt her kick.' Tentatively, I explore Mum's tummy. 'Is that her foot I can feel? Or am I imagining it?'

'So your money's on a girl? Mine, too.' Mum places her hand over my own and says, 'I was really nervous about telling you, darling. I thought you might be angry. Or embarrassed.'

'If you and Dad are happy then I am too,' I declare. 'If this had happened when I was younger, I might have felt jealous or something. But I'm not exactly fifteen...'

I know we are both thinking the same thing.

Mum says, 'You're right. When I was pregnant with you, I was scared. Scared what people would say. Scared that I'd never even held a baby before, let alone been responsible for keeping one alive. Scared that Dad and I wouldn't be able to manage. And then, once you become a parent, scared never really stops.' Mum laces my fingers into her own. 'You've turned out so well, despite all the millions of things I've done wrong. You're kind. Intelligent. Generous. And beautiful. As for me, I'm scared all over again. Scared I'm too old to be a mother. Scared I won't have the energy to get up in the middle of the night and then do a twelve-hour day. Scared I'll have to resort to nannies, and the baby will think I'm its grandma. And scared that if I do take proper maternity leave, they'll replace me with someone younger.'

'You mean you're not going to give birth live on air?'

'Is that supposed to be a joke, Juliet? I'm planning to have a water birth right here at home. In the kitchen, actually. Although now you come to mention it, maybe we should invite the cameras in…'

A few horrified seconds pass before I realise Mum's teasing me.

Hmm, water birth.

Remind me to be working late that day.

Or night.

'You know how you just said I've turned out OK?'

'Is my gorgeous, grown-up daughter fishing for compliments?'

'Not exactly. There's something that's been bugging me for months. And talking of water…'

'Darling, what's wrong?'

'You remember when we went to the spa?'

'How could I ever forget?' Mum throws back her head and laughs. 'Oh Lord, that naked man. I'm soon going to be as fat as he was! No one will ever mistake me for Fiona Bruce again. What about it?'

'Mum. Why did you give me a tub of wrinkle cream?'

Perhaps not the best moment for a confrontation, but I really need to know.

'Why did I *what*? What are you talking about?'

'That present. You left it in my locker. In the changing rooms.'

'Oh, I remember. Look, I realised the spa wasn't exactly as you had intended, and I felt dreadful I had to bale out on you like that, so I wanted to make it up to you. You know how I'm always getting freebies. I thought I was giving you a year's supply of royal jelly, which is terribly good for you. I've been taking it for years. Must have given you the wrong package. Wrinkle cream? Oh, my poor darling. Why didn't you say something? You're the last person in the world who needs wrinkle cream! Talking of which, I have to tell you, I'm getting through almost a litre of virgin olive oil a week. Slathering myself in the stuff every night before I go to sleep, to try to avoid stretch marks. Ruining the sheets! Have you still got the wrinkle cream? I could definitely use it! Probably why they gave it to me in the first place.'

'Actually, I gave it to Natasha.' And I tell Mum the whole story of how I'd forgotten Natasha's birthday and ended up insulting her.

We're both roaring with laughter when Dad finally arrives with the tea.

'If you don't mind, I'm going to take mine up to bed,' I say. 'I've got an early start in the morning.'

I kiss both parents goodnight. 'Is it OK for me to tell Rob and Theodora?'

Mum and Dad exchange glances. 'Yes, of course,' Dad says. 'Goodnight, sleep tight.'

I'm halfway up the stairs when a sudden thought occurs.

'If it's a boy, you have to promise not to call it Romeo,' I shout down. 'Neither of us would ever forgive you.'

Chapter Twenty-Four

'Exciting news,' Freddie Ford tells me. 'Doublekay has hired some sort of elephant whisperer to communicate with Jasmine, and the three of them are working on a reinterpretation of the *Mona Lisa*. Can we get your techie people to sort out a webcam link by tomorrow? We've got five American publishers bidding for the rights, and the auction's on Friday. There's even talk of Spike Lee coming in with an option. Apparently, he wants to call the movie version *Tusk*!'

'Who've they got in mind to play Jasmine?'

Freddie acknowledges my gag with a grin. 'Funny old business. Talking of which…'

I open my bag, pull out a document, and hand it to Freddie. 'Here are my ideas for five possible novels.' I sound calmer than I feel. I've spent days trying to dream up storylines and I'm not confident about any of them. Freddie starts to read and I take in my surroundings.

It's the first time I've been to his office. It's airy and bright with a superb view of the Thames. The desk is chrome and pristine glass – at least until I leave a sweaty finger mark on it – and the walls are lined with books from floor to ceiling.

While Freddie studies my ideas, I study Freddie. He's looking well, and seems considerably more at ease than I am, sprawled in his swivel chair, absent-mindedly running a finger through that thick hair of his, and rocking gently from side to side while he reads.

This is the fourth time we've met since the Night of the High Heels (excluding the Swimming Pool Incident). Up until now I've been on home territory – in the Cognita boardroom – and we've kept strictly and scrupulously to Doublekay business.

On the surface, the only thing that's changed is Freddie's aftershave. His new choice reminds me of cucumber dipped in saltwater. But today, we need to clear the air and move on. As I said to Theodora last night, 'I'm going to give Freddie the benefit of the doubt and decide he was just being gentlemanly when he grabbed me that night in Dean Street.'

What finally convinced me he's on the level is that Dad knows him reasonably well. He told me how Freddie's been quietly heartbroken since his wife died. Skiing accident in Colorado, the Christmas before last. They'd only been married a few months and were terribly in love. After the funeral, Freddie sold the home they'd bought together, moved to a bachelor pad in Canary Wharf, set up a literary prize in his wife's name, and became a total workaholic. Mum and Dad reckon the hours he puts in are a substitute for having a breakdown.

Looking at Freddie now, you'd never guess he's been through so much. His Cupid's bow puckers into a smile as he finishes reading.

Is that good? Or bad?

I don't have time to torture myself. Freddie plonks the document on the desk and says, 'Well, I'm glad you've decided to dump Dickens and go for something contemporary.'

'Which one do you like best?'

'I was about to ask you the same question, Juliet.'

The way Freddie says my name makes me squirm. 'Look,' I say. 'Before we go any further. About me telling you I was an orphan…'

Freddie's smile grows broader. 'Yes, I meant to say I was impressed by your ability to improvise like that. Sign of a decent storyteller. Start with a single falsehood and follow where it leads you. Not that I ever meant to put you on the spot. The opposite, in fact. The moment you mentioned Beth, I was going to confess she put me up to coming to Cognita in the first place. And then make it plain that my interest in you as a potential author is an entirely separate matter. Great news about the baby, by the way.'

'I'm trying to get my head around the idea of not being an only child any more.'

'I can imagine. Now. About these ideas of yours.' Freddie pops a Murray Mint and obliges me to sit through ten seconds of nervy silence. 'Say I put a gun to your head and said, "Pick one or I'll shoot." Which would it be?'

'The one about Celine. The girl who starts a blog about marketing after she's been unfairly dismissed and finds herself corresponding with the hottest movie star in Hollywood. With the final scene at the Oscars.'

Freddie twirls his Murray Mint wrapper into a cellophane butterfly. 'I know you know about marketing, so that's a good start. I also like the twist where we discover Celine lost her job because she's agoraphobic and can't make it out of the front door, let alone get herself to Hollywood. And *Tinseltorn* will do as a working title for the time being. Now go.'

'Pardon?'

'Off you go and start writing, Juliet. Let me know when you've got fifty pages to show me. Until then—' Freddie gets up and I follow suit. He opens the office door and pecks me on the cheek in single, fluid movement.

'Have fun with it. Oh, and by the way—' Freddie gestures at my Patricia Crocs which have wedge heels so tiny they're almost non-existent '—love your shoes. Careful how you go.'

Beth strapped herself into one of her new maternity bras. The firm elastic straps, broad under-bust band and generous cups were definitely more *Vorsprung durch Technik* than *Hello Boys*, and a far cry from the usual

Rigby & Peller that Matthew was so fond of tinkering with.

A gasp of relief as she finally adjusted the alien garment so it sat comfortably on her ever-expanding frame. Accompanied by an undeniable thrill of excitement that she no longer needed to subdue. All those weeks she had spent agonising over how Juliet – and the rest of the world – would react to her pregnancy. What a waste of nervous energy that had turned out to be.

Now she was no longer nursing her big secret, Beth felt back in control. So foolish to have feared the baby would finish her career. On the contrary, now the news was out in the open, business propositions were flooding in. Would she care to put her name to a new collection of maternity clothes? Follow in the footsteps of Princess Diana and become a special trustee at Great Ormond Street?

And then there was Freddie. Wooing her relentlessly with 'the mother of all deals'. Apparently, all she had to do was to agree to put her name to a book – the topic seemed not to matter – and her place in best-seller charts was a foregone conclusion. 'I'll find someone really good to write it for you,' Freddie promised.

Of all the offers on the table, that one had been easiest for Beth to resist. There would only ever be one author in the Jackson family, and her name was Juliet.

Daily News, 15 December 200–

MY WEEK

TALES FROM THE HOME FRONT WITH BETH JACKSON
Christmas Gets Earlier Every Year

You're never too old to have an advent calendar – as Juliet always reminds me midway through November.

This year, I found one that has a chocolate behind each window.

Big mistake.

Christmas came early this year...

...Which is to say my daughter managed to confine herself to a single daily chocolate for precisely three days.

After which, she yielded to temptation and scoffed the lot in a single sitting.

Only Scrooge could blame her.

Beth's own Christmas gift was certainly going to come early this year. A twitching movement in her stomach made it seem as though baby Vishnu was paying attention to her mother's thoughts – a lovely idea, even though it was more likely the unborn baby had hiccups.

'I can't wait to see you,' Beth said softly. 'You'll be with us on Christmas Day. Just a few weeks old. With your big sister, and her boyfriend. I think one day he's going to be your brother-in-law. Maybe you'll be old enough to be a bridesmaid by the time that happens. I'd better hurry up and invite them for Christmas, before they get a better offer.'

After she had emailed Juliet and Rob to say how much she hoped they would be free on 25 December, Beth went to her bag to fetch a credit card. Then she returned to her computer. Five minutes later, an advent calendar was on its way to Juliet.

Carved from walnut wood, it measured four feet, and had twenty-four compartments, carved in the fronds of its Christmas tree shape, each one containing a handmade chocolate. Organic, of course. The calendar came with an eye-watering price tag, but Beth rationalised the purchase with the thought that the wood had been sourced from sustainable forests, and her money would help to support cocoa farmers in Belize.

Not only that.

The tree would make a wonderful heirloom for her children to hand down for many generations to come.

Podolski's we-want-our-money-back deadline expires in fourteen days. But Rob's not giving up without a fight.

'It's impossible to get hold of Mr Podolski on the phone. I'm sure he doesn't have a clue what's going on,' Rob told me when I arrived in Primrose Hill after my meeting with Freddie. 'You can see how well we're doing!' Rob gestured at a vast quantity of blended orange and lime juice, being decanted into hundreds of eco-friendly plastic bottles. 'We're a viable business, and it's just not right to pull the rug out from underneath us. Mr P needs to know we've got seven new FruityFul franchises in the pipeline. So Danny and I are going to Poland to plead with him in person. He seemed such an honourable man when we met him. And it's our last hope.'

Since Feliks Unpronounceable is still no-one-knows-where in South America (I've renamed him Feliks Untraceable) the least I could do was agree to look after Asbo.

Danny warned me, 'The only thing worse than a noisy Asbo is a quiet Asbo, so keep a careful eye on him.'

Clearly an exaggeration: the little beast has been behaving beautifully and, to my surprise, I'm actually enjoying being his minder.

Mum and Dad are letting me keep his basket in my bedroom – although the moment I turn off the light, he leaps onto the bed and curls up on Kylie Minogue's face – and as Rob's forbidden me to say anything to my parents about FruityFul's predicament, I've told them the boys are on a business trip.

To my surprise, Skunk has been perfectly amenable to me taking Asbo to the office for a few days. Enthusiastic, even. Probably because he used to own a Jack Russell. Yesterday afternoon, instead of steering

Cognita to even greater heights of success, our glorious leader spent two hours ensconced in his office, teaching Asbo to do high-fives. ('Three things, Asbo. Sit… Stay… PAW IN THE AIR!') The pair of them have spent so much time together that – now I come to think of it – Asbo's calm demeanour and insatiable appetite probably mean he's permanently stoned.

Meanwhile, Theodora has bagged herself a Sex God off the internet!

Noah.

The sand sculptor she met on Skype.

Noah is the kind of guy who gets scouted by model agents three times a week. Amazing eyes. A very cool accent. And he gets cheap flights because his dad works for an airline.

'It was such great timing!' Theodora was gleeful when she told me Noah was on his way to London. 'He split from his girlfriend a few days before we started hanging out online. I joked that if he could suss out how to move my sculpture in one piece, I'd find a way to mend his broken heart. Seems he's taken me at my word, so now I have to keep my end of the bargain!'

Even though he's been here for barely forty-eight hours, Noah's determined to see Europe. Yesterday morning, he went online and snapped up a bargain trip to Paris. 'The most romantic city in Europe. I want to experience it with you,' he told Theodora.

So my only chance to get to know him is to show up here at the Champagne Bar in St Pancras Station.

Straight from work.

With Asbo.

A stern-looking woman declares, 'No dogs allowed!' the moment we all walk in together. But Noah immediately hypnotises the woman into a change of heart, confiding he's already had one bitter disappointment today – the discovery that Harry Potter's legendary platform nine and three-quarters next door at King's Cross does not exist – and he needs a drink to get over the shock.

Moments later, the woman reappears purring like a pussycat, bearing a bowl of water plus a dainty dish of cheese puffs for Asbo, along with a suggestion whispered into Noah's ear that the Champagne All Day Brunch is our best bet.

'My treat,' Noah says. 'I'm just so sorry you can't come with us to Paris, JJ.' All three of us know that's not true, though it's kind of him to say so.

Once we're settled in at our banquette, Theodora reminds me, 'You promise you'll text me your verdict on the sculpture, won't you?'

'Of course.'

I'm disappointed Theodora won't see my reaction when I finally come face to face with *Pride and Prejudice*. But I can't remember the last time I saw her so happy. She deserves Noah, just as much as she deserves the cash and clout that winning this competition will give her. Whatever I think of the sculpture – even if I don't understand what on earth it's supposed to be – I'll tell the people doing the filming how wonderful it is. Make sure they realise Theodora is the next Barbara Hepworth or Michelangelo or ... who was it who did those Elgin Marbles? I must get onto Google and memorise the names of a few famous sculptors before Sunday, so I can pretend I know what I'm talking about.

'You said you had a list of instructions to give me,' I remind Theodora.

'Yes, babes. You know what TV people are like – *so* bossy. You have to sign a release so they can use whatever you say in their programme. Here's all the paperwork.' She gives me a thick envelope.

Before I can check its contents, Asbo makes a lunge for my freshly arrived scrambled eggs.

'OFF!' I command. Asbo backs off and looks reproachfully at me until I weaken. 'Here you go.' Without chewing even once, he inhales a crust of thickly buttered rye toast.

'You can go through everything later,' Theodora says. 'But make sure you post the release back to them today.'

'Can't I just give it to them? Who's going to be interviewing me, anyway? You must know, but every time I ask you, you go all vague.'

Theodora hesitates.

Maybe it *is* Piers Morgan fronting this programme.

She's already denied it, but I have my suspicions. According to *Digital Spy*, he's currently working on a new UK project.

'Um … the filming's all a bit *Big Brother*,' Theodora says. 'They've rigged up a bunch of hidden cameras and put them on automatic or something. You let yourself into the studio, and take it from there. It'll all make sense on the day. Promise.'

'So I'm in for a surprise?'

'You'll definitely be surprised, babes.'

I can tell Theodora's holding out on me. 'Surprised in a good way?'

'I hope so, yes'

'And you're saying I'm going to be in the gallery on my own, talking to myself like they do when they first go into the *Big Brother* house?'

'Not quite. You'll be with one other person.' Theodora tries to look enigmatic, and fails dismally. There's definitely a lot more to this than she's letting on.

Noah's checking his watch. 'We need to go get our train, honey.' He turns to me and adds, 'You'll love what Theo's done with the sand. I just know you will.'

'Give me a clue.' It's worth a try.

'No way! I want to keep myself in Theodora's good books.'

The pair of them look like something out of Mills and Boon, I think, as I walk them to the Eurostar terminal.

'Just remember,' Theodora says before she goes through the ticket barrier, 'you're not allowed to tell anyone you're going to the viewing. Not even Rob. It has to be kept one hundred per cent private. Or you'll ruin the surprise.'

Now I know it's Piers Morgan.

Which means I've got four days to make myself an expert on sculpture.

And decide what to wear.

Chapter Twenty-Five

Mum has spent almost the whole day in bed, complaining of backache. And I've discovered there's an enormous difference between being twenty-nine weeks pregnant and thirty weeks pregnant: five whole inches.

Or as Mum herself put it when I took her breakfast, 'I'm running out of room to expand!'

I've been reading up on pregnancy (through half-closed eyes in a vain attempt to bypass the procession of full-on gory images that keep appearing on my screen). Wayne Vishnu currently measures almost sixteen inches from head to heel, and weighs about the same as a prize-winning cabbage. No wonder Mum's so tired and uncomfortable.

With Theodora luvved up in Paris, Rob still in Poland and even Dad away – he's halfway up Ben Nevis with a bunch of year elevens – it's been a long weekend.

I've taken Asbo on three big walks to help pass the time. Apart from the heart-stopping moment when he was determined to come between a toddler and her sandwich, he's a great companion, and I've almost forgiven him for peeing on Kylie's hair this morning, instead of keeping his paws crossed while I showered.

'So what's it to be? The red or the blue?' I used to think people who talk to their pets are just plain sad. But now I get it. Asbo's fiercely interested in everything I do – literally dogging my footsteps – and seems to have a firm opinion on everything from literature (he's chewed the cover of my new Sophie Kinsella) to food (I swear a rasher of bacon disappeared from my plate while my back was turned making coffee).

The sound of my voice prompts Asbo to thump his stubby tail on the carpet, and I interpret this as a vote in favour of my lacy blue top. I think it strikes the right note for appearing on an arts programme – casually smart and flatteringly cut – and it looks great teamed with skinny jeans and my new black jacket.

To be honest, it's hard to decide what I'm more excited about. Finally seeing Theodora's sculpture after all these months of hard work and secrecy. Or being interviewed by Piers Morgan.

Theodora finally conceded in a text that I *will* be talking to a famous person.

Someone I like?

Not allowed to tell u ny more babes x

Go on!

Don't spoil the surprise 4 urself. And don't wear hi heels x

I slide into my Melbourne Crocs – Mum says they could easily be mistaken for proper shoes – and read my notes again. In between almost-looking at pregnancy stuff I've been swotting up on sculpture. My crib sheet includes the following:

- Michelangelo was left-handed.
- The wingspan of the *Angel of the North* is the same as a jumbo jet's.
- The world's first (and I suspect only) underwater sculpture park is located in clear waters off Grenada.

If I manage to make myself sound like an expert, my on-camera praise for Theodora will sound all the more sincere – and no one will ever realise that most of what I know about art is courtesy of Doublekay and his elephant.

I give myself a final once-over in the mirror, and wonder if I should tell Mum I'm going out. She's probably still asleep, so I'll leave a note in the kitchen saying I'll be back some time this evening.

There's just one thing.

Asbo.

I'm suspicious of the way he's rolling his eyes at me. As if to say, *What do you mean you're off out? Take me with you. Or Kylie gets it again.* Poor, freshly laundered Kylie.

Besides, everyone thinks Asbo's cute, so he'll look good on camera.

'C'mon. Walkies.' Whether it's the sound of my voice or the fact I'm waving his lead, Asbo understands we're out of here, and on our way to a television triumph.

Despite Mum – because of Mum – I've never been on the telly before. She once invited me to appear on some show she was doing about student life, and naturally I turned her down. Far too embarrassing. But this time feels different. And besides, it's not about me. This is Theodora's big moment. I'm just helping her to shine even more brightly.

I've allowed plenty of time to get to Shoreditch. Asbo and I successfully negotiate the Northern Line (which is to say there are no witnesses when he cocks his leg in the lift at Hampstead tube), then take the bus from Old Street to Bethnal Green Road.

The gallery is even grimmer than Theodora made out. A concrete monstrosity with three rows of tinted glass slits where a normal person would have put windows. It makes the VitalVitamins headquarters in South Norwood look like the Sistine Chapel.

The building has no signs, but eventually I work out the tallest glass slit is probably the front entrance. It's locked, so I press the buzzer and wonder if I'm in the right place. I'm still fishing around in my bag for Theodora's instructions, when I hear footsteps coming towards me from inside the building. Then the soft purr of an electronic lock opens the heavy glass door and a man in a janitor's uniform appears.

'I'm here for the sand sculpture viewing,' I tell him uncertainly. 'I was told to be here at four o'clock sharp.'

'Sorry to keep you waiting. I was brewing a cup of tea, and you're early. But come on in.' The man sounds friendly enough, and I follow him through the narrow entrance into a surprisingly plush reception area with a huge bare marble desk and half a dozen stone chairs arranged around a glass table in a semicircle. Better not sit down, in case they turn out to be Art.

'They didn't tell me anything about a dog.' The janitor has spotted Asbo.

'Didn't they?' I inject just enough surprise into my voice for the man to think Asbo's entitled to be here.

'Expert on modern art, is he?'

I smile politely and check my watch.

Three minutes to four.

Any minute now, I'm going to see Theodora's soon-to-be-prize-winning sculpture. Five months in the making, and I still don't have a clue what to expect, other than some sort of giant sandcastle.

Mind you, if Jasmine the elephant can invent her own version of the *Mona Lisa*, I suppose anything is possible. I only hope Theodora's piece is something I recognise, and not an abstract. There's only so much you can say about weird shapes – 'Mmm … interesting,' sums it up for me – and frankly, I reckon the best place to display some of the stuff I checked out online *is* underwater. Please don't let it be an abstract.

'Here we are.'

The janitor points to a screen above the marble desk. Hidden security cameras are trained on the street outside the building – you can't see a thing through the so-called windows – and a black Mercedes has just pulled up.

A chauffeur gets out and goes to open the back door. I lean forwards, eager for my first glimpse of Piers Morgan.

No.

That can't be right.

It just can't.

What is my mother doing in this part of town?

Especially when she's at home.

In bed.

Except she's not.

She's here.

Coming in through the black slit of a door that magically opens when the janitor punches a code into a black keypad that's attached to his belt.

'Hello, I'm Beth Jackson and I'm here to—'

'What are you *doing here?'*

It's not often my mother and I say the same thing at the same time. In fact, I'm pretty sure this is a world first.

'Are you here to interview me?' I ask.

'What? No. I'm here to see Theodora's sculpture.'

'But so am I.'

'She never told me you were coming.' Mum's voice is accusatory, as though I have no business to be here.

'Ditto.'

The janitor clears his throat. 'According to my list, you're both definitely expected. The gallery is all set up for you and my instructions are simply to lead the way, then leave you to it.'

Asbo trots obediently by my side as we're taken down a short flight of steps into the basement and then along a white-walled corridor with low ceilings and overhead lighting so bright you can feel the heat radiating from the bulbs. Ahead of us is a closed wooden door.

'I'll leave you to explore,' the janitor says. 'Enjoy!'

We wait until the echo of his retreating footsteps has disappeared. Then Asbo begins to scrabble towards the door. We follow.

The door has a large sign on it. Black type on white board with a heading that reminds me what Theodora's sculpture is about.

TRANSIENCE: LASTING FOR ONLY A SHORT TIME AND QUICKLY COMING TO AN END, DISAPPEARING OR CHANGING

A second block of words headed 'ARTIST STATEMENT' sits underneath. Very grand! I begin to read, hearing Theodora's voice in my head as I do so: The material chosen for my sculpture, sand, is not precious in an economic sense. But it has been transformed by love, care and sheer hard work, which makes it a reflection of the subject it portrays.'

So what does that mean?

I'm about to find out.

Mum's turning the door handle, and Asbo's pulling on the lead. 'Remember everything we say will be recorded on camera,' she reminds me. 'Do you need to comb your hair?'

'Are you meant to interview me?'

'Theodora didn't say anything about that.' Mum shakes her head and I notice she's also rubbing her aching back. 'She said my response to the work could help her win this big prize. And of course I'm intrigued to see what she's been up to. But she's been annoyingly mysterious. No clues at all. Even though I gave her a good grilling. She stood up to my questions a damn sight better than most of the people I interview. Only the other day—'

'Mum!' Unless I interrupt her now, we could be standing in this corridor for another half an hour. 'Let's go in.'

I usher her through the door and we find ourselves in another expanse of windowless white space. A big room, empty apart from a couple of expensive-looking creamy leather sofas in an L-shape over in the corner and an ornately framed mirror on the wall.

I leave my bag and on the couch, and Mum follows suit.

Mum points at a large white screen. 'It must be on the other side of that,' she says.

I lead the way.

Oh my God.

Chapter Twenty-Six

OH MY GOD.
OH MY GOD.
OH MY GOD.

I am finally up close and personal with my best friend's sand sculpture.

Very personal.

How could she have done this?

How did she *do* this?

One thing's for sure.

It's definitely not an abstract.

I take a few steps back, as though the sculpture might spring to life and bite me.

'Fucking hell.' My mother sums up the situation accurately, eloquently and with admirable brevity. Then she remembers the hidden cameras are rolling and adds, 'Mmm ... interesting.' But there's an enormous smile on her face as she says this. Then she turns to me and enquires, 'What do you think, darling?'

I think I am going to kill Theodora next time I see her.

Bury her up to her neck in sand.

It's not that I hate what she's done.

What she's done is astonishing. I had no idea a carving from sand could end up looking as detailed as a statue made of stone.

But why didn't she warn me?

Why didn't she *ask* me?

That's easy.

I'd have said no.

Noooooooooooooooooo!

Mum taps her toes while she waits for my answer.

I can't see the cameras.

But the cameras can see me.

'I think it's brilliant,' I say.

Cautiously, we advance the final few paces towards Theodora's creation.

'It's like Mount Rushmore,' Mum declares. 'You know, that mountain in America, where the heads of their presidents are carved out of granite.'

She's right about that.

Except for one big difference.

I can identify the faces on this particular sculpture.

They're mine.

Mine and Mum's.

In fact, my whole life is standing here in front of me.

Cast in sand.

Like those statues on Easter Island.

Theodora's sculpture is about four times taller than

I am. It's more or less triangular in shape. At the pinnacle, a young woman – really no more than a girl – stands cradling a baby.

Madonna and child.

I recognise the pose from a picture that sits in a silver frame on Mum's dressing table. And, of course, I recognise Mum herself, with her shoulder-length hair and those dreadful 80s clothes she was wearing when the local rag took that photo of her a few days after I was born.

Even in sand, my baby face looks like it belongs to Winston Churchill.

And finally, I understand what Theodora meant when she first talked about *Pride and Prejudice*.

Mum's pride in me is self-evident in every grain of sand.

Which leaves prejudice…

I suppose that was Theodora's jokey way of telling me I'm too hard on my mum.

That might have been true a few months ago, but Mum and I seem to get on so much better these days. All those bags of sand forcing me to move back home… In a manner of speaking, Theodora's brilliant sculpture has saved our relationship rather than demonstrated its fragility.

Who says I don't understand art!

Before I can take in any more, Asbo strains at his lead.

'Mum, I'm just going to settle Asbo down at the other end of the gallery. Back in a moment.'

'Sure. Have you noticed the detail over there?' Mum points to the right of the sculpture, just below the summit. I am about five years old, and Mum and I are carving a Halloween pumpkin. I've got a huge grin on my face and (unlike the pumpkin) I have no front teeth.

There's more to see, but Asbo is trying hard to yank my right arm from its socket, making it impossible to concentrate. I let him off the lead, and he follows me back to the leather couches. 'You stay here,' I tell him sternly. In response, he puts his head to one side, apparently considering my instruction. Then he leaps onto the nearest couch, curls himself into a ball and closes his eyes. Gingerly, I remove a pig's ear – Asbo's favourite thing in the whole world apart from Danny – from the plastic bag I've brought with me and throw the disgusting treat on the floor. He'll gobble it up the moment he wakes. I put his favourite toy, a much-chewed Tony Blair doll with its nylon brains hanging out, next to him on the couch, and then return to Theodora's spectacular rearrangement of three hundred and thirty-six bags of sand.

As I reach the screened section of the gallery, I pause for a longer-distance view of the sculpture. But my eye is immediately drawn to Mum. She's slightly stooped and clutching her tummy.

'What's wrong?'

'Nothing.' Mum straightens up. 'Nothing at all. I'm just so immensely impressed with Theodora. What an awesome talent! You've only seen the front view so far, darling. Come round here and look at the back.'

I do as I'm told.

'That's *so* clever!' I say. The sculpture's entire rear façade has been carved into a huge tableau of me and Mum at the seaside. I'm brandishing a bucket and spade, while Mum supervises the construction of an intricate fortress, complete with drawbridge, moat, a Union Jack flying from a turret, and a pair of seagulls so lifelike I expect them to screech at any moment. I vaguely remember the photo Theodora must have used for reference.

'That was when we were on holiday in Margate, wasn't it?' I ask Mum.

'You were nine. And convinced that if we dug a big enough hole in the sand, we'd end up in Australia. Or France.'

Geography never was my best subject. 'Let's have another look at the front,' I suggest. I take a few paces but Mum doesn't follow. 'Mum! Something *is* wrong. Tell me.'

'I just need to sit down on those couches for a few minutes. No need for you to come with me, darling.'

'Don't be ridiculous! Of course I'll come with you.' All at once, I'm scared. 'Is… Is it the baby?'

'There's certainly been a lot of movement all day. Even more than usual.' Mum sounds calm, which reassures me. She walks the last few yards to the couches and manoeuvres herself into a seat.

I'm about to join her when I have a brainwave. The screens surrounding the sculpture are basically five folding panels. It takes me only a moment to figure out how to dismantle them, and shift them to the side of the gallery.

'Great idea,' Mum calls out. 'Now we can see the whole of the front from here.'

I join my mother on the couch and we study Theodora's masterpiece.

'Theodora's so right about transience,' Mum says. 'You wouldn't believe how often I look at you and wonder where all the years have gone. Talk about the sands of time…'

'I love how Theodora's used your press cutting.'

From this view, the sculpture's centrepiece – a square block of sand that works as a pedestal for the Madonna and child – is a newspaper page with a story Mum wrote when I left for uni. Theodora has not only carved the headline – EVERYTHING CHANGES – into sand, she's reproduced the entire article. Must have taken her hours.

'And the two cornerpieces are especially lifelike,' Mum says. 'Not to mention life-sized. Clever of her to have you on the left at your graduation, and me on the right, receiving that Mother of the Year award.'

'Not to mention the fact that she's used the space in the middle to show the pair of us having a nose-to-nose fight! I wonder what you were telling me off about.'

'Could have been any one of a million things. And you still don't stack the dishwasher properly. Or change the loo roll.'

'But at least we don't shout about it any more.'

'No. It's been good having you back at home, Juliet. I feel I've had a second chance to get to know you all over again.'

Mum's words bring a lump to my throat. 'Are you going to do things differently with the baby?' It's a question I've wanted to ask ever since she told me she was pregnant.

'Differently? How do you mean? Did I really do such a bad job with you?'

'It's just that … well, I know I was a mistake. So this time, now you're, um, older and wiser, will you…' I trail off into silence.

'Are you asking me if I'm going to *feel* differently? For goodness sake. Once and for all. Yes, Juliet, you *were* a mistake. But, darling, you're the best mistake I ever made in my life. I thought you knew that.'

'It's so good to hear you say it.' Just about the best thing anyone's ever said to me. 'I sometimes think that if you hadn't had me, you'd have ended up being the Foreign Secretary. Or Director-General of the BBC.'

'I could certainly give the ones we've got now a run for their money. And I haven't entirely ruled out the BBC. Listen, darling. There's something I need to tell you. But before I do, you have to promise me you'll—'

'Did you see that?' I interrupt Mum because it looks as if the sculpture is moving. 'Over on the left. The bit with my graduation. About three feet from the bottom. I could swear my gown is shedding sand. Look, it's happening again.'

I run across the gallery to the sculpture.

Yep.

Part of my gown has disappeared.

And my left leg has been amputated below the knee.

How can that be happening?

I scoot round to the back of the sculpture to see what's going on.

'NO! FUCK! GET OFF! MUM! ASBO'S DIGGING IN THE SAND!'

The little bastard has tunnelled most of the way from the back to the front. A big chunk of the fortress lies in ruins. Even as I take in the catastrophe, Asbo wags his tail vigorously from side to side, and a mini sandstorm lands on my Crocs.

'MUM!'

'Darling, I need you to come back over here for a moment.'

'I can't! You have to help me mend the sculpture. Asbo, don't you *dare* roll your eyes at the other corner, or—'

I aim a kick at the unrepentant animal, who nonchalantly grabs his Tony Blair doll between his jaws and moves beyond reach.

What's keeping Mum from coming to the rescue? And what was it she called out to me just now?

I peer round the sculpture.

What I see makes me race back across the gallery.

Mum is crouching down by the side of the couch, and the look on her face is like nothing I have ever seen before.

Pain so raw I can feel it myself.

The spasm ends and Mum's face relaxes. 'I need you to call an ambulance,' she manages. 'I wasn't sure before. But I'm having contractions. That's the third in twenty minutes. And it's much too soon. I'm scared.'

'Should I call nine-nine-nine?'

Mum nods.

I whip out my phone and punch in the number.

I'm scared, too.

Terrified.

Back at the other end of the gallery there's a heavy thud.

I look up just as my entire graduation gown succumbs to gravity.

And why is no one answering my phone call?

I check the screen and discover there's no signal in this dungeon of a gallery.

'Mum,' I say gently. 'I'm going to go upstairs and get us some help. I'll find the janitor. My phone's not working down here.'

'Be quick.'

But when I get back to reception, there's no sign of the janitor.

And I soon discover the building is located in a mobile dead zone – too much concrete, most likely.

I'll call from the street.

But the front entrance is locked.

A trickle of sweat runs down my face.

What if Mum has the baby?

I'll never survive it.

I'll panic.

Or faint.

Or worse.

This place must have a landline. But there's no sign of a phone on the marble desk. Or anywhere else. 'HELLO!' I shout. 'ANYBODY THERE?'

Only the sound of my own voice.

I go back to the gallery, fighting my own fears every step of the way.

Mum is back up in a sitting position, and she greets me with a wan smile. 'Tell me the ambulance is on its way.'

'Um, afraid not. My mobile's not working, I can't find a landline and the janitor's buggered off somewhere.'

'I'm feeling a bit better,' Mum says. 'Could you look in my bag? See if you can find the Bach Rescue Remedy?'

Reassured Mum's asking me to do something within my capabilities, I fish out a brown glass bottle. 'Here you are,' I say.

But Mum shakes her head. 'No, darling. It's for you. I know what you're like around medical things. Let a few drops dissolve on your tongue. It'll help keep you calm.'

I squirt a powerful jet of Rescue Remedy down my throat.

Followed by another.

'So…' I pluck up the courage to ask, 'have your waters broken?'

'Not yet. Since we're trapped in here I think it's best if I just lie still. And I'll keep babbling away, because that seems to work best for both of us. About your medical phobia, darling. I'm afraid that's all my fault. When you were twenty months, they diagnosed a hole in the heart. Much more complicated to fix in those days than it is now. You were in and out of hospital a few times, and I think the experience must have left its mark.'

Wow. 'But how come I don't remember? Surely you wrote about it?'

'Of *course* I didn't write about it.' I'm reassured by the fact that Mum sounds distinctly irritated. 'It was nobody's business except our own. JESUS CHRIST. Here comes another one…' Mum howls with the pain.

'I'm going to get help! I'll break a window and shout down into the street or something. Fast as I can, I promise.'

There's another gallery on the second floor. I burst through the doors and vaguely register twisty, inter-twined lumps of metal.

That's not going to help.

Ah!

Halfway up the next set of steps there's an exit. I press down on the safety bar and the door opens onto a metal staircase.

The fire escape.

Thank God.

I redial 999 and almost immediately a calm male voice says, 'Emergency services. Which service do you require?'

'Ambulance.'

'Connecting you.'

'Hello, my mother's gone into premature labour. We're in an art gallery in Shoreditch, and we're locked in, and—'

Before I can get any further, the woman on the other end of the phone takes over and starts asking questions. I give her the address of the building, and explain

Mum's only thirty weeks pregnant. 'Is she going to lose the baby?' I ask.

'Don't you worry. Your mum's going to be fine. We've got an ambulance coming, and I'm calling in the police in case we need to force entry to the building. You go back and stay with your mum.'

When I get back downstairs, I'm greeted by a surprise.

Two surprises.

The good thing is that the janitor has appeared. He's sitting next to Mum, who's leaning against him for support, and seems quite calm again. The two of them are in quiet conversation.

The other thing is Theodora's statue...

It's ruined.

Asbo has managed to dig from front to back, hollowing out a space just below the bit where the teenage me was depicted having a shouting match with Mum.

The dog is cowering in the little archway he's created. As well he might. From where I'm standing, it looks as though Asbo's destructive paws have triggered a domino effect.

What used to be the upper part of the sculpture – the pumpkin carving – has toppled onto the floor. And what's left of the Madonna and child has been shunted to a crazy angle. It's hanging in the balance, like the Leaning Tower of Pisa.

I'm still staring at what appears to be the badly wounded corpse of a seagull that has crash-landed on the gallery floor, when I hear the two-tone screech of a siren.

'You'd better go down and let them in,' I tell the janitor. 'Otherwise they'll break down the door. I'll stay here with my mother.' I sit down next to her and ask, 'How are you doing?'

'Not too bad.' Mum's face is ghostly pale.

'What can I do to help?'

'As soon as you get home, I need you to get hold of Dad. He's got to get back from Scotland as soon as he can.'

I hesitate. Then say, 'I'm not going home. I'm coming with you to the hospital. I know you wanted a water birth and Dad by your side and all that, but you're just going to have to make do with me instead.'

I never thought I'd say this, but being inside the ambulance is pretty exciting. Like something out of *Casualty* (not that I've ever watched *Casualty*) with surround sound sirens all the way to the nearest maternity hospital. Mum and I hold hands all the way. I'm getting used to the contractions now, and I've started to time them – that was the second in ten minutes – and I only notice the perspex cabinet that bristles with needles and syringes on the way out, so I don't have time to panic.

Someone's waiting to wheel Mum into the maternity unit. I have a wobbly moment when that unique hospital smell I've successfully avoided for so many years hits me, but apart from that I'm managing.

The two of us have been alone in the Labour and Birth Room for the past few minutes, and I can tell Mum's trying to stay cool. Her waters broke while we were in the ambulance, and the contractions are coming every three or four minutes.

Mum's in a hospital gown, sitting up on a narrow green bed, and she's insisted I sit in a chair at the top of the bed, facing towards the door. That way, the only piece of medical apparatus I can see is a tiny cot with white plastic sides. Which isn't scary at all – not even when Mum tells me it's actually an incubator.

I've tried calling Dad. No answer, so I've left what I hope is a reassuring, don't-panic-but-please-get-back-to-London-right-now message.

A woman about the same age as me comes into the room. It takes me a second or two to realise she's the midwife.

'Let's have a look.' But before she does anything, Mum spasms into another contraction. This time it lasts longer, and seems even more vicious. Mum grunts her way through it like a tennis player serving in a Grand Slam.

When it's over, the midwife does a quick

examination. 'Mrs Jackson, you're almost fully dilated. Thirty weeks, you said?'

'Yes. I need gas and air. Or an epidural. Or drugs. Anything.'

'Too late for the epidural, I'm afraid. Let me organise the gas and air.'

Mum takes the mouthpiece and inhales deeply.

Then she says, 'Hang on. I'm sure this baby's moving down. But surely it can't be doing it yet. It's too soon. Can't you do something to stop it?'

The midwife takes a look. 'Beth, your body's taking over.' Her voice is so conversational, she could be gossiping to a girlfriend. 'Just go with it. Your baby's about to be born. I can see the head.' Then, to me, 'Could you nip down to the reception area and ask the obstetrician to pop in.' In the time it takes me to get to the door, she adds to Mum, 'The neonatal team's already on standby. Trust me, Beth. We have plenty of healthy babies born at thirty weeks.'

In reception, a couple of white-coated guys are sharing a joke. 'WHERE'S THE OBSTETRICIAN?' I yell. 'We need him in the delivery room.'

The taller guy gets up from his chair. 'Let's go,' he says. But there's no sense of urgency, and I practically have to push him all the way back to Mum's room.

Oh my God.

Mum is giving birth.

Right this very second.

I am seeing a part of my mother that I never expected to see.

It's mesmerising.

'Mum, I can see the baby's head. The eyes are open.'

Seconds later, a body slides into the midwife's hands.

I see an incredibly long cord, tangled around its shoulders.

And then a terrible silence.

Chapter Twenty-Seven

The baby is dead.

Mum's right. It was born too soon.

Tears are streaming down my face.

How will we ever get over this?

The obstetrician has untangled the cord and massages the body's tiny, tiny shoulders.

And the most beautiful sound I have ever heard fills the room.

A shrill wail of protest – long and loud – from my brand-new brother.

Or do I have a sister?

The midwife says, 'Congratulations, Beth.'

'Is the baby all right?' Mum asks.

By way of an answer, the obstetrician places a blanketed bundle into Mum's arms. 'It's a boy. A beautiful boy. We're going to cut the cord quickly, and pop him into the incubator.' He turns to me and says, 'Would you like to do the honours?'

I take the scissors from his hand and snip where he shows me, between a pair of clamps. All I can think is, I mustn't let my hands shake. In case I hurt my brother. The cord is thick, and difficult to cut – a bit

like gristle on a piece of meat – and my fingers end
up splattered with blood.

I feel Mum's hand on my shoulder.

Then the midwife says, 'It's not over yet.'

And three minutes later...

...I also have a baby sister...

And we are a family of five.

Book Three
Is that it?

Chapter Twenty-Eight

Beth needed to get back to the hospital – back to her babies – as soon as she could. So strange being parted from them, even for a couple of hours. But it was good to be home, too. And the designers were bound to make mistakes with the nursery unless she was there to brief them in person.

The car was waiting outside, but first she needed to do something that really couldn't wait. Beth located a pair of scissors and returned to the bedroom, where her scrapbook, the newspaper and a tube of glue were waiting.

Daily News, 27 September 201–

MY WEEK
TALES FROM THE HOME FRONT WITH BETH JACKSON
My Daughter The Heroine

It's been a while since I filled these pages with news of my beloved Juliet.

The truth is, now she is grown up with a life of her own, I had resolved never to do so again.

But every rule is made to be broken. And the lovely people

at the *Daily News* have been kind enough to allow me to say a public thank you to my darling daughter for her brave support when I went into premature labour on Sunday.

The twins (we haven't yet decided on their names) owe their lives to their big sister.

Juliet Jackson, you have made me the proudest mother in the world.

I salute you.

Beth pressed down on the newsprint, smoothing out the wrinkles. Then she closed the scrapbook and placed it in her bag.

The scrapbook no longer belonged in her Treasure Chest. She wanted Juliet to have it.

Chapter Twenty-Nine

'It's the hormones talking,' I say to Theodora, forcing her to shove the *Daily News* back into her bag. 'It's not like I did anything except clamber onto the fire escape and call for an ambulance.'

'You were there for your mum when it mattered most. You went into a hospital – you, the girl who faints in cupboards – and you cut two umbilical cords. I'm proud of you too, babes! You deserve to be making headlines. Are you ready to go inside?'

I'm about to introduce Theodora to the twins. Which means I have to walk through several hospital corridors. I can do it … I can do it … close my eyes until that possibly dead man on the gurney gets wheeled into the lift…hold my breath until we're well past the horrid smell…turn away from the woman tugging drip equipment in her wake…final left turn. And yay! I've made it to the neonatal unit without disgracing myself.

Now for the real test.

As usual, my heart lurches

I still can't get used to the sight of my siblings.

Yes, they are living miracles.

But so tiny.

So fragile.

So purple.

Mum has barely left their side in the six days since they were born. Which means the entire hospital's been turned into a mobile television studio.

I mean, who in their right mind would want to take maternity leave when the alternative is fronting daily 'Hospital Fundraiser' shows – '…at least that's scuppered Jeremy's plans for the bloody Autumn Makeover…' – resulting in:

- Two million pounds pledged by viewers.
- Three thousand cuddly toys descending on the hospital.
- A fire-cracking interview with the Secretary of State for Health that almost put the poor man in the cardio unit when Mum asked why an NHS bigwig whose wards were so filthy they helped kill twenty-five patients was handed a £275,000 pay-off instead of a writ for manslaughter.

I am as proud of my mother as she is of me.

She has just finished today's broadcast – a passionate plea urging viewers to donate their unused medicines to a charity that ships them to health centres in Africa – when we arrive.

Theodora and I slip into the blue gowns and face

masks we have to wear whenever we go onto the neonatal – very *Avatar* – and wave hello to Mum and Dad.

My parents are as close to the incubators as they can be, without actually being inside them. Theodora bounces up to the nearest machine and meets my brother for the very first time. (My brother! I have a brother!)

'Ahhhhhhhhh! He's *so* sweet,' she coos. 'How long do they have to stay here?'

'They're coming out of the incubators tomorrow, and we're hoping to bring them home in about three weeks,' Dad says. 'Even though they turned up so early, they're fine. Putting on weight by the hour. We're all very lucky.'

Dad is sporting panda rings around his eyes, and his five o'clock shadow is on the cusp of becoming a proper beard. Even though he's dishevelled, his whole being radiates happiness. He gives me a huge hug and says, 'How's my favourite older daughter? Still thinking of retraining as a midwife?'

I bring Dad up to speed with the latest developments in my life. Good old Skunk has given me afternoons off for the whole week. 'I bunked off to the movies yesterday, and I've been tidying the house today so it'll be spick and span when you and Mum get home.'

What I don't tell Dad – news I haven't shared with anyone – is that Skunk's benevolence is down to the fact that Podolski has authorised VitalVitamins the five million pounds they need to bring wellness, spa treatments and superfluous exclamation marks to Gdansk and all points south.

Yesterday, while Skunk was chuntering on about the imminent increased ad spend and asking if I thought we should recruit a native Polish speaker, all I could think was, if Podolski's still lending money to British businesses, how come they're pulling the rug from underneath FruityFul? It's a question I still can't answer, no matter how hard I try.

I look across the unit and see Mum and Theodora poking their hands through the access holes along the side of the other incubator. They stroke my sister's tiny legs, their heads close together, deep in a low buzz of conversation.

I hear the words 'sand', 'sculpture' and 'sorry', and strain to hear more. But the chief paediatrician has arrived to give the twins their eight-hourly inspection, and Theodora and I are ushered out of the door.

On the bus and tube back to North London, Theodora barely stops talking about Noah. 'It's as if we've been together for years!' she informs everyone on the top deck of the 242.

'You mean you've given up shaving your legs. And he's permanently in charge of the remote control?'

'No need to take the piss.'

But Theodora knows how happy I am for her. Although also a little concerned. 'How long's he staying?' I ask.

'Another week. At least.'

'And then?'

'He's got a big sand-sculpting gig coming up in California.'

'I suppose there's always Skype.'

'He's invited me over in November. Thanksgiving. Meet the parents.'

'So it's really serious?'

'I think he might be The One.'

'And you don't really need to be in London to be an artist. Do you?' A test question. I'd be gutted if I lost Theodora from my everyday life.

'Guess not. Quick, babes, or we'll miss our stop.'

We travel together as far as Camden Town. Theodora's off home, where Noah is waiting, and I'm about to find out from Rob and Danny exactly what happened in Poland.

Before we part, I say, 'Look, we've got to talk some more about the sand sculpture. I'm mortified by what happened.'

To my amazement, Theodora's face creases into a grin so broad it eclipses even Mum and Dad's present state of bliss. 'Noah and I went straight to the TV production company when we got off the train this morning,' she says. 'They've started editing the footage.

JJ, it's hilarious. Asbo starts off trying to bury that pig's ear you gave him. When he realises scratching the stone floor won't work, he just aims higher. As soon as the first bit of sand lands on him, he goes crazy. Digs for all he's worth. And when the big collapse happens, he growls at the sand. Gives it a good telling-off, but I think it frightened him. Meanwhile, at the other end of the gallery, your mum's in labour.'

'No! I didn't realise they had cameras hidden there as well! So what happens next?'

'Babes, I didn't win. But it's not your fault.'

Oh crap.

'If only I'd taken better care of that damn dog it never would have happened.'

'Honestly, it's not a problem. The sculpture succeeded beyond my wildest dreams. All I ever wanted was for you to realise your mum loves you to bits. From the moment you were born. I know I've told you that before. More than once. But you wouldn't have it. So I thought that if I could show you the pair of you more or less growing up together, I might finally get the message across. That's what it was all about, JJ. Not winning a stupid competition.'

'But the prize. Fifty grand.'

'Yeah. Well, that might have bought a few plane tickets to Vermont.'

'How can I make it better?'

'Just make up for lost time, babes. Transience and

all that. Draw a line in the sand. If you'll pardon the expression. Realise your mum doesn't expect you to be some sort of version of her. She'd be happy if you were sweeping the streets.'

'She so would not!'

'Bad example. But you know what I mean. And at the same time, you have to let her be who *she* is.'

'Thank you.' My voice catches in my throat. 'That's the best present anyone's ever given me. The truth.' I pause for a moment, then continue, 'And I guess Asbo's made me realise how easy it is to destroy something precious without meaning to.'

'Hearing you say that means much more to me than winning the competition,' Theodora says. 'Oh, by the way,' she adds, 'I almost forgot to tell you. The judges thought Asbo had been trained to dig up the sculpture. Just to make a point about transience. Wankers. The only reason I lost is because they've arranged to have the winning piece dragged around the world on some Arts Council tour next year. So they've invented a second prize. I'm getting a video installation in the Tate Modern of Asbo destroying my work of art. That and twenty grand!'

I wish we could have hit the town with a huge celebration. Or that I had time to look at the battered old scrapbook Mum thrust into my hands when I left the hospital.

Both will have to wait.

Rob's texting to find out what's keeping me, and Theodora's desperate to spend every moment with Noah.

By the time I get to Primrose Hill, it's dark and starting to rain. Danny is outside the flat, loading up a van with the latest bottles of juice.

Indoors, Rob greets me with a tall glass of mango and coconut blend – a combo that works surprisingly well. Even before I get my coat off, I sense something has finally gone right.

'So did you get hold of Mr Podolski after all?' I already know the trip to Poland was frustrating in the extreme, with Rob and Danny taking it in turns to keep permanent vigil in the bank's lobby. To no avail. One of Mr P's assistants confided her boss was in London but the boys were convinced she only said that to try to get rid of them.

'As if.' Rob shrugs. 'But there *is* a ray of hope.'

'Tell me!'

Before he can do so, Asbo slinks into the room. I'm desperate to share Theodora's wonderful news. But first things first.

'So last week, Wednesday I think it was, Danny was killing time in a wi-fi café in Krakow. He posted on FruityFul's Facebook page that we're seeking business angels. Made a good job of it, too. Made it sound like a really good business opportunity, and omitted to mention we're staring bankruptcy in the face.'

'You *are* a good business opportunity.'

Before Rob can tell us any more, Danny strolls into the living room.

'I was just bringing JJ up to speed,' Rob says. 'About Facebook.'

'How far have you got?'

'I was just about to tell her about Brian Brinkley.'

Brinkley.

Where I have heard that name before?

Got it!

After all, he and I have something in common.

Cupboards.

'He's that boy from school, isn't he?' I say. 'The one you locked up when you were in the Upper Fifth or whatever. And you met him back in the summer at the school reunion.'

'Full marks,' Danny says.

But I'm puzzled. 'Didn't you tell me the reunion was a bummer?' I ask Rob. 'That they all thought you were failures because you didn't have big jobs and tons of money?'

'Something like that,' Rob admits. 'But that's not the point.'

'Brian Brinkley's the point,' Danny butts in. 'He got in touch within a couple of hours. Very interested in FruityFul. And full of praise for what we've achieved in such a short time. Loves the viral marketing campaign, by the way. And Asbo.'

The dog recognises his name – or maybe just his master's voice – and leaps onto Danny's lap.

'We had a three-hour meeting with him today,' Danny continues. 'And it looks as if we have a deal.'

But Danny's voice is hardly sparkling with excitement, and I notice the look that passes between him and Rob.

'And the problem is?' I ask.

'Brinkley will own more of the company than we do.' Danny sighs. 'He's insisting on fifty-one per cent of FruityFul in exchange for six hundred thousand quid.'

Rob takes up the story. 'We've tried to negotiate. But he won't budge. Told us he was in no hurry, and to go away and think about it. But, of course, we don't have time. Podolski's deadline is start of business on Wednesday. So we've got— ' Rob consults his watch '—roughly eighty-five hours to come up with three hundred thousand quid.'

'What are you going to do?'

'We've told Brinkley to draw up a contract and let us have it first thing in the morning, latest. Soon as he sends it, I'll have my dad look it over. At least we'll save on legal fees. I've told Dad what's going on, and he says he'll try to get a few bob more out of him. On principle,' Rob says.

'So once we've paid off Podolski, we'll pocket three hundred thousand between us. At least Brinkley's not insisting we use the extra cash as working capital. So that's not too shabby for a few months' work.' Danny's smile doesn't quite reach his eyes.

'And that means fifteen grand for you, sweetheart.' Rob's doing his best to be upbeat as well.

'Fifteen grand? How come?'

'You're forgetting you're a shareholder in FruityFul,' Rob reminds me. 'Congratulations!'

Suddenly, we're all swimming in money.

Rob.

Danny.

Theodora.

Now even me.

My student loan will be – almost – a relic of the past.

And yet the FruityFul windfall leaves a bitter taste.

'You're certain there's no other option?' I ask.

The boys nod their heads.

'So tell us about the twins.' Rob's obviously keen to change the subject. 'They got names yet?'

Before I can answer, Danny chimes in, 'And I want to know all about Theodora's sculpture. I still don't understand why you said it was too complicated for a text or an email while we were away. Haven't you worked out how to send pictures on that phone of yours?'

I spend the next ten minutes explaining exactly what happened when I went to view the sculpture.

'So Asbo's a hero. Sort of.' Danny concludes when I've finished. 'And he's going to be in a video at the Tate Modern! That's the best news I've had in weeks.'

And even though it's gone ten o'clock, we all go round to Theodora's, picking up half a dozen bottles of wine on our way.

It takes so long for her to answer the door, it's clear we've dragged her and Noah out of bed. Even so, they're pleased to see us.

Reasonably pleased.

No surprise that the following morning I've got a hangover.

I've also got Asbo. Looking after him while Rob and Danny meet Brian Brinkley to sign their deal with the-devil-they-know.

Strange to think that this time last week the main thing on my mind was what to wear for my non-interview with Piers Morgan.

I feel as though a new chapter has opened in my life.

Perhaps even a different book.

I'm supposed to be working on *Tinseltorn*, but it's impossible, because I've been reading all the articles Mum wrote and kept in the scrapbook she's given me.

It's amazing!

It s also living proof that I have seriously misjudged my mother.

Memory plays strange tricks. All these years I've been convinced Mum's stories mocked me. But now I'm able to read the cuttings as an adult, her love for me shines through with every word.

But I mustn't spend the whole day reading them again. Especially as I've already wasted the past hour going through the papers from cover to cover. Even the sports section.

Asbo is lolling on the jumble of Sunday supplements spread across the bed. Like me, he's restless. I'm sure he knows that his owner is currently sitting across a table from his old schoolmate, haggling over the fine print of a contract that runs to over thirty pages. Either that, or he thinks I ought to be getting on with *Tinseltorn*.

I fight a sudden, strange impulse to scrub the kitchen floor and force myself to focus.

My heroine, Celine, is being egged on by her loser boyfriend to take the advertising agency that just sacked her to an employment tribunal. But she doesn't want their money because she's determined to make big bucks of her own.

I manage a couple of paragraphs. Then another. And I'm beginning to think Celine's going to dump the bf even before she finds out he's been lying all along about being a prospective Member of Parliament.

Ooooh!

Three pages later, it turns out the closest he ever got to Westminster was canvassing on an estate in Sheffield during the general election. And the bastard had an affair with the candidate's wife. No wonder he left for London in such a hurry.

Poor Celine.

But if that really happened, I'm going to have to backtrack and—

My thoughts are interrupted by the sound of running water.

That's weird.

It's coming from the middle of my bed.

What has *that dog got against Kylie Minogue?*

I can tell just by looking that Asbo has cocked his leg on the exact spot where Kylie's mouth would be, even though my bedspread is – happily – protected by the newspapers I was reading earlier.

'Get off, you little bugger!' I yell.

Asbo has the temerity to give himself a final shake, landing a few drops more onto the soggy newsprint, before he leaps from bed to floor.

I'm clearing up the mess when I notice a couple of paragraphs on the front page of the Business Section.

Oh my God.

Chapter Thirty

OH MY GOD.

OH MY GOD.

OH MY GOD.

What if I'm too late?

I whip out my phone and call Rob.

Answer.

For God's sake answer.

Don't let it go to voicemail.

Please not voicemail.

'JJ. What's up?' Rob's irritated. 'Can't it wait? Has something happened to the babies?'

And I shout, 'Don't sign! Whatever you do, don't sign that contract!'

I never knew I could run so fast.

Ten minutes later, I arrive in the lobby of the Holiday Inn at Camden Lock so breathless I can barely speak. Rob and Danny are outside the building, pacing up and down.

'You realise I had the pen between my fingers when you called?' Rob says.

'And I've already signed the contract,' Danny chimes in.

'So what is it that's so important?' Rob is perplexed. I can see he's wondering if he was right to trust me.

'Where's … where's Brinkley now?' I gasp.

'Cooling his heels in the restaurant. He was about to pop the cork on a bottle of Champagne when I told him we had to deal with a family emergency. He wasn't best pleased.'

'I bet he wasn't.' I shove a damp copy of the *Sunday Times* Business Section into Rob's hands. 'Read this,' I say.

It takes him only a few seconds. 'Holy Christ,' he says. Then he passes the article to Danny.

Danny studies the article closely. 'Yes, but it's not conclusive,' he says. 'Could just be a coincidence.'

'No way!' I retort. 'You never thought it was suspicious, Brinkley crawling out of the woodwork like this? Someone who's never liked either of you, ever since you were kids.'

'Alternatively, he's just an opportunist who recognises a sweet deal when he sees one.' Danny can be as stubborn as his bloody dog.

'So what are we going to do?' Rob is in practical mode. 'I mean, you've signed already, Danny. And Brian's going to be seriously pissed off if we say we need more time at this stage. That would just make us look like idiots. Unless we tie things up today, the funds won't be in place in time to meet Podolski's deadline. Even if the article's true, I still don't see we have any alternative.'

'Follow me,' I say.

And I lead the way into the hotel.

I am already predisposed to dislike Brian Brinkley.

On sight.

And I do.

Maybe it's the way he looks me up and down, and then dismisses me as being of no interest.

Or the limp handshake he offers when Rob introduces me as his partner.

Or the fact that when I take a seat opposite him, he turns to Rob and drawls, 'Might I suggest your *partner* goes and powders her nose until we've concluded our business.'

Before Rob has a chance to defend me I say, 'Actually Brian, or may I call you Mr Brinkley, I'm a shareholder in FruityFul. So you'll be needing my signature on these documents as well. Maybe you could get me a coffee while I go over the small print one more time.'

'I'll do no such thing,' Brinkley snaps. Then he changes his tone, as if remembering he's about to go into business with Rob and Danny, and adds, 'This is most irregular.'

I flick through the pages of the contract for a few moments, giving myself time to think. Then I say, 'You'll have to forgive the boys for not explaining I'm late for our meeting because I was held up with the due diligence aspects of this deal.'

'Due diligence? What do you mean?'

I'm not entirely sure. But I know Sister-of-Skunk has been doing due diligence on VitalVitamins' new business partners in Central Europe, so I cross my fingers underneath the table and hope for the best.

'And in the interests of full disclosure,' I continue, 'I have to say I'm most concerned – we're all most concerned – that you haven't seen fit to mention your involvement with Podolski.'

Brinkley's response reminds me of the time I forgot I'd left a pair of gel hand-warmers bubbling away in a pan on the stove for an hour and a half instead of ten minutes.

First he bubbles.

'Podolski? What do you know about Podolski?'

Next he simmers.

'I fail to see the relevance, bearing in mind this is a private arrangement between myself, my valued old school friends, and apparently yourself.'

Then Brinkley boils.

'Whatever you think you know, whatever it is you're accusing me of, I'd love to see your proof. Come on, where is it?'

And finally he explodes.

'Besides, anything you've found out about Podolski is confidential. I insist you name your source.'

Brinkley obviously hasn't seen the papers this morning. But there's no need to tell him that. 'Look, I know exactly what you're up to,' I say. 'And I'm sure you'll agree, your bank's involvement with Podolski while simultaneously trying to steal FruityFul from us is going to be of enormous interest to the Prudential Regulation Authority.' I know no such thing, but Feliks Unpronounceable always says he lives in fear of breaking PRA regulations, so it's worth a try.

Brian Brinkley picks up a pen that's lying on the table. He looks as if he wants to stab me with it. 'Again, I insist you name your source,' he spits.

I cross my fingers even tighter. 'Mr Podolski himself.' A barefaced lie if ever there was one, but I'm not the only person in this room who's being economical with the truth.

'Just got back from Krakow, have you?'

Something in the way Brinkley asks the question makes me retort, 'As it happens, Mr Podolski and I had breakfast together this morning. Due diligence. As I said.'

My second untruth has a startling effect.

Brian Brinkley's shoulders slump.

He puts his head in his hands.

He runs his fingers through his unattractively gelled hair.

'So you know everything?' he whispers.

'Every last detail,' I say firmly. 'But Rob and Danny

are still missing a few pieces of the jigsaw. If you want
to avoid the PRA, I think you'd better fill them in.'

Brian Brinkley stares at the table in front of him
and begins to talk in a low monotone. 'Gavin Brinkley,
he's my uncle, as well as my boss at the bank. When
he told me we were in merger talks with Podolski, I
saw an opportunity. I knew FruityFul had borrowed
from Podolski because of the adverts you've been
running. Once we got into serious negotiations, the
balance sheet showed you guys were in hock for three
hundred grand. To land you in it, I only needed to
grease the wheels with a certain young lady in the
corporate lending department. All it took to get your
loan called in was for me to persuade her – you know
what I mean by that, I'm sure – to hit a few keys on
the computer.' Brinkley makes eye contact with me for
a split second. 'But how did you and Wyktor Podolski
know about that?'

'You just told me.'

Finally, I uncross my fingers. Then I pick up the
contract, turn a few pages and circle the third clause.
'And this, I take it, is some kind of typographical
error?'

I slap the document in front of Brinkley.

'Ah … that.'

Danny leans across and takes a look. 'God Almighty.
Not only have you been bribing people at Podolski,
you also reduced the amount you were going to pay

for FruityFul. By two hundred thousand pounds. Shame on you.'

Brinkley gives all three of us a look of pure hatred. 'I knew you were so desperate to sign you wouldn't sit here and read the contract all over again. So I made a few changes. You also overlooked the clause on page fourteen, which would have entitled me to sack you both in three months.'

Rob returns Brinkley's look with one of his own – pure contempt – then turns to Danny and me and says, 'We're done here.'

'Now look.' Brinkley gets up and puts his hand on Rob's shoulder to try to stop us leaving. 'I'll get your loan reinstated first thing tomorrow. Maybe even today. Then we'll call it quits, shall we? No harm done. I was just having a laugh. Like you were, when you locked me in that cupboard.'

I link arms with Rob and Danny. 'I'm sure you'll be hearing from Mr Podolski,' I tell Brinkley. 'As well as the PRA. I've even got a feeling the Fraud Squad's going to want a word with you.

'Now if you'll forgive me, I need to powder my nose.'

Chapter Thirty-One

The past few weeks have been really hectic.

The twins are out of hospital.

I'm moved back in with Theodora.

Feliks Unpronounceable was finally released by immigration officers in Buenos Aires, who'd taken umbrage at the fact his passport was about to expire.

My Kylie Minogue bedspread has gone to the dump.

Rob and Danny have sold another eight FruityFul franchises. And they're about to take a lease on a production unit near Wembley.

Mum tells me she has it on the highest authority that Piers Morgan bought a Parson Jack Russell the day after Theodora's *Transience* video installation hit YouTube, sparking instant global mirth.

Oh, and the merger between Podolski and Brinkley's bank (or rather, the bank Brinkley no longer works for) has been quietly called off.

I'm sitting at my desk in Cognita when the internal phone rings.

Carlotta, Skunk's PA, says, 'He's finished smoking his lunch. Ready for you now.'

Ravi gives me a thumbs-up sign.

Natasha tries not to give me a dirty look.

She was closeted in Skunk's office for ninety minutes this morning, going through the new agency brochure. Given her recommendation that Cognita should abolish it altogether – 'Brochures are so last century. A wicked waste of rain forest and sustainable resource' – I'm surprised the meeting was over so fast.

She says it went well.

Skunk showered her with praise.

And he's going to make an announcement to the whole agency once he's seen me.

'JJ. Take a seat.' Skunk gestures at the chair opposite his own.

And my heart hits a speed bump.

'I'm not going to beat about the bush,' Skunk tells me. 'Congratulations, JJ. Never any real doubt about your promotion to Creative Group Head. Three reasons. VitalVitamins. Doublekay and that elephant of his. And the new budget from FruityFul. You've increased Cognita's revenue by thirty per cent and I'm enormously grateful.'

Everything I ever wanted.

I'm overwhelmed.

'So grateful I'm giving you a budget to furnish your new office.' Skunk beams.

Wow. I've always wanted one of those sexy Aeron

chairs. And a glass coffee table. Maybe even a mini-fridge.

Skunk mistakes my daydream for some kind of negotiation ploy. 'You'll be getting a cab allowance,' he continues. 'And, of course, the agency will pick up your phone bill from now on.' My boss looks at me uncertainly. 'You're obviously expecting a hefty pay rise. Why don't you tell me what you have in mind, so we can haggle before I give you what you want.'

'Look, I won't drag this out either. It's fantastic that you're offering me this opportunity. And I'll always be grateful to you for taking a chance and getting my career started. But I'm afraid I'm going to have to turn you down.'

Skunk jerks back in his chair so violently, a shower of grey ash and glowing embers falls from his spliff to his shirt. For a moment, I think my almost-ex-boss is about to self-combust. He gives himself a shake and says, 'My sister was right. She warned me it was only a matter of time before you'd be headhunted. Which agency are you joining? One of the big boys, I suppose? Is that it?'

Skunk looks so crestfallen, I feel dreadful.

'If it's any consolation, I'm getting out of advertising altogether. For a while, at least.'

Now he looks baffled. 'Why would you want to do that?'

'I had a long talk with my mum the other night,' I

begin. 'She asked if I thought she should take a break to look after the twins. Terrible idea. My mother wouldn't be my mother if she didn't have a big career. So we started talking about childcare arrangements, and I realised Mum's really nervous about having a stranger look after them. Even a well-qualified stranger.'

Skunk looks more puzzled than before. 'Don't tell me you're about to turn into Mary Poppins?' he says.

'Not exactly. But my mum and dad have done a lot for me, and this is my chance to give them something back. We're going to choose a part-time nanny together. And I'm going to look after my brother and sister for four afternoons a week.'

'That's the craziest thing I've ever heard,' Skunk declares. 'Were you and your mother smoking this?' A nod at the Prince George biscuit tin in which he keeps his stash. 'You'll go crazy. Begging me to take you back within a month.'

'You're right,' I say. 'Looking after those kids full-time would probably leave all three of us needing psychiatric care. And I wouldn't trust Mum not to make a film about it! But that's my plan. I'm going to be spending the mornings trying to write a novel. Mum's going to fund me for a year, and we'll see what happens after that.'

'In that case—' Skunk gives me a rueful smile '—I wish you the very best of luck. And now, I suppose I'd better go tell the troops Natasha's the new Group Head.'

'Could I make a couple of suggestions?' I ask.

'Of course.'

'Since I'm not going to be around any more, I think you need to give Ravi a decent pay rise. He really deserves it.'

Skunk nods assent.

'And how about you tell Natasha she's got the promotion on merit. Rather than because I've turned it down. No one else knows the exact value of the business I've drummed up. And we can delay the news about me leaving for a few days.'

'Three reasons why I should promote Natasha. Quickly, JJ.'

'She's a hard worker. Some of her green ideas are good. And she'll be thrilled you're choosing her instead of me.'

'I wish I didn't have to.' Skunk sighs. 'I'll miss you. Make sure you come back and visit.'

Rob's been working even harder than usual.

So tonight he's taking me out on the town.

Our favourite restaurant in Soho.

The last time we were there was on my birthday.

I arrive a few minutes late.

Rob's already sitting at the table.

We kiss hello, the waiter pours the wine, and we clink glasses.

Rob seems subdued.

Whenever he's worried or upset, his face seems to age. Heavy bags appear under his eyes, and the cute frown line between his eyebrows turns into a deeper ridge. Tonight, it's more like the Grand Canyon.

He's only picking at his food.

But knocking back the wine.

This is horrible.

I hear myself making one-sided conversation. Even when I ask how Tottenham are doing, all I get is a shrug. 'The usual,' he mumbles.

The waiter brings dessert menus. But the only thing I'm interested in is what's bugging my boyfriend.

'Rob, what's up?'

He sighs heavily. 'I wanted to wait till after the meal. But this is killing me JJ. I'm no good at pretending.'

This doesn't sound good.

'Problems with FruityFul?'

'No. Everything's fine at work.'

'Something up with your mum and dad?'

A shake of the head.

We lapse into silence.

'The thing is...' Rob looks at me. 'Help me out, JJ. You know what I'm trying to say.'

Oh God.

'Are you breaking up with me? You are. Aren't you? Bringing me here to our special restaurant, so I can't make a scene. After all we've been through. And now, just when— '

Book Four
It is!

Chapter Thirty-Two

Breakfast was chaotic.

Mum insisted we all sit round the table – even though I pleaded with her to stay in bed. My pancakes turned out too crispy, and poor Dad wasn't even allowed to douse his burned offering with whipped cream, because Mum's insists he's showing the first signs of middle-age spread.

But seeing as how today is Mother's Day, you-know-who gets to call the shots.

(Also, Dad reckons it's never a good idea to argue with a woman who's holding a bread knife.)

Lorcan threw up all over my brand-new Jayna Crocs. And the only thing Izara wants to eat is her own toes.

We're hoping it's just a phase.

At eleven o'clock, we turn on the television to watch a special edition of *At Home*.

Extra special for me.

In that it is missing Beth Jackson.

Mind you, Mum's producer, Jeremy, is still sulking.

He had this dreadful idea.

Wanted to bring the cameras into our living room for a programme called *At Home With The Jackson Five*.

Like that was ever going to happen.

Instead, Jeremy's having to make do with a model-turned-WAG-turned-actress-turned-presenter who recently discovered she and her husband can't have children.

Mum watches carefully. 'Not bad,' she says. 'I like the way she did that last link. Touching. Yet dignified.'

Dad's watching Mum. 'Scared you've got competition?' he asks.

'These days you're over the hill at forty. Any day now, they'll replace me with a younger model.'

Mum doesn't sound worried.

Hardly surprising, when you consider she's never been busier.

The day the twins were baptised, Mum got talking to Theodora and Noah.

And the day after that, the three of them formed their own TV production company.

The pilot for their show *Desert Storm* is about to be filmed.

Reality show.

Featuring sand sculptures.

The artists do their thing, and at the end of each show, viewers decide who gets voted off.

Their piece is then destroyed.

By a tank.

Or maybe a plane armed with water bombs.

Contestants also have to cope with natural disasters.

Such as tidal waves.

And Asbo – leading a canine Charge of the Light Brigade.

I'm lobbying for Piers Morgan to present the show, but I think Mum's going to put Noah in front of the cameras.

Guests are starting to arrive for our open house brunch.

I say guests, but really it's our extended family.

Danny, Theodora and Noah arrive together with Asbo.

Followed by Freddie Ford – Lorcan's godfather – who slopes off upstairs with Dad for a game of snooker.

And now here's Rob, with his mum and dad.

Automatically, I twist the silver band on my finger.

Rob was really, really wonderful when I explained I wasn't quite ready to live with him. This year is so important for us both. He and Danny have got huge plans for FruityFul. And I've got my work cut out with the twins and *Tinseltorn*. In the circumstances, setting up home together would be a pressure, rather than a pleasure.

'But I'm still putting this ring on your finger,' Rob said that night in the restaurant.

And he did.

Produced it from his pocket.

A perfect fit.

'I'll never take it off,' I vowed.

'But you have to.'

And, when I did, I saw what had been engraved inside.

I know they say it's possible to inscribe the Lord's Prayer on the head of a pin. Even so, I was astonished how many words fitted inside my ring: *That that is, is. That that is not, is not. Is that it? Other than the fact I love you, it is!*

After today's brunch, I shan't need to eat for a week.

Even though I'm weary, I think I still have it in me to write for an hour or so. Theodora and Noah are babysitting the twins, so the flat is nice and quiet.

I sit down at the kitchen table and open my laptop.

But before I settle down to work, I spend a few minutes staring at the wonderful gift Mum gave me today. 'I was clearing out some cupboards,' she said, 'and I came across this. Thought you might be amused by it.'

A yellowed envelope with 'MUM' written on the front in crayon. And inside, a home-made card that announces, 'You are the prettyest mother in the world.'

Something else to treasure for the rest of my life.

I go back to the kitchen, and *Tinseltorn*.

The truth is, I'm a bit stuck.

I'm worried about Celine's mum. She's an architect

working for the local council. Designs schools and leisure centres. But she doesn't exactly leap off the page at you. She's dull. And what I know about architecture could be written on a grain of rice.

'Write what you know! And make sure there's lots of conflict.'

That's what Freddie's always telling me.

So...

...What if Celine's mum worked in television.

Maybe she's a producer.

And the first time we meet her, she says to Celine, 'I'm worried about work. These days you're over the hill at forty. Any day now, they'll replace me with a younger model.'

Oh my God.

Chapter Thirty-Three

OH MY GOD.
OH MY GOD.
OH MY GOD.

I'm turning into *my* mother!

Acknowledgements

Thanks first to my dear friend, mentor, and fellow novelist, Beverly Swerling, who knew exactly how to save this book from oblivion and showed me how to knock it into shape the day I declared I was about to delete it from my hard drive.

The subsequent long road to publication has been strewn with interesting and unexpected turnings and adventures and special thanks are due to Andreina Cordani and everyone involved with the Good Housekeeping Novel Competition, and to the organisers of the Lucy Cavendish College Fiction Prize 2013 – especially Joy Haughton.

Others have said Madeleine Milburn is the best agent in London; I am delighted to report they are correct. Gillian Green not only came up with this book's brilliant title, but also took a risk on a new novelist, and I shall be forever grateful to her and to the team at Ebury Press, especially Emily Yau and Ellie Rankine, plus Sandra Ferguson, Carol Lamble and Jessie Ford.

Thanks also to: Yvonne Antrobus, Gareth Bale, Jo Barnett, Richard Barnett, David Benedictus,

Carol Clifford, Malcolm Craddock, Mel Croucher, Malcolm Davidson, Sue Davidson, Francesca Drake, Jeff Drake, Ken Dytor, Fiona Gamwell, Alison Gillow, David Goldstein, Penny Guy, Lynda Hand, Randy Haunfelder, Harvey Ingram, Dotti Irving, Sylvia Jacobs, David Jackson, Eddie Levy, Lynne Orton, Marianne Jones, Ross McGrath, Catherine Pace O'Shea, Philippa Pride, Miriam Rankin, John Reiss, John Ryan, Primrose Hill Books, Gloria Stewart, Angela Torpey, Tottenham Hotspur FC, Juliet Warkentin, Tim Whiting, Neil Wilson, Debbie Wilson. All of you have helped or inspired me in one way or another and I am grateful.

Final thanks to Scrabble. Who is a dog. My dog. A dog whose misadventure at Fendi in Puerto Banus (from which we are both, alas, still banned) was the direct inspiration for the events that take place towards the end of this book.

THE MEMORY BOOK

by Rowan Coleman

*The name of your first-born. The face of your lover.
Your age. Your address...*

What would happen if your memory of these began to fade?

Is it possible to rebuild your life? Raise a family?
Fall in love again?

When Claire starts to write her Memory Book, she already knows that this scrapbook of mementoes will soon be all her daughters and husband have of her. But how can she hold on to the past when her future is slipping through her fingers...?

**Original, heartwarming and uplifting,
The Memory Book is perfect for fans of Jojo Moyes.**

EBURY
PRESS

THE LAST WINTER OF DANI LANCING

by P. D. Viner

Something very bad happened to Dani Lancing.

Twenty years later, her father is still trying to get her to talk.

Her best friend has become a detective, the last hope of all the lost girls.

And her mother is about to become a killer…

A hauntingly original debut that will stay with you long after the last page.

EBURY
PRESS